WITCHBREAKER

Also by James Maxey

Books of the Dragon Age

Bitterwood
Dragonforge
Dragonseed

The Dragon Apocalypse

Greatshadow
Hush
Witchbreaker

WITCHBREAKER

BOOK THREE *of the* DRAGON APOCALYPSE

JAMES MAXEY

SOLARIS

First published 2012 by Solaris
an imprint of Rebellion Publishing Ltd,
Riverside House, Osney Mead,
Oxford, OX2 0ES, UK

www.solarisbooks.com

ISBN: 978 1 78108 061 0

10 9 8 7 6 5 4 3 2 1

A CIP catalogue record for this book is available from the
British Library.

Designed & typeset by Rebellion Publishing

Printed and bound by CPI Group (UK) Ltd, Croydon, CR0 4YY

For Joy, Gina, and Joseph
fellow wanderers

CHAPTER ONE

A CONVERGENCE OF DRAGONS

SORROW SHIVERED AS she opened the blanket clasped around her shoulders long enough to feed the last shards of the kitchen table into the stove. Commonground was a tropical port, and Menagerie's houseboat had been ill-stocked to deal with the blizzard that had settled over the city for the last week. The small stove had been designed for cooking, not for heating, and Sorrow had quickly exhausted the firewood Menagerie had stocked; so when the mercenary failed to return after leaving to speak to the Black Swan days earlier, Sorrow had started burning his furniture. This was perhaps crossing a boundary as a houseguest, but the shape-shifter struck her as being practical. She was certain he'd understand.

The room was pitch-black save for the glowing red square of the open oven door. Yellow flames danced as she slid the table-legs onto the coals. She paused a moment in the improved light to study her feet. She'd returned from the Great Sea Above with her ankles covered in hard black scales. They had grown and spread in the intervening days, leaving her shins covered in overlapping diamond-shaped plates that felt hard as iron.

Despite this unexpected physical change, she didn't regret her decision to hammer a fragment of Rott's tooth into her brain. Doing so had opened a portal within her that allowed her to tap the primal dragon's power of decay. She'd made generous use of his abilities when she'd fought to keep Hush, the dragon of cold, from killing Glorious, the dragon of the sun. For most of her life, she'd pursued the power she would need to change the world more to her liking. Gaining control of a fundamental force of nature was more than she'd dare to dream.

Of course, none of this was going to matter if she froze to death. She wanted to be anyplace other than here, in a snow-covered floating shack miles from civilization. Her desire to be elsewhere felt physical, as if an invisible rope was wrapped around her soul, with a team of horses dragging her elsewhere.

She reached to close the oven door, and a red claw thrust out of the flame and grabbed her by the wrist. She jerked her hand back, gasping, her eyes growing wide as the red claw retreated back into the dancing flames.

As she stared into the fire, twin yellow eyes formed in the swirling incandescence to stare back. The last table leg she'd added split along its length, like opening jaws lined with teeth of jagged blue-white jets.

The crackling fire spoke to her: "Rott has been summoned to the convergence. It's rude that you keep him from answering the call."

Sorrow swallowed hard. "But I—"

She was unable to finish her thought as the red claw once more shot from the open door. She tried to scramble backward, but the talons closed around her face. She felt something tear and suddenly she was floating above herself, watching her limp body collapse on the floor. It was shocking to see herself from this perspective. She wasn't unfamiliar with her own face; she shaved her scalp daily, and was well used to seeing herself in a mirror. But the body that lay upon the floor looked quite different now that it was soulless. It was still breathing, and Sorrow was vaguely aware of a heartbeat, but she still was repulsed by how much her shell looked like a rather ill-kept doll made of skin and bones and meat. She was only twenty-five, but the frown lines and furrowed brow of the meat-mask that covered the skull before her looked much older.

"There's no time to study your human aspect," the flames crackled. "It's the dragon within you that's required. Come."

Suddenly, the sensation of a rope tugging her soul became fantastically real. Only instead of a rope, it was a cord of braided silver. The silver stretched down through the floor of the houseboat. The material world faded before her spiritual eyes and she found herself falling through a cloudless blue sky.

She now saw that the silver cord stretched taut beneath her for what looked like miles. At the other end, Rott tumbled lifelessly toward a green ocean far below. When she'd encountered Rott in the Sea of Wine, his body had been half submerged, and all that she'd seen was his serpentine spine, miles in length. She'd not realized he had limbs, or tattered wings that fluttered uselessly as they fell.

At last, he splashed into the emerald waves. She was dragged down until she was nearly submerged herself. At last, the huge corpse floated back to the surface. The water around him turned white with what she assumed was foam, until she realized it was maggots boiling from beneath his scales.

Repulsed, she willed herself to fly away. She was high in the sky before the silver cord snapped tight, whipping her around to look back at the scene below.

A chain of islands formed into a rough circle directly below her. Though mostly equal in size, the topography and climate of each island was radically different.

The northernmost island was a deep blue mountain of crystalline ice, surrounded by gusting snow. The upper edge of the ice was a saw-tooth ridge that looked like a dragon's spine. Avalanches spilled down the slopes as the mountain lifted her head. This was Hush, the primal dragon of cold, and she looked out toward the other islands with unveiled contempt.

The stony island to her east was wreathed with a rapidly churning circle of storm clouds. The hurricane swirled into a serpentine mass. A dragon's head emerged, opening its massive jaws to lick the land beneath with a tongue of lightning. Thunder rolled across the green waves, forming a voice, shouting, "Who dares summon Tempest, Lord of Storms?"

To his side was an island of granite. The earth grumbled and cracked and quaked as the dragon stirred from his repose. Dirt slid from a hill-face to expose two enormous diamonds, which narrowed into angry eyes. Sorrow knew enough dragon lore to deduce that this was Kragg, the dragon of stone.

On the island beside Kragg, lava spilled down the slopes of a steep volcano until all the land was ablaze. The smoke and flame snaked together as it stretched into the sky, curling into a dragon's neck and face.

"I have issued the call," roared Greatshadow, the primal dragon of fire.

The bone-white cliffs of the island next to Greatshadow began to crack, releasing rivers of blood. A thousand animals jumped free of the red torrent, multitudes of beasts, from common house cats to lumbering elephants, from swarming ants to slithering boa constrictors. The menagerie marched together, sinking their teeth into the flanks of their neighboring beast, digging their claws deep into flesh, until the writhing, shrieking mass formed a dragon, a towering creature part lion, part snake, and part eagle. This was Abundant, the dragon of animal life. She shrugged her long back as she looked out upon her brethren.

She was beside Rott, who floated belly up in the water, looking like a long chain of tar-covered islets that smelled like a city dump. Rott's unblinking eyes were half submerged, his jaws agape, his yellow teeth cracked and broken.

The dragons glowered at one another, then one by one glanced toward the heavens. Sorrow wondered if they were looking at her, until she looked up to see the sun high in the sky, looking for all the world like a huge disk of gold floating above them.

"What's he doing here?" Abundant asked, with a voice formed by wolf-howls and baboon yowls and the chorus of a thousand robins.

"The sun still respects the pact we made long ago," Greatshadow said. "No primal dragon may ignore the summoning."

"He's not a dragon," Kragg rumbled. "He's an interloper."

"He's here," said Tempest. "This is more than I can say for Abyss."

"It's unlike our brother to be tardy," said Abundant. "I sense he draws near."

The water of the sea in the center of the islands began to boil. From the depths a giant turtle rose, as large as any of the islands surrounding it. Waves spread across the green sea, crashing onto the shores of the other dragons.

"You dishonor us with your delay, brother," Hush growled. "I expect Rott to be late, but you've no excuse."

The turtle turned its head toward the north. With a voice formed by crashing waves, it spoke: "You know the reason for my sluggishness. The cold you've unleashed has frozen my form further south than you've ever before encroached. I normally keep silent about your intrusion into my domain, but this is inexcusable."

"*Your* domain?" Hush asked with a scoff.

"All here recognize the sea as my abode," said Abyss.

"The sea is nothing but molten ice," said Hush. "You borrow it at my pleasure."

"I would argue that the reverse is true," growled Abyss.

"His is not the only domain you've invaded," Greatshadow said as the pillar of crackling flames that formed his body swirled to face Hush. "You dare blanket my earthly home with snow? How can you justify this insult?"

"It's more than an insult," howled Abundant. "It's an assault! Your blizzards have killed countless tropical beasts who've never known winter. If Greatshadow had not summoned us to the convergence, I would have. We understand you have reason to be angry, but this doesn't excuse the magnitude of your sins."

"You dare to speak of me of sins?" Hush answered with a trembling voice. It sounded as if she was on the verge of tears. "I'm the one who cries for justice! I shall not call back my blizzards until one particularly vile beast is wiped from the earth: man!"

Tempest let loose with rumbling thunder. "We understand your grief, sister. However—"

"You understand nothing! Men killed Glorious! At the moment of my greatest happiness, when my one true love had finally opened his heart to me, he was cruelly slain by a human!"

"You would punish all mankind for this crime?" asked Kragg, with a voice like vast stones grinding together.

"It was not the act of a lone man. These creatures have banded together and declared war upon us all." She stretched an icy claw toward the volcanic island. "Greatshadow! You barely survived when the Church of the Book sent men to hunt you! Surely you must share my thirst for revenge!"

"I think not," the dragon of flame answered. "You've thrown your blizzards throughout the earthly realms. Men have responded by building fires and lighting lanterns. Why should I think ill of those who feed me so faithfully? The time has come for your tantrum to end."

"But the threat the humans pose—"

"—can be contained," said Greatshadow. "I survived the best that mankind could throw against me. The only reason they wounded me at all is that they came bearing a weapon carved from the spiteful ice that once was *your* heart. In failing to kill me, they've left me stronger. I admit, I'd grown complacent. Now, I keep a watchful eye for their schemes."

"You admit there is a threat?" said Hush.

"Yes," said Greatshadow. "Though I'm not certain that humans are the ultimate source."

"What do you mean, brother?" Tempest thundered. "Speak, if you know something."

"I'm hesitant to sully this sacred space with mere speculation," said Greatshadow. "I simply find it curious that the Jagged Heart was stolen from the ice-ogres by members of the Storm Guard, only to wind up in the possession of the Church of the Book. The Storm Guard wouldn't invade the domain of another dragon without your permission, nor would they be so careless with their treasure."

"You say you will not engage in speculation," Tempest grumbled. "But you offer only opinions, not evidence."

Greatshadow nodded. "My apologies." He turned his attention once more to Hush. "If I confine myself to statements of simple fact, here is one that is indisputable. The only reason that Judge Adamant Stern, the murderer of Glorious, had reached the Great Sea Above was that you gave him passage there."

"Lies!" said Hush.

"I watch mankind through every candle flame," said Greatshadow. "And I listen to the conversations of ice-ogres through their cook-fires. I know what I know. You personally accompanied Stern on the hunt for Glorious. I accept that you had a change of heart, and would have spared him. But what does that matter? Stern was your murder weapon. You loosed a bow, and now blame the arrow because your feeling toward the target changed while the missile was in flight."

"You've hated me for centuries!" Hush screamed. "Can anyone ever expect a fire to give honest testimony about the cold?"

"Do you have proof of your accusations, brother?" asked Abundant.

"I've spoken with an eye-witness," he said. "You may trust my testimony."

"Such grave accusations must be backed up by more than hearsay," said Abundant.

Greatshadow turned toward Tempest. "Perhaps there are others among us who may shed light upon recent events."

"Again you speak to me with veiled accusations," said Tempest. "I do not like your tone, brother."

"I've simply asked myself, who would benefit most from the death of other primal dragons?"

"Obviously, the Church of the Book," the storm dragon answered.

"A church you've a record of manipulating through blackmail."

"I've been a target of their plots as well," said Tempest. "I've merely been alert enough to thwart them before they endanger me."

Greatshadow kept his jaws shut as he glared at the storm dragon with eyes of flame.

Hush shook her head, sending tornadoes of snow swirling about her. "Greatshadow, you've grown too used to being fed by mankind. It's left you soft. What's more, your smoldering hatred toward me distorts your judgment. Do you think your kindred dragons will sit idly by while mankind schemes against them?" She looked around the isles. "Or will the rest of you join with me to end their threat once and for all?"

Abundant was the first to speak. "Men are arrogant beasts, foolishly believing they are superior to other animals. Yet they are still beasts, and all living creatures are dear to me. I cannot allow you to harm them."

"Even though these monsters killed Glorious? Even though they killed Verdant? How many more of us must die?"

"We dragons have killed far more of our fellows than men have," Kragg answered.

Thunder rumbled as Tempest responded, "It's true that men are dangerous. Yet I've learned a great deal by studying them. Men have built their civilization by taming wolves and boars and oxen. Animals that once threatened them have been trained to do their bidding. I've taken inspiration and mastered the art of taming men. I cannot permit you to harm my livestock."

Abyss lifted his head from the water and said, "I care nothing for what happens to men who dwell on land, but there are still Wanderers who respect the pact they made with me long ago. I will not let you harm them."

"You're fools, the lot of you," growled Hush. She turned to Kragg. "You cannot love these animals. They riddle your body with mines and steal your precious gems and metals!"

Kragg writhed, stretching his back. There was a rumbling that echoed long after as boulders larger than houses tumbled down his slopes. "With a shrug, I've plunged an entire city into a vast cleft in the earth. Men are little more than annoying fleas. I can hardly be blamed for scratching them. I care nothing if they all die, but I also am unconcerned if they live. They aren't worthy of my sustained attention."

"It's five to four in favor of the death of mankind," said Hush. "The rest of you must respect the will of the majority!"

"I fear that the cold has frozen the part of your mind capable of math," said Tempest. "Greatshadow, Abundant, Abyss, and myself all vote that mankind shall live. Kragg's position seems to be one of neutrality. This leaves you alone in wishing the extinction of mankind."

"We must count the votes of our fallen brethren!" Hush howled. "Verdant, slain by humans, votes for vengeance! Glorious, slain by humans, votes for vengeance! And Rott, though his mind is too long gone to give voice to his wishes, is the embodiment of destruction! Is there any doubt how he would vote?"

"The Rott I remember was more complicated than you give him credit for," said Abundant. "For him, life and death were part of a unified whole. He might argue that the deaths of Verdant and Glorious were inevitable. Despite our great powers, we're not gods. We're living creatures who've risen to dominate our chosen environments, but this does not make us immortal. Dragons die just as surely as men. You cannot count Rott's vote for your side."

"You can't count any vote as being on your side other than your own," said Tempest.

"I don't need your approval to destroy mankind. This isn't a democracy!"

"You were the one who brought up voting!" roared Greatshadow.

"The rest of you can't stop me," growled Hush.

"I could," said Kragg. "I could shatter the earth beneath your feet and plunge your frozen lands into the raging flames within the heart of the world. Greatshadow would no doubt welcome you with open claws."

"That will not be needed," said Tempest. "Hush, we've tolerated your invasions of our abodes for a little time, and are not without sympathy for your grief. But you must withdraw to the ordinary boundaries of your domain. It would cause me great anguish if, when we dragons converge once more, you failed to answer the call."

"Is this supposed to be some sort of threat?" sneered Hush.

"It is my promise," said Tempest. "If you continue your campaign of global destruction, I will take whatever actions I must to defend my domain."

"It will not come to that," said Greatshadow. "Hush, you're angry. You've already killed thousands of men with your actions. But this is true each year; never does the human race emerge completely unscathed by winter. If you spare mankind now, think of the suffering you may inflict for centuries to come. Will this not satisfy your thirst for vengeance?"

The great snow-dragon ground her teeth as she glared at her brethren. She answered them after a moment of silence, her breath rolling out in a great fog. "Very well. I will not darken the memory of our fallen companions by turning my wrath against other dragons. For now, I shall withdraw my blizzards. My cold will follow the normal order of seasons. But know this: when the day comes that humans turn against you, Abyss, or you, Tempest, and rip you body and soul from the earth, I will shed no tears. I will instead savor the cold satisfaction of knowing you were warned."

"I'll take that chance," said Abyss.

"We're decided," said Greatshadow. "Mankind shall be spared."

Greatshadow turned his face upward, gazing directly at Sorrow. He bared his teeth. Sorrow wondered if he was trying to smile.

Abyss sank back into his sea, disappearing beneath the waves. The storms forming Tempest slowed their churn, dissipating into fluffy white clouds. Abundant fell apart, the various animals that formed her disappearing from sight beneath a black cloud of cawing ravens.

Rott began to sink beneath the waves, pulling Sorrow closer and closer to the water. As the other dragons vanished, she looked up at the yellow disk of the sun and shouted, "Stagger! Stagger, are you there?"

She thought, perhaps, that a faint voice answered, just on the edge of her hearing, but it was drowned out by the sloshing, maggot-tipped waves beneath her. She was dragged into the water, sinking into the calm silence beneath the surface, with curtains of light shimmering around her. She sank beyond the light, and there was nothing but darkness, and the cold.

"SORROW?" A WOMAN asked.

Sorrow sat up with a gasp. Though she was drenched in sweat, her teeth were chattering. She stared at the open oven door before her and saw that the fire had gone out. She snapped her head to the left as she realized she wasn't alone. A blonde woman in a long fur coat stood by her side.

"Infidel?" she said. "You came back?"

The warrior woman had lit out for the jungle the second they'd returned to Commonground. Sorrow had assumed she'd never see her again.

"Guess again," said the woman.

"Menagerie?" asked Sorrow. The shape-shifter had left the boat in the form of a hound-dog. She'd known that he'd consumed Infidel's blood and could now shape-shift into her double, but she hadn't seen him do so since returning to the material world.

The woman nodded. Her eyes were fixed on Sorrow's throat. "That's a nasty burn."

Sorrow lifted her fingers to her neck and winced. The flesh was covered with blisters.

"What happened? Did you fall against the stove?"

"Something like that," she said softly.

Menagerie glanced around the room, and sighed. "It's bad enough you burned the furniture. Did you have to take the doors off the cabinets?"

"I burned them early on. They seemed extraneous," she said as she wrapped the blankets around her.

"Burning the boat itself seems like a dead-end plan," Menagerie said. The shape-shifter nodded toward Sorrow's sea-chest in the corner. The lid was open, exposing Sorrow's books, journals, and maps. "Bound parchment burns rather nicely in my experience."

"I've been keeping journals since I was ten," said Sorrow. "But I didn't spare them solely due to sentimentality. I suspect historians may one day find my diaries of value."

"Ah," Menagerie said with a smile. "Still planning on ruling the world?"

"Quite the opposite," she said. "I'm planning to free the world from tyranny."

Menagerie stooped in front of the chest and thumbed through one of the journals without asking permission. "Nice handwriting. Precise and tidy. Nothing immediately tips a reader off that you're insane."

"Just because you're mad that I've burned your furnishings is no need to be insulting."

Menagerie closed the book and stood. "I mean no insult. But I've earned my living as a mercenary since before you were even born. I'm a good judge of people." The shape-shifter stared at her face with a penetrating gaze. "Mentally, you're one of the most dangerous people I've ever met."

Sorrow smiled.

"I didn't mean that as a compliment."

"I've spent a great deal of my life in pursuit of the goal of becoming more dangerous. As have you, if the stories about you are true."

"My goal wasn't to be dangerous," said Menagerie. "My goal was to be effective. I always knew what I was fighting for, and I always knew the steps I would take to reach my end game."

"As do I."

"Do you?"

"My end game is a more just world," she said.

Menagerie nodded. "And step one toward achieving this is to gain power. That's why you've got a head full of nails and scales all over your legs."

"Correct."

Menagerie crossed his arms over his breasts. "And what, exactly, is phase two of your plan?"

"I… I'm still in pursuit of the first phase. Once I have the power I need, I'm confident the path forward will be clear. One thing I do know about my path is that I'll need allies. Infidel rebuffed me. Will you consider my offer? You know I can pay your wages."

Menagerie shook his head. He asked, "Did you know there's a hell?"

"So the church teaches."

"I just spent what I felt was eternity there," he said. He pressed his lips tightly together and took a long breath through his nose. "It's… not a place I'm eager to return to."

"Don't tell me the legendary Menagerie has lost his nerve?"

"Menagerie died when an angry god tore his soul into a thousand tiny shreds," he said. "Whoever I am now, I have a clean slate. I've got a chance to make a new life."

"As a woman," Sorrow said. "If you return to the civilized world, I suspect you'll find that people treat you much less equitably than they did when you were a man."

Menagerie shrugged. "I guess I'll find out. I've sold this boat to the Black Swan. I'm using the funds to head for the Silver Isles for a taste of civilian life."

"You won't last a week in that city of hypocrites," Sorrow said. "You've lived too long in Commonground. People here are thieves and murderers and scoundrels, but at least they're open and honest about it. The so-called civilization of the Silver City is nothing but a den of vipers."

"I guess I'll find out. If it's not too much of a burden, could you try not to destroy civilization while I'm still using it?"

"I can make no promises," said Sorrow.

CHAPTER TWO
GRAVEDIGGERS

SORROW'S KNUCKLES WERE white as she gripped the sides of the dugout canoe. The Dragon's Mouth, the river that fed into the bay at Commonground, was normally a broad, placid body of water, but snowmelt had swollen the river beyond its banks. Ancient trees felled by the snow bobbed in the current, forming an ever-shifting maze.

The river pygmies she'd hired to ferry her to the Knight's Castle navigated silently through the treacherous waters. When the four canoes had first departed Commonground, the pygmies had been chatting and laughing with one another. Now they paddled without saying a word, their eyes barely blinking as they studied the roiling river. Their faces were hard, stoic masks.

There were eight pygmies, two in each canoe. She was their only living passenger; the rest of the canoes held her gear, plus Trunk. She'd left him inert for the moment. She didn't want to alarm the pygmies with his unusual appearance. That said, the pygmies struck her as difficult to alarm. She'd allowed her hood to slip as she boarded the canoe and they hadn't even taken a second glance at her head. River pygmies dyed their shaved bodies blue and cut fish scale scars along their shoulders and backs. Her scalp studded with nails probably struck them as positively banal.

The terrain around the river grew more rugged and rocky. She wondered if the pygmies would be up to the task of carting her gear to her destination. She'd made her needs quite clear to the pygmy leader, Eddy (his full name, translated, was White Foam

Curling Past an Eddy, which she found rather mellifluous). He'd assured her that his men were the strongest of their tribe, but the tallest of pygmies barely reached the bottom of her ribs, and she'd not packed lightly. She'd come into the jungle seeking the lost Witches' Graveyard, and was prepared for an extensive dig when she found it. The canoes were heaped with picks, shovels, wheelbarrows, ropes, tents, and enough food for a six-month expedition.

After several hours of paddling against the fierce current, their immediate destination came into view, the towering, vine-draped walls of the ruins known as the Knight's Castle. She'd lost Stagger's map in the rush to abandon the *Freewind*, but his directions were simple enough. Locate the Knight's Castle and head east. Here, she'd find rows of evenly spaced depressions in the ground. Stagger had been certain the place was a graveyard but had always assumed, since the graves weren't marked, that it had been used to bury people of little importance. It seemed unpromising, and no treasure hunter had ever done the hard work of digging there. But she'd come seeking knowledge, not treasure, and the thought of the waiting graves filled her with an almost childlike excitement. For the rest of the world, the burial of hundreds of executed weavers was ancient history, but for Sorrow, if this was a graveyard of witches, it would be a repository of lost secrets needed to give birth to a new golden age of witchcraft.

The pygmies guided the canoes between two enormous walls. In the flooded gap was a broad avenue, draped by shadows. Sorrow strained to see in the dim light. At the end of the avenue, steep stone steps rose from the water, leading to the top of the walls. Her canoe shuddered as it scraped unseen rocks beneath the coffee-colored river.

Eddy leapt from the tip of the canoe, his feet splashing loudly as he landed in knee-deep water. His muscles bulged as he pulled the canoe to rest on one of the broad steps hidden just inches below the surface. Eddy wasn't a young man, but his muscles were well-sculpted beneath his leathery blue hide. Sorrow was embarrassed that she'd doubted the pygmies' capacity to cart her gear. Despite their small stature, these men needed immense strength to survive this savage land.

Sorrow rose from her canoe as the other pygmies brought their vessels to rest on the steps. The pygmies still looked nervous, but she felt relieved to be away from the worst of the river.

She said, "Well done, Eddy."

Eddy frowned as his men gathered around Sorrow.

"It's time for us to take our moons," said Eddy.

"You'll be paid when we reach the graveyard. Three moons each. We were clear on this subject."

"At the market, my brother saw you pay for provisions with a purse full of moons."

"Perhaps he did," said Sorrow. "I don't see how that matters."

"It matters because we're eight warriors," said Eddy. "You're a lone woman, far removed from any long-men who could hear your cries."

Sorrow crossed her arms. "It's bad enough that you would renege on an agreement. I can't believe you're trying to threaten me."

"No, no, no," Eddy said, laughing gently. "You misunderstand. I make no threat. I'm merely saying that, in such a hazardous landscape, you'll give us all your coins. You can hand them over willingly, or we can take them after we are done amusing ourselves with your corpse."

He raised his hand and brought his thumb and little finger together. At this signal, all seven of his companions drew knives from their belts.

Sorrow sighed. "I see. Fortunately for you, I abhor settling disputes with violence, and wish to avoid doing so now. Here's my counter proposal: your men will drop their weapons. You'll unload the canoes in a neat and professional fashion. After this, we shall part ways. In exchange, none of you will die in unimaginable agony. At least, not today. "

Eddy drew his own knife. "You've a bold tongue, witch. We'll see if you're still as arrogant when I cut it from your mouth."

Sorrow stepped back as Eddy ran toward her. She snapped her fingers, then extended her hand as Eddy leapt high in the air, swinging his knife at her torso. She caught him by the arm just as a second pygmy attempted to stab her in the back of her thigh. She felt his blade tear through her pants and skitter along the hard scales beneath as she toppled backward.

Meanwhile, Trunk had heard the snap of her fingers and stirred. Her last golem had been built of driftwood, but she'd had no patience for rooting around on a snow-covered beach looking for appropriate timber. Trunk's torso was a heavy cedar chest; his limbs were thick, sturdy boards. His fingers and toes were built of oak dowelling. For a head, she'd used a bucket so new it had never been touched by a mop.

As expected, most of the pygmies turned toward the wooden man as he rose with a clatter. She had only to deal with Eddy, who was straddling her torso, attempting to press his knife to her throat, and the thigh-stabbing pygmy she'd fallen upon.

Dealing with Eddy was simplest. She relaxed her arm and allowed him to press his iron blade to her throat. The second it touched her flesh, she willed the knife to crumble and it did so, rusting instantly to the core and snapping as Eddy pressed down.

The pygmy she'd fallen on had managed to untangle himself from her legs and rose on his hands and knees directly in front of the soles of her boots. This was an unfortunate place for him. While she wasn't happy about the scales covering her legs, she'd discovered that the external changes were accompanied by internal changes, including superhuman strength in her lower limbs. She kicked the pygmy squarely in the chest and he went flying, smacking into the vine-draped wall twenty feet away.

"Now, Eddy," she said as she grabbed the diminutive robber's face in both hands, "it's time for me to teach you a lesson in keeping promises."

She could have been merciful and killed the man. Instead, she closed her eyes and focused on the dragon's tooth in her skull. In her mind's eye, it was like a tiny black doorway. She opened the door a crack, allowing the smallest fraction of Rott's power to surge from her bare palms.

Eddy howled as his flesh sagged on his face. She pushed him away and he fell on his back, writhing in agony. He wailed as his teeth turned black, falling from their sockets. His muscles shrank as his skin grew paper thin. He raised his hands before his face as they twisted into arthritic claws. Mercifully, he didn't have long to stare at his deformity. Thick cataracts fogged his eyes, turning them into twin white marbles.

She rose on trembling legs. As before, she found the after-affects of using Rott's power unpleasant. The energy hadn't flowed from her cleanly. Her whole body tingled. She nearly gagged as she exhaled; the odor of her lungs was like rotten meat.

Eddy's mewling whimpers of pain drew her focus back to her immediate surroundings. When pressed into violence, she killed as efficiently and coolly as possible. She despised those who took pleasure at inflicting pain. Yet a smile crossed her lips as she looked down at the man who'd threatened her with such swaggering confidence. She fought back the urge to taunt him, but not the urge to educate him.

"You called me a witch," she said, standing over the now ancient man. "It's a term commonly used to describe women inadequately subservient to men. I, however, embrace the word's true meaning. I command forces you can never hope to comprehend. I'm heir to an ancient and awesome power. You should not have betrayed me."

She glanced behind her and found Trunk standing in ankle deep water surrounded by six headless corpses. She shook her head slowly. She'd hoped at least one survivor would bear witness, to spare her further trouble from the locals.

There was always Eddy, weeping at her feet, splayed out like a rag doll, covered in his own bodily waste. She doubted there was enough left of his mind to pass on her warning.

"What's the point in teaching lessons if there's no one around to learn?"

Then, because she was disturbed by the satisfaction she was taking from his feeble, wet sobs, she placed her boot upon his throat and pressed until his suffering ended.

She had Trunk dispose of the corpses in the river while she sorted through her supplies. They would have to cart her gear in one load at a time. Fortunately, the dug-out canoes would prove handy for storing what they left behind. Trunk turned over one canoe and placed it atop another. She used her power over wood to weave the two halves together, forming a sealed container that held most of her provisions. For now, Trunk would cart only tools and a few days' worth of meals.

She led Trunk up the stairs to the top of the wall. She shielded her eyes from the fierce noon sun as she studied the jungle, gray and withered, devastated by the cold. From her vantage point, she could see a slope of black beyond the trees, evidence of the recent lava flow. If Stagger's description was correct, it looked as if the lava hadn't covered the area of the graveyard.

Two hours later, she'd barely made it a hundred yards into the jungle. The ground was mushy, and Trunk kept sinking up to his knees. Sorrow grew coated in mud herself as she worked to free him and drag their supplies forward. She lost one of her boots in the sucking mire. She pressed her lips tightly together as she stared at her now bare foot.

She wasn't overly sentimental, but she missed her toes. After her strange dream of witnessing dragons debating the fate of mankind, the changes in her legs had gotten worse. Her feet were now covered in overlapping bands of scales that tapered to points. If she pressed hard, she could barely feel the bones of her toes still present beneath the hard surface.

The uncertainty over whether her physical changes had halted added a sense of urgency to her quest to find the Witches' Graveyard. The few remaining practitioners of the art of weaving placed great value in their privacy, and the handful she'd tracked down had seldom given Sorrow a warm welcome. Sorrow's pursuit of power had earned her more than a few enemies; no living weavers wanted to make themselves a target of the forces allied against her.

Her hope of pushing her education further now lay with dead weavers. She was certain that if she could study the skulls of witches, she could learn a great deal by documenting how they'd placed nails into their brains. With any luck, she wasn't the first weaver to tap the power of a primal dragon. She might yet discover the secret to using Rott's power without corrupting her body.

It was nearly sunset when she finally found the hilly slope covered with rows of long narrow depressions that Stagger had described. Her nostrils twitched as she hacked her way through the spiky vines that draped the area. Was she smelling fire? Or was it just a lingering odor from the volcanic eruption?

She sliced her way through a curtain of dying vines and found herself in an area relatively free of undergrowth. The canopy of trees here was particularly thick, blanketing the area in a perpetual gloom that suppressed smaller plants. She looked up the hill and saw a granite bolder, nearly the size of a house, shaped something like a heart. It looked top heavy and a little out of place despite being girded with thick vines. She suspected it had rolled down the mountain many years ago. Next to the boulder, she saw a small makeshift tent, little more than a large blanket stretched over some branches. Near this was a smoldering fire pit.

She cocked her head. She could hear voices from the other side of the boulder.

She looked toward Trunk and motioned for him to drop his pack. She opened a bundle of tools and supplied him with an axe, then nodded for him to follow. Armed with her machete, she crept silently up the hill. Stagger had warned her that treasure seekers often tried their luck around the Knight's Castle. From what she knew, these were desperate men of low morals who might not behave honorably. She had no fear that they were an actual danger to her, but if they did look problematic, she saw no reason to waste the advantage of surprise.

She pressed herself against the heart-shaped boulder and listened to the voices from the other side.

"Here's another one!" said a man in a curiously high-pitched, falsetto tone.

"Gold?" a second man asked, sounding hopeful.

"No. It's green. Maybe more glass? The light's getting bad."

"Let me see," said the second man.

Sorrow furrowed her brow. She'd heard these voices before. What were they doing out here? Then she realized why she hadn't been able to find her map when she abandoned the *Freewind*.

She marched around the boulder and saw a mound of damp earth piled a few dozen feet away. A tall blond man was standing in the pit beside the mound, visible only from his bare shoulders up.

"Brand!" she shouted, stomping toward him.

The blond man looked up. His eyes grew wide. "Sorrow? I didn't expect to see you out here."

"I'm sure you didn't!"

He grabbed a root near the edge of the pit and started to pull himself up. He was half out of the hole when she placed her boot on his shoulder and knocked him back in. He landed next to the second figure in the pit, a pot-bellied dwarf wearing a platinum blonde wig.

"Villain!" the dwarf shrieked, shaking his fist. "You'll pay dearly for striking the scion of King Brightmoon!"

"It's okay," said Brand, rising to his knees. "I think there's been a misunderstanding."

"You stole my map!" said Sorrow.

"Technically, I found a map in the rubble when we were hastily packing. How was I to know it was yours?"

"It was in my cabin!"

"Things got sloshed around when the ship capsized. There's no telling where it originally came from."

"You knew it wasn't yours!"

Brand nodded. "Okay, sure, that's true. But, honestly, when I found it, I saw the word 'treasure' in large letters, underlined, and thought it was a joke. I doubt that most people who hide buried treasure do that."

"You took it seriously enough to come out into the jungle."

"Also true," said Brand. "But after Gale fired me, all the princess and I had were the clothes on our backs. We need to raise some scratch to get back to the Silver Isles. What did we have to lose?"

"The princess?" Sorrow rolled her eyes. "Bigsby still thinks he's Innocent Brightmoon? And you're still humoring him?"

"'Him'?" asked Bigsby. "Who's she talking about?"

Brand shrugged.

"I should just fill in this hole with both of you in it," grumbled Sorrow. "The world has more than enough thieves."

"Have a care, commoner," said Bigsby, wiping a muddy strand of blonde hair from his face. "We don't care for your tone or your accusations."

"I'm not a thief," said Brand. "I'm just lucky at finding stuff."

"Like those shovels and pickaxes? Since you're broke, you obviously didn't acquire them honestly."

"It depends on how you define honest. We holed up on the *Black Swan* for a few days during the worst of the blizzard. I earned a few moons reading palms for the patrons."

"You read palms?"

"To the extent that anyone reads palms, sure," said Brand. "It's a talent I picked up traveling with the circus."

"He's very good," said Bigsby.

Sorrow clenched her fists. "You've no magical powers. I'd spot it in your aura if you did."

"I didn't say I knew magic," said Brand. "Fortune telling

is ninety per cent listening to your clients, and ten per cent repeating their words back to them with a twist."

"So you swindle fools," said Sorrow. "All the more reason the world won't miss you if I fill in this pit."

"I didn't swindle anyone. My clients are very happy with my work. Let me do you."

"I think not," said Sorrow. "You've nothing to tell me about myself I don't already know."

"I can tell you you're not going to bury us," said Brand.

Sorrow sighed. "No, I suppose I'm not. I'll let you out if you promise to leave peacefully. If you refuse, you know what I'm capable of."

"How about this?" asked Brand. "We get out of the pit, we all eat dinner together, and tomorrow we work as a team to look for the treasure, whatever it is."

Sorrow studied Brand's face. He smiled at her, but this didn't help his cause. She hadn't much liked him when they traveled together on the *Freewind*. Brand was little more than a prostitute, a pretty young man who served as the sexual toy of Captain Gale Romer, a woman old enough to be his mother. On the other hand, one reason that Gale had been so smitten with him was that Brand was a rather impressive physical specimen. Having a gravedigger with broad shoulders and a strong back could speed up her search.

"Fine," said Sorrow. "But you'll work as my employees, not my partners. I'll pay you a set fee to dig graves. What we find will be mine alone. At least you won't be digging blindly with the chance of winding up empty-handed. I'll compensate you and Bigsby a moon for each grave you excavate."

"I'm not Bigsby!" the dwarf shrieked. "Why does everyone keep calling me that? Has the whole world gone mad?"

Sorrow closed her eyes and rubbed them. It wasn't too late to have Trunk dismember them both with his axe.

She sighed. She'd always thought of herself as a defender of those outside of the mainstream of society. An insane cross-dressing dwarf certainly fell into that category. How much did she truly believe in her own cause if, when confronted by a person who was an even more of an outcast than her, her first instinct was to bury him in an unmarked grave?

"Sorry, Innocent," she said softly. "I'm just tired. I got confused."

"You're still confused if you think you can address me in such a familiar fashion," Bigsby said huffily.

"Sorry, your highness," she said.

"The apology is accepted," said Bigsby. "But we reject your offer. Any treasure we find is rightfully ours."

"Hold on," said Brand. "We only need enough money to get passage back to the Silver Isles. We'll be rich once we're home. Why be greedy?"

"That's quite rational of you," said Sorrow. "You wouldn't be trying to trick me?"

"Nope," said Brand. He grinned. "If you can't trust royalty, who can you trust?"

"By the pure metals," Sorrow said, shaking her head. "I'm probably going to regret this."

She turned toward Trunk. "Help them out."

Brand helped Bigsby steady himself as Trunk lifted him to the surface. Brand didn't wait for Trunk to bend back again, but once more grabbed a root and scrambled out.

"If it was your map, do you have any idea of what it is we're looking for?"

"Some," said Sorrow.

"I don't suppose we're looking for very fancy knitting needles, are we?" Brand asked, holding up a slender jade shaft.

"You found one!" said Sorrow. "Where's the skull that held it?"

"There wasn't a skull," said Brand. "If these pits used to be graves, any human remains rotted away a long time ago." He pulled two more of the shafts from his pocket. "We also found these rods of onyx and glass."

Sorrow took the glass rod, feeling both excited and disappointed. She already had a nail of glass, and saw no benefit to adding a nail of jade or onyx. "How much do you know about my abilities?"

"We know you're a witch," said Bigsby.

Sorrow nodded. "More precisely, I'm a materialist. By using these nails, I can gain mastery over objects made from the same base materials."

"How?" asked Bigsby.

"You really don't want to know."

"I do! I command you to tell me how to use these items!"

Sorrow drew back her hood, revealing her shaved scalp. "Fine. You take a hammer and nail these into your head."

"Really?" Bigsby asked. "It's that simple?"

"I wouldn't call it simple. A misplaced nail can kill a weaver. If you're lucky enough to live, you're marked forever as a dangerous heretic who can be legally put to death on sight. All power comes with a price."

"But you could show me how to place one of the nails in my scalp?" asked Bigsby. "I could gain your powers?"

"Only women can do it. For reasons I'm not sure of, men always cripple themselves if they try."

"Why should that be a problem for me?" Bigsby asked.

"It's a problem because we're royalty, sister," said Brand. "We represent not just our people, but our religion. Since the Church of the Book says that witches are sinful, imagine the scandal if a princess showed up in court with a nail in her head."

"Good point," said Bigsby.

Sorrow had to admire the calm tone Brand used in addressing Bigsby. She wasn't certain he was doing the right thing by manipulating the dwarf's delusions, but he seemed good at it.

She said, "You can keep these nails. They will be of interest to collectors. The jade nail might be worth a hundred moons. What I'm looking for are nails I've never seen before. And skulls. Especially skulls." She looked around the darkening jungle. There were hundreds of depressions. She shook her head. "Why did you choose to dig here?"

Brand pointed down the hill. "This is pretty much the highest point among the graves, so I didn't think we'd have to deal with a lot of groundwater. The graves further down would probably fill up with water faster than we could dig."

"Probably," she said. "Still, I hate to think that our search is going to be so... random. This could take a long time."

"Do you know anything that might help us pick the best targets?" Brand asked.

Sorrow shook her head. She glanced at the smoldering fire of their pathetic campsite. She said, "Why don't the two of you get that fire going again while Trunk and I unpack? No point digging further tonight. We can eat dinner, get some sleep, then figure out the best way to tackle this in the morning."

Bigsby looked the golem up and down. "I confess, I've not been as good a student of theology as I should have been. Why does the church hate witches? Being able to build a helper like this seems rather useful."

"Indeed," said Sorrow, giving Trunk hand signals to clear ground to pitch their tent. "Perhaps a bit too useful. Weavers lived in peace for a long time among the rest of humanity until Avaris, Queen of Witches, used her powers to carve out her own kingdom. She upset the existing order of the world by crafting a society in which women were held in higher esteem than men. The church's hatred of witches has more to do with politics than theology."

Trunk tossed aside a small boulder nearly a yard across that had to weigh several hundred pounds. Bigsby looked impressed as the rock rolled down the hill.

"This thing's as strong as Infidel," he said.

"Probably," said Sorrow. "And much more cooperative. I don't know why I wasted my time trying to persuade Infidel to join my cause. If there's one thing I've learned from life, if

I'm to truly have companions I can rely on, I must build them myself."

SORROW LAY AWAKE through the night. Though she had pitched her tent twenty yards distant from the brothers, she could still hear Bigsby snoring. But that wasn't the main reason she couldn't sleep. Partially, there was a sense of anticipation. She'd first heard about the Witches' Graveyard almost seven years ago, and it felt unreal that she'd found something she'd been searching for after all this time. The fact that three nails had been discovered in the first grave was a good omen. Honestly, she hadn't expected to find any. If these were the graves of victims of Lord Tower, the Witchbreaker, she would have guessed the nails would have been removed either before or after execution. Perhaps only valuable nails had been treated this way. Jade and onyx resembled colored glass; perhaps they'd been left in the grave by mistake.

Underlying her excitement was dread. There had been no skull, or any bones at all. What if she'd come all this way in vain? What if she spent the next year of her life digging for secrets and found none?

She was almost tempted to put Brand's fortune-telling talents to the test. Almost. He'd as much as admitted his skills were mere trickery. But perhaps there was some value in having someone listen attentively as she spoke. She'd kept her talks with the Romer family short and professional. They'd been employees, not friends. She'd opened up a bit with Infidel, but, in the end, they'd had little to say to one another.

She found it interesting that Brand might be a good enough listener that other people paid for the service. Perhaps it was worth spending a moon or two for a demonstration.

Still unable to sleep, she turned on her side, lowering her hand to scratch her left ankle. Her nails slid along the hard, glassy surface of the scales without managing in the least to relieve the itch. She scratched with more pressure, and succeeded only in slicing open the tip of her finger along the edge of one of the scales. She sat up in her tent and reached for her belt. She used the hard surface of the buckle to scrape her ankle vigorously.

She stopped scraping as she heard someone laugh directly behind her.

She spun around and found a pygmy standing not a yard away. How had he gotten into the tent? At least he didn't appear menacing. For starters, he was elderly, his face looking like wrinkled leather over his skull. He was so thin she could have counted his ribs. He was bald, devoid of any of scars that most pygmies sported. He was also missing the pygmy dyes that rendered river pygmies blue. He was white as cotton, save for his eyes, black and empty sockets in the dark tent. The skull-like quality of his face was enhanced by his grin, which showed his teeth.

She reached out to grab him as she said, "How did you get in here?" He stepped backward and her fingers closed on empty air. He laughed softly, then sighed, shaking his head.

She lunged, this time trying to grab him with both hands. He jumped backward. He laughed as he watched her hands flail uselessly in the space he'd stood a heartbeat earlier. But his back was now pressed against the wall of the tent. There was no more room to retreat.

"You aren't going to think this is funny when I'm through with you," she said, reaching for his throat.

He stepped backward, fading through the tent as if it were made of fog instead of heavy oilcloth. Her hands smacked into it with a thump. She stared at the empty wall. Was she dreaming again? Admittedly, she was exhausted, and had been drifting in and out of the antechamber of sleep. But she was definitely awake now. Wasn't she?

From outside the wall, the pygmy giggled.

She scrambled to the door of the tent, wearing only her cotton slip. She ran around the canvas walls and found the pale pygmy glowing in the moonlight. He was standing a few feet in front of the heart-shaped boulder. He laughed harder as he saw her, tears running down his cheeks.

"What's so funny?" she asked.

"You," the pygmy gasped, pointing at her. He spoke in the Silver Tongue, but she didn't recognize his accent. "The demons in the Forest of Torment told me I should bear witness to the return of the Destroyer." He wiped his wrinkled cheeks. "I can't believe they mistook you for something so dangerous."

"Demons? Forest of Torment? What the hell are you talking about?"

The pygmy shook his head. "It's precisely hell that I'm speaking of, but there's no point in explaining. You're nothing but a desperate and foolish girl." He sighed. "Demons. I should have known they were trying to trick me. The dragon will devour you and return to his slumber."

"The dragon?" she asked. "Are you talking about Rott? What do you mean, he'll devour me?"

"You're nothing but a tick, clinging to Rott's flesh. You may feast upon him only a little while before he catches you between his teeth."

"Who are you? How do you know this?"

He turned away, facing the boulder. He glanced over his shoulder and said, in a serious tone, "I've had my fill of conversation with the dead this day. At least those other souls accepted their fate." He took another step toward the boulder before looking back again. "Struggle if it amuses you. In the end, this is all there is of life. Take some comfort in the notion that your death may serve as a cautionary tale for others. Now, I must depart. I'm late for the Inquisition."

There was the sound of leaves crunching from the left side of the boulder. Brand appeared around the corner and asked, "Who are you talking to, Sorrow?"

Sorrow glanced at him, then back to the pygmy. But the pygmy was gone.

She ran forward and placed her hands on the rock. "Did you see him?"

"See who?"

"A pygmy. He was albino."

"They're all albino, I think," said Brand. "They just dye themselves different colors."

"Did you see him?"

"No."

"But you heard us talking?"

"I heard you talking, sure," said Brand. "But not the other half of the conversation. I thought you might be sleepwalking."

She shook her head. "I think I saw a ghost."

"Really?"

"Don't sound so skeptical," she said. "You've been to the Sea of Wine. You know that souls survive death."

"I don't doubt the existence of ghosts," said Brand. "But I've never met one. I have, on the other hand, met sleepwalkers. And crazy people."

"I'm neither."

"Just throwing out some theories." He stretched his back and yawned. "What time is it?"

"Time for us to dig," said Sorrow, heading back to her tent.

"Can't we wait until dawn?"

"You can go back to sleep if you wish. I've got things to do."

"Like what?"

"For starters, I've got to move this boulder."

"What? Why?"

"Because I'm pretty sure the pygmy just walked into it."

"You think it's hollow?"

"I don't know. But it occurs to me if it really did roll down the mountain and came to rest here, it's probably sitting on top of more graves. Maybe no treasure hunters have ever dug here. With a house-sized rock on top of them, on this high ground, maybe these graves have been protected from rain. Maybe the skeletons haven't rotted."

"That's a lot of maybes. While you strike me as a person who generally gets what she wants, I highly doubt that golem of yours is strong enough to move this boulder."

"I have more tricks up my sleeve than mere brute force," she said, looking back at him as she reached her tent.

"Fine," he said, scratching his head. "You can show me your tricks in daylight. Right now, I'm going back to... to..."

His voice faded off as he stared at her. She followed his gaze and realized he was staring at her feet.

"Are you... are you wearing..."

"These aren't boots," she said. "I think... I think I might be turning into a dragon. I'm hoping I can find something in one of these graves that will help me avoid that. Perhaps you can grasp my sense of urgency."

"I see," said Brand. He nodded, then headed back toward his tent. "Let me grab my shovel."

CHAPTER THREE
CLATTER

As Brand went to wake Bigsby, Sorrow ran her hands along the boulder. The surface was heavily weathered and cracked. Vines had dug deep into crevices in the rock. Sorrow closed her eyes and leaned her forehead against the stone. She took a deep breath and calmly expanded her senses. Since tapping into Rott's power, she'd been more aware of the decay that surrounded her. She'd noticed it first when she'd returned to the *Freewind* from the Great Sea Above. The second she'd stepped onto the ship, she'd felt the torn and broken wood fibers in the timbers beneath her feet and been keenly aware that the ship was doomed.

Worse, when she'd looked at Gale Romer, the ship's captain, she'd been able to see that Gale was dying. Not in an immediate, urgent sense, but Gale was well along the path of her inevitable fate. Gale was only forty, robust and active, strengthened by life at sea, but Sorrow's new awareness had focused on the woman's gray hairs and weathered skin. It was as if she could watch Gale's life slowly but inexorably seeping away.

Save for dealing with Eddy, she'd barely used her powers since returning to the material world. Her hyper-awareness of the creeping decay had faded. But it was time to summon that sense once more. Just as humans didn't last forever, this imposing mound of stone before her was on a one way trip toward becoming sand. She spread her arms across the rock and could feel the veins of weakness that radiated through the seemingly solid surface.

She closed her hands around the vines that corseted the rock. The roots and tendrils had weakened the stone over the centuries, but now the thick vines did as much to hold the boulder together as tear it apart. Fortunately, they were easily removed. She closed her eyes and found the dark doorway inside her, carefully opening it. The vines in her grasp crumbled to dust. She opened her eyes as the rot spread through the remaining vines, which twisted and crackled as they withered. In moments, the last of the vegetation peeled away, leaving a ring of dirt around the boulder. She took a deep breath and willed the portal to close. It wasn't so difficult, when things were quiet and calm. But could she ever control the force during the heat of combat?

"Not bad," said Brand, who stood behind her holding his shovel.

"I'm just getting started," she said. She motioned for Trunk. He was now armed with a large sledgehammer. Sorrow pointed toward the top of the stone, where it dipped down into a narrow depression that formed the indentation of the heart-shape. "Climb," she said.

Trunk's inhuman limbs had no trouble scrambling up the cracked surface. Sorrow guided him with a string of commands to what she sensed was the boulder's weakest spot.

By now Bigsby had left his tent and found his brother. He looked like he was still half-asleep. He mumbled, "Whash going on?"

"Sorrow's hunting for ghosts," said Brand.

"Ghosts?" asked Bigsby, rubbing his eyes. "That's crazy."

Sorrow bit her lip to avoid responding. She couldn't let the dwarf distract her. She finally had Trunk right where she needed him.

"Strike the crack before you!" she shouted. "Use your full strength!"

Trunk swung the hammer back behind him. It cut through the air with a loud *WHOOSH* and smacked into the rock with a deafening *BANG*. All throughout the waking jungle, monkeys and birds screeched in alarm.

Sorrow turned and said, "Gentlemen, I'm fairly certain I know how the stone will fall, but I suggest you take a few steps back as a precaution."

Bigsby's eyes narrowed. Sorrow could tell she was about to be scolded for addressing the two men as 'gentlemen.' She quickly added, "You also, your highness."

Behind her, the stone was popping and trembling as the shock of the impact continued to reverberate. She stepped away as the loudest crack yet made her flinch. She looked back in time to see the two halves of the heart-shaped boulder split, then tumble away from each other. Both of the top-heavy pieces flipped as they tumbled down the respective halves of the hill they'd been perched upon.

Trunk had been straddling the crack; he tumbled into the shallow pit of black earth left by the departing stones and landed on his feet, looking none the worse for the experience. She was deeply satisfied by the performance of the golem. The moons she spent on top quality lumber were an excellent investment.

"That was a lucky break," said Brand. "What would you have done if the stone had split, but just sat there?"

"That wasn't going to happen. I could sense the tension between the two halves of the stone. Each half was held in balance by the other, but doomed to fall once split. Once you know how to look at the material world, it's not that difficult to understand."

Brand shook his head as he looked down the hill to where half of the boulder had come to rest. "I think there's a metaphor here about broken hearts, but I'm too deprived of coffee to piece it together."

"I shall record in my journal that on this day you were at a loss for words," said Sorrow.

Brand laughed. "I don't think I've heard you make a joke before."

Sorrow shrugged. "I'm not certain why you think I've made one now."

She grabbed a shovel and carried it to Trunk, swapping it for the sledgehammer. The compressed earth beneath the boulder was broken and jumbled from the movement of the stone. There were no clues to guide her to a likely place to start digging, other than the fact that the other graves seemed to be laid out in predictable rows. Following from the row that led up the hill, the stone possibly covered a half dozen graves. She eyeballed the nearest grave and used it to locate what might be the first grave in from the edge. Brand used the same strategy to find a grave on the opposite side.

"Shall we race?" Brand asked as he pushed his shovel into the soil.

"It really wouldn't be a fair contest. Trunk is far stronger and never tires."

"You're on," Brand said, as dirt flew over his shoulder. Bigsby grabbed a shovel and joined his brother.

"Dig," she said to Trunk, feeling a slight urge to complain that the brothers had a head start. But she'd never agreed to a contest. Why should she be concerned about who would win?

Of course, ten minutes later, when Trunk's shovel struck something hard, she couldn't resist the urge to shout, "Victory!"

Brand and Bigsby had barely dug a pit four feet deep, while Trunk was already in a hole down to his shoulders.

"Congrats," said Brand. "What did you find?"

Sorrow knelt to see better. What *had* she found? Trunk continued to remove dirt, revealing a layer of flat black slates, looking for all the world like roofing shingles. The boulder had been as big as a house, but she hadn't expected to find an actual structure under it.

Brand climbed out of his hole and wandered over.

"It looks like a roof," Sorrow said.

The shingles were rectangles two feet long and a foot wide, with rough edges. Once Trunk had made the hole wide enough, Brand dropped in to help clear the dirt. It soon became apparent the slates were stacked into an arch. The structure was about five feet across, but she couldn't guess how long as they hadn't found either end yet. So far, about six feet of the arch was exposed.

Brand knelt and tested his luck at lifting one of the shingles. He let out a little grunt as he lifted it to his chest, then stood and pushed it out of the hole.

"Are those heavy?" she asked.

"They ain't light," he said.

"Climb out. Let Trunk remove the stones."

Brand did so. Trunk lifted the shingles with no hint of effort, revealing another layer of stones beneath. Under this, something glinted through the gaps. Sorrow leaned low to be certain. As, one by one, the stones were pulled away, she could see that they were exposing what looked to be a coffin made of solid glass.

That wasn't the only thing being exposed, however. For as Trunk stood to lift out a slate tile, a shaft of sunlight fell upon the first rectangle of open glass, illuminating the contents. While Sorrow had little personal experience with male anatomy, she couldn't help but think that what the light revealed strongly resembled the naked crotch of a hairy man.

Brand and Bigsby apparently noticed as well.

Bigsby asked, softly, "Is that... what I think it is?"

"I'm almost certain it is," said Brand.

Of course, there was more beneath the glass than preserved genitalia. As Trunk continued uncovering the glass coffin, he revealed the man's torso. The body was covered in kinky black hair over skin white as cotton. Despite his deathly pallor, the man was an impressive physical specimen. He was muscular almost to the point of grotesquerie. Sorrow wondered if he might be a half-seed of some kind, perhaps a man blended with a bear. His shoulders were far broader than any she'd ever seen on a living man. His beastly appearance was compounded by fingernails at least four inches long, thick and gnarled.

Yet when his face was at last revealed, she abandoned any thought that the figure before her was anything other than human. Though his face was mostly concealed by a thick black beard, and despite the long hair draping around his head having the fullness of a lion's mane, there was something deeply human about the man's face. There was a gentleness to it, a look of peace that reminded her of a sleeping child.

"Is he breathing?" Bigsby asked.

Sorrow furrowed her brow as she stared intently at the man's chest. It was perfectly still. She also noted the man didn't possess an aura. All living things carried a faint glow of energy she'd been trained to detect, and this man was completely devoid of inner light. "I'm almost certain he's dead."

"Quite well preserved, isn't he?" Brand asked.

"Perhaps he isn't even real," said Sorrow. "You can craft a figure out of wax that looks eerily lifelike. It's difficult to believe anything that once lived has been buried for centuries without rotting."

"He's in glass," said Bigsby. "Maybe he's pickled."

Sorrow suspected the light would refract differently if the coffin had been filled with fluid. But she did notice that the coffin didn't appear to have any seams. Since she knew the art of glass weaving, she knew it was possible to craft a container, heat it to drive out air, then seal it before it could refill, creating a vacuum. The weaver who'd taught her this trick many years ago had used it to preserve flowers. Could the effect be scaled up to preserve a body? Were walls of thick glass enough to hide this corpse from Rott's gaze?

"Well, as treasure goes, this is something of a dud. He's not even wearing any jewelry," said Brand.

"Really?" Sorrow asked. "We encounter something this mysterious and all you can think about is the lack of loot?"

"The Black Swan might buy him," said Bigsby, now speaking in his normal, male voice. "She used to buy all kinds of weird stuff from Stagger."

"I'm here for knowledge, not wealth," said Sorrow. "Somebody went to a lot of trouble to preserve his body. Aren't you curious who cast the spell? For that matter, aren't you even more curious who he is?"

Bigsby nodded. He said, once more in his annoying *falsetto*, "Maybe it's the knight."

"What knight?" she asked.

"You know. The knight from Knight's Castle."

"Stark Tower? The Witchbreaker?"

"Why not?" Bigsby squeaked.

Sorrow sighed. "You know, real women don't sound like that. Just use your normal voice."

Bigsby put his hands on his hips and pushed his voice even higher as he said, "This is my normal voice."

Sorrow was sorry she'd brought the subject up. She returned to the topic at hand. "I can't imagine it's Tower. He was a hero to the church. They wouldn't bury him naked in the middle of nowhere."

"Do you want me to smash open the coffin?" asked Brand.

"No," said Sorrow. "I can weave glass, so opening the coffin isn't a problem. But I don't want to tamper with anything before I get the chance to do some research. We'll need to pull this coffin out and take it back to Commonground. I'm not selling anything to the Black Swan, but she might have some information as to who he is."

"That sounds like a lot of work," said Brand.

"I'll see that you're well compensated for your efforts. For now, let's continue digging the hole you started. Perhaps our mystery man has a brother."

The second grave went quickly, thanks to the combined efforts of both Brand and Trunk. They were aided by the fact that the soil of this grave was bone dry, starting a few feet below the surface, and crumbled easily beneath the assault of the shovels. Sorrow stood near the edge of the grave, chewing her nails. What if this grave held another preserved body? Of all the things she'd imagined digging up, a naked man had never entered her list of possibilities.

At the same depth as the first grave, they again hit a stone arch. The structure soon proved to be much larger. They spent hours clearing out an area twice the size of the original grave, and still had failed to find the final shape of the building.

Impatient that their efforts weren't yielding results more quickly, Brand dropped to his knees and pulled away a layer of slate tiles. His efforts only revealed more stones. He was completely drenched in sweat as he kept pulling aside fresh layers. Finally, two feet down, he reached the last of the slate. Glass glinted in the now dimming light. He leaned in close to stare into the dark interior.

"What do you see?" asked Sorrow.

"Nothing," Brand said, sitting up and pushing aside more stones. "I need more light."

As he cleared away more slate, it soon became obvious that insufficient light wasn't the problem. Instead, the coffin beneath the stones was made of smoked glass, almost tar black, hiding the contents.

Brand brushed aside dirt, cupping his hands to block reflections on the dark glass, but shook his head when this failed to produce results. He blew on the edges of his hands where they'd touched the glass. "Ouch. That's kind of hot."

"Hot?" asked Sorrow.

"Everything feels hot to me right now," said Brand. "A side-effect of digging holes. But this glass is like an oven."

"Climb out," Sorrow said. She grabbed Trunk by the hand and said, "Lower me."

"What are you going to do?" asked Brand.

"I'm a glass weaver," said Sorrow. "I'm going to alter the glass to make it transparent."

"Nice trick," said Brand as he pulled himself out of the hole.

Sorrow dangled from Trunk's grasp until she was a few inches above the stones. She dropped down and knelt over the glass.

She touched it carefully. Brand had exaggerated its heat. It was far shy of an oven, more like a freshly poured cup of hot tea.

She placed both palms on the glass. Pulses of energy flowed into her shoulders, feeling almost like ants crawling just beneath her skin. "There's extraordinary power here," she whispered. "I've never felt anything quite like it."

"That would have been a very funny thing to say when we first exposed the contents of the other grave," Brand said as he sat on the edge of the pit.

Sorrow ignored him. She concentrated on the substance beneath her fingers. Glass was easy to manipulate. Ordinarily, it would yield to her fingers as if it were a slightly sticky dough. But she didn't want to change the shape of the substance, only its color. There must be foreign material in the glass to create the smoky hue. Could she isolate this and draw it out?

Her brow furrowed as she found that the foreign material was caked mostly on the interior of the glass. The exterior parts of the glass she was touching were actually transparent already, but backed with a dark substance that swallowed all light.

She gave the glass a slight push, hoping to dislodge the darkness. She was pleased when it worked and a chunk of inch-thick sooty blackness fell away. Unfortunately, all this revealed was gray smoke swirling in the interior.

Suddenly, she was tossed a foot into the air as the stones around her jumped, as if they'd been struck from beneath. She landed as black smoke billowed up from cracks in the stone.

She tried to call out to Trunk, but wound up coughing violently. Her eyes clamped shut as the acrid fumes burned them. The ground beneath her surged again, throwing her onto her back.

A man's hands closed on her forearm. With a tug that felt as if it would pull her arm from its socket the unseen man lifted her, rudely throwing her over his shoulders.

"Hold tight!" Brand called out, though not to her. She managed to crack her eyes open ever so slightly and saw that she was thrown over Brand's shoulder. She twisted to see that he had one hand on a shovel thrust down into the hole. At the edge of the grave, Bigsby lay with his head and shoulders out over the pit, holding the handle of the shovel down. Brand grabbed the shovel and used it to climb. This resulted in an ungraceful tangle of limbs as Brand pushed Sorrow from his shoulder onto Bigsby's back as he crawled out over both of them.

She was too weakened by her inhalation of smoke to protest as she was sandwiched between the two men. They were all tossed into the air by a powerful shock wave that sent huge stones flying straight up from the grave. Another jolt followed swiftly. There was a loud *SNAP* and a chunk of smoky glass that must have weighed a hundred pounds shot fifty feet skyward before falling back into the grave and shattering with a loud crash.

"Trunk, get us to safer ground," Sorrow croaked as she wiped her stinging eyes. She didn't even see where her golem was, but he proved to be within range of her commands. His gloved fingers closed around the belt of her pants and lifted her butt-first from the trembling earth. It was apparently too much to expect to be rescued with any hint of dignity today.

Trunk paused to keep his balance as the earth shuddered again. Bigsby lay near the golem's feet, flat on his back. Sorrow reached out to him. As Trunk started running, her hand closed around the dwarf's fingers and she dragged him as they dashed for safety.

Brand was left behind, but by now he had managed to make it to his feet, nimbly dodging the heavy stones that fell to earth around him. He danced across the shuddering landscape, leaping up to grab a low hanging vine. He used the makeshift rope to pull himself up into the branches of a swaying tree, then leaned out to peer into the smoking grave. The plume was so thick Sorrow wondered if they'd somehow dug into an active volcano vent.

A bony black claw rose from the pit, digging into the earth. This was followed moments later by an ebony reptilian skull snaking through the billowing fumes. The eye sockets were lit by flickering embers.

"Greatshadow?" she whispered.

The beast opened its jaws, and jets of black smoke poured out. It looked as if were roaring, but no noise came from the beast save for the clatter of bone against bone and the sizzle of damp earth as it dragged its skeletal body to the surface.

The creature now stood revealed as a skeletal dragon, as tall as a warhorse, perhaps thirty feet in length from the tip of its snout to the last smoldering vertebra of its serpentine tail. Within its blackened rib cage roiled organs of smoke and flame. The beast spread its bone wings and flapped, a futile gesture as it had no flesh to catch the air.

Brand was almost directly above the dragon, stretched between branches, now utterly still.

Before the beast could gaze in their direction, Sorrow shouted, "Trunk! Stop!" The wooden man instantly froze. She froze as well. She wasn't certain, but there was a strong possibility the dragon was an expertly constructed bone-golem. In the absence of their creator, these mindless beasts would obey predetermined criteria as to whom and what it should attack. "Anything that moves" was one likely criteria, so until the beast turned its gaze elsewhere, she wasn't twitching an eyebrow.

Unfortunately, Bigsby didn't share her caution. He twisted free from her grasp and ran for a pickaxe that had fallen nearby. He brandished the tool overhead and cried, "For the glory of King Brightmoon, I smite thee!" The "thee" trailed off into a high-pitched battle-shriek as he charged the dragon.

The beast whipped its head toward the dwarf, extended its neck, and let out a whirlwind of smoke. Bigsby disappeared in the swirling smog, but his cry continued undiminished. To Sorrow's surprise, Bigsby leapt up from the smoke a yard away from the beast's snout, swinging the pickaxe with both hands to drive the tip into the monster's nose. Sparks flew as iron bit into bone. The creature jerked its head sideways, throwing

Bigsby in a spinning arc through the air. He landed with a bounce, bounced again, and wound up tumbling into the grave where the naked man had been uncovered.

The dragon turned toward the grave, apparently intending to give chase. Sorrow ground her teeth. As tempting as it was to not hear Bigsby's voice again, she couldn't sit by and watch him get slaughtered. She commanded Trunk to put her down and pointed at the dragon. "Stop that thing!"

Her golem lumbered forward, but she could see he would never cover the distance in time before the bone-dragon dove into the pit and finished off Bigsby. As the beast reared back to lunge, Brand swung down on a length of vine and kicked the creature's right hind leg out from under it. The beast stumbled, craning its neck around to see who had attacked it. Brand somersaulted backward as the beast snapped at him, then scrambled up into the trees with the speed of a hyperactive monkey. The bone-dragon's jaws bit into bark where his feet had rested half a second before.

The dragon dug its claws into the tree and started to give chase. Brand eyed the surrounding vines, planning his next leap. But before the beast could force him from his perch, Trunk reached the bone dragon and grabbed the creature by the tail, yanking it from the tree with a loud clatter.

The dragon spun around with its jaws spread and neatly clipped off Trunk's right arm. The golem swung with his left, delivering a blow to the side of the beast's skull that send a cloud of soot flying from the creature's bones. The dragon responded with a swipe of its dagger-like fore-claws, tearing Trunk's wooden-bucket head from his torso.

Sorrow circled through the trees, then darted toward the bone-dragon from behind. She had no direct command over some other witch's golem, and her power of decay would have little effect on smoke-cured bones. Her one hope was that the beast's skeleton had been fixed together with iron or copper wires. She could command these metals to corrode, reducing the beast to a pile of disconnected bones.

The dragon's tail whipped unpredictably as it continued to tear Trunk apart. Despite her best efforts at dodging, the tail caught Sorrow in the gut, knocking her backward. Her fingers briefly closed around a vertebra, but she sensed no metal at all within the creature. The smoky bones were held together with enchanted sinews. She fell to her hands and knees, unsure of what she would do if the dragon turned its jaws toward her.

Fortunately, the dragon was distracted as Brand leapt from the trees and rolled in front of it. He darted away from the beast, waving his arms and screaming, "Over here!"

Sorrow wondered if this was to save her, then saw Brand glance toward the open grave where Bigsby had fallen. The dwarf was climbing from the pit, in full sight of the dragon. The dragon crouched, eyeing the struggling dwarf like a cat stalking a mouse. Brand waved his arms even more vigorously, and the beast's glowering eyes turned to study him.

For a few seconds, the dragon paused, its arcane programming unable to choose between two inviting targets. Sorrow struggled to her feet, running toward the tall tree Brand had climbed earlier. Her powers of rot might not be able to affect the dragon directly, but with luck she might yet be able to strike a blow. The beast had gouged thick claw marks into the wood as it had chased Brand. With a grunt, she drove her hands and boots into the splintered wood and climbed, scrambling to reach the thick branch Brand had stood on, a good thirty feet off the ground. The dragon's hips were almost directly beneath the branch. Breathlessly, she stretched her right arm up until her fingers touched the thick limb, almost a tree in its own right. She felt Rott's dark energy flow through her into the tree. In seconds, there was a loud *CRACK* as the branch snapped from the tree.

Unfortunately, the beast had by now decided between its targets as Bigsby reached the top of the grave and stood, shaking the dirt from his tangled wig. Something about the shimmering locks triggered the dragon's instincts to strike.

The dragon leapt in a graceful arc like a tiger, its jaws opened to consume the dwarf. Luckily, the falling branch caught the last few vertebrae of his tail as it fell, robbing the creature of momentum. Instead of landing on Bigsby, the bone-beast tumbled snout first into the open grave. There was a crash as the glass casket shattered beneath the dragon's weight.

Brand ran and grabbed Bigsby, tossing his diminutive sibling over his shoulder like a sack of potatoes. Bigsby waved his fist at the dragon flailing in the grave and shouted, "We must not retreat! The honor of the Brightmoon name demands victory!"

Brand probably wasn't persuaded by this argument, but it proved not to matter. Graceful as he was, he stumbled on the uneven ground, thrown off balance by his flailing brother. They both slid down the leafy hillside just as the dragon fully emerged from the grave. Sorrow scrambled down the tree, planting both her feet firmly on the ground.

She placed one hand on the tree trunk. She knew that if this didn't work, she was dead. She waved with her free hand and cried out, "Dragon! Face me! I've come to steal your treasures!"

She felt a curious thrill as the monster turned toward her.

"Come and get me," she growled, as she sank her fingers into the thick tree trunk. The entropic force flowed from her and she tore out chunks of crumbling wood by the fistful as the dragon charged. The tree began to creak. She was reaching into the core, up to her shoulder now, and the tree groaned as it leaned in the direction of the dragon. At last, the wood splintered, snapped, and fell. She nearly laughed that her plan had worked, until the falling tree came to a halt at a thirty-degree angle, its upper branches tangled in the branches of its neighbor.

By now, the dragon was mere yards away. She stared into the beast's open jaws. What exquisite irony that her quest to restore the weavers to their full glory was to be brought to a premature end by this unthinking relic crafted by her predecessors.

The creature jerked to a shuddering halt, its jaws snapping half an inch from her nose. Soot and cinders washed over her face. She fell to her knees, blind and gasping. The beast sounded like a thousand castanets clacking as it wheeled away from her.

Low to the ground, she forced her eyes opened. Through tears, she could barely make out a large, naked man standing in the first grave, his muscles straining as he held the dragon by the tail. The man let go as the dragon turned in its tracks, its open jaws aimed for the warrior's head.

Sorrow blinked. Her vision improved slightly in time for her to see that the man was definitely the person who'd been buried in the glass coffin. His long hair whipped behind him as he leapt from the grave to meet the dragon's charge. He held a slab of slate the size of a shield in his hand, one of the roofing stones she'd barely been able to move.

The man thrust the slab into the dragon's snapping jaws. The stone shattered, but took with it several of the dragon's teeth. The beast's mouth opened again, and the grave-man thrust his hands into the gap, grasping the upper and lower jaws. His face contorted as he forced the dragon's jaws open wider, then wider still. The warrior showed no sign of pain as the beast's fore-claws slashed out and tore bright red ribbons across his chest. With a *SNAP*, the right half of the beast's lower jaw broke free, leaving the warrior holding a long, toothy club of bone.

Sorrow made it back to her feet, wiping her eyes, coughing out the last of the smoke, only to have her vision blocked as the dragon unleashed another torrent of black vapors, completely engulfing the warrior. From the black cloud came a succession of grunts and bangs and cracks. Suddenly, what was left of the beast's skull spiraled into the air, landing thirty feet away.

Unfortunately, decapitating a golem wouldn't kill it. As impressive as the warrior had been so far, the fact that he'd bled when cut hinted to her that the dragon would likely emerge the victor. She looked around, but couldn't see Brand and Bigsby anywhere. Sorrow wondered if it might not be time for her to make a strategic retreat.

A voice called from above, "Get out of the way!"

Brand was in the vines overhead, with Bigsby struggling to climb to his level. They both had knives, and were slashing at the vines and branches that held the tree she'd attempted to topple. The dragon was still well-positioned to be crushed. Unfortunately, so was the warrior, although she couldn't see his exact location within the smoke.

"You'll crush the man!" she yelled, as Brand sawed through the sturdiest vine holding the tree.

"These things happen!" Brand cried.

Sorrow had no time to argue, as the vine snapped and the tree lurched down, gaining momentum as more and more of the smaller branches holding it broke. She ran clear as the massive tree slammed to the earth behind her. She spun, and saw a tornado of smoke rising. Shards of black bones bounced in every direction across the broken ground. The tree had fallen dead on, crushing the beast's rib cage.

Off to one side, a black claw twitched as the magic that animated it drained away. She ran to the fallen trunk and clambered over it, searching for the warrior.

To her relief, he hadn't been crushed. He was on his feet, looking down at the jawbone in his hand with glazed eyes. His chest and arms were striped with blood from dozens of gashes. His once white flesh was now black with soot. Perhaps the loss of blood had weakened him, for he swayed on his feet, his legs trembling.

"Are you all right?" she asked, standing on the tree, looking down at him.

He didn't look at her. He looked down at his arms, coated with soot and blood. He lifted his hands, and silently stared at his long, curling nails. His brow furrowed in confusion.

She felt confusion all her own. Even though the man was plainly alive and breathing, she still couldn't detect any hint of a life aura. It was as if she were looking at a walking corpse. Hesitantly, she asked again, "Are you all right?"

"Aye," he whispered, then collapsed, landing face down in the leaves.

CHAPTER FOUR
CHAMBER OF SECRETS

"OKAY, WHAT JUST happened?" Brand asked as he dropped from the tree.

Sorrow shook her head as she climbed down to the fallen warrior. "You know everything I do."

She knelt over the man. He was still alive, despite his wounds and missing aura. She could see down to bone through the neatly parallel slices across his ribs. Blood gushed freely from a deep gash on his left arm.

"Give me your shirt," she said. "We need to stop the bleeding."

Brand obeyed, though his shirt was sweaty and covered with dirt. "He'll get infections unless we use clean cloth."

"I think the more urgent problem is his imminent exsanguination," said Sorrow, tearing the shirt into strips. "Once we staunch the bleeding, I can clean and stitch his injuries."

Brand dropped to his knees and wadded up one of the shirt rags, applying pressure to a nasty wound on the man's thigh.

The man began to shiver violently.

"Is he cold?" asked Bigsby, looking over her shoulder.

"He's hot as a furnace," said Sorrow, placing her hand on the man's brow.

"We should feed him," said Bigsby.

"What?" Sorrow asked.

"If he has a fever," said Bigsby. "Feed a fever, starve a cold."

Sorrow started to point out that the man was bleeding to

death, not fighting the flu, but pressed her lips tightly together, determined not to get drawn into the dwarf's madness.

"It's starve a fever, feed a cold," said Brand.

Bigsby crossed his arms. "You don't know what you're talking about."

"Which is it, Sorrow?" asked Brand.

"How should I know?" she asked.

"Women learn that kind of stuff from their mothers," said Brand.

"My mother died in childbirth," said Sorrow. Fortunately, this left her companions silent, allowing her to focus on the task at hand.

"I think we've got the worst of his limbs," Sorrow said to Brand. "See if you can lift him so I can work on his ribs." Brand shifted around, placing both hands beneath the man's shoulders. The man groaned as he was lifted. His eyes fluttered open, but were unfocused.

"Can you understand me?" Sorrow asked. "We're trying to help."

The man's eyes fixed on her. Perhaps it was her imagination, but the faintest hint of a brave smile flashed across his lips. Then he fainted once more.

She wrapped his chest and ribs with the longest strips of the shirt, putting as much pressure as possible to close the wounds. The dragon's claws had been sharp as razors, resulting in wounds that meshed together quite nicely with a little pressure. A cut with a duller instrument would have left torn and ragged edges that would have resisted her hurried attempts to close them.

"Bigs—I mean, your highness, run to my tent and bring us blankets," said Sorrow, as she helped Brand lay the warrior back down.

"I'm not some common servant," said Bigsby.

"I'll go get them," Brand said wearily. He glanced at Sorrow and gave an apologetic shrug.

Dusk dimmed into night as she continued working on the fallen warrior's wounds. Brand built a fire and boiled water, then constructed an impromptu shelter of blankets, since Sorrow didn't want to risk transporting the man to her tent. As she carefully cleaned each wound, she stitched them using fine silver wires no thicker than a hair. The man's fever abated as she worked. Indeed, he was now cold and clammy to the touch. Despite their best efforts, he'd lost a lot of blood.

The man slept through most of her treatment, though from time to time his eyes would flicker open. Once, he arched his back, gritting his teeth as he sucked in air. She'd grabbed his hand and he'd squeezed until she was certain her fingers would snap, before his spasm passed and he lapsed into stillness once more.

"You're good at this," Brand said as he inspected the zig-zag stitches along the man's ribs.

"I wish I were better," Sorrow said. "If I was a bone-weaver, I could manipulate bodies as if they were clay. Alas, I've never tracked down a living bone-weaver to learn the art. Still, I've learned a great deal about human anatomy. I was fortunate enough to study with Mama Knuckle, who has no peer as a necromancer."

"You studied necromancy?" She could tell from Brand's tone that he equated necromancy with evil.

Sorrow shrugged. "If she hadn't taught me the art of soul catching, I couldn't animate my golems."

Brand leaned over to the fire and poked at the logs with a stick. "Trapping the spirits of the dead seems, um, not nice."

"You were about to use a stronger word."

"I like to be diplomatic."

"You're entitled to your opinion. The souls I capture are doomed spirits who would eventually fade from existence. It's not as if I'm snatching souls off clouds in heaven."

"You believe in heaven?"

"How can you not? You've been to the Sea of Wine. You have the evidence of your own senses to know that our world is surrounded by numerous abstract realms where the dead dwell for a time. Why shouldn't heaven be among them?"

"I didn't think you believed in the teachings of the Church of the Book."

"What I believe is of no importance. The abstract realms are shaped from human collective consciousness. Hundreds of thousands of people believe in heaven, so they've no doubt created it by now."

"By that logic, shouldn't the Divine Author exist as well? The same number of people believe in him."

"Perhaps he does exist."

"And you'd wage war against a god not noted for his tolerance of sinners?"

"If there is a Divine Author, he's the creation of men, reflecting all their flaws and weaknesses. He's the embodiment of hatred and fear and injustice, and I shall fight to my dying breath to oppose him. If I have the courage to overthrow earthly kings, I can muster the will to battle a heavenly one."

Brand chuckled and said, "Wow."

"What's funny?"

"I just haven't met many people, male or female, ballsy enough to take on gods."

Sorrow kept quiet as she finished stitching the last wound on the warrior. She was determined not to respond to Brand's choice of words, but in the end, she couldn't hold her tongue. "I'm decidedly not 'ballsy.' Courage isn't dependent on male anatomy."

"All I'm saying is that you're bold. I meant it as a compliment."

"Yet you managed to turn it into a slight against the entire female sex."

"In addition to being bold, you're also more than a little brittle," Brand said with a frown.

"I'm paying you to dig graves, not judge me."

"That I'll do for free," he said, grinning. "Ever since I learned the art of reading people's hidden natures, I've been unable to turn it off."

"Nothing about my nature is hidden," said Sorrow. "I pride myself on being open in my goals and motives."

Brand laughed.

Sorrow scowled at him.

"You honestly believe that?" Brand asked.

"You've no reason to doubt my word."

"Maybe you should try a little doubt. I would say there's a very good chance you've been deceiving yourself."

"By what right do you think that you know me better than I do?"

"Let's put it to a test. I'll ask you three questions. You answer me as honestly as you can, and I'll tell you what you truly mean."

"I won't engage in such an absurd exercise," she said, with a dismissive wave.

"You just said you were proud to be open. I think we've exposed the first false notion you have about yourself."

She fixed her eyes upon him with a fierce glare. She didn't like having her own words thrown back in her face. Worse, he was smirking. He regarded this conversation as an amusing way to pass the time, while she found it to be an unwelcome intrusion. She owed him no answers.

On the other hand, what did she have to hide? She felt certain she could wipe that smug expression from his face.

"Fine," she said, crossing her arms. "You may ask what you wish."

"Okay," he said. "But don't make it so easy."

"I assure you, it will be easy to disprove your delusions."

"Not with such transparent body language," said Brand. "Crossing your arms like that is like trying to build a little wall between the two of us. You're entering into this as a hostile witness, rather than an open-minded seeker of truth."

"Just ask your first question."

"Why did you tell us your mother died in childbirth?"

"It's factual," she said. "It explained why I didn't feel like answering Bigsby's insane babbling."

"But if you've studied healing well enough to stitch this man back together, I'm guessing you probably know how to treat a fever."

"Yes," she said. "But he was bleeding to death. The fact he was hot was the least of his problems."

"You could have said that. Instead, you played the dead mother card."

She frowned. "This wasn't a poker hand. My mother's death is not a card."

"That's no doubt true, but you brought it up at a very odd time for no other reason than to shock us."

She shrugged. "It brought that ridiculous discussion to a halt."

"True. But it also revealed to me your mother's death has left you feeling entitled."

"Entitled?" she scoffed.

"Perhaps your father overcompensated for your mother's death. Doted on you a bit more than he should have. You could probably play upon his sense of guilt to get your way by invoking your dead mother. As an adult, in times of tension, you still resort to pleading that your loss in childhood should give you special privileges."

Sorrow shook her head and laughed ruefully. "That's your analysis? It's so pathetically wrong I don't know where to begin. No one who knows my father thinks of him as doting. Our family name is Stern. He's the living embodiment of the word."

"Wait... you wouldn't happen to be the daughter of Judge Adamant Stern?"

"I am. Was that your second question?"

"Is it true your father hung his own mother for being a witch?"

"Is that your third question?"

Brand looked lost in thought. "So, I'm guessing you think you hate your father?"

"I don't think I hate him. I know I hate him with every fiber of my being. His sins against mankind, all women, and his own family are beyond forgiveness."

"He's a captain in the king's Judgment Fleet. He has a duty to be tough."

"Did he have a duty to hang his own mother? I was ten years old when my housekeeper snuck me into the public square to witness the execution. As they pulled the hood over her head, my grandmother shouted, 'How can you betray your mother?'" She shook her head, as the memory burned fresh within her. "My father answered, 'How could you betray your god?' And then he gave the command to open the gallows door. I tried to scream, but my housekeeper clamped her hand over my mouth. That unborn scream... it's still inside me. It drives me to this day. All that I do, I do to destroy the institutions and laws that gave birth to a monster so vile as my father."

Brand rubbed his chin. He opened his mouth, about to speak, then fell silent.

"Is there something you wish to say?"

"I suspect I'd deeply regret saying it. I don't know how open you'd be to understanding your true motives."

"I won't be bothered by anything you say. Your supposed insights are merely part of a circus act. The pattern so far is that I tell you something in perfect honesty, then you tell me I meant the opposite of what I just said. Now that I've explained how much I hate my father, I imagine you'll tell me that means I truly love him."

"Oh, it's something much more powerful than love," said Brand. "Don't you see? Your father has provided your template for adulthood. Your whole life has been a quest to become him."

Sorrow rolled her eyes. "You're as insane as Bigsby."

"Your father's a judge. His daily life is devoted to deciding who's right and who's wrong. Now, you've fashioned yourself into a judge. But you've gone one step further. Your father pronounces witches and heretics and common criminals worthy of death. You've decided that all of civilization is guilty and must be destroyed."

"All people are judges," said Sorrow. "To say I'm like my father in this respect is unremarkable. We both eat bread and drink water. It's too trivial to be noteworthy."

"It's not just that you're both judgmental," said Brand. "You're both so certain of your cause it pushes you to do the unthinkable. Your father hanged his own mother. You've hammered nails into your brain."

"I do what I must," said Sorrow. "I've witnessed the true source of evil. Now that I can see what's wrong with the world, I cannot shut my eyes. My father's blind belief in the law has turned him into a monster."

"An interesting choice of words from someone whose legs are covered in dragon scales," said Brand.

His voice was calm as he said this, but Sorrow felt as if he'd grabbed her by the throat and shouted into her face. She rose. "I'm tired. It's late. This conversation is over."

"I haven't asked my third question."

"Your senseless speculations following your previous questions haven't left me eager to continue speaking. Besides, it's absurd talking to you about truth when you so openly live a lie. Bigsby isn't the missing Princess Innocent. The king has no son named Brand. I wouldn't believe you were brothers at all, if it weren't for your eyes."

Brand nodded. "They are similar, aren't they? I'm certain that Bigsby truly is my brother. But you're right. I'm no prince. I'm Brand Cooper, son of Grand Cooper."

"Of the Cooper Barrelworks?"

"The same."

"Forgive me for being dubious. Grand Cooper is one of the wealthiest men alive. Why would his children be wandering the world as coinless vagabonds?"

Brand chuckled. "That's kind of a long story. But who needs coins when we have dragon bones?" He held up a blackened rib.

Sorrow's eyes opened wide. She hadn't even thought of the fortune scattered around them. Dragon bones were worth their weight in gold at blood houses. Even bones burnt black would bring a good price.

"Since we all worked together to kill this dragon, I assume we split this treasure three ways?" he asked.

Yesterday, she would have argued. Their verbal contract said that anything they dug up would belong to her. But Brand had delivered the final killing blow. The division seemed fair. She nodded in agreement.

"This will buy us passage back to the Silver City," he said. "Hell, it will buy our own ship."

"If you're Grand Cooper's son, I'm surprised you don't already own a whole fleet."

Brand shrugged. "I do, technically. But it's been a long time since I've been back home to enjoy any of the trappings of my wealth. My father... he's something of a perfectionist. When Bigsby was born, he couldn't bear the thought of his first son having stunted, malformed limbs. So he commanded the midwife to take the baby away and kill it. He buried the body in a closed coffin so no one could see the freak he'd produced, and told the world the child had been stillborn."

"That's awful," said Sorrow.

"Fortunately, the midwife didn't kill the baby. Freaks are a valuable commodity. She sold the child to a circus."

Sorrow shook her head. "It's a sign of this world's corruption that such things can happen. How did you learn of his fate?"

Brand fed a new log into the fire, coughing at the smoke it stirred up. When he caught his breath, he said, "The midwife spent her money a bit too freely. My father thought she was stealing from him, but soon learned the truth of what had happened. He kept the secret for almost thirty years. During this time, I was born." He sighed. "I tried to be a good son, but sometimes he just seemed so unhappy. I didn't know that every time he looked at me he was almost paralyzed with guilt."

"He deserved his guilt," said Sorrow. "Though he failed, he'd conspired to commit infanticide. I can only imagine how much you hate him."

"No. I don't hate him. He made a mistake, but he's not evil. Four years ago, he suffered a stroke. His body was half-paralyzed. On his sick bed, he confessed everything to me. Said he'd been a fool to expect perfection from mere human flesh. He begged me to find his lost son and bring him home."

He looked at the sparks that rose from the fire. "The ensuing years have been a pretty wild adventure. I'm a different person from the naïve kid who left home. It's going to be strange going back. Stranger still when I tell Dad that his long lost son isn't only a dwarf, but also completely flipping insane."

"You could…" Sorrow shook her head.

"What?"

Sorrow ground her teeth together. "It causes me almost physical pain to say this, but a truthspeaker might be able to help you."

Brand's face brightened. "You're right. They could command Bigsby to remember who he truly was. It's an excellent idea."

He rose, picking up a branch from the fire. He used his makeshift torch to aid him as he gathered up dragon bones into a pile next to the warrior. "Maybe we'll run into a truthspeaker on the journey home who'll be amenable to a bribe."

"I think they prefer their compensation to be referred to as offerings."

As Brand turned his back to her, Sorrow allowed herself the luxury of scratching her itching thighs. Her stomach tightened as she felt how hard and stiff her skin was beneath the fabric of her britches.

Brand wound up near the pit the dragon had first erupted from. He crouched down, and held out his torch.

"Look at this," he said, sounding excited.

Sorrow welcomed the distraction and walked to the pit. To her surprise, Brand doused his torch on the broken ground as

she neared. She held her hands before her as her eyes adjust
to the sudden darkness.

Now she saw what Brand saw. The pit was glowing faintly.
She carefully crept across the uneven ground to gaze into it.
Thin beams of pale light seeped up through cracks in the slate
lining the bottom of the grave.

"I got so swept up in the fight and saving the mystery man's
life that I never stopped to think there might be something else
in the hole," said Brand. "I mean, I glanced in here while I was
gathering firewood, and all I saw was rock. But what if that
thing was meant to guard something?"

Sorrow slid down the dirt wall into the pit. She grunted as
she pushed one of the large flat stones aside. More light seeped
up from below. She kept moving stones until she nearly fell
through the widening gap. Carefully removing more stones, she
revealed the opening to a set of spiral stairs. She was looking
down the center of the spiral, and though this was the source
of the glow, she couldn't make out anything beyond the stairs.

Brand asked, "Should we wait until daylight to—"

Sorrow didn't wait for him to finish. She swung her feet
forward, then slid into the gap.

"Let's think this through," said Brand. "We're both
exhausted. I don't have it in me to fight another dragon."

"I'm just going to peek," said Sorrow, placing a hand on
the stone wall as she stepped gingerly down the stairs. She
knew Brand was right. The smart move would be to wait until
she could build a new golem and use it to explore the space.
But she'd come to the Witches' Graveyard expecting her life
to change forever. She felt certain she'd arrived at a pivotal
moment of her quest.

The steps opened into a circular chamber twenty feet across
and six feet tall, the walls, ceiling and floor hewn from a single
piece of slate. A glorystone was set into the center of the slate
floor, no bigger than a pea yet sufficient to fill the chamber
with light. Alas, the chamber appeared to be completely empty.

There wasn't even any dust. Her heart sank, disappointed that such a promising lead had come to nothing.

She clenched her fists. This couldn't be all there was. There must be some hidden passage. She moved to the nearest wall and rapped the stone with her fingers, then turned when she heard footsteps on the stairs. Brand crept down, with a dagger drawn.

"It's safe," she said. "Give me your knife."

"This was worth guarding with a dragon?" he said, crouching as he entered the room to hand her the dagger. "I mean, the glorystone will bring a good price, but—"

"This isn't about treasure," she said, tapping the wall with the hilt of the dagger as she held her ear close to the stone.

"What are you doing?"

"Checking for hollow spaces," she said.

"Right," he said, drawing another blade. He started tapping the ceiling as she worked the walls.

They worked for ten minutes, not speaking, just tapping.

"Wait," she said, holding up her hand.

"You got something?" he asked.

She tapped the wall, pressing her ear to it. There was a definite hollowness to the sound. "I think so." She ran her fingers across the slate. "This stone is perfectly smooth. No mason could have finished it to this precision. It has to be the work of a weaver with command over stone."

"How do we open it?"

"I don't know. I've never even heard of a slate weaver. It must be a lost art. A witch with power over slate could simply will the stone to move aside."

"Where there's a will, there's a way," said Brand. "Wait here."

He darted up the stairs. Sorrow scraped at the slate with her dagger blade, marring the finish, then began to hunt for another space behind the stone. Three minutes later, Brand came panting back down the stairs with a pick-axe in hand.

"Where was it?" he asked.

She pointed toward the mark she'd made.

He lined himself up. In the low space, he had to swing sideways. The pick-axe struck sparks and bounced off the wall. The force of the blow caused Brand's back to straighten and his head bumped the ceiling.

"Ow, ow, ow," he said, rubbing the top of his scalp. He ran his fingers where he'd struck the wall. "Barely even a scratch." He sighed. "The pick is more of a digging tool than a smashing tool. We need a sledgehammer."

"Go get one."

"I couldn't find it. Your golem was carrying it when the dragon tore him apart. Maybe it's under the tree."

"Give me," she said, grabbing the pick-axe. "I can't mold stone, but I'm an artist with iron." The rigid metal turned as soft as clay between her fingers. Brand looked impressed as she squished, squashed, and sculpted the relatively slender arms of the pick-axe into a sturdy hammer-head.

When she handed the hammer back to him, he said, "This should do the job."

This time, he got on his knees, shifting his grip on the hammer to allow for an overhead swing. The hammer hit with a thunderous CRACK and the slate splintered into a dozen shards.

The space revealed was no bigger than a breadbox. Within was a glass bottle, lidless and seamless, inside which was a rolled-up sheet of parchment.

"A message in a bottle," said Brand.

"A message only a witch can open, as there's no stopper," said Sorrow as she carried the jar into the light.

Brand snatched it away from her. "I think you may be overlooking a more direct approach." Before she could react, he smashed it on the ground, then bent down to pick up the parchment.

"Give me that," she grumbled. He offered it to her with a grin on his face. It was closed with a small band of silver. She could have used her powers to remove it, but decided to simply slide it off the end.

67

She unrolled the thin leather sheet. From its color and texture, she had the uneasy feeling the scroll might have been made from human skin. Brand looked over her shoulder at the looping script written upon it.

"I can't read a word of it," he said.

Sorrow frowned. "It's weaver script. Unfortunately, I can only read a little."

"They didn't teach you the secret code in weaver school?"

"I'm mostly self-taught," she said. "I've picked up bits and pieces of the script here and there, but never studied with anyone fluent in the language."

"Can you make out anything?"

"I recognize this symbol," she said, tapping on a small mark that looked like a sword or dagger. "It's the symbol of the Witchbreaker."

"The knight?"

"Either the knight or his sword. His sword was almost more feared than the man."

"Why?"

"Legend has it that the sword was forged from iron stolen from the gates of hell. Supposedly, this gave the sword the ability to open a direct path to the underworld for the soul of anyone it killed."

"That's worthy of a legend, I guess."

She traced her fingers over the symbols adjacent to the sword. "This is the symbol for death. I think... this symbol here is *rejoice*, or *celebrate*. And... hmm. I think this reads, 'Rejoice, sister, the Witchbreaker is dead.'"

"Maybe that was him buried in the grave," said Brand. "You might have spent the better part of the night saving the life of your greatest enemy."

"Maybe. But probably not. I can't understand why they would have saved his body." She furrowed her brow as she tried to puzzle out more symbols. "'In the midst of defeat, we have,' um, cooked? Tasted? Feasted on victory? I think it says 'we have feasted on victory.'" She ran her finger further down the page. "'But... they must abandon...' uh, 'abandon the... weapon'?"

"The sword?"

She shook her head. "No, I know that symbol. This is kind of a blend of the symbol for tool and the symbol for war. I'm reading *war-tool* as weapon. The symbol after it stands for 'man.' Maybe *war-tool man* is the way they wrote 'warrior'?"

"Keep reading," he said. "Maybe it will make sense in context."

"The... um. Hmm." She scratched her scalp. "The first one? 'The original is ours'?"

"The original?" he asked. "The original what?"

She sighed and shrugged her shoulders. "I'm lost. I got off to a good start, but I'm guessing at three out of four words. I think these are instructions to leave the 'war-tool,' whatever that is, and meet up at the 'dancing castle,' wherever that is."

"Dancing castle?" asked Brand. "That sounds kind of fun."

"I'm probably reading it wrong. But one thing I'm sure of is that I know this mark." She touched a skull-like symbol at the bottom of the parchment. "This was signed by Avaris herself."

"The old Queen of Witches?"

"Maybe the current queen," said Sorrow. "It's common folklore that Avaris is still alive, made immortal by her powers, living in a hidden castle until her enemies eventually perish. I guess if you're immortal, you can just wait people out."

"Immortal or not, she's got a long wait. The Church of the Book is still anti-witch, and it's not going anywhere soon."

"It will if I have a say in it."

"Right."

"But my task would be easier if I could find Avaris, and have her teach me the full arts of weaving."

"Maybe the dancing castle in the letter is her secret hideout," said Brand.

"Maybe. And maybe some of these symbols I can't read are directions. I think this might be the symbol for 'east.'" She tapped the page. "On the other hand, it might be the symbol for 'star.' A lot of these glyphs look alike."

Brand chuckled.

"What's funny?" she asked.

"You weren't happy with the idea that the church could help my brother. What if I told you the church could help you?"

Sorrow frowned.

"There are monks who spend their whole lives studying dead languages and copying ancient documents," said Brand. "I'm guessing somewhere in the church there's a monk who could read this letter."

"I can hardly stroll into a monastery and ask," she said.

"I could," he said. "My father is a great patron of the church. I'm guessing a little name dropping and a few coins in the poor box would have this thing translated in no time."

"An interesting theory," she said, keeping her voice neutral. Would it be that easy? Could she risk placing such a potentially valuable document into the hands of her enemies?

"I need to think about what to do," she said.

"Whatever." Brand shrugged. "It's past my bedtime. I'm dead on my feet."

"There might be more hidden chambers," she said.

"Holding letters we can't read? That's totally worth staying up all night."

"There's no need for sarcasm."

"See you in the morning," he said, going up the stairs.

As soon as he was gone, Sorrow scratched her thighs beneath her buttocks vigorously. She listened carefully at the stairs to make sure he wasn't coming back, then undid the buttons on her pants. Slipping her britches down her hips, her heart froze when she found both her thighs now oily black, covered with smooth scales. Her genitals were still untouched, but only just barely.

Had the changes stopped? Her skin itched almost to her belly button. Worse, the bones of her legs ached, as if invisible vises were clamping down, slowly warping them, the way her toes had been fused and reshaped into a tapering point.

She pulled up her pants and sat down on the stone floor. She took a deep breath. She'd always known that her quest for power would involve sacrifices. She'd forever scarred her own scalp, reworking her very brain with self-inflicted surgery. If she wound up covered in scales, well, what of it? She would pay any price.

Just as her father would have paid any price for what he believed in.

Was Brand right? Her father still had the physical form of a man, but at some point he'd turned into a monster. Had he felt the change? Had he understood the moment when humanity slipped away from him? Would she know if she herself crossed such a threshold?

She swallowed hard. Her vision blurred as she looked down at the letter. She wiped tears from her cheeks. "Don't be silly, girl," she whispered to herself, her voice trembling. "You're stronger than this."

She didn't feel it. Brand was right; she was exhausted. She lay flat upon the stone floor, staring up at the flawless black of the slate roof. It was like an endless void, and she felt as if she were perched upon a precipice, ready to fall into the dark.

She turned her head, staring at the glorystone, a small fragment of the sun. She idly reached out and ran her fingers along its faceted surface. She wondered what had become of Stagger. During the height of the blizzards, she hadn't been able to tell if the sun was following its normal path, though now that the storms had withdrawn the length of a day felt right to her.

She sat up as she heard a faint voice say her name. Craning her neck, she saw she was still alone. Had it only been her imagination?

Stranger still, she recognized the voice. She placed her fingers on the glorystone once more. She said, quietly, "Stagger?"

And then she fell.

CHAPTER FIVE

ART THOU A DEVIL?

THE SLATE CHAMBER vanished as Sorrow once more found herself falling through blue sky toward a vast green ocean. Before, she'd been only a disembodied spirit, affixed to Rott by an ethereal silver cord. Now, wind rushed across her skin and her stomach lurched as she tumbled. She landed with a splash in the warm ocean, gasping for breath as she floundered to the surface. She shuddered in horror as she looked down.

Her legs were gone. Her hips now flowed into a black, serpentine neck leading to Rott's body. Her still human torso served as the primal dragon's head. She had little to judge scale by in the trackless ocean, but she felt as if the human portions of her conjoined body had grown to giant size to better mesh with her draconian half.

She looked around and found the ocean empty. None of the other islands were present. Above, the golden disk of the sun hung motionless.

"Stagger!" she shouted.

A giant face appeared in the disk of the sun, with a scraggly beard and a mostly bald scalp. The face opened its eyes in a look of surprise. "Sorrow?"

"Where are we?" she shouted. "How did we get here?"

"I don't know!" Stagger said. "Something happened like this a few days ago, but I thought I was daydreaming. Things are a little boring up here. My mind wanders."

"I had the same dream!" she said. "The primal dragons were debating whether or not to destroy mankind!"

"The Black Swan told me she was trying to stop the dragons from wiping out mankind," Stagger said. "But, except for Hush and maybe Kragg, the dragons didn't seem keen on the idea."

Before they could speak further, the sea erupted in the distance as steam and stone shot into the air. In seconds, a mound of glowing stone rose from the boiling ocean. Flame spewed from the tip of the still growing mountain, curling and coiling into a giant serpent of fire.

"Greatshadow!" Stagger shouted.

The flame-dragon nodded. "I see you've learned to journey to the convergence on your own."

"The convergence?" Sorrow asked. "What is this place?"

"This is neutral ground," said Greatshadow. "Here, we dragons may meet in private without doing great harm to the world. If we met in the material realm, our combined might could shatter the earth beneath us."

"How did we get here?" asked Stagger.

"You must have called one another," said Greatshadow. "Do not do so again. When the other dragons learn that the two human interlopers have met in private to scheme against them, they will not be happy."

"We're not scheming against anything," said Sorrow. "I don't even know what I did to come here, or why I look like this."

"Your form reflects your truth," said Greatshadow. "When you first joined your spirit with Rott, only the faintest trace of your soul seeped into his elemental form. But as you've continued to use his power, more and more of his essence bleeds into your world, finding purchase in your body. In exchange, more and more of your spirit flows into his form. Rott's mind perished long ago. He survives only as a bundle of instincts; his chief drive is hunger. As he consumes you, Sorrow Stern, your mind will flow into the vacuum of his now absent will. For a time, you will be the intelligence in command of his power, until the entropy destroys your mind as well."

"There must be some way to stop that," she said. "Help me avoid that fate!"

"If a thing can be avoided, it was not truly fate," said Greatshadow. "For now, I bid you both to depart. You've each stumbled onto the discovery that, like other primal dragons, you're no longer bound to a single physical body. I recommend that you master your new abilities quickly. You may need to defend yourselves sooner than you guess."

"From what?" asked Stagger.

"Return to whence you came," Greatshadow said, turning his back to them.

Sorrow's eyes snapped open. At first, she thought she was blind, until she realized she was simply staring up at featureless black stone. She sat up and banged her head against the rock. She rubbed the top of her head, utterly confused. Had the ceiling gotten lower or had she somehow gotten taller?

She looked down and began to scream.

SORROW SLID THROUGH the hole that led from the top of the stairs into the grave. Already she could hear Brand's footsteps as he ran toward the pit. She pulled the flat slate slabs surrounding the hole closer, concealing her body from the waist down. She finished just in time. Brand skidded to a halt at the edge of the pit a moment later, his body a dark silhouette against the pink morning clouds.

"Are you all right?" he asked, panting.

"Of course," she said, faintly. She swallowed hard, then said, in a louder, raspy voice, "Why wouldn't I be?"

"We heard screams. We thought it was you."

"Oh, that," she said. She did her best to force a feeble smile. "I had a nightmare. I'm fine now."

"It sounded like you were being murdered!"

"Obviously I wasn't."

Brand looked skeptical. "Are you sure you're okay? You're voice is kind of quavering."

"I slept all night on cold stone," she said. "I'm a little congested."

Brand nodded. "Come on out and we'll warm you up with some breakfast."

"I'm not hungry," she said. "And I don't want you spending any more time at my camp. Pack your things and go."

"Your camp? Aren't you being kind of possessive?"

"Nothing of the sort," she said. "But... having thought further about our discussion last night, I've decided that I no longer care for the company of a person who thinks that I'm in any way like my father."

Brand squatted at the edge of the hole as he said, "Oh. That. I guess I did cross a line. I'm sorry. You shouldn't take what I said too seriously. Fortune telling is mainly the art of maintaining a straight face while spouting bullshit."

"I don't accept your apology. Take the dragon bones and go. You came here looking for wealth. You've found it. You've no further reason to stay."

"You came here looking for knowledge," said Brand. "Have you learned what you needed to learn?"

Sorrow shook her head. "I believe I know less now than I did when I came here. But mapping the contours of my ignorance has its own value."

"I'm not going to argue myself into more digging," said Brand, standing up and stretching his back. "I'm sore as hell." He looked around and said, "So, how do you want to divide up these bones? Are there any parts you—"

"Take them all," she said.

"But—"

"Take them all and go!"

Brand furrowed his brow. Finally, he turned away. She could hear him moving around. Less than a minute later, he was back at the edge of the pit.

"Your kicking us out wouldn't have something to do with our missing patient, would it?"

"Who?"

"What do you mean, who? The guy we dug up."

"He's missing?"

"There's just an empty blanket where he was sleeping. You didn't know this?"

"I haven't left this chamber," she said. "How could I know?"

"Climb out and let's look for him," said Brand. "He might be wandering around in delirium."

"What do I care?"

"He saved your life!"

"And I saved his. He was free to leave anytime he wished. Just because we saved him doesn't make him our property."

Brand scratched his head. "Are you sure you're okay? You just seem—"

"Leave!" Sorrow said, clenching her fists. "Stop wasting my time with your prattle!"

Brand grumbled something she couldn't make out as he turned away. Time slowed to a crawl as she listened to Brand and Bigsby gathering bones around the grave. The sun grew ever higher in the sky, and she adjusted the slate tiles around her to better support the weight of her elbows as she leaned forward. She couldn't believe how much time the two men were taking.

At last, Brand and Bigsby both returned to the edge of the pit.

"We've packed all we can carry," said Brand. "Are you sure you don't want us to stick around? It's dangerous out here alone."

"I believe I've shown myself capable of handling any threats," said Sorrow.

"I bet she's found a bigger treasure," said Bigsby. "She doesn't want to share, so she's getting rid of us."

"Or maybe I'm just sick of the company of a brain-damaged dwarf!" Sorrow snarled. "Get out of here, you little freak!"

Brand shook his head woefully as he and Bigsby turned away. "You weren't exactly friendly before, but I didn't think you were flat-out mean."

"This just proves how bad you are at reading people," she grumbled.

Brand and Bigsby left. She could hear their voices for a little while, growing ever more distant. She waited until they'd had time to move far beyond the graveyard. Then she waited another hour.

Sorrow knew she couldn't sit in the hole forever. Despite her... handicap, she'd obviously had the power to make it to the top of the stairs. She just needed the courage to push on a little further and make it back to her tent. She placed her hands upon the edges of one of the stones, prepared to push it aside. She stared for a long time as her arms refused to move the slate.

Finally she set her jaw, took a deep breath, and pushed the rock away. She moved the other stones that concealed the lower half of her body one by one, studiously keeping her eyes fixed upon her hands, avoiding what lay beneath.

She stared up into the canopy, at the patches of blue she glimpsed beyond the trees. She wiped her brow, wet with sweat, perhaps from the effort of moving the stones, or perhaps due to the rising heat of the day. Or perhaps from the undertow of terror that had accelerated her heart since waking.

"I can do this," she said, clenching her fists, gathering her courage. She swallowed hard, then looked down.

From the top ridge of her hipbones, the pants she'd worn had decayed into a fringe of tatters. Her boots had experienced a similar rapid degradation, devoured by mildew and mold until they'd fallen apart at the seams.

Some other time, the loss of control of her entropic magic would be quite worrisome. But now, she was focused on the all-but-vanished clothing because it provided a welcome distraction from a much larger and more deeply existential trouble.

The truth was, she didn't need to worry about trousers or boots any more. She finally allowed her eyes to focus on the reason her heart was beating with a speed to rival the wings of a hummingbird.

Her legs were gone. From her hips down, she now possessed an enormous black serpent's tail. She stared at her scales for only a moment before she had to turn her face away and stare at the walls of the pit.

"You're already in a grave," she said out loud. "Why waste the effort of crawling out?" She choked back tears. Never before had she contemplated suicide. She held nothing but contempt for those who threw their lives away. But did she even have a life as a human now? She was more snake than woman. If the changes continued, and she lost her arms... she shuddered at the thought.

Should the day come when she lost her arms, she'd curse herself for not ending her life when she'd had the chance. She cast about the broken ground with her hands until she found a shard of glass from the dragon's coffin.

She placed the sharp edge against her wrist. She studied the blue veins beneath her pale skin and set her jaw.

After a moment, she threw the glass away. She wasn't afraid of death, but she couldn't bear the thought of her long war against the church coming to an end due to a moment of weakness. If her life had lost so much value that she found death an acceptable option, wasn't this a liberation? She had nothing left to lose. She could throw herself into her quest to destroy the church without fearing for her own survival. Perhaps she'd been too concerned for herself, too cautious. Now this timidity no longer stood in her way.

"I'm a monster," she whispered. She found that the words didn't hurt. She said, in half a shout, "I'm a monster!"

The thought calmed her. She'd been a freak and an outcast since the day she'd shaved her head and driven in her first nail. Brand had perhaps been right after all. Her father was a moral monster. It had been only a matter of time before his blood pulsing through her veins drove her to the same inhuman extremes. Let the world see what she had become. If she was to be a monster, better it be in body than in soul.

"I hereby promise myself that I shall never surrender," she said. "Let my enemies gaze upon me and know fear!" She raised her fists in defiance. She was certain she was more ready than ever to take the fight to her foes, if not for the non-trivial problem that she had no idea how to climb out of this hole. Her mind, trained in the art of placing one foot in front of the other, couldn't quite make sense of the sensations coming from beneath her hips.

She could feel the length of her serpentine form spiraling down the stairs, and sensed the weight of her new body pressed against the edges of the stone. But how to move? She had no memory at all of crawling to the top of the stairs, but she'd obviously done so, with enough precision that only her human half had reached the surface. Her new body was obeying her will, at least on an unconscious level.

Perhaps the key was not to think of moving. Her body had responded to her fear of being seen by Brand. Now, what she wanted more than anything was something to drink. She'd not had even a sip of water since before they'd fought the bone-dragon. She imagined the canteen in her tent, fixing the image of it in her mind, hoping her body would carry her there.

To her delight and horror, her serpent body began to undulate. Her torso was pushed into the air, until she had risen above the lip of the grave. She looked down. Her serpentine length was now fully exposed. Before, she'd stood five feet, five inches in her boots. Now, her legs had been replaced by a tree-trunk thick expanse of black coils almost twenty feet long. She was standing—if standing was the right word—on the lower ten feet of her serpent tail, which was looped into a rough circle. This left ten feet of her scaly trunk rising into the air, with her human torso balanced atop it. She was suddenly thirteen feet tall. It was oddly empowering to look upon the world from such a vantage point.

As she crawled from the grave, a large fragment of black glass caught her eye and she momentarily forgot about her thirst. She stretched out her hand toward a particularly large remnant and her body obeyed her unspoken will to lower her toward it. She picked up the glass, a good fifty-pound smoke-blackened chunk.

Glass was one of her favorite materials to manipulate. She had only to touch it and think and it would flow to whatever form she imagined, unlike iron or copper, which she had to physically sculpt. In moments, she'd coaxed the glass into a long flat plane, which she rested against a tree trunk.

She willed herself before it. The midday sun that pierced the leafy canopy was bright enough to turn the dark glass into a mirror. She stared at herself for a long time. The scales of her tail glistened as if they were wet, though when she touched them, they were dry, smooth as polished wood, slightly warm, and hard as bone. But despite the hardness, she could feel the pressure of her fingers in the muscles below. Sliding her hands around, she even found that she could feel a pulse. She wondered how her heart found the strength to push blood such a length. And where had she gained all of the new mass? While she could shape glass and wood and other materials, she couldn't create these from thin air. Nothing new was added or subtracted from the total mass of the objects she sculpted. Why should this new nail giving her command of decay suddenly allow her to magically create matter?

She thought about Greatshadow's words. She wasn't creating mass. She was channeling it. Rott manifested himself as a giant black serpent. Her new body hadn't come out of thin air. Somehow, she'd opened a gate. Her own body was now a door that the dragon was slipping through. Why? And, more urgently, would he continue to do so? Had the changes stopped?

Pressing her lips together, she untied her blouse. She shed it, and stood naked before the mirror. From her pubic mound up, she was still completely human, with no hint of scales. She turned and peered back over her shoulders. Her buttocks blended into the serpent body. The line of transformation seemed to mirror the shape of her pelvis.

Frowning, she pondered the gross yet practical matter of how she now went to the bathroom. The loss of her reproductive organs was tragic, yes, but it wasn't as if she'd been using them. But even if she never planned on having children, she did still plan to eat and drink, and these actions had consequences.

With a sense of both revulsion and curiosity, she ran her fingers along her front. The scales of her back and side were the shape and size of the heads of garden spades, but her front scales were more like ringed bands. She explored the length of her body until, three feet from the tip of her tail, she found a gap between the bands that her fingers slipped into. She withdrew her fingers at once; the flesh within the gap was tender. She furrowed her brow. This was a very long way for food to travel. And there seemed to be only the one hole. When she returned to civilization, she would have to seek out a naturalist who could explain the intricacies of snake anatomy.

Ah, yes. Returning to civilization. That might prove to be a challenge. Even in as wild a port as Commonground, full of half-seeds and the most jaded of humanity, she couldn't imagine she would get a warm reception. She bent down and picked up her blouse. She slithered once more toward her tent, paying little attention to her surroundings as she buttoned her clothes shut once more.

Twenty feet from the tent she stopped, looking up. She heard something.

She stared at the silk walls. Was there someone moving inside? Had Brand and Bigsby tricked her?

In answer, the tent flaps opened and two forest pygmies walked out, carrying a basket filled with dried meats and cheeses, provisions she'd packed for her expedition. The two forest pygmies had dark green skin the color of moss and were naked except for bright red gourds they wore over their penises. Their green hair was pulled back into braids. Each carried a short spear tipped with a stone point. They moved as quietly as cats, craning their necks around to make sure no one had seen them.

They both looked right at Sorrow as if she wasn't even there. They turned their backs to her and began to walk away, then, in unison, froze and slowly looked back over their shoulders. Both of their mouths fell open at exactly the same time.

Sorrow felt like being tall and she became so, rising up on her tail until she loomed above them by several body lengths.

"Drop the basket and no one gets hurt," she said.

They dropped the basket, though whether they understood her words was debatable. They began to shout in a language she didn't recognize, their voices deep and booming despite their diminutive stature. Both reared back and threw their spears. Sorrow swayed out of the path of one missile, but the second spear struck her on one of the scaly bands where her knees had once been. She flinched, but the spear bounced off.

Sorrow ran her fingers along the impact point to make certain she was okay. She couldn't even feel a scratch. In addition to being tall, she was also spear-proof. At least, parts of her were.

When she looked up, she found that the two pygmies were at least a hundred yards away, leaves and dirt flying as they fled headlong over the graves before finally vanishing in the underbrush.

Sorrow picked up the basket and removed a hunk of beef jerky. She chewed it slowly as she contemplated what would've happened if the spear had flown a yard higher. She suspected that, unless she could find a way to reverse the changes to her body, she would have to get used to people's first reaction being to throw things at her.

After washing the jerky down with water from her canteen, she slithered back to the hilltop. Despite the massiveness of her new form, her motions were surprisingly silent. The whisper of her smooth scales sliding across one another was much quieter than her footsteps had been. She also took note of her speed. Though she didn't feel like she was moving terribly fast, she made it back up the hill as swiftly as if she'd sprinted. She would have preferred not to be a hideous reptilian abomination, but she tried to take some comfort that her new body had its strong points.

Of course, while the new parts of her physical form were stronger and tougher, she was still greatly concerned about the safety of her old, non-spear-proof human parts. Fortunately, the dragon's shattered coffin provided plentiful raw material to ameliorate her vulnerabilities. Glass had a reputation for brittleness, but during her years of working with the substance she'd learned it could be spun into long, thin, interweaving fibers that could be sealed inside a matrix of smoother glass. This woven glass was practically shatterproof, much lighter than iron, and quite tough.

She found a large piece of black glass and held it above her head. Her fingers sank into it as it liquefied, turning into slow moving black molasses that seeped down her arms and flowed over her shoulders. Inspired by the diamond pattern of her lower half, she willed the threads to form overlapping scales of black glass. In a few moments, she'd turned the glass into a suit of jet black scale armor that matched her bodily scales in gloss and shape. There was just barely enough material left to form a dark, gleaming helmet to conceal her face. Only her hands remained bare; her magical abilities required her to touch the substances she commanded.

She returned to the mirror she'd made earlier. It was almost impossible to tell where her armor ended and her scales began. With her face hidden, she looked even less human. For some reason, this was a relief. Before, she'd been a freak, a woman sewn onto a snake. Now, she looked like some ancient demi-god who'd crawled out of hell. Despite the underlying horror she felt, she was quietly pleased to look so formidable.

For the greatest part of her life, she'd been nearly invisible. There had been advantages of being a young woman of petite build. Concealing her shaved scalp beneath a cloak, she'd been able to walk down city streets unnoticed. Hiding in plain sight was no longer an option. Brand had laughed at her boldness; at last, she looked as dangerous as she felt.

She decided to increase her air of menace by crafting a pair of curved swords from the picks and shovels she'd brought to the site. She had no training in fighting with such blades, but she anticipated she might need to learn swiftly. In all her recent fights, she'd relied on Rott's power to vanquish her foes. Wielding such might had almost become addictive. But it was plain that there was a connection between using this power and losing her legs. She wanted to hold onto what remained of her humanity. She dared not use Rott's abilities again.

She packed the few belongings she thought she might need into a large satchel, which she slung over her shoulder. She decided she would travel lightly; she would create a case from the leftover glass and bury all but her current journal for later retrieval. She wished to make it back to Commonground as swiftly as possible. She felt certain that a complete translation of the letter she'd found would provide clues to finding Avaris, if she was still alive. Brand's suggestion of finding a monk to translate was definitely not an option. But a more likely translator was nearby—the Black Swan. The unofficial empress of Commonground's underworld, the Black Swan had a reputation for uncovering secrets. Sorrow felt it likely that the Black Swan could read the ancient script, or employ someone who might be able to.

She set off as the sun was low in the sky. Soon the forest was a maze of shadows. Her difficulty in seeing her path made the feel of her serpentine body slithering over roots and rocks and slimy leaves more unsettling. She wouldn't have enjoyed walking through the jungle barefoot, and now she was effectively crawling through it on her belly. On the other hand, if she'd navigated this root-filled wilderness on foot in such poor light, she couldn't have gone twenty feet without tripping. Her new body moved across the dark terrain with confidence.

At last, she made it to the river and crawled out onto a long sandy bank. Now that she was out from under the trees, the night was awash with moonlight. She wondered what to do now. Should she swim? Could she, given that she was wearing armor?

She looked down river and spotted the hulking remains of the Knight's Castle. She wondered if the canoes were still there. Her body was now longer than a canoe, but perhaps if she lashed two together with poles, she could create a craft that might support her weight. She slithered toward the dark ruins. If nothing else, she could take shelter and wait out the night before deciding her next move.

She reached the fortress wall and leaned back to look at its upper edge, eighty feet above. She wondered if she could find a path to the top now that she had only starlight to guide her. As she thought about reaching the top of the wall, her body slithered forward with a mind of its own. Her torso slammed into the stone. She barely managed to push herself back as she was forced higher up the rock. In seconds, her body was moving vertically along the wall, as her belly scales grasped imperfections in the rock face. Before she could really focus on how she was moving, her head popped over the top of the wall. There was a small tree here, growing from a crack in the stone. She grabbed it with both hands, steadying herself as her body continued to snake upwards.

Realizing she was now fully atop the wall, she let go, and slithered to the center of a ten-foot-wide pathway that ran the length of the ruins.

"That was interesting," she said, swaying back out over the edge, looking down at the ground far below her. Interesting and unnerving. Was she actually in control? Or did her serpent tail genuinely have a mind of its own, listening to her thoughts, but acting independently? Was there a second intelligence inside her?

"Stop scaring yourself, Sorrow," she whispered.

She turned, and was scared by someone else. Standing directly behind her, covered in tattered and muddy bandages, his wild mane of hair tangled with twigs and vines, was the man they'd found in the grave. His eyes were narrow slits as he lunged toward her.

She swayed back, avoiding his arms, but discovered that it hadn't been his intention to tackle her. Instead, as he leapt past her, he grabbed both of the iron swords affixed to her belt and tore them free. He rolled as he landed, and sprung back to his feet, before whirling around and placing the tip of one blade atop the glass scale directly over her heart.

In a thunderous voice, he barked, "Art thou a devil?"

"No." Sorrow's hand flashed to the blade. She calmly bent the iron tip into a u-shape. "I'm a pissed-off witch who's going to teach you some manners."

CHAPTER SIX

SLATE

THE SHAGGY WARRIOR responded as Sorrow knew he would, driving his unbent iron blade into her serpent coils. Given her command over metal, he might just have well attacked her with a wad of damp clay. It folded like an accordion against her scales.

The warrior spent no time dwelling on the loss of his weapon. He spread his arms and unleashed a savage growl, driving forward on his powerful legs to tackle her. His arms wrapped tightly around her body in roughly the area where her feet would once have been. He squeezed her in a bear hug that caused jangling pain to dance along her extensive spine. She fell backward, writhing uncontrollably as she felt two of her new ribs snap.

Though she was too rattled to think clearly, her tail possessed its own battle tactics. Her body looped into great coils around the man, crushing him as he crushed her. Unfortunately, she failed to catch his legs. To her great surprise he managed to rise, lifting her easily despite her new mass. To her greater surprise, he charged toward the edge of the wall.

They plummeted toward the earth below. She barely had time to think before she slammed into the wet sand at the base of the fortress. Her body slackened as the impact stunned her. The warrior hadn't even been winded by the fall. Her crushing coils had the unanticipated effect of cushioning him.

He kicked himself free of her limp form as he clawed up the length of her body.

"Foul devil!" he growled as he straddled her human torso. "Thou shall trouble the human world no more!"

He raised both his fists together over his head and swung them with a loud grunt, delivering a strike to the faceplate of her helmet as powerful as if he'd been swinging a sledgehammer. Spots danced before her eyes as she clawed at the bandages covering his chest with her bare fingers. She knew she could save herself if she unleashed Rott's powers, but, try as she might, she couldn't summon the dark energy. If she released the entropic force again, the dragon might swallow all that remained of her humanity. Perhaps she would die because of this fear, but at least she would die with her own face.

While Rott's powers couldn't save her, her dragon half came to the rescue anyway, as the tip of her tail whipped up and slapped the warrior in the side of his neck as he was preparing a second blow. The force knocked him sideways. With her vision blurred, she couldn't see where he'd gone, but it was enough that his weight no longer pinned her down. Her tail lifted her into the air until she stood at her ordinary human height. She clenched her fists as she craned her neck, trying to see where the man had fallen.

Her head jerked to the left as a sudden motion caught her eye. The warrior leapt toward her, swinging a branch as long and thick as his arm. She tried to raise her hands, but was too slow. The club slammed into the lower edge of her helmet and her world exploded into showers of bright sparks. She was vaguely aware of her helmet flying from her head as she fell backward into the muck.

The glowing sprites before her grew in intensity, becoming a uniform white light that blotted out the jungle. All she could hear was a loud whistle, rising in shrillness, building as a great wave of pressure in her skull. When the sound stopped, the world went dark.

SHE WOKE WITH the worst headache of her life, a significant milestone for someone who voluntarily hammered nails into her own skull. Her eyes snapped open, then immediately clamped shut in the intensity of the light before her. Her nose wrinkled as she breathed in smoke. She turned her head, coughing. She opened her eyes once more and found she was sprawled on a dark, sandy beach. The left side of her body was considerably warmer than her right side. From the sound of crackling nearby, she deduced she was near a fire.

Who'd built it? Why? Where was she?

She turned toward the fire, squinting against the glare, feeling nauseated by the sensation of her brain sloshing around. She could barely make out a dark, vaguely human shape beyond the flames.

Suddenly, she remembered what had happened. Her body whipped into the air, balanced atop her tail. She felt certain she would vomit, but managed to suppress the urge long enough to demand "Who are you?" of the shaggy-haired warrior who sat on the opposite side of the fire.

The man slowly shook his head, and said, in a soft voice, "I don't know."

"Excuse me," she said as she spun away. She could no longer hold in the contents of her stomach. Green bile erupted as she collapsed to the ground, supporting herself on her hands. She continued to throw up much longer than she would have thought humanly possible. Of course, she wasn't human anymore. She had no way of knowing how large her stomach was now. The quantity of fluid that spilled from her seemed enough to fill a bathtub.

In the aftermath, she slithered into the river. She was still wearing her armor, though she had no idea where her helmet had wound up. She plunged her face beneath the surface. The water was chilled by snowmelt. Under ordinary circumstances, the cold would have been unbearable and she would have exited the water with utmost haste. Now, she left her head and shoulders immersed, allowing the icy river to numb her throbbing skull. She noted that, just as her stomach seemed larger than it had once been, her lungs had apparently also been altered. Several minutes passed with her head beneath the surface, yet she felt no great urgency to rise for air.

Finally, the frigid waters froze the sloshing contents of her skull into something less soupy. She rose from the river and sucked in air in a long gasp. She wiped her face with her hands, then slowly turned back toward the fire.

"Why didn't you kill me?" she asked.

"Thou art the woman who tended my wounds. I did not recognize thee at first."

"You remember fighting the dragon? You remember me stitching you up?"

"Aye. And nothing before."

"Nothing?"

He shook his head.

"You must have some memories," she said. "You remember how to fight, obviously. You seem to have a grasp of traditional theology judging by all the devil talk. You must have learned this somewhere."

"Aye. I must."

"But you don't remember who you were before you climbed…" She let her voice trail off. She decided not to tell him she'd found him in a grave. "I mean, before you attacked the dragon?"

He scratched his shaggy mane. "My first memory is the bone dragon rattling above me. I acted to save thee from the beast. Are we… are we not companions?"

She shook her head. "I'm sorry. You just sort of, um, showed up. I don't know anything at all about who you were before you jumped in to save my life."

Or did she? The ghost pygmy said he'd come to witness the birth of the Destroyer. He'd not been impressed with her. Maybe he'd been looking at the wrong person.

She asked, "Does the name Stark Tower mean anything to you?"

He shook his head.

"Avaris?"

He furrowed his brow. "She is… a queen?"

"Yes. Queen of what?"

He looked lost as he sadly shook his head.

"Do you know what a weaver is?"

"Aye," he said. "A witch. Thou art one."

"Why do you say that?"

He tapped his fingers against his scalp.

"Right. The nails. You know what I am."

"A woman. Not a devil."

"Not everyone thinks kindly of weavers," she said.

He shrugged. "I've no cause to hate thee."

"Right. But if you know what a weaver is, you had to learn it somewhere. Forget about remembering yesterday or last week. What about your childhood? Who was your father?"

He didn't answer.

"Your mother? Do you have any siblings?"

He shook his head.

"No siblings? Or you don't remember."

"I've no memories of anything before fighting the dragon."

"You knew how to build a fire. How did you learn?"

He looked toward her leather satchel. "I found a flint and steel within. I know how to use them, but don't remember where I learned."

"You can't be a completely blank slate."

He shrugged, looking apologetic.

She crossed her arms, tapping her glass-covered biceps with her fingernails as her mind raced. Maybe this man was brain-damaged, but, as a fighter, he put any golem she'd ever built to shame. Infidel and Menagerie hadn't been interested in joining her mission, but this hairy brute didn't seem like he had anything better to do with his time.

But what if his memories returned? What if this was Stark Tower, the Witchbreaker, somehow returned from the dead?

Shouldn't she end his miserable life here and now, in payment for his crimes? If he was Tower, and his memories returned, he'd almost certainly attempt to kill her.

On the other hand, what if he wasn't Tower? The letter had a symbol that blended together the glyphs for war, tool, and man. Was the man before her some sort of living weapon?

She squinted as she looked at him. Though some auras burned more faintly than others, she was certain that the man before her had no inner-light whatsoever. She'd met such people before. The Skelling ice-maidens had been abused to the point that their spirits were extinguished, though their bodies stubbornly carried on. Could lost memories produce a similar effect?

A more fantastic possibility was that she was in the presence of an elaborate flesh golem. She'd discovered with Stagger that the remnant souls that animated golems could retain aspects of their former personalities. Short of tearing open this man's chest and seeing if it held a golden cage instead of a heart, she was unsure how to test her theory. When cut, he'd bled. Would this be true of a flesh golem?

She uncrossed her arms. "Did you find the food in my pack? Have you eaten already?"

"I found the food," he said. "But I'm no thief."

"It's good that you know that about yourself."

"I was greatly tempted," he said. "I was delirious when I first woke. I felt... I felt a pull that drew me to this place. I didn't think of food, or clothing. Thou must think me quite the savage, wandering through the jungle nude, little more than a beast."

"You've more manners than a beast," she said, slithering over to the pack. She dug out a package bound with string and tossed it to him. "Here's some jerky."

"Aren't thou also hungry?"

She shook her head. She felt hollowed out inside, but could still taste snake bile on her tongue. "It might take a while to recover my appetite."

She watched as he untied the string and her heart froze as he laid the open package on his lap, lowered his head, and clasped his hands together. He closed his eyes and sat a moment in silence.

"Are you... praying?" she asked.

He looked confused. "I don't know. I just... if I'm praying, I can't remember who I'm praying to. But the motions... felt natural."

She looked up at the ruins beside them. "Like coming here felt natural?"

He shrugged. "I... was delirious. I was dreaming as I walked. I imagined a fortress, resplendent with banners. I found only these ruins."

She pressed her lips tightly together. This was certainly tilting the scales toward him being Lord Tower.

"Are you a knight?"

He tilted his head, looking slightly surprised by her question. He nodded slowly. "Aye," he said. "Aye. I believe I am."

She resisted the temptation to curse. Just because he was a knight didn't mean he was the Witchbreaker. A knight who couldn't remember the god he served might be a valuable commodity.

"If you're a knight, I happen to be a damsel in distress," she said. She felt cheap describing herself in this fashion, but she knew it was the truth. "As you may have noticed, I've got a bit of a problem." She waved her hand along the length of her body.

"Once I saw your scalp, I assumed you were a bone weaver. They often alter their forms."

She wondered how he knew this, but decided not to press the issue. "I didn't voluntarily choose this form," she said. "I'm dealing with a little bit of a curse right now." Neither statement was completely true, but neither was completely false. "I'm hoping to find Avaris, Queen of the Weavers, so she can help restore my human form. Will you aid me in this quest?"

"Aye," he said. "I cannot deny a damsel in distress. I pledge my strength and my sword to thee, my lady."

She smiled, almost despite herself. "Thank you." She extended her open hand to him for a handshake. "All this serious talk without a proper introduction. My name is Sorrow."

He surprised her by taking her outstretched hand in his and kissing the back of her fingers. Ordinarily, she would have been repulsed by a gesture with such romantic undertones. But his face seemed so innocent, she couldn't find it in herself to be offended.

"I fear I'm at a loss," he said, as he released her hand. "I don't know what you shall call me."

"Slate," she said, looking into his dark gray eyes. "In honor of your eyes."

Though, in truth, it was because, if his mind was a blank slate, it would be her hand that filled that empty void with knowledge, shaping him into the ally she needed him to be.

IT WAS WELL past sunset the following evening before Sorrow slithered once more into Commonground. Slate was at her side, dressed in glass armor similar to her own. She'd returned with him to the Witches Graveyard, telling him she needed to gather the raw materials to outfit him. In truth, she'd wondered if the sight of the grave where he'd been buried might stir further memories. The hunt for memories had proven unsuccessful, but she'd cut up the fabric of her tent to fashion undergarments for Slate, molded glass to fit his form, and equipped him with a fresh sword. He looked quite formidable in his black armor.

When she'd last walked these docks, no one had given her a second glance. Now all eyes were upon her and her muscular companion. But unlike a town in more civilized parts of the world, no one seemed afraid or repulsed by their appearance. They were being sized up as competition. They were rough customers in a city of rough customers.

They arrived at length at the floating saloon known as the *Black Swan*. She'd spent several weeks here not long ago, designing and building a body for the eponymous owner. The Black Swan was the unofficial queen of Commonground, a woman so wealthy she could purchase the loyalty of anyone she wished. She also had a reputation as a powerful sorceress, a reputation only enhanced by the fact that she continued to oversee her business concerns after death as an animated skeleton. It had been rumored that the Black Swan was a weaver, but Sorrow had held the woman's skull in her hands and saw no signs that it had ever been punctured by nails. Despite the rather intimate connection she'd had with the Black Swan while fitting her skeleton into a new iron shell, she'd been unable to learn the true nature of the woman's abilities.

Sorrow pushed open the doors of the saloon and slithered into the room. Few people even looked up from their cards as she entered. She wrinkled her nose at the cigar smoke combined with the strong perfumes of the painted women who accompanied the men at the tables.

The fact that no one found a woman blended with an enormous serpent more interesting than their cards was partly the blame of the man tending bar. Battle Ox was a half-seed, an eight-foot-tall minotaur with broad shoulders and iron-clad horns. Despite his fearsome aspect, during her time at the bar, she'd discovered that Battle was actually a rather gentle soul.

"Battle," Sorrow said, drawing up to the bar, her head just above the level of his own. "Good to see you again."

He looked up, his brow furrowed. She could see her black helmet reflected in his eyes. She pulled her helmet off and his expression changed.

"Sorrow! This is a new look for you. Are you on stilts or something?"

"Something," she said, realizing that most of her lower body was hidden by the bar. "My additional height is one reason I'm here. I need to see the Black Swan."

"Are you sure?" he asked.

"Pretty sure. Why wouldn't I be?"

"Ever since you left, the boss has been griping that you cheated her."

"What gall! She complained about a thousand completely fictional defaults in my workmanship and tried to avoid paying my wages. She was the one who attempted to cheat me!"

"But she did pay you. And now that she's had time to adjust to her new body, she hates her voice."

"She's lucky to have any voice at all," Sorrow said. "She has no lungs or throat. That I was able restore her power of speech using bellows and reeds borders on the miraculous."

"In any case, when you see her, you'll get an earful."

"I'll risk it."

"Fine. But don't laugh when she's chewing you out. She hates that. It's just... she does kind of sound like a duck."

"If people think that, I'm hardly to blame," said Sorrow. "She's the one who chose to name herself after a waterfowl."

Battle cast his gaze toward Slate. "Who's the big guy?"

"I'm called Slate, *half-seed*."

"He's agreed to help me with a problem I'm trying to solve," said Sorrow.

Battle nodded. "Let me go tell the boss you're here." He disappeared behind a curtain that covered a door behind the bar.

Sorrow turned to Slate and said, "Try not to sound so contemptuous."

"Contemptuous?"

"The way you said 'half-seed.' It sounded judgmental."

Slate shrugged. "His mother sullied herself with animal seed. His inhuman soul was fated for damnation from before his birth. How can you not judge such a beast?"

"Considering you don't remember who your own parents are, you might want to keep an open mind."

"I may not remember them, but the evidence of my own eyes testifies that they were human."

Battle returned a moment later and said, "She'll see you. But your bodyguard stays here."

Sorrow had expected as much and made no protest as she slithered around the bar.

"So," he said, as he finally saw her full form. "You've, uh, got an interesting new look."

"Indeed," she said. "It's given me a new appreciation for the plight of your kind."

Battle tilted his head. "Plight?"

"You didn't ask to be born half-animal," she said. "It's a cruel fate, and it disgusts me that you're treated with contempt by thoughtless fools."

"You know what I hate more than contempt?" Battle asked. "Condescension. I happen to be proud of who and what I am. I'm bigger and stronger than any of the pathetic pink-skins who think they're better than me. And I'd wager I'm better hung than anyone else in this port."

"There's no need to be crude," she said as she felt her cheeks go red. "I'm sorry if I've offended you. I just... I'm certain you've had a difficult life. I was trying to convey my empathy."

"You don't feel empathy. You feel pity. That's just another form of judgment."

Sorrow started to say that it was possible that a lifetime of poor treatment had left him unable to realize when someone was actually being nice, but decided to hold her tongue.

Battle opened the door at the end of the hall. "Madam, Sorrow is here to see you."

"How delightfully ominous," said a reedy, squawking voice.

Battle stepped aside and Sorrow slithered past. The room beyond was lit by lanterns. When last she'd been here, the room had been stripped bare, but now it was crowded and cluttered with old dusty furniture that must have been quite lovely in its day. On a low velvet couch, the Black Swan waited, stretched out in what might have been a relaxed pose, if her body were still capable of looking relaxed.

Sorrow had been hired by the Black Swan to build an iron shell to encase her old bones. Any fair-minded person would have judged Sorrow's handiwork to be a masterpiece of sculpture. The Black Swan's new skin was, of necessity, much less flexible than a body of flesh. The lacy black dress that the Black Swan wore over her iron limbs somehow made her look even stiffer. She brought to mind a manikin that had toppled over. Still, with her slender limbs and long fingers, the old witch possessed pleasant echoes of the female form. Indeed, her face might even be thought beautiful, though her eyes were made of glass and her eyelashes fine wires. But one had to admire the symmetry and proportions of her visage. The plates that formed her cheeks slid silently as the Black Swan's iron lips parted. Her polished teeth chopped the squeaking notes produced by the bellows and reeds inside her chest into a voice that was eerily musical.

"I know why you've come," the Black Swan sang. "You've found a letter."

Sorrow raised her eyebrows. "How could you know that?"

"Because Brand arrived yesterday. Only I had the resources to negotiate a fair price for such a large hoard of dragon bones. When he recounted the story of their discovery, he mentioned that you'd found a letter signed by Avaris herself."

"Oh," she said. "Right. Brand. Do you know if he's still in port?"

The Black Swan shrugged. "He seemed eager to depart for the Silver City. Perhaps you'll meet him there."

"Doubtful. I was merely curious as to his whereabouts. I'm hardly going to follow him to a city full of my worst enemies."

"You will if you wish to have the letter translated."

"You can't translate it?"

The Black Swan shook her head. "Why would I know the lost script of the weavers? For this, you need an authority on dead tongues. The person best fitting this description is Equity Tremblepoint, who resides in the Silver City."

"Tremblepoint? Why do I know that name?"

"Given your upbringing, my dear, I'm surprised by your ignorance. Lord Tremblepoint was the author of a dozen of the world's most beloved plays. Equity is his descendant."

"Oh," said Sorrow. "You'll have to forgive me. I fear I've limited education in the fine arts."

The Black Swan released a string of squawks that might have been laughter. "I would hardly describe Tremblepoint's work as fine art. He was a horrid playwright, possibly the most dreadful of all time. He acquired his family name because, in each scene, his stage directions require the actors to tremble and point as they deliver their melodramatic soliloquies."

"I thought you said his plays were beloved?"

"Indeed. While his works are meandering, long, and riddled with inconsistencies, they're also rife with the lowest forms of humor. The public has a hunger for jokes involving bodily output and the most shameful forms of sexual congress. His works have been popular for centuries. Equity Tremblepoint makes a healthy living as a thespian due mainly to the fame attached to the family name."

"And this actor is also an authority on dead languages?"

"Indeed. The Tremblepoint family has collected a library of literary manuscripts that date back centuries. It's only natural that Equity would learn to read them."

"And you're certain you can't read the letter?"

"Why would you doubt me?"

"Because, despite your denials, the world believes you to be a weaver."

"This would not be the first time that a thing commonly believed has proven baseless. I've not a single nail in my skull," the Black Swan said, tapping the solid dome of her forehead with a razor-sharp fingernail. "You know this."

"True. But I recently encountered a ghost named Purity. She hinted that the nails were only one crude method of becoming a weaver. She said emotions could be as powerful as physical spikes, and that hatred and the thirst for revenge had opened channels in her mind to grant her powers."

"Interesting. Might I suggest you discuss this matter with her?"

"Unfortunately, Purity was intent on murdering the sun. Stopping her required killing her."

"And in the course of stopping her, you took the drastic step of merging your soul with that of Rott."

Sorrow frowned. "Brand couldn't have told you that. I never explained my powers to him."

"My dear, you crawled into the room on a serpent's belly. You're covered in dragon scales. There's a nail in your scalp of a matching ebony hue."

"Fine. You've diagnosed my problem correctly. Is there nothing you can do to help me?"

"You drove that nail into your scalp seeking great power. Why did you do so if you weren't willing to pay the price?"

"I had no idea my body would change like this. I want it to stop."

The Black Swan shook her head slowly. "It won't stop. I'm sorry, Sorrow, but your fate was sealed when you chose to access Rott's powers. As a dragon, Rott had centuries to study the elemental force he blended his soul with, and still his mind was decayed by entropy."

"Perhaps my mind is stronger," said Sorrow. "My life has toughened me."

The Black Swan shook her head. "You risk the world if you approach your current problem with arrogance. You've been given a great opportunity to change the fate of mankind, but doing so will require that you alter your goals."

"But my goal *is* to change the fate of mankind."

"By waging a pointless war against the church, when the true threat to humanity lies with the primal dragons. What use will it be to overthrow your fellow men if humanity is wiped from the world by the collective power of these beasts?"

"I'll deal with the dragons when and if they're a problem," said Sorrow. "For now, I know who my enemies are. It's just my friends I'm still having trouble identifying."

The Black Swan nodded. "We may not be friends, but I feel I owe you the courtesy of a warning."

"A warning against what?"

"Despite your confidence, Rott is an ancient power whose will far exceeds your own."

"I met Rott in the Sea of Wine. He's dead. I don't think he has any will at all."

"You saw his physical body in the Sea of Wine. His form would only persist if some flickering hunger for survival were left within him. By blending your soul with his own, you may stir this hunger enough to wake the dragon. If the beast awakes while he shares your form, the dragon will devour your spirit and digest your intelligence to nourish his own quiescent mind."

Sorrow found that she'd unconsciously begun to chew her fingernails. She pulled her hand away from her lips. "You can't know that. You're like all prophets, speaking in vagaries."

"Let me say this as directly as possible. I believe that Rott's energies are too powerful for you to control. You can halt your slide toward total domination by the beast by removing the nail you carved from him and giving it to me for safe-keeping."

"That's not going to happen," said Sorrow. "I finally have the power I've sought for all these years. I'm going to learn to control it."

"How?"

"I don't know, but that's never stopped me. I've become an expert at defining my most dangerous areas of ignorance, then learning what I must to survive. I know it's possible to tap a primal dragon's power without losing one's intelligence because Purity did it. I saw it with my own eyes. If a thing can be done, it can be duplicated."

"You're a fool," said the Black Swan. Her iron fingers clanked as she clamped them to her chest. "If you have such command

and control over your abilities, why did you produce such poor work on my breasts?"

"By the vacant moon," said Sorrow, closing her eyes and rubbing them. "They're made of iron! They're never going to look real!"

"So you admit you've delivered an inferior product," the Black Swan said. "I insist you remain here until they've been remade to my satisfaction."

"You've lost your mind," Sorrow muttered. "When the worms ate your brains, they shat out your sanity."

"I was a fool to have faith in you," the Black Swan said in a low squawking tone that might have been intended to convey disappointment, though she sounded more like a duck with a sore throat.

Sorrow curled around to face the door, resisting the urge to curse. She slithered down the hall and found Battle and Slate leaning on opposite sides of the bar, engaged in an arm wrestling contest. A score of gamblers had gathered around them, staring intently at the match. Slate had removed his helmet, and his face showed signs of strain. The cut on his neck she'd stitched shut was bleeding freely again.

Suddenly, Slate's arm went down, and the crowd erupted in cheers. Battle pumped his fists in the air. Slate rose, rubbing his wrist, then extended his open hand.

"An honorable victory," he said. "Well fought, my friend."

Battle shook his hand. "You had me worried for a minute, buddy. Thought we'd break the damn bar. The Swan would take that out of my pay."

Slate chuckled as he nodded. Sorrow slithered around the bar and grabbed him by the arm.

"We're leaving," she said.

Slate allowed himself to be pulled toward the door. "Must we depart in haste?"

"I don't need you rough-housing in here. Battle's right. The Black Swan will bill us for any damage."

"No harm was done," said Slate as they stepped outside.

"I suppose I should be happy you just arm wrestled instead of getting into a brawl."

"We had no cause for combat," said Slate. "Ours was a friendly contest."

"Fifteen minutes ago you thought he was an unholy abomination. Suddenly he's your friend?"

Slate shrugged. "We talked as we waited. Beneath his beastly exterior, he's a good soul." He sighed, and leaned against a piling on the dock. He removed his glass gauntlet. His arm was covered in blood. "I could have bested him if my stitches hadn't torn."

Sorrow shook her head. "Was it so important to find out who was stronger that you'd risk hurting yourself?"

He grinned. "A day isn't well lived until I've spilt a little blood, even if it's my own."

"You don't have much extra to spare," she said. She removed her helmet and took his arm to examine her torn handiwork. "Let's find a room for the night. I need to fix you up again."

Slate chuckled. "How is it, if thou art the damsel in distress, I'm the one who requires constant mending?"

Before she could answer, a voice called out, "Sorrow?"

The curious thing about the voice was that it came from directly overhead.

CHAPTER SEVEN

CIRCUS

SORROW LOOKED STRAIGHT up. A teenage boy with curly black hair was floating fifty feet above her. She raised her hand and cried, "Jetsam!"

Jetsam smiled broadly as he kicked his legs to swim down through the air. When she'd parted company with the Romers, the family had been the most miserable creatures in all of creation, Wanderers without a ship. The *Freewind* had been transportation for Sorrow, but for the Romers it had been home. They'd escaped with little more than the clothes on their back. Now, Jetsam was outfitted in a crisp white uniform of cotton breeches and vest, with a bright green sash for a belt and a matching bandana serving as a cap.

"Zounds!" Slate cried as he spotted the flying teenager.

"Zounds?" Jetsam asked. "What are you, an actor?"

"An actor?" Slate asked, confused.

"The only place I've heard that word was in the Tremblepoint play, *The Merchant of Monkeys*."

"When would you have seen a play?" Sorrow asked. "You've lived your whole life on a ship."

Jetsam's head reached the level of her own when he stopped swimming down through the air. He spread his arms and brought himself to a halt, his feet still sticking straight up. "I've done more than seen the play. I performed in it. I played the role of second monkey when I was eight. The show was staged on the fo'c'sle of the *Horizon*."

"I had no idea Wanderers had thespians among them," said Sorrow.

"We're sailors, not barbarians. One of the reasons Commonground even exists is so we can get together and enjoy plays, concerts, dancing, and so on."

"How is it that thou dost fly?" Slate asked.

"'Thou dost?'" Jetsam responded, eyebrows raised. Then he shrugged and said, "My family rescued a mermaid princess. As a reward, each member of my family got to blow a note on the mer-king's magical conch. We all wound up with different powers, based on our names, more or less." He performed a loop in mid-air, righting himself so his feet were pointing down. "I got the best power, if I do say so myself."

"Aye. 'Tis quite a talent."

Sorrow said, "Forgive me. I was so surprised to see you, I haven't made the proper introductions. Jetsam, this is Slate. Slate, Jetsam."

The two men shook hands.

"Speaking of surprises," Jetsam said, glancing at her serpent tail. "You, uh, look… different… somehow." A few awkward seconds passed, before he asked, cheerfully, "Have you lost weight?"

She sighed. "I'm surprised you recognized me, to be honest."

He laughed. "I have an unusual level of experience with looking at the tops of people's heads. Believe me, even from fifty feet up, the second you took off your helmet I knew who you were."

"I take it from the uniform you've found work on a new ship? Was your family able to remain together?"

"Yep and yep. You'll never guess who we're working for now."

"Brand Cooper," she said.

"You're a better guesser than I gave you credit for."

"I happen to know that Brand recently came into some money, and a ship was one of the things he mentioned buying. Your mother must have mixed feelings about working for him."

"Nah. Ma's fine. It's Mako who's pitching a fit."

"And Brand's going back to the Silver City?"

"Yep."

"Might he be interested in taking on passengers?"

"I can't answer for him, but I know Ma wants you back on board."

"Really? Why?"

Jetsam shrugged. "I just heard her telling Sage that there's never a witch around when you need one."

"What do they need a witch for?"

"Who knows? But come on back to the ship. Everyone's asleep, but I'll wake Brand and let him know I'm bringing you aboard."

"We're most grateful," said Sorrow. "Where's your ship?"

"Right here!" Jetsam pointed to a clipper docked next to the *Black Swan*. The name on the bow was *Circus*. The figurehead beneath the bowsprit was a buxom woman painted to look like a clown. "Used to belong to some wealthy gambler. Well, wealthy before he came to Commonground. When he tried to skip town on his debts, the Black Swan sent her enforcers after him. They were kind of messy. It smelled like hell when we came aboard. We've spent our whole first day cleaning up dried blood and worse from all the nooks and crannies."

Jetsam led them up the gangplank. The timbers creaked as Sorrow slithered onto deck. The ship smelled strongly of soap, with only a hint of rotting meat. Yet even that masked whiff made her stomach growl. She'd not had a thing to eat since she'd been sick at the Knight's Castle, and she was now undeniably famished. When she realized it was the scent of putrefied human remains triggering her hunger, her appetite fled once more.

Jetsam led them to the aftcastle and softly rapped on the door. They waited in silence for a moment; just as he was about to knock again, the door creaked open and Brand looked out. Sorrow's eyebrows shot up.

"You've cut your hair!" she said.

Brand ran his hands along his closely cropped scalp. With his long locks gone, he looked older. His face seemed squarer, less feminine. "I'm a businessman now. I figured I should clean up a little." His eyes focused on Sorrow. She could see his whole body tense up.

"Let's play fortune teller," she said. "I can tell you what you're about to ask."

"What happened to your legs?"

"You said it too fast."

"But—"

She held up her hand. "It's a long story."

He looked at Slate. "Is he part of the story?"

"This is Slate," said Sorrow. "He's agreed to help me find Avaris."

Brand wiped the sleep from his eyes, then silently contemplated Slate. "Does he... I mean..."

"Can we talk privately?" Sorrow asked. "We'd like to book passage to the Silver City, and I dislike discussing money in public."

"Come in," said Brand.

"I'll be out in just a moment," Sorrow said to Slate and Jetsam. She slithered into Brand's cabin. It was pitch black when he closed the door. There was a soft click and the room filled with light. Blinking, she saw that Brand was now sitting on his bunk, holding a small open locket in his hands. The pearl-sized glorystone inside produced enough light to rival a large lantern.

"The big guy looks like he's survived his injuries well enough," Brand said. "I guess the next question is, who is he? Or maybe, *what* is he?"

"Excellent questions," said Sorrow. "He has no memories. At least, no memories of a personal nature."

"Is it safe for him to be on board?"

"Why wouldn't it be?"

"Buck naked, he beat a dragon half to death with its own jawbone. I hesitate to think what he might do now that you've armed him."

"He seems friendly enough. And the fact I made his armor means I can keep him on a short leash. All I need to do is touch him and I can cause the armor to fuse into a single piece, trapping him. I'm surprised you're worried. You've never struck me as possessing an excess of caution."

"Things have changed a lot in the last day. I own a ship now. I have responsibilities. I don't want to do anything to place my crew in danger."

"Slate won't be a danger to them. But I have to wonder about you."

"Me?"

"You buy a ship, then conveniently hire the woman who's the object of your unrequited love as your captain?"

"Gale's experienced. And, on a purely economic level, hiring the Romers is a bargain. When Rigger's on deck, he's like twenty men working, but only one mouth to feed."

"So you admit you're exploiting Rigger. What about Gale?"

"What about Gale? Her family needed a ship. I needed a crew."

"You've placed yourself in a position of power over her," said Sorrow, crossing her arms. "You now feed and clothe her and her entire family. If you invite her back into your bed, can she refuse you?"

"I should be insulted that you think I'm some sort of manipulative pseudo-rapist, but I'm more bugged that you think so little of Gale. She's not a whore who's going to crawl into my bed because I throw a few coins her way."

"You crawled into her bed when the tables were turned."

He raised his eyebrows. "You think I was sleeping with her because she used to be my boss?"

Sorrow shrugged. "Not many men wind up involved with women old enough to be their mothers."

"But the reverse is so common it barely merits mention," he said. "My father has wed three times, each time to a younger woman. His latest wife is only two years older than me."

"This is one of the things I despise about the world," said Sorrow. "There cannot be equality in such a marriage."

"Equality is a vastly overrated commodity. I didn't enter into a relationship with Gale because I thought she would be my equal. I expected her to be my superior. I wasn't disappointed. The things I learned in her bed opened my eyes to –"

Sorrow raised her hand. "Stop. I really don't want to know. I will point out, however, that a woman who sought out lovers to increase her experience would be shamed and branded a slut. As a man, you're free to openly boast of your experience."

"I suppose it's a bit of a double standard," said Brand. "But it's all behind me. I'm changing my ways now that I've found the only woman who could ever complete me."

Sorrow stared at him, wondering if he was trying to fool her, wondering even more if he was fooling himself.

He shook his head. "How the hell did this conversation become about me? You're turning into a giant snake and this isn't the main topic of discussion?"

"What's there to discuss? I've lost control over some aspects of my magic. Regaining control is my immediate priority. The next person who might be able to help me is Equity Tremblepoint, who resides in the Silver City. Will you give us passage there?"

"Of course," he said. He furrowed his brow. "Tremblepoint? Like the playwright?"

"Am I the only person who's never heard of him?"

"I don't think Equity Tremblepoint is a him. I think she's a she. Maybe."

"You're not sure?"

"I've seen her, or maybe him, in a couple of plays. In a *Midwinter's Fantasy*, Equity played the Fairy Queen. But in *Brightmoon the Eighth*, she played the king. Amazing performances in each role, by the way."

"If she's adept at playing both genders, perhaps she can give Bigsby a few tips," said Sorrow, though she instantly regretted the words. It was cruel to mock a person who was genuinely mad.

"Maybe," said Brand, clearly taking no offense. He stretched his arms and yawned. "It's still a long ways until dawn. We can let Slate bunk with the boys. With your, uh, different configuration, I'm not sure you'll fit anywhere but the cargo hold."

"I won't be choosy," she said. "I'm sorry if I sounded scolding earlier. I know you're a good person at heart."

"That goes both ways. For a person with a head full of nails, you're nowhere near as mean as you look."

Sorrow glanced down at her tail. "My head is now the least frightening part of my body. I hope my appearance won't prove alarming for the younger Romers."

Brand chuckled. "The Romers used to routinely take shortcuts through the Sea of Wine. From what Gale told me, nearly getting chewed by Rott on their last trip was one of their less eventful journeys. I don't think any of the Romers are that easy to shock."

THE CARGO HOLD was mostly empty save for a few barrels and large sacks of grain in the corner. Jetsam turned the space into a makeshift bedroom by supplying pillows and blankets, along with a jug of fresh water and a basin.

"Not fancy," he said.

"It's fine," she said.

Slate was already in the bunkroom shared by Mako, Rigger, and Jetsam. It had only three bunks, but one of them was always on duty, so no one was inconvenienced.

Jetsam closed the door, leaving Sorrow alone. She was weary down to the center of her bones. She quickly shed her glass armor. The suit fit her like a second skin, but the hard edges chaffed beneath her armpits and especially around her hips, where her human flesh turned dark gray before blending with the ink-black scales.

She ran her fingers along the band of transitional flesh. The chafed, scraped skin that her armor had rubbed proved to be a surprising source of encouragement. The raw flesh formed a rough band around her belly, providing a visible limit of where her human skin had ended when she'd first donned the armor. While wearing the suit, she'd been paranoid that her itching midsection might be changing further. Fortunately, however, the scales had not advanced. Had she halted the changes by refraining from further use of her powers?

She poured water in the basin and washed herself. She was especially careful around her face. There was a knot on her temple that felt like an egg under her skin where Slate had clocked her. She wondered how long it would be before the swelling went down.

Once she was cleansed of jungle grime and sweat, she lowered herself to the blankets. She normally slept on her back, but this was all but impossible now. She crossed her arms beneath her head, wondering if she would ever get to sleep like this.

She soon had her answer, as the sound of waves lapping against the hull lulled her into slumber. She'd not even had to extinguish the lantern Jetsam had left behind.

Her eyes snapped open. She lay perfectly still, listening.

Scritch. Scritch. Scritch.

The sound was coming from behind the sacks stacked in the corner.

Scritch. Scritch. Scritch.

She knew it was rats. She had no particular fear of rats, nor was she overly fond of them. Under ordinary circumstances, she might have thrown a shoe in the direction of the noise, scared off the pest, then gone back to sleep.

Of course, she no longer had shoes.

She rose, her head nearly touching the beams. The noise stopped suddenly as her shadow shifted across the wall. She held her breath, waiting. She felt paralyzed. It wasn't fear that stilled her, however, but something else. Not for the first time, she had the sensation that there was a second intelligence within her body, and it was now exerting its will.

Scritch.

Her ears precisely fixed the sound of the rat clawing into the sack. Her body whipped forward. In less than a second she arced over the sacks and shot down, arms outstretched. The rat jumped as her fingers brushed its fur.

Mindlessly, she crammed the squealing rat between her jaws and snapped its head off. The hot blood filling her mouth sent a wash of electric ecstasy through the length of her body. She swallowed the head whole, the whiskers still twitching, then crammed the rat into her mouth, pushing, shoving, crushing the bloodied flesh between her teeth. She wanted to scream, but couldn't, as her throat was distended by the rat's torso. She wanted to vomit, but swallowed instead, then swallowed again, and again, until the rat's slender tail slipped between her lips.

As she shoved the last of the rat into her mouth, she once more gained control of her hands. She held them before her face and found them covered with blood and fur and feces.

Despite the horror, she continued to swallow.

She raced back to the basin to wash the blood from her hands. As she loomed above it, she could see herself from the shoulders up, reflected in the water. Her neck was bulging and contracting, swollen so that it distended out past her chin. Her clavicles felt as if they would break as the mass in her throat pressed outward. She still couldn't breathe.

With one last gulp, the rat cleared her windpipe and she filled her lungs. She started to scream, but clamped her hands over her mouth, stifling her cries. She couldn't bear the thought of anyone rushing into the hold and finding her in this condition.

She plunged her face into the wash basin, scrubbing it roughly, then rubbed her hands in the water until they felt raw. She was acutely aware of the hot lump now swelling her stomach. She grabbed the pitcher and poured water into her mouth, but didn't dare swallow the foul hair and ooze that it washed off her tongue and teeth. She spat out gray sludge, then rinsed again.

At length, there was no more water, and nothing left to scrub off.

She leaned against the door to be certain it would not open. After a moment, a spasm ran the length of her body, and she began to weep.

SHE WAS STILL awake many hours later when there was a knock on the door.

"I'm not decent," she whispered. "Come back later."

"It's Gale," said the voice on the other side. "Open up."

"I'll be out in a little while," said Sorrow.

To her consternation, Gale tried to open the door.

"Can't I have a little privacy?" she asked, throwing her weight against the wood so that it only opened a crack.

"Privacy is exactly why we must talk now," said Gale, her voice little more than a whisper through the gap. "Jetsam just went to bed. Mako has gone to the crow's nest. Everyone else is asleep. This is a conversation that must not be overheard by prying ears."

Sorrow sighed. "Fine. Just give me thirty seconds."

"Agreed."

Sorrow grabbed a blanket and wrapped it around herself. Her belly still seemed grossly distorted, but perhaps it was only her imagination. She said, "Enter."

When the door opened, she discovered that Gale wasn't alone. Sage Romer was with her, dragging the wooden figurehead that had once decorated the *Freewind*. Sage was Gale's oldest daughter, a serious-minded fifteen-year-old who shared her mother's curly black hair and athletic build. She was a talented clairvoyant, and Sorrow had witnessed her ability to boss around her older brothers with the same forcefulness as her mother.

Gale closed the door behind her. Sage placed the figurehead against the wall, then removed the spyglass she carried in a holster on her hip. She stared into the spyglass even though the end was capped, then announced, "Jetsam's sound asleep. Mako's focused on the *Maelstrom*, probably hoping Sandy will come above deck. Poppy's awake, but she's reading that book about knights. We're clear."

"You can see in any room?" Sorrow asked. She wondered if Sage could possibly have seen what had happened earlier. Were they here to discuss the danger she posed to their family?

Sage nodded. "I do my best not to invade the privacy of others. Alas, some of my siblings don't feel the same way."

"Jetsam eavesdrops at every opportunity," said Gale. "Mako can hear things much better than an ordinary man. It's difficult to keep secrets from them."

"What secret do you think I need to keep?" Sorrow asked.

"You?" Gale asked. "I imagine that is between you and your conscience."

"Jetsam warned us about your condition," said Sage. "I don't see how you could keep it secret if you wanted."

"Then what—"

"Can we trust that nothing we say will leave this room?" asked Gale.

"You have my word," said Sorrow.

Gale motioned toward the figurehead. "This is all that's left of the *Freewind*. I've saved it not because I'm sentimental. I rescued it because my mother's soul is trapped inside."

Sorrow looked at the wood. "I fear you're mistaken. I would see an aura."

"I see the aura," said Sage. "But it would be concealed from you. When grandmother's soul was bound to the ship, steps were taken to conceal her spirit from Rott's gaze. Otherwise, the *Freewind* couldn't sail the Sea of Wine unmolested. This same spell of concealment hides her from the gaze of other magically aware individuals such as yourself."

"Okay," said Sorrow. "What do you need me to do?"

"We can't leave her trapped in this figurehead," said Gale. "Before, my mother's ghost could roam the *Freewind*. Watching her family carry on was her own personal heaven. Now the magic that sustained her has been damaged. We don't know if she can see us or hear us. If she's withering away, deaf and dumb, she may be in her own private hell."

"How long has your mother been dead?" Sorrow asked, tracing the lines of the figurehead's face.

"Eighteen years," said Gale.

"Are you certain her soul is still in the wood? Souls don't last forever in the material world. They're like the residual heat from a fireplace. Once the fire dies out, the heat may linger a long time in the stones, but it isn't eternal."

"I know this," said Gale. "But mother's soul drew power from the Sea of Wine every time we crossed it. The Sea of Wine embodies the dreams and myths of all Wanderers. It sustains our souls for all eternity."

"Can you not return to the Sea of Wine? I was under the impression this was one of your magical talents."

Gale shook her head. "I could trigger the transition, but mother was the true cause. When she bargained with Avaris to bind her soul to the ship, she didn't know that her state, bridging the gap between life and death, would weaken the fabric of reality, to the point that the *Freewind* could tear through."

"Wait. Avaris? Your mother knew her?"

"So I've been told," said Gale. "Truthfully, my mother's biography is a complicated matter. She really did live a life of grand adventure. Alas, she was also prone to, shall we say, fabricating certain elements of her history."

"If we found Avaris, she could explain the spell she used to bind your mother to the ship."

"We know a good deal about the process," said Sage.

"Grandmother was quite ill when she made her bargain with Avaris. She knew she had very little time left. So she allowed Avaris to kill her. All the blood was drained from her body. The blood was diluted in wine, then soaked into to the *Freewind* board by board."

"This is why our former ship had such a distinctive hue," said Gale.

"Right," said Sorrow. "But problematic. Since your mother doesn't have any blood now, we couldn't duplicate the original binding."

"If we can't place her spirit into a ship once more, can we release her? Better to swim on alone into the Sea of Wine than to live in a prison of wood."

Sorrow nodded. "I agree. But we shouldn't give up hope. As it happens, I'm on a quest to find Avaris. I think she can help me with my, um, skin condition. If your mother's soul can last until then, Avaris may know some new trick to save her. Right now, my best hope of finding her lies in the Silver City, so it's fortunate you were heading there, yes?"

"Good fortune indeed," said Gale. "We're departing later in the day. We can—"

Gale was interrupted by a knock on the door.

Sage whipped out her spyglass. "No one's there," she whispered, confused.

There was a second knock.

"Who is it?" Sorrow asked.

"Slate," a deep voice answered.

Sage lowered her spyglass as her mouth went slack.

"I'm getting dressed," Sorrow said. "Go find the galley and get some breakfast. I'll join you later."

"May I prepare something for you?" he asked.

"I'm not even a little bit hungry," Sorrow said, doing her best to ignore the feeling of fullness in her abdomen.

She heard Slate's heavy feet as he climbed the stairs up to the deck.

"You look spooked," Gale said to Sage.

"I didn't see him!" Sage said. "I mean, once he started talking I realized I could see him, but I hadn't seen him the way I normally see people. He's like a big, walking sack of meat. He has no aura at all!"

"Is he undead?" asked Gale.

"He breathes, he sweats, he bleeds," said Sorrow. "He's alive in every way I've thought of testing."

"Sounds like you were pretty thorough in your testing," Gale said with a sly grin. "I don't blame you. Jetsam makes him sound like quite a feast for the eyes. Is there any sort of agreement between the two of you? A partnership that it would be impolite to intrude upon?"

"What? Are you... are you asking if we're lovers?"

"You said you'd tested him in every way you could think of. I know the first thing I'd test."

"By the pure metals, no! It's nothing like that."

"Good. I'd thought that, since you slept alone, you might not be possessive of him."

"I'm not, but, really, I don't think you should, um, test him yourself."

"I agree!" said Sage. "I'm not even certain he's human!"

"Also, you would drive Brand absolutely insane," said Sorrow.

"Brand employs me," said Gale. "He's not my husband. He has no say as to whom I share my bed with."

"You know he's in love with you."

"I know he *thinks* he's in love with me."

"You're not worried he's trying to manipulate you by providing you with a new ship?"

"I'm certain he is. But no matter. Brand may make any attempt he wishes to seduce me. I can see through his every action. When we share each other's bed again, it will be due to my actions, not his."

"When?" Sorrow asked. "Why would you..."

Gale shrugged. "Since we can no longer shorten our journeys

via the Sea of Wine, we'll be between ports for weeks at a time. In times of boredom, a woman can be forgiven for seeking… amusement."

"When I tried to find amusement with Will Fortune aboard the *Monsoon*, you practically broke my arm," grumbled Sage.

"You'll thank me later. He wasn't the right man for your first time."

"It wasn't going to be my first time. We were going to just fool around a little."

"Fooling around a little is how I wound up pregnant with Levi when I was sixteen," said Gale.

Sorrow folded her arms across her chest. "I'm not really comfortable with this discussion."

Gale nodded. "My apology. I forgot that you were raised to follow the tenets of the Church of the Book. It's no wonder they've become the most populous faith in the world, considering how they discourage the discussion of sex."

"Wouldn't refraining from discussing sex have the effect of reducing the population?" asked Sorrow. "The less the mind is focused on the topic, the less feverish it becomes."

"So the church teaches. But all their efforts lead only to ignorance. Men and women among the faithful are left to rut like animals on pure instinct. The men know nothing of seduction, and the women know very little about how to entertain themselves without spilling out babies."

Sorrow thought this was an odd attitude for a woman who had seven children, but let the matter pass.

Gale wasn't through, however. "In most other cultures, sex is an act of the body. Wanderers, by being free to discuss the act, have turned it into an act of the mind. Until you've experienced the difference between the approaches, you can never understand how one is superior to the other. Perhaps you can speak to Brand about it. He was an enthusiastic student."

"It's not a topic that's ever interested me," said Sorrow. She looked down at her tail. "For obvious reasons, it interests me even less now."

She led them toward the door. "If you'll give me a moment, I'd like to get dressed. I'm sure you both must have a million things to do before this ship can leave port."

"True," said Gale. Sage lifted the figurehead.

"You know that Mako sneaks out to see Sandy, and you never say a word," Sage muttered as she passed her mother.

"Mako doesn't stand a chance with Sandy," said Gale. "She doesn't like his teeth."

"How can you know that?" asked Sage.

"A mother knows," said Gale, as Sorrow closed the door behind them.

Sorrow dressed, finding her armor no tighter than it had been before. The bloated sensation in her belly was all in her mind. She ran her hands along the remnants of her pelvic bone, letting her fingers pause where her crotch had once been.

She sighed. "I wasn't using it anyway."

CHAPTER EIGHT

CHILD'S PLAY

SORROW SPENT THE following day in the hold. The ship had departed at dawn, and when Sage had come below to bring breakfast, Sorrow claimed to be suffering from sea-sickness. In truth, she wasn't, but she suspected it wouldn't take much to nauseate her considering her most recent meal. As horrible as the rat had been going down, she couldn't bear the thought of having it come back up. She felt her best course to avoid the experience was just to remain in the dimly lit hold and try to sleep until she was certain her unanticipated late night snack was completely digested.

She attempted to distract herself by updating her journal. Writing always took her from the realm of emotion into the realm of objective analysis:

It was only meat. For most living creatures, my meal was a completely natural event, barely worth note. Lions and wolves and housecats survive on raw meat; certainly humans can tolerate the diet. In some respects, the convention of gutting and skinning a beast, draining it of blood, cutting out the bones, then cooking only the muscles seems wasteful.

I should feel proud to have moved beyond such unnatural prissiness. Civilization has done all it can to suppress the hunting instinct that lies within us all. To have this instinct reawakened is an improvement, not a curse.

She closed her journal with a sigh, not convinced of a word she'd written. She began to think that her self-confinement was keeping her from moving past the incident. If she would only go up on deck, she could be distracted by the activities of the Romers.

If all the Romers had been adults, her decision would have been simple. She could hear Poppy and Cinnamon on deck, and they were ten and twelve, respectively. It had been one thing to slither into Commonground and face the stares of scoundrels and ruffians. If they were given nightmares by her appearance, she felt no pity for them. But Sorrow had seen things no child should see at Poppy's age, and didn't want to give the girls nightmares. Still, she couldn't hide below deck for the entire voyage, could she?

Her self-imposed exile in the hold came to an end with a knock on the door. The hold was dark save for the lantern. She threw her blanket around her shoulders to conceal herself before opening the door.

It was Brand, looking concerned as he slipped into the hold.

"Can I help you?" Sorrow asked.

"You've been hiding out since we left port. I was wondering if you needed help."

"I'm just feeling... queasy. I've more stomach to upset than I used to."

Brand held up a gnarled, tan root. "Ginger. Chew on this and you can handle rough seas. Gale's powers do push a ship across the waves faster than most people are used to."

Sorrow took the root. It looked tough and fibrous. She had doubts about putting it into her mouth.

"So what's the real reason you're hiding?" Brand asked.

"Why do you doubt that I'm sea-sick? On my previous travels aboard the *Freewind* I spent most of my time in my cabin."

"Some company would be good for you."

"I've been too busy for company," said Sorrow. "I've been updating my journal."

"Is there a section about how I killed the dragon?" Brand asked with a grin.

"You've been mentioned, yes. As an aide in my successful gambit to stop the beast."

"Do you also talk about me being a good listener with interesting insights into your true feelings and motives?"

"No." She rolled her eyes.

"I think you're hiding down here because you're ashamed of your appearance."

She crossed her arms. "I've been seen by half the Romers already. What do I have to hide?"

"It's the only explanation I can think of for why you're letting Slate run around the ship without you watching his every move. Considering you went to that graveyard digging for answers, I can't believe you don't have the biggest question you found under constant surveillance."

"Slate's... running around the ship?"

"He's playing with Poppy and Cinnamon on deck right now."

Sorrow frowned. What had she expected? That he would spend his journey lying in his bunk immobile as a corpse? She shouldn't have been surprised to discover that Slate was interacting with the crew. He'd been quick enough to make friends with Battle Ox. After she'd eaten the rat, all thoughts of trying to figure out who and what Slate might be had faded in importance.

Sorrow sighed. "Let me get dressed and I'll come up top. In truth, I'm feeling better adapted to the waves now that we've been under way for so many hours. I'd reached the decision to go to the deck on my own just before you knocked."

"Right," said Brand.

She dressed in her full armor. She knew that this was pointless attire aboard the ship, but she felt stronger when she wore it. She did modify the helmet, opening the faceplate to reveal her features from eyebrow to chin. When she was done, she slithered from the hold up the stairs to the deck.

When her torso rose above the edge of the hold she ducked, as she found herself in the midst of battle. Poppy was wearing a bucket on her head and lunging at Slate with a mop handle. Slate parried her blow with a mop handle of his own. Slate had shed his armor, and was dressed in the same white cotton uniforms sported by the Romers.

The mock sword battle between Poppy and Slate was being watched from the aftcastle by Cinnamon and a short woman that Sorrow didn't recognize. She did a double take and realized that the woman was Bigsby. The dwarf had his platinum blonde wig piled on his head, where it was held in place by a dazzling silver crown studded with emeralds. He was wearing a cream-colored silk dress adorned with abundant frills. His face was powdered to the point that it almost resembled a white mask, with bright red lips, pink cheeks, and thin arched eyebrows penciled on.

"Glad to see you've joined us," Brand said from behind her.

She turned around and asked, "Where does he keep getting these outfits?"

Brand shrugged. "He knows a seamstress in Commonground named Rose Thirteen. She apparently has a whole wardrobe full of outfits his size."

Sorrow was confused.

Brand shrugged and said, "I didn't ask questions. I had a million things to do to get the *Circus* ready. And Rose was a little too friendly for my taste."

"You found a woman to be too friendly?"

"I didn't think it was possible either, but she asked if I wanted to marry her about five minutes after we met."

"That's too friendly."

Brand nodded.

Sorrow turned back to the sword fight between Poppy and Slate. Slate obviously had the upper hand, but Poppy was making up for her lack of experience with speed and agility. Slate parried every blow, but she easily tumbled and rolled away from any attack he launched. She ducked beneath his latest swing, jumping forward, rolling into a ball, then springing back to her feet only inches in front of Sorrow.

"Sorrow!" Poppy said. "Slate's teaching me to be a knight!"

"Girls can't be knights!" Cinnamon shouted from her seat on the aftcastle.

"Not true," Bigsby answered. "Like my ancestor Queen Alabaster Brightmoon, I'm also a famous knight of the church."

"Then why aren't you down here training?" Poppy asked, placing her hands on her hips.

"My abilities are innate in my royal blood. Before I could even walk, my father placed me in the saddle atop his finest steed and I bested twenty men at jousting. I need no training."

Poppy fixed her eyes on Sorrow. The girl circled her finger next to her skull as she silently mouthed, "He's crazy."

"Be that as it may," Sorrow said, "your sister is correct that you can't be a knight."

"Ma says that a Wanderer can be anything she wants to be."

"But being a knight isn't merely a profession," said Sorrow. "It comes with a lot of religious baggage. Wanderers can't be knights because they don't believe in the Divine Author."

"I'll convert," said Poppy.

"Please don't let your mother hear you say that," said Brand. "She'll skin me alive for giving you that book."

"What book?" Sorrow asked.

"When I took possession of the ship, I found a dog-eared copy of *Champions of the Book* tucked in behind the mattress in the captain's cabin. It's a history, sort of. Mostly its blood-drenched legends of knights battling monsters, witches, and dragons. I immediately thought of Poppy."

"Why?"

"Did you ever see the books she read on the *Freewind*?"

"No."

Poppy said, "I like reading about battles. The bloodier, the better."

"Is that appropriate reading material for a child?" Sorrow asked.

"No!" said Cinnamon. "It makes her mean. She's always hitting people!"

"I'm not mean," Poppy grumbled. "You're just a—"

"Poppy is rambunctious," said Slate. "Full of energy and daring, but lacking formal training. She would make a fine warrior."

Sorrow raised an eyebrow. "So... you believe it's okay for women to fight? That's not exactly a tenet of chivalry."

Slate shrugged. "I suppose it's not. But, somehow, it feels right to me that women should engage in combat. You certainly held your own in battle."

"By the seven stars!" Poppy exclaimed as she bent over to look down into the hold at Sorrow's serpent form. "It's true!"

"Don't be alarmed by my appearance," Sorrow said. "I'm still the same woman you knew."

"Alarmed?" Poppy said, dropping to her chest and stretching her arm down. "This is amazing!" She ran her fingers along Sorrow's scales. "You're like a dragon!"

Cinnamon was suddenly at the hold as well, bending over to stare at Sorrow's tail.

"Come out into the light!" she said.

Sorrow was surprised by the reaction, but complied by slithering up the steps until she was completely on deck.

"I thought Jetsam was lying," said Cinnamon.

"You look just like Avaris!" said Poppy.

"What?" Sorrow was bewildered. What could this girl know about Avaris?

Poppy ran across the deck and grabbed a bag lying next to the mast. She pulled out a book and ran back. The tome was leather bound and thick, with dog-eared pages and a spine that had seen better days. She flipped through the yellowed paper until she found the page she was seeking. "This is Avaris!"

An old woodcut portrayed Avaris as a demon with a serpent's body from the waist down. Avaris also had fangs, and fins for ears, not to mention menacing talons in place of hands.

"Beyond the obvious, I don't see the resemblance," said Sorrow.

"Your scales are so smooth," Cinnamon said. She was running her fingers along Sorrow's hide so lightly that Sorrow hadn't noticed until the girl pointed it out.

"It's impolite to touch others without permission," Sorrow said.

Cinnamon drew her hand back, looking hurt.

"They're children," said Slate. "It's natural they'd be curious."

"My scales are sharp," said Sorrow. "She could injure herself."

"You have to play with us!" said Poppy. "You can be a dragon, and Slate and I will be the knights that slay you!"

"I'm uncertain why I would find that entertaining."

"It's merely play," said Slate.

Sorrow furrowed her brow. She hadn't expected the dragon-slayer she'd allied herself with to play well with children. To possibly be a destroyer worthy of discussion in hell, Slate was proving to be unexpectedly... *nice*.

"Is something bothering you?" Slate asked.

"'You'?" she said, noting the change in his grammar. "What happened to the *thous* and *thees*?"

"No one else speaks that way," Slate said with a shrug. "I've adapted."

Sorrow regretted wasting so much time below deck sulking. If Slate was a magical creation, it's possible he was programmed to adopt the mannerisms of those surrounding him to better fit in. She should be the one shaping his personality rather than leaving him in the hands of children.

"If you need a sparring partner to hone your skills in combat, you shouldn't battle these girls," she said. "As it happens, I've spent much of my life avoiding hand to hand combat, but suspect that will be more difficult from now on. I can craft swords of unnatural sharpness. You can teach me to use them effectively."

"It would be my honor," he said, bowing toward her. "But I shall continue training Poppy, as she continues to teach me."

"He's forgotten a lot about being a knight," said Poppy. "He didn't remember the code."

"The code?" Sorrow asked, thinking of the letter she couldn't read.

"The Code of Knighthood," said Slate. He straightened his spine and pulled back his shoulders, placing his hand over his heart. "A knight shall be brave, courteous, and kind, obedient to his king, a defender of his faith, and a champion to all men of virtue."

Sorrow crossed her arms. "That might mean more if you could remember your king or your faith."

"Aye," he said, wistfully. "I mean, yes."

"Even if he's lost his memory, he's still brave, courteous, and kind," said Poppy. "You can see it in his eyes."

Sorrow looked at his face. His dark eyes still reminded her of cold, hard stone. Despite his newly revealed gentleness, she could still see in his visage that Slate was a man capable of remorseless violence. Perhaps Poppy saw in his eyes only what she wished to see.

"I think his eyes are dreamy," Bigsby chimed in. He gave Slate a dainty wave with his gloved hand.

Slate looked uncomfortable as he turned his back to the dwarf and said to Sorrow, "Let's go below and examine your swords. If you wish advice on how best to use them, I should be familiar with your weapons."

They headed down the stairs. Once they were out of sight of Bigsby, Slate whispered, "I'm told that the short, portly woman is a princess. But I'm beginning to suspect she may not even be female!"

Slate looked bewildered as Sorrow laughed so hard that tears came to her eyes. It was a relief, of sort, to discover she still had the capacity to find something funny. When she wiped the last of the tears from her cheeks and caught her breath, she realized her ribs were now sore. She had a lot of ribs.

* * *

HER RIBS CONTINUED to suffer abuse in the coming days as Slate made good on his promise to train her. Her strength and speed were better than ever, but he still had no trouble slipping past her best defenses and whacking her flanks with the flat of his wooden sparring sword. After nearly a week of training, she grew frustrated, and threw down her blades.

"I give up!" she said. "I don't know why I thought I could do this."

"You can do it," he said. "You've learned a great deal in the last week. Once or twice you've actually turned my sword aside."

"My ribs are black and blue. I thought that one of the virtues of a knight was to be kind. What's kind about beating me to a pulp?"

"Do you enjoy pain?"

"No!"

"Then you definitely wouldn't enjoy having a real sword cut into your flesh. I tap you just enough to provide you with an incentive not to get hit."

"But the problem is that this isn't real combat," she said. "When I do engage in violence, I always strike to kill. I've never been in a fight that lasted more than thirty seconds. I can't really attack you with the full force of my powers. I've no desire to hurt you."

"Perhaps I need to hit you harder. You need not hold back against me."

Sorrow clenched her fists, thinking of the entropic forces she'd managed to suppress so well for the last week. Her body hadn't changed since she'd stopped using those powers. She said, "Let's hope, for both our sakes, I continue to hold back."

Before their conversation could go further, Sage shouted from the crows nest, "Ship!"

Sorrow rose to twice Slate's height and scanned the

surrounding sea. She saw no ship, but Sage's abilities allowed her spot a ship many miles away.

"Where? How many?" Gale shouted from her position at the wheel.

"Only the one. Just beyond the horizon, dead ahead."

"What flag do they fly?"

"The flag of King Brightmoon, but it's probably a deception," said Sage. "I know that ship. It's the *Seahorse!*"

"Wonderful," said Gale, with a sigh.

Sorrow slithered back toward the wheel where Gale stood. "Is there a problem?"

"The *Seahorse* is a pirate ship," said Gale. She shook her head. "A real pirate ship, I mean."

Sorrow understood Gale qualification. Her entire family had been branded pirates after they'd freed slaves from a fellow Wanderer's ship. The Wanderers had recently engaged in a civil war over whether it was against their values to accept slaves as cargo. Gale's family had been on the losing side.

"So the *Seahorse* might try to board us?" Sorrow asked.

Gale shook her head. "We won't be getting anywhere near them. Between my control of the wind and Sage's ability to see them before they see us, we'll just slip around them."

"Of course. It's just that you sounded bothered when you learned it was the *Seahorse*."

"To be honest, the only good news I heard during the length of the pirate wars was a report that the *Seahorse* had been sunk by Brightmoon's fleet. Captain Stallion and I have something of a history."

"A romantic history?" asked Sorrow.

Gale looked genuinely offended. "No. Eight years ago, he raided my cousin's ship, the *Stormfront*. Piracy is just a day-to-day part of the business when you make your living on the sea, and my cousin attempted to dissuade Stallion from harming her ship or crew with a sizable bribe. Many pirates are merely businessmen, but Captain Stallion is motivated by sadism even more than greed. I'll spare you the details of what unfolded on the *Stormfront*, and say only that he occupied the ship for three days, misusing and abusing the crew in the most horrific fashion. Under other circumstances, I wouldn't steer away. I'd race right toward him for the chance to hang his head from my bowsprit. Alas, I may be captain of the *Circus*, but I'm not the owner. My first duty is to keep the ship and its passengers safe. My revenge against Stallion must wait."

"We need not endanger this ship," said Mako, coming back to join the conversation. Mako was the eldest of Gale's children aboard, at twenty-one. He was tall and sleek-muscled, with long ink-black hair that hung down his back in a perfect glistening stripe. Despite the near-perfection of his body, his face was disturbing to look upon. His mouth was twice as wide as an ordinary man's, and when he spoke he revealed row upon row of saw-like teeth in his muscular jaws. "It was sheer luck Stallion escaped when we ran into him near the Isle of Apes. I've nothing to fear from him. I'll just swim over to his vessel and bore a hole in the bottom. When his crew hits the water, I can easily finish them off."

"No," said Gale. "We've been hired to sail to the Silver Isles. We aren't being paid to settle old grudges. Also, we don't even know if Captain Stallion's still alive. Just because he once captained the *Seahorse* doesn't mean he's still in charge."

"Oh, he's still alive," said Sage, looking down from the crows nest. "I see him on the deck. Even if I didn't have my magic, he's not a tough figure to spot."

Sorrow wondered what that comment meant, and apparently Gale read the question in her face.

"Stallion is only human from the waist up," she explained. "From the waist down, he has the body of a jackass."

"Inhuman scum," Mako cursed, the syllables spilling without a hint of irony from his shark-like jaws.

"He's a half-seed?" asked Sorrow.

"No," said Gale. "Ten years ago he was human. But, as I

mentioned, he has a sadistic streak. Unfortunately for him, he got rough in the sack with the wrong woman. One of his victims proved to be a bone-weaver. She used her power over flesh to graft his torso onto a donkey. She told him if he was intent on behaving as a jackass, she would make him look like one as well."

"Maybe we should stop chit-chatting and start taking some evasive action," Sage called down. "They're heading directly toward us."

"Do they see us?" asked Gale.

"I don't see how," said Sage. "We're still over their horizon. But if I didn't know better, I'd say they were adjusting their course to intercept us."

"Luckily, they don't know who they're dealing with," said Gale, turning the wheel hard to starboard. "Mako, go wake Rigger and Jetsam. I want all hands on deck until we're well clear."

"Sure, Ma."

"Sure, *Captain*. We're employees now. We must be more professional."

"Right," Mako said tersely. "Captain."

The ship lurched as the wind shifted and the *Circus* turned due north. They sailed on this course for about five minutes before Sage reported, "They're turning. They're on a course that will intersect ours."

"That can't be a coincidence," said Rigger as he came back to the wheel. Rigger was a few years younger than Mako, a thin, lanky figure who always had bags under his eyes. "There's no reason for them to change direction out here on the high seas."

Gale said, "How are they seeing us?"

"Another clairvoyant?" asked Mako.

"Look up," said Rigger.

All eyes turned toward a sky mottled with clouds. A small dark speck drifted across an expanse of blue between the white puffs.

Sage stared into her spyglass. "Crap," she said. "It's another half-animal like Stallion. This is an old woman with wings like a vulture. She's looking straight at us, and pointing in our direction with her toes. Stallion is watching her with his spyglass."

"Get Brand," Gale said to Mako.

Brand had gone below deck to have breakfast with the Princess in her cabin and had yet to come back. Mako ran to get them and five minutes later everyone aboard the ship stood on the deck.

Sage pointed toward the horizon with her spyglass. "They're getting closer."

Indeed. Sorrow could see the white sails as specks bobbing on the horizon. They were still quite distant. She squinted, but the ships were still too far apart for her to see Captain Stallion. If he really had run afoul of a bone-weaver with sufficient talent to weave together a man and a donkey, she wanted to learn that weaver's identity.

"Here's our first option, sir," Gale said to Brand. "We keep heading toward the Silver Isles. I'm fairly confident I can outmaneuver them, but can't guarantee it. I may hate Stallion's guts, but he wouldn't still be alive if he weren't a damn good sailor."

"What's the second option?" asked Brand.

"We turn tail. They're only getting closer because we're heading in converging directions. If we turn, I'm certain I can outrun them. I know nothing about their aerial spy, but she can't stay aloft forever. Assuming she can't see us at night, we turn back toward the Silver Isles at sunset and slip past them in the dark."

Brand stroked his chin. "Effectively, we'd lose a day of travel. That doesn't seem such a high price to pay."

"Why should we pay any price?" asked Mako. "Option three: we take the fight to them. Stallion has a price on his head. We can come out of this with a profit."

"Mako!" Gale said. "We don't kill people for profit. If I've sacrificed everything to not trade in live bodies, I'll be damned if I'll sully myself by trading in dead ones. If we kill Stallion, we do it for justice, not to collect a chest full of moons."

"Yes, *Captain*," said Mako. "But you don't have the final word on this matter. Brand does."

Brand looked thoughtful as he said, "So, we'd be ridding the world of a known pirate and earning a nice reward?"

"If rewards are your only motive," Gale said, "how do we know you won't one day turn us in? The gold on our heads spends just as well."

"Oh, that won't be a problem," said Bigsby, drawing back his shoulders and thrusting out his stuffed cleavage. He took a deep breath and stretched out his hands, as if encompassing the whole of the ship, as he said, in formal tones, "In the name of the Brightmoon throne, I hereby grant all members of the Romer family an immediate and unconditional pardon!"

"Well, that's a weight off my shoulders," said Rigger.

Brand sighed. "Mako, I'm sure you could take these jokers out by yourself, but I don't see any reason to risk it. I've been gone from the Silver City a long time. I'm returning home with a new fortune and long-lost family." He placed his hand on Bigsby's shoulder. "I'm not going to risk it all just to teach some pirate a lesson."

"Well reasoned, sir," said a voice from the bow.

Everyone looked up. A young boy, no older than ten, stood on the bowsprit. Water beaded on his golden-tanned skin and seeped from his white cotton breeches. He was skinny; you could count the ribs on his shirtless torso. His black hair was cropped close to his scalp, and his eyes were dark and intense as he looked at them.

"Who the devil are you?" Brand asked.

"An interesting choice of words," said the boy. "For it seems my role in life is to be the eternal adversary. Once, I believed I was the savior of mankind. Now, I suspect, I'm the death of it. But, today, I'm merely enjoying the carefree life of a seafaring scoundrel. We've come to take your ship, your treasure, and your women."

"Oh, heavens," gasped Bigsby, placing the back of his palm against his forehead.

Gale put her hands on her hips. "Aren't you a little young, boy? Why do you need women? To have your diaper changed?"

"Amusing." The boy chuckled, hopping to the deck next to the anchor.

"Grab this idiot before he hurts himself," Gale said to Mako.

"Idiot?" said the boy. "You wound me. I assure you, I'm the most educated person on this ship."

"Certainly the most talkative," said Mako, stalking forward.

The boy waited patiently. He was unarmed. Mako was at least two feet taller. Yet the boy's spiky red aura radiated out several yards around him, making him look like a giant in Sorrow's eyes. "Be careful," she warned.

"Yes," said the boy, with a grin. "Be careful. You don't know who it is you face."

"In fairness, Brand did ask your name," said Mako, reaching for the boy's arm.

As he leaned forward, the boy took him by the wrist and spun his shoulder into Mako's guts. Mako toppled heels over head across the railing. "What the..." he cried, before a loud splash muffled his voice.

"You! Down below!" the boy shouted toward Mako as he grabbed the anchor. "Be a friend and hold this for me, will you?" Though the anchor had to weigh more than he did, the boy tossed it overboard.

The chain went *clackety-clackety-clackety* as the weight dropped.

"Luckily, it's too deep out here for the anchor to catch," said Rigger.

"I would have thought an experienced sailor such as yourself could deduce from the color of the water that there's a sea mount directly beneath us," said the boy.

Just then, the ship whipped to a halt, dipping forward and throwing everyone from their feet.

Sorrow, lacking feet, remained upright, her tail wrapped around a mast to keep her stable. Not that her stability helped much. The boy somersaulted across the pitching deck faster than Sorrow's eyes could follow. There was a loud smack to her right and when she turned her head she saw that both Rigger and Gale were flat on their backs, unconscious.

Sorrow looked up. The boy was in the rigging directly above her, grinning down.

"Want a job?" he asked. "I've been staffing my pirate empire with half-seeds and braided-beings. You'd fit right in."

Suddenly, there was a grunt off to Sorrow's side. The boy reached out his hand almost casually and caught a belaying pin that had just been thrown at him by Slate, who'd made it back to his feet. The boy flicked his arm like a whip and the small wooden club flew back at his attacker, bouncing off the center of Slate's forehead. The big man winced, but seemed unharmed. With a growl, he leapt into the rigging and began to climb after the child.

"Sorry for the interruption," the boy said to Sorrow as he climbed higher. "By now, it should be apparent that I'm winning. Care to join my crew?"

"Who are you again?" Sorrow asked, utterly befuddled.

"My name is Numinous Pilgrim. You may have heard of me as the Golden Child, or perhaps the Omega Reader."

Sorrow's eyebrows shot up. She *had* heard of him. "You're the perfect being that the Church of the Book has been waiting for?" The words sounded odd as they came from her lips. The book that the church was founded upon was far too sacred for any ordinary man to dare open. For the last thousand years, the church had been awaiting the arrival of the Omega Reader, the flawless human who could open the book without its holy purity burning out his sinful soul. She'd never believed in such a being, but she'd never seen an aura like this before.

Numinous leapt to the mast, then bounced to another set of ropes, easily avoiding Slate's outstretched arm.

"I didn't expect the Omega Reader to be a common pirate," Sorrow said, as Jetsam rose silently in the air behind him. Jetsam was carrying the light rapier that she'd seen him use to great effect. She almost wanted to call out a warning to Numinous—she would have preferred to capture a child his age without harming him—but held her tongue. The boy had already proven himself too dangerous to play with.

"I would hardly call myself common," said Numinous. He shifted sideways as Jetsam lunged, and the tip of the thin blade poked the air where his belly button had been a moment before. Numinous snatched the rapier away, then kicked Jetsam in the throat, sending him to crash on the deck below, gagging.

Numinous stretched the rapier toward the rigging Slate was climbing and made two fast slices. Slate frowned as he found that the ropes supporting his weight were no longer attached to anything. He fell to the deck, his head smacking hard on the wood.

Sorrow asked, "Why, exactly, if you're the savior that the church has been waiting for, are you out here robbing boats and threatening women?"

"The Omega Reader is both savior and destroyer," said Numinous. "If it's my fate to bring an end to this wicked world, I thought I should first investigate the true nature of sin. So far, the *Seahorse* has been an entertaining classroom."

Numinous dropped from the rigging as Brand started to rise. He'd been knocked unconscious earlier when the ship slammed to a halt, and had been sprawled face down. Numinous drove his foot into the back of Brand's skull, smashing his face into the deck, rendering him still once more. By now, Poppy had recovered. She grabbed a belaying pin and pressed it against the mast. When she let go, it shot toward Numinous. Her mermaid gift was the power to 'pop' whatever she touched, turning anything she placed her hands on into an impromptu missile.

The boy made a show of yawning as he leaned three inches to the left so that the pin flew past his ear.

He cast a quick glance toward Sage in the rigging, then his eyes darted back to Poppy, who was fishing about for something else to fire at him, and Cinnamon, who was hiding behind the hatch that led to the cabins below. He looked back to Sorrow. "Your only remaining allies are three unarmed girls. Ready to switch sides?"

Sorrow rose, riding her serpent body ever higher, until she loomed over Numinous by a good ten feet.

"You seek an education in wickedness?" she asked, drawing her swords. "You've just met your final teacher."

CHAPTER NINE

SPOILS OF WAR

BEFORE SORROW COULD act, Poppy somersaulted toward Numinous, bouncing high enough that she could land perched upon his shoulders. Numinous grinned as he stood frozen, almost as if he was looking forward to the attack.

Poppy's hands pressed down on his shoulders as Slate rose from the deck barely two yards away, shaking his head. He wasted no time in spotting the boy and lunged, attempting to tackle Numinous by driving his shoulder into his gut.

Unfortunately, Slate's tackle came just as Poppy bounced off and Numinous shot straight up with the speed of a cork popping from a champagne bottle. Instead of Slate hitting Numinous, he wound up slamming into Poppy as she dropped back to the deck. The force of his blow was powerful enough to send the girl flying. Her head banged against the ship's rail with a loud *WHACK* and she tumbled limp into the sea.

"That was unfortunate," Numinous said from above. He was standing on one the yardarms of the foresail. He'd apparently escaped being launched completely off the ship by grabbing a rope. "I know that legends say that Wanderers can't drown, but I wonder how they fare unconscious in shark infested waters while bleeding from a head wound?"

Sorrow knew Numinous was trying to taunt her into jumping into the sea to rescue Poppy. But if she rescued the girl, she would leave everyone else aboard to the mercy of this boy.

She'd already made her choice when Slate jumped to the railing, scanned the waters beneath him, then dived in.

"Noble, isn't he?" Numinous asked. "I wasn't certain which way he'd go. Something is masking his aura." He squinted as he stared at Sorrow. "Either that, or he has no soul. While you, intriguingly, seem to have two."

"Then you're outnumbered!" Sorrow cried out, brandishing her swords as her serpentine body uncoiled to launch her heavenward. Numinous smiled as he jumped to meet her attack. His feet flashed over her face and he landed on her back. He slid along her smooth scales, zipping along her spine to reach the deck.

Sorrow twisted around and the boy lunged toward her torso. He was trailing a long length of rope that had been coiled near the main mast. He kicked hard and sailed over her head, the rope spiraling behind him. The hemp wrapped around Sorrow's forearms. Her wrists clapped together forcefully enough to knock her swords from her grip, which was fortunate since her bound fists smacked against her throat as the line went taut. Despite her supernatural strength, she was helpless as the boy formed a makeshift pulley by running the rope through the base of the anchor chain. He reeled her in, until the top of her helmet smashed against the large iron loop. As she struggled, she felt something tighten around the tip of her tail. The lower half of her body began to rise into the air. She caught a glimpse of a rope whirring through a pulley high in the riggings. In seconds, she was completely upended, stretched with the tip of her tail high in the air and her bound neck and wrists fastened to the deck in such a fashion that her armored shoulders were pressed hard against the polished wood.

Numinous crouched beside her. "I apologize for the rough treatment. I hope you'll take a moment to calmly contemplate your circumstances. It should be obvious that I can anticipate your every move. I see your truths quite plainly. Your predominant narrative is that you crave power. This has led you to make use of forces beyond your control. I'm the living embodiment of control. Serve me, and I'll teach you how to see past your own lies. Only in truth will you find mastery."

"I'll serve no one," she growled. "Least of all a brat like you!"

Numinous chuckled. "You'll remain defiant for a while longer. But your surrender is inevitable. I see it quite clearly."

Sorrow bit her lower lip. Was the boy onto something? Perhaps she could simply pretend to surrender. Could she bargain joining his crew in exchange for sparing the Romers?

She grimaced. Whatever the boy thought he knew about her, the one thing she knew beyond doubt was that she'd never surrender. She had only to tap into a fraction of Rott's power and the ropes that bound her would crumble to dust. She could open the gate to Rott's full power and the boy would be devoured by flies. But, if she did so, would she lose even more of her humanity?

"You're afraid of something," he said. "Something you believe is more terrible than me. What is it that troubles you?"

"You don't want to find out," Sorrow whispered.

At that moment, the hatch to the cabins beneath them banged open. Sorrow's eyes darted toward the noise.

Bigsby stood in the opening, wearing a full breastplate and helmet, his limbs draped in chain mail. He brandished a large mace with both hands as he cried, "Face me, villain! You may have bested these common sailors, but you now face Princess Innocent Brightmoon, champion of the oppressed!"

Numinous burst out laughing.

Bigsby clanked and clattered as he advanced across the deck at a pace more akin to a tortoise than a hare. Numinous yawned loudly, crossing his arms as the dwarf approached. He said, "Could you pick up the pace, 'princess'? I'd like to get back to making a deal with the snake-woman."

Bigsby responded by bounding forward and swinging his mace. Numinous leaned back to avoid the blow. To Sorrow's surprise, a loud *WHACK* followed. Numinous fell to his back, clutching his right cheek with his hand.

His eyes were wide as he spat out blood and mumbled, "How did you—"

Bigsby answered by shuffling forward and swinging the mace over his head. Numinous rolled to keep his brains from being bashed in, but Bigsby still managed to strike a glancing blow to the boy's shoulder. Numinous made it to his hands and knees and tried to crawl away, but Bigsby pursued him, driving the mace into the boy's ribs.

Numinous sucked in air through clenched teeth as he rolled across the deck. He stared at the dwarf with terror in his eyes.

"Your reality... it's fractured," he whimpered, his voice trembling. "You exist outside the truth!"

Bigsby swung his mace again and Numinous rolled away barely in time. Sorrow was surprised the blows were even close. Despite her poor skills with weapons, she was certain she could have avoided Bigsby's blows, given that he was weighed down by armor and swinging a weapon twice as heavy as he could effectively handle. Perhaps Numinous wasn't quite as in control of events as he'd like to believe.

Just then, soft footsteps whispered across the deck toward Sorrow. She turned her eyes toward the sound and found Cinnamon dashing from her hiding place with a knife in her grasp. The red-headed girl dropped to her knees in front of Sorrow and whispered, "Hold still." She began to saw at the ropes binding Sorrow.

At the same instant, Sorrow felt vibrations near her tail. The second her wrists were free she turned her gaze upward and saw Sage Romer hanging upside down from the crow's nest, grasping the cord that bound Sorrow's tail. With a slash of a dagger, Sorrow was free. Her tail fell against the main mast and instinctively coiled around it.

"Mind if I borrow this?" she asked as she took the butcher's knife from Cinnamon.

With her tail braced high above on the mast, her torso flew into the air to get a better view of the fight between Bigsby and

Numinous. The boy was now near the back of the ship, with a fresh cut above his left eyebrow. Bigsby had apparently gotten in another lick.

Bigsby had the mace swung back over his shoulders with both hands and was lumbering forward to deliver another blow. Numinous furrowed his brow as he studied the dwarf's motions.

Bigsby swung. Numinous jumped aside at the last possible second before bouncing forward and grasping Bigsby's shining helmet with both hands. He snatched it from the dwarf's head, revealing the platinum blonde wig.

Numinous clasped the dwarf by the cheeks, stared into his eyes, and shouted, "Your madness shall lift! Be healed!"

He let go of Bigsby's face. The dwarf staggered backwards, tripping and falling on his butt. He reached up and pulled the blonde locks from his head and stared at them with a look of terror. He looked around and saw Sorrow, Sage, and Cinnamon staring at him.

"Oh, god," he whispered.

Numinous picked up Bigsby's mace from where it had fallen.

He limped toward the dwarf, lifting the mace high. He spat out blood as he grumbled, "Enjoy your moment of clarity, 'princess.' It will end when I splatter your brains across this deck."

Sorrow flashed toward Numinous. The boy saw her coming and leapt aside, but his actions were plainly impaired by his injuries. She failed to grab him, but her fingers did close upon the shaft of the mace. He released it, dancing across the deck to land on the railing near the anchor chain. He looked back over his shoulder and grinned.

Sorrow's heart sank. The *Seahorse* was now barely a hundred yards away. Fifty pirates stood upon the deck, many holding grappling hooks. Most were bestial blends of man and animal. A single ten-year-old boy had left the *Circus* all but defenseless against a crew of monsters.

"You win, kid!" Sage shouted from high in the riggings. "As the most senior officer still conscious, I'd like to talk surrender!"

Numinous looked up. He frowned as he said, "You're lying. You're trying to distract me so –"

At that moment, Cinnamon rose from behind an overturned barrel and dashed toward Numinous. He turned, facing her, and jumped for a rope overhead. Her fingers barely brushed the tips of his toes as he climbed into the rigging.

The small contact proved sufficient. Cinnamon had the power to control a person's taste buds. The boy's face contorted in a mask of horrified disgust. His body convulsed as he began to violently vomit. His trembling fingers lost their grip on the rope and he fell to the deck, landing hard. Any hope he would be knocked out by the fall was quashed as he rose to his hands and knees, his body heaving as he threw up once more.

Sorrow assumed that Numinous was too busy trying to purge the foul taste from his mouth to pay attention to her. She lunged toward him, the knife in one hand, the mace in the other, prepared to put him out of his misery.

Alas, her blows bit into the vomit covered deck as the boy again displayed inhuman reflexes in rolling aside. Spitting with each motion, he jumped to the rails.

Wiping his lips, he whispered, "My troops can finish you!" He spat again, and flipped backward into the sea.

"Mako!" Cinnamon cried, leaning over the rail. "Mako! Catch him!"

"Mako can't hear you," Sage shouted. "He's at the *Seahorse*. He headed there the second Numinous threw him overboard."

"He left us even though we were under attack?"

Sage shrugged. "I doubt he thought we'd have a problem beating a little kid. You know he'd rather tear into a ship full of bloodthirsty pirates than fight a boy half his age. How much longer before the kid stops feeling sick?"

Cinnamon shook her head. "I had contact for less than a second. But I hit him with weeping cheese."

"Weeping cheese?" asked Sorrow.

"Sometimes cheese aboard ships gets infested with a kind of translucent, gelatinous maggot," said Sage. "When they break through the rind, it looks like the cheese is crying."

"It's the worst thing I've ever put in my mouth," said Cinnamon. "But some rich people consider it a delicacy."

"Let's hope there are no rich people among these half-seeds," Sorrow said as she watched the *Seahorse* draw to within a hundred feet. "We're about to be overrun."

"I can assure you that we aren't," said Sage, pointing toward the stern of the *Seahorse*.

Mako was climbing the massive rudder. He was biting through the heavy iron bands that held the beams together. The *Seahorse* lurched as her rudder suddenly tore loose. Even from a hundred feet away, Sorrow heard Captain Stallion curse, "What the devil?"

A dozen pirates ran to the stern and peered over. Mako reached up and flung the closest few into the waves, then leapt to the stern rail and shouted, "Fight for your lives, you scurvy dogs! I take no prisoners!"

Cinnamon ran past Sorrow on her way toward her mother. She grabbed Gale by the shoulders. The older woman's face contorted, her nose wrinkling, and she suddenly sat up, spitting.

"Sorry," Cinnamon said. "I had to wake you fast. You should be tasting mint now."

Gale wiped her mouth on her sleeve. "That's much better." She looked around. "What's going on?"

Sage shouted down the current battle status as Cinnamon moved to revive Rigger.

Sorrow wondered what had happened to Poppy and Slate, and moved to the rail to see if she could spot them. She found the big man climbing the anchor chain with the now conscious Poppy clinging to his shoulders.

"Are you both okay?" she shouted.

"I'm fine!" Poppy cried.

"I'm eager to hit someone," said Slate. "Where's the boy?"

"He went into the water," said Sage. "For some reason, I can't see him. But if you need a little violence, we have a whole ship at the ready."

"You can't touch Stallion," Gale cried. "He's mine!"

"I'm not sure that got explained to Mako," said Sage.

"Jetsam and Brand are awake!" Cinnamon shouted.

"Where's Bigs—the princess?" Brand asked groggily.

Bigsby stumbled past, his wig in his hand, the kohl around his eyes running down his cheeks. "She's going below to find a bottle of rum," he said softly as he unclasped his breastplate, which clattered to the deck.

Gale paid the dwarf no mind as she readied her twin cutlasses and jumped to the railing.

"Ready, Rigger?" she asked.

"Bring the wind, Captain," the young man answered as he took the wheel.

On the *Seahorse*, chaos had broken loose. A half-dozen pirates now flailed in the waves behind the ship. Mako had liberated a cutlass from one of the cutthroats and was busily cutting throats. Sorrow couldn't guess how many dead bodies lay around him. Suddenly, a short, shirtless pirate covered with quills broke from the pack and flicked his arms toward Mako, unleashing a hail of barbed darts. Mako flinched as the tiny missiles turned his face into a pincushion. His eyes scrunched shut from the pain. Blinded, he dropped his cutlass and dove back into the sea.

The *Circus* turned toward the *Seahorse* and was closing fast. Brand intercepted Bigsby before he went below deck.

"Don't take off your armor just yet, Princess," Brand advised. "There's about to be a big fight. Time to bring a little Brightmoon justice to these pirates!"

"I'm not a princess," Bigsby said with a sigh. "I'm a fishmonger. You know that."

Brand raised an eyebrow. "I'm just happy to hear that you know it!"

"Happy? Now that my secret's out, I'm ruined," Bigsby moaned. "It's hard enough being a dwarf among the ruffians of Commonground. Now that everyone knows about my... other wardrobe... I'm doomed."

Sorrow's attention turned to a discarded element of Bigsby's wardrobe. She slithered over and picked up the gleaming breastplate from the deck. The front and back halves of the armor clanged together on their leather straps as she lifted them, taking a closer look to see if they'd work for the plan she had in mind. Despite the smallness of his limbs, Bigsby's torso was as large as most men. "If you don't need this any more, I've got a use for it."

"Take it," Bigsby said, shaking his head. "I can't fight. I'm nothing but a coward."

"I don't believe that," said Brand. "I watched you charge at a dragon without batting an eye. If Princess Innocent was brave, you're brave."

Sorrow had no time to listen to Brand's attempt to cheer his despondent brother. She snaked around and headed for Slate, who stood at the rail with his fists clenched as the space narrowed between the two ships.

She held Bigsby's mace toward him. "I'm sure you can bang some heads together with your bare hands, but you might do more damage with this."

"Aye," he said, taking it from her.

"I thought you might also benefit from a little armor," she said, presenting him the breast plate.

"It's too small," he said.

"I can adapt it," she said, lining the iron plate up to his chest. "Hold still."

She bent the edges of the plate outward, stretching them to fit over Slate's impressive musculature. She spun him around and worked on the back, molding and sculpting the metal to his form. She tightened the leather straps, then spun him back around. She glanced toward Bigsby's discarded helmet. She flicked it with the end of her tail, sending it bouncing across the deck toward her, then caught it and plopped it onto Slate's head. Satisfied that it fit without any further adjustment, she ran her hands along Slate's chest to smooth out her handiwork. Slate stared at her intently as she worked.

A little too intently.

She suddenly felt awkward. Was she really trying to perfect his armor? Or were her fingers lingering on his muscles for reasons she was unwilling to admit?

"That should be good enough," she said.

"Your eyes," he whispered. "I... remember them."

"We see each other every day. You've not had a chance to forget them," she said.

"No..." His face sagged as he shook his head. "It's... it's like a memory from... long ago. Of you outfitting me for battle. But now... it's gone."

Sorrow pressed her lips tightly together. Was he merely remembering when she'd fitted him with his glass armor?

But there was no more time to ponder such things, because the *Circus* was now within grappling range of the pirate vessel.

Captain Romer leapt beside Slate and Sorrow. "The three of us lead the charge," she said. "Mako's already in the water and Jetsam's heading down. Knock everyone you can into the drink. My sons will make swift work of them."

Cinnamon ran up, with Sorrow's swords in her grasp. "I figured you might need these."

Sorrow grabbed the blades. She looked across the narrow gap to the assembled pirates. Despite Mako's attack, there were still at least three dozen. Among the pirate ranks she spotted a half-bear, a half-boar, and a long-jawed monstrosity that might have been half-crocodile. This wasn't going to be an easy fight.

Gale cried, "Poppy! Clear a path!"

She stepped aside as a barrel shot past her, splintering against the horns of a goat-man at the rail of the *Seahorse* and knocking him backwards. Gale raised both her cutlasses and leapt across the six-foot gap dividing the ships, shouting, "The moment you chose to be pirates is the moment you chose to die!" She landed where the goat-man had stood and severed the head of a dog-faced boy who'd had the misfortune of standing too close.

Slate followed Gale's lead, easily crossing the gap between the rolling ships despite his new burden of armor. He plowed into the crowd, swinging his mace in wide arcs that sent pirates flying.

Sorrow stretched across the gap. She had the misfortune of facing off with the half-bear, who slapped away the blade she drove toward his left shoulder and swatted her face with his massive right hand, full of claws. Her helmet spared her any cuts as the man-bear's nails slid along the glass, but the impact left her seeing stars.

He opened jaws full of ugly teeth and made a thrust for her neck. The pirate's charge was halted by Slate's mace, which drove his snout-like nose back into his brains.

She had no time to thank him. Her serpent half had now slithered fully on board and was being attacked by a dozen swords at once. Her scales proved impervious to the combined assault. As if it had a mind of its own, her muscular tail whipped back and forth, knocking pirates overboard.

Sorrow turned to face the alligator-man as Gale flew past, swinging over the battle on a rope, to land on the upper deck where Captain Stallion watched the fight unfolding in the company of the porcupine half-seed. The quill-covered creature bristled as it readied an attack on Gale, but with a flash of steel its head tumbled from its shoulders.

Stallion turned, looking at first as if he might be getting ready to flee, but instead he kicked with his back hooves, catching Gale in the chest. She went flying, falling to the lower deck, where a mob of pirates jostled for the chance to finish her off.

None reached her. Instead, the rigging unknotted and snaked to life, catching the pirates attacking Gale by their necks. All were jerked from their feet by impromptu nooses. Sorrow glanced over her shoulder to find that Rigger had come aboard and was standing on the rail, his hand upon a line leading up to the main mast.

A few of the remaining pirates on the deck turned pale as they looked at their brethren kicking overhead. They had no need to fear death by hanging, however, as Slate plowed through their ranks, bashing skulls and breaking limbs.

Gale bounced back to her feet and again leapt for Captain Stallion. The half-horse cursed as hurricane winds whipped his hair and carried Gale toward him. However, fast as Gale moved, she was no match for his equine legs. He chose flight over fight, making a magnificent leap over the railing. He hung in the air with a look of defiance, before dropping, legs kicking, arms flailing, toward the shark-infested water.

Sorrow lingered for half a second as she tossed a pig-man into the drink, studying the water below. She never saw Stallion surface. The waves were crimson with blood and countless shark fins churned the water. Mako was climbing up the anchor chain and Jetsam had jumped into the air and was swimming up to the level of the deck.

Sorrow turned back toward the action, only to find there was none. The only two animal men still alive were rather pathetic. A half-rabbit was curled into a fetal ball by the mainmast, tugging his ears.

"I-I-I-I s-s-surrender!" he shrieked.

"We both surrender," a turtle man said in a thick, slurred voice as he slowly raised his fat, wrinkled hands.

"The b-b-boy made us d-do it!" the rabbit man cried. "I n-never wanted to be a p-p-pirate!"

Mako advanced on the cowering figure, drawing his bloodied lips wide as he growled, "I said we would take no prisoners!"

Gale placed her hand on Mako's shoulder. "Hold! I gave no such command."

"We dare not show mercy!" Mako screamed as he spun to face his mother. "These crud aren't even fully human!"

Jetsam laughed. "That just seems funny when you've still got bits of pirate stuck between your teeth."

Mako frowned as he glared at his brother. He ran his fingers between his lips and dug around, producing an earring, and what once might have been an ear.

"There's no need to hurt us," the turtle man said. "Hopper is right. We were kidnapped by the others, but the only dirty work we ever did was swab the deck."

Mako shook his head. "If you've eaten their food, you've shared in the spoils of their plunder. Honest men would have fought their captors!"

"They w-would have k-killed us!" said Hopper.

"Better to die an honest man than to be moved by fear to wallow in a life of sin," said Slate.

"Let's just put them out of their misery," said Mako.

Gale shook her head. "We gain nothing by killing these two. If they give us no trouble, we'll spare them."

Mako crossed his arms and slunk away, sulking.

"I suppose you're not going to let us keep any of the good stuff we find, either?" Jetsam asked as he crouched over the body of a dead cat-man who had a beautifully crafted rapier in his now limp grasp.

"A Wanderer must never kill in order to enrich himself," said Gale. "But we did initially attempt to avoid this fight. They brought this battle upon themselves. We may claim the spoils of a justly fought war."

She made a hand gesture toward Sage, still back in the crows nest of the *Circus*. The girl pressed her eye to her spyglass. Sorrow guessed she was searching the ship for any lurking dangers.

"Will we take possession of the *Seahorse*?" asked Rigger.

"I don't see the wisdom of laying claim to the only ship on the ocean more hunted than the *Freewind* was," said Gale.

"W-will you g-give us s-safe passage?" asked Hopper.

"No," said Gale.

"But the two of us aren't enough to sail this ship," said the turtle man.

"You couldn't steer if we'd left all the crew alive, what with your rudder torn to splinters," said Gale. "You're at the mercy of Abyss now. Perhaps his currents will guide you to land before you run out of food and water."

Before the half-men could beg for a different fate, Sage shouted, "You won't believe what I just found!"

"I'm almost certain I will," said Rigger, leaning against the foremast. "I've lost all capacity for surprise."

"Is it treasure?" Jetsam called out. "The proverbial pirate chest of gold?"

"It's a painting," said Sage.

Rigger furrowed his brow. "I retract my statement. I can't believe you're excited about finding a painting."

Jetsam scratched his head. "Is it... you know... a naked lady?"

Gale smacked the back of his head.

"I really think you should take a look at it," said Sage. "It's in Captain Stallion's cabin."

Sorrow was nearest to the door. She grasped the tarnished brass handle and turned it. The room stank worse than a horse stall. She covered her mouth to cut the stench, and still couldn't quite bring herself to slither into the filthy chamber. In the dim light, she could see a painting bolted to the wall. It was a large canvas in a gilded frame. The painting was difficult to make out; the varnish had darkened, leaving only shadowy figures. Yet there was something about the colors and the poses that reminded her of paintings that had adorned the wall of her father's mansion. If this was the work of an old master, it could be a far more valuable prize than any gold or jewelry.

"It doesn't look like much," Mako grumbled as he pushed past Sorrow. If the stench of the room bothered him he gave no indication. He tore the frame off the wall, more roughly than Sorrow thought necessary. If it was valuable, why damage it?

Mako carried the painting into sunlight. Now the colors were brighter, the shapes clearer, though it was also more apparent that much of the painting had been splattered with various forms of filth over the years, obscuring the images. Sorrow recoiled as she understood the subject matter.

Jetsam, now well out of Gale's reach, said, "I was right! A naked lady!"

Indeed, one of the foreground figures was an unclothed female. But the painting didn't portray her as a figure of beauty set against some pastoral landscape. Instead, the woman was bound with her wrists stretched overhead, fastened to a hook on a wooden pole. Kindling was stacked around her legs to the midpoint of her thighs. The woman's face was a mask of terror. Her head was shaved and bleeding from numerous holes in her scalp.

This was a painting of a witch being put to death.

Judging from the apparent age, the canvas could possibly have been painted during the war against the witches those long centuries ago. A trio of men stood near the woman. A truthspeaker was present, reading from a scroll. Beside him was a large man in ebony armor, carrying a sword that was painted charcoal black. He was pointing toward the woman's feet, seemingly issuing a command to the third man, a ghostly white pygmy who stood by the piled kindling with a torch in his hand.

"Isn't it amazing?" Sage asked.

Sorrow jumped. At some point, Sage had left the *Circus* and was now standing right beside her.

"I'm not amazed," said Sorrow. "My father had an extensive collection of similar art. I heard him say that one painting he most wanted for his collection had been stolen from its last known owner. The painting was called *The Witchbreaker*."

"The guy with the sword that could send you straight to hell?" said Jetsam.

"If the sword did have such power, then death by flames was an act of mercy," said Slate.

Sorrow frowned at him.

"If you were to be put to death by fire, you would have time to repent your sins while the flames were building," Slate explained.

"So you think the painting's worth something?" asked Jetsam.

The painting wasn't in the best of shape, given the way the varnish had colored and cracked. Nor had Captain Stallion taken care with it. What looked like mustard hid the face of the truthspeaker, and what was almost certainly manure was smeared across the face of Stark Tower, which gave Sorrow a certain grim satisfaction. But, despite the painting's poor condition, she knew it would easily find a buyer. "My father would no doubt pay to have this in his collection. The halls of our family home are adorned with similar atrocities. To keep it from his hands, I'll negotiate whatever price you consider fair. Then I shall destroy it."

"What?" Sage said. "You can't destroy this!"

"Why not?" asked Mako.

"You stumble onto a mystery like this and your first instinct is to destroy it?" asked Sage.

"What mystery?" asked Sorrow. "The Silver Isles are rife with such paintings. The Church of the Book is ever eager to celebrate the torturers of women. Entire cities are named for these ancient witch slayers."

"But—" Sage shook her head and chuckled softly. "Sorry. I'm an idiot. I sometimes forget that not everyone sees the things I see. Look." She licked her thumb and rubbed the grime obscuring the truthspeaker's features. Details of his face emerged. He was a dark-haired man with his hair pulled back into a severe ponytail. Oddly, a large red 'D' was painted on his forehead. "Don't you know who that is?"

"I can't say that I do," said Sorrow.

"That's Zetetic the Deceiver! He came to us a few years back seeking passage to the Sea of Wine."

"We didn't do business with him," Gale said. "He offered good money, but how can you enter a contract with someone who openly calls himself a deceiver?"

"It does kind of look like him," said Jetsam. "But it can't be. Zetetic is, what, maybe forty? This painting's got to be hundreds of years old."

"I'm positive it's him," said Sage.

"I admit there's a resemblance," said Gale. "But I'm sure it's just a coincidence."

"Maybe," said Sage. "But what do you make of this?" She pulled down the sleeve of her blouse and spat on it, then scrubbed away the filth that covered Stark Tower's face.

Gale's eyes widened. Jetsam let out a low whistle. Mako's monstrous jaws gaped. Sorrow's breath caught in her throat.

In unison, they all turned to stare at Slate.

Slate cocked his head as he realized he was the target of their combined gaze. "Does something trouble thee... I mean, you?"

"I think we have a clue as to why you talk like you've walked out of another century," said Jetsam.

CHAPTER TEN

SUCH A BAD THING

THE ROMERS WERE still sorting through the items found aboard the *Seahorse*. Sage could identify some of the rightful owners of the stolen objects, and there was a great deal of political goodwill they could purchase among their fellow Wanderers by reuniting them with property taken by Stallion.

Slate had grown quiet after discovering his resemblance to Lord Stark Tower. Sorrow had been speaking with Sage about the possible fate of Numinous when she'd noticed Slate discarding his armor and returning to the *Circus*. Her initial instinct had been to let him have time to think things over. Perhaps his memories would be jogged further. But she noticed that Poppy was also absent, and wondered if the girl might be trying to cheer him up. The girl's romantic notion of knights bore little resemblance to their real world cruelty, and she worried that Slate might receive false impressions from her.

Sorrow found Slate and Poppy in the galley.

"You should be excited," Poppy said to Slate as Sorrow slithered silently through the door. "Stark Tower is one of the best knights ever. He saved the whole world from evil witches!"

"Your book tells you this?" Sorrow asked.

Poppy turned her head swiftly, looking startled that Sorrow was right behind her. She swallowed, then said, "I know that not all witches are bad."

"Your book tells you that?"

Poppy shrugged. "The book really only has one kind of witch. But you're a nice witch. Aren't you?"

Sorrow frowned. It was a simple enough question. Why couldn't she bring herself to say, "Yes, I'm nice?" Instead, she said, "Can I speak to Slate in private?"

"I guess," said Poppy, who looked a little worried as she glanced at the big man. He was normally cheerful in her company, but now his expression was completely neutral.

"Leave us," he said.

Poppy left the table, leaving her book of knights resting where she'd been sitting.

The door closed behind her. Slate and Sorrow eyed each other without speaking. It had been a long day. The daylight was fading. Neither made a move to light the lantern.

"You knew who I was," he said.

"No," she said. "I didn't. And I don't. So what if you happen to look like him? I know nothing about who you really are, or who you were before we met."

"Tell me again how we met."

"You know. You were there. I was attacked by a dragon's skeleton and you jumped up to save me."

"Jumped up."

She pressed her lips tightly together.

"Tell me everything," he said.

She sighed. "This is everything. Brand and I found you buried in the Witches Graveyard. You were in a glass coffin. We thought you were dead, but you made a remarkable recovery after the bone-dragon smashed open your casket."

Slate placed his hands upon the table and stared at them. "My nails... my hair...."

"Were rather long, yes," she said. "You may have been underground for a while."

"Then... I am Tower? Returned from the grave? Due to your magic?"

"I can assure you that I don't have the power to raise the dead. If I did, I can also assure you that I wouldn't use that power on the Witchbreaker. He deserves to rot in whatever hell may hold him."

Slate pulled the book toward him. He ran his beefy thumb along the edge of the cover.

"According to this book, the man was a hero," said Slate. "He abandoned his comfort and fortune in the Silver Isles to lead the battle against the greatest threat ever faced by the Church of the Book. He literally traveled to hell and back to acquire the weapon that turned the tide of history."

"Don't believe everything you read," said Sorrow, crossing her arms. "You saw the damn painting. The witches didn't have a traditional army. They mostly lived in peace among all the different kingdoms of the time. Tower's war didn't involve him testing his might against hordes of armed warriors in battle. It mainly involved him kidnapping women from their homes and torturing them into confessions. That's not heroism."

"According to the book, Avaris commanded an army of devils and beasts that threatened all of mankind."

"History is written by the victors. I believe her crime was building a following of women and offering them an alternative to the oppression they faced elsewhere. If she threatened anything, it was to improve the lives of half of humanity."

"Why should I believe you? You hid the full truth of how you discovered me. I was a fool to trust you."

"You're right. I should have told you everything." She shook her head slowly. "In perfect honesty, I seldom feel I have people's trust. It leaves me a poor steward of the commodity when I do stumble upon it. Can you forgive me?"

"Let me turn the question upon you," he said. "If I am Stark Tower, would you forgive me? Or are we enemies by blood, forever? A witch and a witchbreaker?"

"Whoever you used to be, as far as I'm concerned you crawled out of that grave a new man. There's no need for us to be enemies."

"Even if I'm a champion of the Church of the Book?"

"But you're not!" She slammed her fist onto the table. "You barely remember anything about the church. Your mind's a damned blank slate! How can you want to be a champion of something you know nothing about?"

Slate grinned slightly, looking bemused.

"Did I say something funny?"

"I fear I'm a slow learner. Until just now, I didn't comprehend why you decided to call me Slate. What is it that you wish to write upon me, Sorrow?"

"What do I wish to write?" she said. "Only the truth."

"Indeed? And you hoped to bring me to the truth by lying about my origins? By stringing me along by your claim to be a damsel in distress?"

"I didn't want to confuse you. I was going to tell you more when the time was right."

"I'm ready to hear what you wish to tell me."

She sighed. "Fine. All cards on the table. Maybe I have been stringing you along. I've even been trying to manipulate you. I don't have a lot of friends, Slate. I've been fighting most of my battles alone for a long time. I thought... it would me nice to have an ally."

"An ally against what?"

She took a long, slow breath. "Against the Church of the Book. My life's goal is to destroy it."

His eyebrow's raised.

"Forget what Poppy's fairy tales have told you. You may not have any memories, but I have a lifetime of moments I can never forget. My father was a judge. I watched him hang his own mother after she was accused of being a witch."

"Was she?" asked Slate.

"How can that possibly matter?" Sorrow asked. "He. Hung. His. Mother. He killed her because he loved his church more than he loved his own flesh and blood. I was ten years old when I witnessed this. I learned the truth of the world that day. My father wasn't wicked; he was the product of an entire society of wickedness. The supposed laws of a supposed god had been warped and twisted to make evil seem like good and good seem like evil."

Slate looked thoughtful. He said, "But if she was a witch?"

"If she was a witch, she was like the vast majority of those who practice weaving, and used her powers in secret for the good of those around her. Weavers don't seek glory or fortune. We seek knowledge and use it to help our friends and neighbors. Weavers are sought out by mothers for potions to cure sick infants. They're consulted by farmers who wish to learn the best nights to plant. Unlike the church, which tells men that they'll have a better life in some distant, spiritual kingdom, we teach men to make the most of their time in the material world. We make life better here and now. How can anyone be put to death for such a thing?"

Slate didn't answer.

"Now you know my true intentions are good intentions. I want to change the world. I want to rescue it from the cruel ideology that has corrupted it. Will you join me?"

He shook his head. "A knight shall be brave, courteous, and kind, obedient to his king, a defender of his faith, and a champion to all men of virtue." He sighed. "If I were to go against this code, I doubt I could look Poppy in the eyes."

"You can't make the sole guide for your life the opinions of a ten-year-old girl."

His head tilted slightly to the side. He studied her a moment before he asked, "Haven't you?"

FOR THE REMAINDER of their journey to the Silver City, Slate barely spoke to Sorrow. Nor could she think of a good way to once more initiate conversation. It wasn't that the air between them was hostile. Instead, Slate's formerly jaunty nature had been replaced by a haunted sullenness. Sorrow had no idea what to say that might console him.

She chose to stay below deck as they sailed into Salvation Bay. From her porthole, she could see the vast walls that lined the bay. The Silver City was a fortress encompassing several square miles with walls taller than the trees on the Isle of Fire and towers that vanished into the clouds. The whole of the city sparkled in the morning sun. She felt a curious swell of sentimentality as she returned to her childhood home. But the warmth quickly faded as she glimpsed the mirrored spires of the Cathedral of the Book looming above the massive walls.

Brand, Bigsby, and Slate were on deck directly above her cabin. If she focused, she could just make out their conversation.

"Cheer up, gentlemen," Brand said. "You seem so glum when you're about to start new lives in the most wonderful city ever built."

"If it's so wonderful," Bigsby grumbled, "why do so many of its inhabitants come to Commonground looking for happiness?"

"I would argue they come to Commonground looking for booze and loose women," said Brand. "Which, admittedly, are in short supply here. But there are parks and theatres and opera halls and museums. Something wonderful to see every day, if you're high-minded."

Bigsby replied, "High-minded? I'm a fishmonger whose sole pleasure in life is wearing women's clothing."

"You were almost killed by Greatshadow. People do crazy things after that much stress."

Bigsby sighed. "I can't blame the dragon for my insanity. I started stealing women's underwear from clotheslines when I was still in the circus. I'm wearing Sorrow's pantaloons right now."

Sorrow started to say something, but held her tongue.

"When on earth did you get your hands on those?"

"I rummaged through her bags before we left camp," said Bigsby. "As luck would have it, she's not had a reason to spot their absence."

Sorrow had to admit she hadn't even noticed that portions of her wardrobe had vanished.

Brand said, in a voice barely audible, "When you meet father, don't break the ice with this topic."

"Why not?" Bigsby asked. "Will it embarrass him? Will it make him disown me? He's ignored my existence for thirty years. Why should I care what he thinks of me?"

"You've every right to feel aggrieved," said Brand. "But take a look at those docks. Do you see the ships being loaded with cargo?"

Bigsby's weight shifted on the planks above. "So?"

"What's that cargo packed in?"

Bigsby sounded puzzled. "Crates? Barrels?"

"Precisely. And our father has a near monopoly on their manufacture. He's a very wealthy man. You, dear Bigsby, are his eldest son, and rightful heir. I'm throwing away a grand inheritance by bringing you here. Is it too much to ask that you at least pretend to be happy about this?"

"Why?"

"Because it's got to be better to be a wealthy dwarf in stolen underwear than a poor one?"

"I mean, why did you come and find me? Why throw away your inheritance?"

Brand didn't hesitate with his answer. "I've seen how father's silent guilt has hollowed him out over the years. If I'd gone on a false quest, and returned and reported you dead, I would have inherited only shame. It's in my own self-interest to do what is right, my brother. It lets me sleep soundly at night."

Bigsby said, "I can live with that."

"Nice speech, Brand." It was Gale's voice, at some distance. "If I didn't know better, I'd say you said it just loud enough that you'd be sure I overheard and thought better of you."

"Did it work?"

Gale laughed. Sorrow thought the laugh sounded derisive, but perhaps it was flirty. She was a poor judge of such things.

"We approach a city of marvels," Brand said, sounding as if he was once more speaking to Bigsby. "Anything can happen."

There was a pause and Brand asked, "Has it changed much since you were last here?"

Sorrow thought this was an odd question to ask of Bigsby, who'd only been in the city as an infant.

It was Slate who answered. "I've no memory of this place."

"If you really are Stark Tower, you've arrived at an interesting time," said Brand. "The current Lord Tower got himself killed fighting Greatshadow. He has no heir, so the family fortune will be fought over by various cousins. If you can find a truthspeaker to verify your identity, you might have the best claim to the estate."

"I've no interest in wealth. What I crave more than anything is purpose. Having no past has robbed me of any future."

Sorrow bit her lip to keep from shouting out that she'd offered him a purpose.

"If you're the Witchbreaker, you might find things kind of boring. There aren't many witches left these days."

"If you were the Witchbreaker, would you kill Sorrow?" Bigsby asked.

The ship had turned so that Sorrow could see Slate's shadow on the water as he placed his hands on the rail. "I'm choosing not to dwell on the prospect."

"It would be a shame to rid the world of a pair of such beautiful eyes," said Bigsby.

"Aye," said Slate, sounding dreamy. "Like emeralds."

Sorrow's jaw went slack. She'd never before heard men describe even a portion of her appearance as attractive. It was unsettling.

"She's bald and covered with scales," Brand said. "You guys need better taste in women."

"Says the man who's moon-eyed over a woman old enough to be his mother," said Bigsby.

"As far as I'm concerned," Brand said loudly, "she's the only woman in the world."

"I'm not," Gale called out.

*   *   *

SORROW WATCHED THE bustle of the docks from the porthole in the master cabin. She found it distasteful to be hiding, but there were simpler ways to contact Equity Tremblepoint that didn't require her catching the attention of guards.

She'd had Jetsam hire a messenger to deliver a letter requesting that Tremblepoint come to the ship to verify the authenticity of an ancient manuscript. She'd thought of offering a fee for the service, but decided against it. A genuine scholar would be drawn by the sheer intellectual curiosity of reading a newly discovered manuscript.

Hours later, when the messenger reappeared at the gates and began to walk toward the docks alone, she wondered if she'd made a mistake. Where was Tremblepoint? Perhaps Jetsam had made a poor choice of a courier. Judging by his unruly hair and soiled clothing, the messenger was from a family of low character, if indeed he had a family at all.

Sorrow frowned as she felt the prejudices of her youth bubbling up inside her. Her father had been disdainful of the poor, viewing them as too slovenly and weak-minded to improve their lot. He'd believed a person's station in life was determined solely by talent and ambition. Strip a wealthy man's fortune away, and he would make another within the year. Perhaps there was a little truth in this, as she'd been without a coin to her name many times in her travels, but always seemed to have an easy enough time getting her hands on whatever funds she needed.

She held her breath as she listened to the conversation above deck.

"Why did you bring the letter back?" Jetsam asked.

"Sorry, sir," the courier answered. "But Equity Tremblepoint has left the city. Just last week, in fact."

"Where has he gone?"

"If you want to know, you have to pay me first."

"You don't get paid. You didn't deliver the letter!"

"I ran five miles across the city. I deserve remuneration."

"I bet you didn't even go, you liar."

Sorrow banged on the ceiling of the cabin. She shouted, "Just pay him so we can find out where Tremblepoint is now."

She listened, but Jetsam was now talking so quietly she couldn't make out what he was saying.

Five minutes later, there was a rap on the cabin door. She opened it and Jetsam handed her the letter.

"I was going to haggle to pay half to find out Tremblepoint's new address before you butted in."

"You were insulting him," said Sorrow. "He would have left."

"You don't know a thing about haggling," said Jetsam. "I'm a natural. I could have talked until he wound up paying me for the privilege of listening to the new address."

Sorrow rolled her eyes.

"Anyway," said Jetsam, "I'm told that Zetetic the Deceiver recently saved the world and has been rewarded with his own private island. He's paying scholars to come live there so he can have sparkling dinner conversations."

"Really?"

"The messenger told me Zetetic is bringing scholars to his island. I'm just guessing about the dinner part."

Sorrow brought her fingernails to her lips, but caught herself before she chewed them. She'd not given a great deal of thought to Zetetic's presence in the same painting as the Witchbreaker. Hearing he was involved with Tremblepoint, even tangentially, made her feel as if she was catching glimpses of larger forces at work. She was only looking for Tremblepoint because the Black Swan had told her she should. The Black Swan claimed to be a time traveler. Did she have something to do with the painting?

"I guess Zetetic has really earned the title of Deceiver," she said. "If he's claiming to have saved the world from

Greatshadow, I heard the real story from Stagger and Infidel, and it was mostly their doing."

Jetsam shook his head. "According to the kid, Zetetic put the sun back on course after it started slipping backward in the sky."

"No, he didn't!" said Sorrow. "That was me! And, you know, Infidel and Stagger."

"Maybe you can explain things to the king and wind up with your own island fortress."

Sorrow chuckled ruefully. "Did you learn where we can find Zetetic's island?"

"Sure thing. It's in the Spittles. That's a string of tiny islands halfway between here and the Isle of Storm."

"I know where they are." She reached for her purse. "I'm going to need you to hire another messenger. We need to get word to Brand to see if we can take the *Circus* to—"

She never completed her thought. Sage shouted above, "All hands on deck! Release the moorings! Hurry!"

Jetsam went to the hatch and called out, "What's the emergency?"

Gale looked into the hatch and said, "You weren't ordered to ask questions, you were ordered to report to the deck."

"Yes, ma," Jetsam said, heading up the steps.

"Captain," said Gale.

"Captain, Ma," mumbled Jetsam as he flew up the stairs.

Sorrow started to follow, but had to slip back into her cabin to avoid Poppy and Cinnamon running past to report for duty. Once they passed, she started out again, only to pull back as Mako jumped down the steps into the hall, charging toward a door near the end.

"Rigger!" he shouted as he banged on the door. "Wake up!"

"What's going on?" Sorrow asked.

"Don't know yet," said Mako. "But this port is the home base of Brightmoon's navy. We knew the second we sailed into this bay that we might have to leave in a hurry."

He pounded the door again, so hard that Sorrow wondered if it would come off its hinges.

A sleepy voice came from the other side. "Whassa...? Huh?"

"Get out of bed, you layabout!"

The door opened. Rigger was unclothed saved for a pair of briefs. Dark bags lined his eyes as he hoarsely protested, "It's still light. I'm not on watch until sunset."

"Get to the wheel," Mako said. "Sage says we need to get to open water."

Rigger sighed. "Let me get some clothes on."

"We may not have time," Mako said, grabbing his brother by the arm and yanking him bodily down the hall. Sorrow followed, blinking as she emerged into full sunlight. She left most of her serpentine form below deck to avoid drawing attention.

Her efforts at caution were perhaps unnecessary. Despite the activity aboard the *Circus*, it quickly became apparent that most people along the docks had their eyes turned toward a commotion at the main gate in the wall leading into the Silver City. Though the gate was at least a hundred yards away, the shouting could be heard from here.

Suddenly, three uniformed guards went flying from the gate. A second later, Slate leapt over their limp bodies with Bigsby slung over his shoulders. Brand followed close on his heels, running as if an army were chasing him.

And, indeed, an instant later a sizeable force of guards surged through the gate only a few yards behind the fleeing men. Slate and Brand had their eyes fixed upon the *Circus*, which already had sails rattling up the pulleys.

As they neared the ship, a score of archers appeared on the city walls. Sage cried, "Incoming!" as the volley of arrows rained down.

Fortunately, the three men avoided injury as strong winds suddenly whipped over their heads, deflecting the missiles. Brand outpaced Slate and leapt onto the ship. Slate threw

Bigsby onto the deck, then spun around, fists clenched, and growled at the onrushing squadron of guards.

Though he was unarmed and they were outfitted with mail and armed with spears, the guards slid to a halt. Sorrow noticed that Slate's knuckles and sleeves were spattered with blood.

A barrel shot past Slate and smashed into the legs of the closest guards, upending them. Slate spun and leapt for the *Circus* as Poppy readied another barrel.

"Stay alert!" Gale shouted as wind filled the sails with a thunderous *WHUMPH!* The ship lurched as arrows began to pepper the deck. "I can't deflect arrows while I'm pushing the ship."

Poppy launched another barrel, but missed the bravest of the guards who ran along the dock and leapt for the *Circus*. His heroic efforts came to naught as Mako leapt to the railing and caught the man square in the face with a punch, dropping him into the water. Mako leapt back as an arrow jutted from the wood where he'd just stood.

"We're sitting ducks," Mako grumbled.

"Only if you're idiot enough to be a target," Sage called down. "Take cover!"

Mako looked around to find that all of his family, as well as Brand and the others, were crouching behind cover. Only Sage was exposed, but she swayed her body back and forth, avoiding the barrage of arrows with ease. Mako jumped to Sorrow's side, pressing his back to the crate that sheltered her.

Bigsby made a dash from his hiding place, shouting, "Out of the way!" as he charged toward Sorrow, whose body was still stretched down the stairs into the hold.

Sorrow retreated below deck as Bigsby tumbled down the steps. Mako swiftly followed. The sound of arrows biting into wood, *thunk thunk thunk,* echoed in the confined hall.

"I didn't ask for this!" Bigsby screamed, rising to his feet with a clatter of metal on metal. It was only now that Sorrow noticed the dwarf's wrists were bound with manacles. "I was happy in my old life! Happy!"

"I take it things didn't go well with your father?" Sorrow asked, snipping the iron links with her fingers.

"He's dead!" Bigsby said. "And apparently our mom is a real bitch!"

Brand bounded down the steps. "She's not our mother. She's a step-mother, and not one I've met before."

"She's an evil witch!" growled Bigsby. He looked sheepish as he glanced toward Sorrow. "Metaphorically. No offense."

"None taken."

"I may have mentioned that my father had outlived several wives," said Brand, looking at Sorrow. "Apparently, before he died, he married wife number five. She's younger than me!"

"You disapprove of such age differences between couples?" Mako asked, sounding smug.

"I don't give a damn about the age difference," said Brand.

"Why bring it up?" asked Mako.

Brand shook his head, then said, "It's not important. What is important is that she accused me of being an imposter, and ordered the town guard to arrest us."

"But you're his true son," said Sorrow. "As much as I hate to say this, couldn't a truthspeaker vouch for your identity?"

"She had a truthspeaker present. But he never got around to testing me. He started off on Bigsby, accusing him of murdering the carnival ringleader who'd once employed him. And Bigsby confessed!"

"Once *owned* me, you mean," said Bigsby. "I was nothing but property to him! I'd stab the bastard again if I had the chance."

"But we were outnumbered ten to one. Why did you attack the guards?"

"They were shackling me!" Bigsby shouted, rattling the links still cuffed to his forearms. "I swore I'd die rather than wear chains again!"

"You almost got to do both," said Brand.

At this point, Slate walked down the stairs. He was covered

in an alarming amount of blood, but didn't seem to be in any pain. "Things may have gotten out of hand," he said.

"You tore that guard's head off," Brand said, sounding mournful as he ran his hands through his hair.

"In my defense, he had an unusually skinny neck," said Slate.

"You fought the city guard?" Sorrow asked. "Even though there was a truthspeaker present?"

"He bashed out the truthspeaker's teeth!" said Brand.

"I was put off by the way he was shrieking as I approached him," said Slate. He shook his head. "I'm sorry. I don't mean to be flippant. The situation quickly grew out of control. Bigsby's life was in danger. I grabbed him and ran, laying low anyone who stood in my way."

"Why?" asked Sorrow. "If he's a confessed criminal and you're a knight, shouldn't you have sided with the guards?"

Slate shrugged. "If I'd thought about it, perhaps. But for most of the life I remember, the people aboard this ship have been my companions. When Bigsby believed he was a princess, he was playmate of Cinnamon and Poppy. A knight is loyal. In my heart, this ship is the kingdom I serve."

The ship lurched hard to starboard. Sorrow glanced at Mako. "You seem calm."

"We've done this before. Things happened so fast they won't have time to blockade the harbor. We'll escape."

"Back to Commonground?" asked Bigsby.

"To the Spittles," said Sorrow.

"The what?" asked Bigsby.

"It's a chain of damp pebbles dead in the center of nowhere," said Brand. "Why there?"

"It's where Zetetic the Deceiver hangs his hat these days. He might be able to answer our questions about the painting."

Before Brand could ask any further questions, Cinnamon bounded down the steps and said, "You can come out now. We're out of arrow range and none of the navy has even hoisted sails yet."

Brand and Bigsby followed Mako back above deck. Sorrow

placed her hand on Slate's shoulder before he could leave. He turned to her with a quizzical look in his eyes.

"You're not going anywhere until I tend your wounds."

"I believe I'm uninjured," he said.

"You're covered in blood."

"I'm confident little of it is mine."

"Humor me. Let's at least get you washed up."

She led him back into the master cabin. A porcelain pitcher of fresh water sat next to a small white basin. She poured water into the basin, then grabbed a towel and moistened the tip of it.

"Wash your hands," she said.

Slate did so, and Sorrow pushed the door shut with her tail. She dabbed away the flecks of blood on his face. He certainly had no injuries there.

His hands were not as pristine. His knuckles were bleeding and bruised. She examined them closely, then said, "I don't think I'll need to stitch you up again. Take off your shirt."

She washed away the blood that had soaked through his sleeves. She inspected his old wounds, the ones he'd suffered from the dragon, and saw that they were still healing well.

She didn't look at his face as she said, softly, "I may know why you found it easy to attack a truthspeaker."

"I acted in the heat of the moment."

"Perhaps. But perhaps you acted as you were meant to act."

"What do you mean?"

She pressed her lips together, certain that what she was about to say was a mistake.

And then she told him everything. Told him about the mysterious man-weapon referenced in the letter. Told him about the pygmy ghost who'd left hell to witness the birth of the Destroyer. Finally, she revealed the information that she most wanted to hide from him.

"You have no aura," she said.

"What does that mean?"

"I don't know for certain. But I want to be honest with you.

It's possible that you aren't human. You might be some elaborate magical construction, created to defend witches, not kill them."

He shook his head. He held up his bruised fists. "I bruise. I bleed. I breathe. I laugh when I play with Poppy. I'm a living man. I've no doubt."

"I have to admit there are many holes in my theory," she said. "But I heard you on the deck. Talking about how you would like to have a purpose. It may be that you already have one. You've been created to make the world a better place by helping me fight the church."

Slate shook his head. "I refuse to believe that I've been created solely as a weapon. I must have a past. It's only my memory that's missing, not my humanity."

Sorrow nodded. "You don't have to be only a weapon. Try to think of your lack of yesterdays as a gift. You've no shackles chaining you to the way things are. You've the freedom to make the world anew. Not having a past gives you an open path to the future."

Slate stared at his bruised hands, lost in thought.

At last, he rose and walked for the door.

"Thank you for telling me this," he said.

As he was halfway out the door, she said, softly, "And thank you."

She was surprised when he turned back and asked, "For what?"

She blushed. But honesty had worked out pretty well over the last few moments. "I heard you compliment my eyes." She looked down at her serpentine body. "I wake up most mornings feeling inhuman. It was... welcome... to discover that someone could still see past this. It's not such a bad thing, to be human."

"Aye," said Slate.

CHAPTER ELEVEN

THE MUNDANE DESTRUCTION
OF ORDINARY LIFE

SORROW'S NOSE WRINKLED as she slithered from the rowboat onto a gray pebble beach filthy with bird droppings. Her body felt stiff as she slid along the cold earth. The Spittles were a decidedly bleak stretch of real estate, cloaked this morning with clouds. Her breath came out in a fog, amidst a drizzle that was half rain, half snow.

Sorrow pulled her cape more tightly about her. She'd left Commonground with little in the way of a wardrobe beyond her glass armor, and was grateful to have a cloak to protect her from the elements. Since regaining his sanity, Bigsby had avoided outright depression by keeping himself busy with constant sewing. Bolts of cloth had been among the booty of the *Seahorse*, and Bigsby had been somewhat obsessive in attacking the raw fabric with scissors, needle, and thread. Sorrow's cloak had been cut large enough that when standing still, it was just barely possible for her to coil her tail beneath her and have it completely hidden by the fabric. Of course, this left her much taller than an ordinary person, so it wasn't as if she was inconspicuous. Further drawing attention was the fact that Bigsby had crafted the hood in such a fashion that, in profile, her head now resembled that of a cobra. She was certain the dwarf had meant well.

She surveyed the cliff of jagged rock that ran the length of the beach. She saw no obvious way to climb it. She looked back to the boat. Slate was pulling the small vessel further up the stony strand, overturning it so it wouldn't fill with rain. Brand was struggling to find a convenient way of holding the canvas-wrapped painting he carried. Bigsby didn't offer to help, but instead stood with his hands in the pockets, looking sullen.

"This doesn't seem like the sort of place a king would build a palace," Bigsby said as he contemplated the inhospitable scenery.

"This isn't a palace," said Brand. "It's a fortress. For centuries the Silver Kingdom and the Isle of Storm fought wars over who would control these islands."

"What's so valuable about them?" Bigsby asked.

"Damn near nothing," said Brand. "After the last war firmly established the land as belonging to the Brightmoon family, there were a few feeble attempts to colonize the place, but the settlements kept dying off. Eventually, the Silver Kingdom abandoned the islands entirely. It was expected that the Isle of Storm would try to claim them, but, apparently, the only reason they ever wanted them was to keep the Brightmoons from having them. Now, all that's left is a few ghost towns and the graveyards of all the soldiers who died trying to hold on to the place."

Sorrow rose up on her tail as high as she could and strained to see over the cliff tops. "Are we certain this is the right island?"

"Sage assures me there's a fortress up there," said Brand. "We couldn't see it from the ship because of the mist, but I've learned to trust what she tells me."

Sorrow looked at Slate and said, "Toss me the rope. My snake half can climb almost anything. I'll go up and throw you a line down."

"That won't be necessary," said a voice from above. If Sorrow had been forced to guess, she would have said the voice belonged to an old man. "If you journey a quarter mile to the west, there are steps carved into the rock. They lead to one of the entrances of our modest little shelter."

"Who are you?" Slate shouted.

"An excellent question," the unseen voice answered. "It's perhaps the sole topic I find of interest these days. But we need not stand in the rain and debate my identity. I'm certain it will be a topic of conversation at dinner. It usually is."

"You're inviting us to dinner?" Brand asked.

"Everyone on this island is invited to dinner," said the voice. "Whether they wish to be or not."

Bigsby shook his head. "I should have stayed on the ship."

"Excuse me," Sorrow called out. "But we've come looking for Equity Tremblepoint. Do you –"

"Equity will join us at dinner," said the voice.

"How about Zetetic?" Brand called up. "Will he be there? There's a painting we're wanting him to look at."

The voice didn't answer.

"Hello?" Brand asked.

"Let's go find the stairs," said Sorrow.

They did so, though the steps didn't lead to the top of the cliff. Instead, they led to the mid-point of the rock face, where they opened into a tunnel. Large oak doors stood ajar, their iron hinges locked with rust. Slate took the lead, advancing a few yards into the opening before turning quickly. He leapt back out into the drizzle, coughing violently.

"Sorry," he gasped. "I wasn't prepared for the smell."

Now that he'd stirred the dank air of the guano filled tunnel, ammonia-laden fumes rolled out in eye-stinging waves.

They fashioned makeshift masks from the silk handkerchiefs Brand and Bigsby had in their pockets and pressed ahead in silence. No one dared breathe deeply enough to initiate conversation. A few yards beyond the door, the tunnel became too dark for Sorrow to see her hand before her face. There was a soft *click* at her back and shadows were cast as Brand opened his glorystone locket. As Sorrow slithered forward, she found she would have preferred the tunnel to remain dark. The roof was black with sleeping bats. The floor was covered with a carpet of thick white filth, fuzzy with mold. Sorrow wouldn't have wanted to walk through this with boots on, let alone crawl across it on her belly. Footprints in the muck showed that they weren't the only ones to pass this way in recent days, though it didn't seem that Zetetic had very many guests. Breathing as shallowly as possible, she followed Slate.

At the end of the tunnel they found another oak door. Tacked to it was a hand-painted wooden sign that read, 'Welcome to the Inquisition.'

"It's not too late to turn back," Bigsby whispered.

"I believe it is," Slate said, pressing his shoulder against the heavy door, his feet slipping in the mire.

The door opened into a vast room filled with casks and crates. Brand's light did little to illuminate the outlines of the space, save for rows of stone columns rising to a vaulted ceiling twenty feet above. The play of light and dark created by the glorystone left Sorrow imagining she was seeing movements in every shadow.

Slate closed the door behind them.

Bigsby lowered his handkerchief. After a few breaths, he said, "It's just as bad in here."

"We've got gunk all over our boots," said Brand. "You'd think they'd at least have a door mat."

"Feel free to wash your feet with the contents of the casks," said the same unseen voice who'd greeted them from the cliffs. "The wine's long since turned to vinegar, but it does rather cut through the smell."

Sorrow's ears pin-pointed the patch of darkness where the voice originated. Whoever the speaker was, he seemed to be clinging to the ceiling.

"Come into the light," Sorrow said.

"It's best that I don't," came the answer. "My appearance can be somewhat alarming."

Sorrow pulled back her cloak, revealing her nail-studded scalp. She coiled up on her tail and said, "We may be more open-minded than you give us credit for."

"Some of you are indeed open-minded." Sorrow heard a faint rustling as the voice spoke. The speaker seemed to be moving. "Once, all minds were open to me. It was as if I was surrounded by men shouting their most sacred secrets. Now I hear barely intelligible murmurs, save for the dwarf. His mind sounds like an old, familiar song."

"I've had my fill of mind-readers!" Bigsby said, shaking his fist. "Get out of my head!"

"Perhaps you should learn to keep your thoughts inside you." There was a further rustling in the shadows. "Your fear amplifies your inner voice into a scream."

"I-I'm not the one afraid," said Bigsby. "You're the one hiding in shadows."

"Ah, but you are afraid. You felt a swell of panic when you saw that our host has labeled this fortress the Inquisition."

"It's an unpleasant name," said Bigsby. "The only time I ever hear the word is when the church is seeking to root out heretics."

"We're all heretics here," the voice answered with a chuckle. "That doesn't mean we welcome fugitives."

"Why would you think we're fugitives?" Bigsby asked.

"You fled the Silver City as wanted men, did you not? Bigsby, you stand accused of murder. The man with no memories killed at least three of the city guard, and maimed uncounted others. Brand is accused of fraud. I see he's innocent, but that will matter little as long as juries can be swayed with bribes and his stepmother controls his family fortune. And Sorrow... I don't care to spend the time it would take to catalogue her crimes."

"If you know our names, tell us yours," said Sorrow.

"Ah. This is an easier question to answer than your original query. If I know nothing else of myself, I at least know what my father called me. My name is Brokenwing."

"That's an odd name," said Bigsby.

"Perhaps. But it is my one precious possession."

Bigsby crossed his arms. "I hardly see how a name can be precious."

"There's one among you who does not know the name given to him by his father," said Brokenwing. "Or, indeed, if he even had a father. Ask him how precious he would consider a name."

Everyone looked toward Slate. Slate shrugged.

"I fear that the hours grow short," said Brokenwing. "Our host is rather insistent that everyone arrive for dinner promptly and in appropriate attire. It will take some time to make yourselves presentable. You look like vagabonds from the sea, and smell even worse."

"If we offend your nose, might I suggest you find a shovel and muck out the path to your front door?" said Brand.

"This is a back door," said Brokenwing. "The other side of the island has a more pleasant approach. For now, if you continue moving forward, you'll find the exit to the cellar. Turn right in the hall and follow it to the third staircase on the left. This will lead you to our guest quarters. By now the servants should have your rooms prepared. Hot baths are being drawn. Dinner is served at sunset. I'll see you there."

"But will we see you?" asked Bigsby.

Brand said, "We really don't want to be rude, but we came here seeking answers, not dinner. Is there no chance we can see Zetetic now?"

There was no answer.

"Nothing is stopping us from going back to the ship," said Bigsby.

"We're staying," said Sorrow. "There's something here that I want more than anything else in the world right now."

"Aye," said Slate. "Answers."

"Those too," said Sorrow. "But I was talking about the hot bath."

THE DINING HALL was lined with fireplaces large enough for a grown man to stand in. Firewood being in short supply in the Spittles, the flames were fueled by small mountains of coal. The fires did an admirable job of chasing away the chill, but the coal gave the room a rotten egg miasma.

While the hall was large enough to seat hundreds, the handful of current guests were seated at three long wooden tables arranged in a triangle so that everyone could easily see each other. Servants led Bigsby, Brand, Slate and Sorrow to seats along one side of the triangle. At the next table sat a liver-spotted old man, two empty chairs, and a person Sorrow suspected was a woman, given the shape of her face and the slenderness of her build. But she was wearing a man's suit and had a mustache, which confused the matter somewhat.

"I don't suppose you're Brokenwing," Brand asked as he eyed the old man.

The old man grinned as he scratched his bald head. "I knew my skin was getting a bit scaly in my later years, but certainly I've not gone that far."

The person at the end of the table said, "I've told you, Vigor, there's something reptilian about your mannerisms."

The old man nodded. "I've spent seventy years studying the beasts, Equity. It's only natural I've picked up a few of their traits."

"Equity?" Sorrow asked. "You're Equity Tremblepoint?"

"Indeed," said the androgynous figure. "And the old reptile is Vigor. I'm glad to see that Zetetic has finally arranged for other scholars to join our little party. Though, I fear, I don't recognize any of you from my normal circles."

"We aren't scholars," said Brand. "I'm Brand Cooper. This is my brother, Bigsby, and my friends Sorrow and Slate."

"If you aren't scholars, what are you?" asked Vigor.

"A weaver, a warrior, a fish baron and a retired circus performer," said Brand.

"Indeed," said Equity, with thinly-veiled disappointment.

There was a moment of awkward silence until Vigor cleared his throat. "I can't help but notice, my dear Sorrow, that you're a rather impressive blend of serpent and human. I'm the word's foremost authority on reptiles, from the common skink to the mightiest dragon. Perhaps later we can meet in private? I would find it most interesting to examine you unclothed."

"I think not," she said.

"She's on to you," said Equity.

Vigor's wrinkled cheeks flushed red. "My dear, my curiosity is entirely scholarly."

"He's nothing but an old letch," said Equity. "He propositions me five times a day."

"I most certainly do not," Vigor grumbled. "I wouldn't risk you saying yes. I've been in your company for over a week and still haven't decided if you're a man or a woman."

Sorrow had been wondering about that as well. Equity was tall for a woman, a little short for a man, and thin for either sex. Equity's hair was cropped in a severe, mannish cut, but her or his face was feminine, with blue-green eye-shadow and lips painted crimson. Above these lips sat a thin, curly mustache that may or may not have been woven from horsehair. Equity's throat, which might have solved the mystery with the presence of an Adam's apple, was hidden by a high collar. The rest of Equity's wardrobe was equally confounding, consisting of pants and a jacket of a masculine styling, but trimmed with frills of crimson lace.

"Actually," Bigsby said, looking at Equity. "I'm a little confused myself."

"You shall remain confused," said Equity. "I'm all sexes, and none. My only gender is thespian. If the world knew the configuration of my genitalia, they would have prejudice in regards to the roles I play on stage. I will not allow my biology to shackle me."

"I'm surprised you haven't been thrown in shackles, period," said Vigor. "I've never been to the Silver City, but from what I know of it, the people there don't think kindly of deviants."

"Then it's wise you've avoided the place," said Equity. "As for my survival in such a conservative enclave, my talent in the theatre places me beyond reproach. I'm honest enough to admit that my family fortune may also play some small role in my relative freedom. When the poor make people uncomfortable by refusing to comply with the prevailing morality, they're imprisoned. Similar transgressive behavior among the wealthy is tolerated as mere eccentricity."

"It must be nice to dress however you want and not worry about it," Bigsby said.

"I wouldn't know," said Equity. "I worry over the finest details of my appearance with what must surely be an unhealthy obsession. Today, I changed my undergarments nine times before settling on the correct pair, despite my certainty that no one but myself will ever see them."

"I just meant it would be nice to have the freedom to look however you want in public," said Bigsby.

"We're all born with such freedom," said Equity. "If you lack the inspiration and audacity to live as you wish, you've no one to blame but yourself."

Sorrow left her spot at the table, gliding toward Equity with her undulating motion as she retrieved from her pocket the scroll that had launched her on this journey. "I haven't come to discuss clothing. I'm informed you're the world's foremost authority on dead languages."

"I dabble," said Equity. "My ancestors bequeathed me a voluminous collection of ancient plays. It would have been wasteful not to read them."

Sorrow unrolled the scroll. "I found this on the Isle of Fire. I believe it may have been written by Avaris, Queen of the Weavers."

Equity picked up the aged parchment. "Hmm. This is the old weaver's script. I'm a bit rusty. There are no plays written by witches, I fear."

"So you can't read it?"

"I didn't say that. I'll need to investigate a few of the words, but the gist of the manuscript is obvious. 'Dear Sisters, our struggle has been a long and difficult one, etcetera, etcetera.'"

"It's the *etcetera* part I'm interested in," said Sorrow.

Equity nodded. "Very well. It goes on to say that the great persecutor is in our possession. There's something about the man-weapon having been hollowed and needing to be refilled. These lines here explain the wisdom of retreat. The author says she will travel to the eastern isle to regain her strength, and encourages her sisters to go into hiding."

"Does it say which eastern isle?"

"If it did, I would have told you."

"Does it say who or what the man-weapon is?" asked Slate.

"No, but—"

At this moment everyone grew silent, as a dragon the size of a small pony limped into the room on misshapen, bandaged limbs. Slate leapt up, sending his chair skittering across the floor. They'd come to dinner unarmed, but Slate wasted little time in changing that situation, bounding to the nearest fireplace and grabbing a heavy poker.

He spun to face the dragon, brandishing the makeshift weapon.

"I told you my appearance was alarming," said the dragon. "Please put that down, sir, before I'm forced to defend myself."

"Brokenwing?" Sorrow asked.

"An appropriate appellation, no?" the dragon asked, glancing toward his back where his wings were braced with wooden splints. "Vigor is doing what he can to restore my limbs."

"We were talking to a dragon?" Bigsby said, his eyes nearly popping from his skull.

"This isn't the first time we've spoken, Bigsby," Brokenwing said. "I paid you a visit in Commonground. You knew me then as Relic."

"You're the guy who wanted to kill Greatshadow!" Bigsby's brow furrowed. "But if you're a dragon, why did you want to kill another dragon?"

"Do men not kill men?" asked Brokenwing. He kept his gaze on Slate, who still brandished the poker. "I'll ask you again, sir, to assume a less threatening pose. Not to mention it's unwise of you to linger so close to the flames. It unsafe to stand between me and my father."

"Your father's Greatshadow?" asked Sorrow.

"And you want to kill him?" Bigsby said.

"Our relationship is complicated," said Brokenwing.

"Stand down, Slate," said Sorrow.

"But... but... dragon," said Slate.

"How eloquent," said Equity.

Slate placed the poker back on its stand. "I suppose I've no cause to hate thee. I mean, you."

Brokenwing removed the chair beside Vigor and drew up to the table. "After I informed our guests of the importance of promptness, I see that Walker and our host have failed to show up."

"Perhaps I've been here all along." All eyes turned to an albino face that rose above the edge of the table next to Brokenwing. It was a pygmy, who climbed up in his chair and walked across the table. He hopped to the main table, and walked to the throne that sat behind the table. "As for Zetetic, it's possible he's too small to be seen. I led him to the mathematical realms earlier. He insisted on pressing on alone to explore past the zero, though I warned him he might return as only a fraction of himself."

He knelt for a closer look and shook his head. "I sense no trace of him."

Sorrow could hold her tongue no longer. "It's you! You're the pygmy who came to my tent!"

Walker nodded. "Indeed. I thought I recognized you. You've engaged in some interesting addition and subtraction of your own."

"You're the one who was looking for the Destroyer?" asked Slate.

"Yes. And you're wondering if you're him."

"Am I?"

Walker shrugged. "It's been, what, seventeen years since I gave the matter any thought."

"It's not even a month since I met you," said Sorrow.

Walker chuckled and shook his head. "No, my poor witch. Eternities have passed. Admittedly, not locally. But I'm seldom in one place for long. I never visit hell without losing track of years."

"Let's get back to the Destroyer," said Slate. "Who was he? What was he?"

Walker shrugged. "In the grand design, we're all destroyers. We trample unseen kingdoms of insects beneath our heels, oblivious to their hopes and dreams, their wars and gods. We destroy nature, enslaving fields to do our bidding, robbing the ocean to steal food from the mouths of sharks. Even seated alone in a room, holding our breath, we grind the past to dust by perceiving the present. Destruction is a synonym for life."

"I suppose that's true, but the mundane destruction of ordinary life hardly seems like the type of destruction discussed in hell," said Sorrow.

"I assure you that ordinary life is the most popular topic of conversation there."

"I mean, demons would probably focus more on a Destroyer that burns cities and topples empires."

"Or one who erects cities and builds empires," the pygmy said.

"You're not really answering our questions," Sorrow grumbled.

"Perhaps you're not really asking them," said Walker, with a broad smile.

"Pay no mind to our pale associate," said Vigor. "He's completely in... sane..."

Vigor's voice trailed off as he stared at the door. A tall man with a black ponytail had just walked backward into the room, completely naked, drenched in sweat and bleeding from a thousand small scratches. The blood was smeared into patterns of lines and squiggles. Sorrow squinted. Were they all numbers?

The man walked backward to his throne and sat, turning his face toward his guests. The large red 'D' tattooed in the middle of his forehead burned with a faint, pulsing glow. His mouth opened. ".reverof no tnew tsuj taht rebmun lanoitarri na htiw tnemugra na otni tog I .gnitiaw uoy peek ot yrroS"

Walker laughed so hard he fell off the table.

"?ynnuf os s'tahW" asked Zetetic.

Walker wiped tears from his eyes, unable to breathe.

"?ereh klat elpoep od noitcerid hcihW .etunim a tiaW" He stood up and walked around his throne backwards. When he said down he said, "Is this better? Do you understand me now?"

"I don't think I've understood anything since I got off the damned boat," said Bigsby.

"You're Zetetic?" asked Brand.

"I certainly hope so," the man answered. "I'm sorry if I've kept you waiting. I'm sure you all must be hungry. Fortunately, I have the power to summon a feast from thin air merely by scratching my nose."

He did so. Nothing happened. Sorrow blinked and suddenly all the tables were heaped with large platters of roasted birds, steaming cauldrons of soup, and bowls stacked high with fruit representing every color of the rainbow.

Bigsby stared at the platter of flaky white cod stacked before him. "I'm glad you didn't live in Commonground," he said. "It's tough enough making a living selling fish."

Zetetic waved his hand dismissively. "Your industry is safe. I never, never repeat myself." He grabbed a quail and tore it in two, shoving the breast into his mouth. With his mouth full, he said, "Forgive me. I'm famished." He glanced at Walker. "Next time, we should pack a lunch. I haven't eaten in three days."

"We just had dinner last night," said Vigor.

"Time moves at different rates in some realms. It can get confusing. When Walker led me through the abode of dreams undreamt, we returned nineteen minutes before departing. I met myself as I was preparing to leave. Those nineteen minutes alone with myself were very educational." He shook his head as a wistful smile settled upon his lips. "Very educational indeed."

"Speaking of things that are confusing," said Brand, "there's a painting in my room I'd like you to look at."

"The one with me, Walker, and the Witchbreaker?"

"You've seen it?"

"It was in my possession for a while. It used to hang in the Monastery of the Book until I stole it. When the church caught me and killed me for a little while last year, I lost track of it."

"Do you know why you and I appear in the painting?" Slate asked.

"I have two theories," said Zetetic. "The first is that, at some point in the future, I'll travel into the past. Walker's in the painting, so I assume he comes along."

"I'm not in the painting," said Walker.

"It certainly looks like—"

"I assure you, I'm not in the painting. Neither are you."

"Are you arguing for the sake of argument here?" Zetetic asked. "Because I know what I've seen with my own eyes."

"Do you?" asked Walker. "Or have your eyes been deceived by a falsehood? The representation of a thing is not the thing."

Zetetic sighed and poured himself a glass of wine. "Some other time I'll puzzle out what the hell it is you're trying to say to me. Right now, I've got too much of a headache to focus on your riddles." He took a long drink, emptying his glass, then poured himself another.

"What's your second theory?" asked Sorrow.

"About what?"

"The painting. How you got into it."

"Oh. Right. My second guess is that I'm a lunatic." He downed the second glass of wine. "Do you know that a few weeks ago I walked into the interior of the sun and talked to the ghost who lives inside?" He ran his finger along the rim of the now-empty glass. "I've a dragon for a houseguest. I've danced across stone stripped of all truths to stare into the eyes of dead gods and witness the end of the world." He let out a long sigh. "Now I'm drinking wine that I've lied into existence. Does any of this sound sensible?"

"I can think of few situations where drinking wine isn't exquisitely sensible," said Equity, raising a glass.

"True. But what if my sanity is so far gone that everything and everyone I experience are merely figments of my imagination? I can't devise any possible test that could determine what's real and what isn't." He threw his glass against the wall, where it shattered into shards. "Did that just break? Did I dream it broke? Was there a glass at all? Perhaps if I clapped my hands forcefully enough, I'd wake myself. Everyone here would vanish, fading as my true life returned."

Sorrow inhaled sharply as Zetetic swung his hands toward one another. With his palms an inch apart, he snapped to a halt. He sat for several seconds, staring at his barely separated fingers. At last, he lowered his arms, and everyone let out their breath.

He grabbed an apple from a nearby bowl. "Now would be a poor time to test my theory. I detest dining alone."

"If you're done scaring us," said Bigsby, "what about Slate?"

"What about him?"

"You said you thought you might go back in time to wind up in the painting. Why's Slate in it?"

"Oh." Zetetic chewed his apple thoughtfully. "I suppose he could also travel through time with me, and become Lord Stark Tower. Or perhaps he's the original Tower, and has somehow managed to sleep all the way into our time."

"Why don't I have any of Tower's memories?" asked Slate.

Zetetic shrugged. "Perhaps you aren't him after all. Avaris was a master bone-weaver. If she ever got so much as a hair from the true Tower, she could have grown an exact duplicate."

"How can I discover the truth?" Slate asked.

Zetetic shrugged. "Today I carved equations into my bare flesh with the thorn of a screaming cactus while sipping wormwood steeped in dragon's urine. It tasted like doubt and despair, but I swallowed every drop so that I might glimpse one hair-thin aspect of truth."

Brokenwing narrowed his eyes. "You've been collecting the contents of my chamber pot?"

Zetetic waved away his query. "Anyway, Slate, I'm sure Walker would be happy to ply you with various pharmaceuticals that would lift you above the confines of ordinary life in order to look down and see the larger patterns. Or if you want to know what Avaris has done, you could stop bothering me and just go ask her."

"That's easier said than done," said Sorrow. "I've been searching for her for years. The letter that brought me here says she retreated to an eastern island, but beyond this I know nothing of where she might be, or if she's even alive."

"Of course she's still alive," said Zetetic. "At least, she was alive three years ago. I studied a full month in her walking castle."

"You know her?" Sorrow asked.

"In every sense of the word," said Zetetic. "She required I make love to her three times every night between the span of two full moons." He eyed Slate. "I recommend a diet high in protein before you seek her out. You look like just her type."

Sorrow slowly lowered her fork to her plate.

Equity studied her face and said, "You look absolutely mortified."

"Avaris was a great champion of women. I can't believe she'd trade knowledge for sex."

"Sexual energy is a vital component of bone-weaving," said Zetetic. "Without capturing procreative energies to animate her creations, Avaris would just be sewing meat together."

Sorrow felt the blood drain from her face. "I suppose I won't be learning bone-weaving."

"Why not, dear?" asked Vigor.

"I learned the truth of what lies in the hearts of men when I watched my father hang my grandmother. I've never felt the slightest inkling of physical desire for a man."

Equity nodded. "I have my own father-issues. But you needn't turn to men for sexual energy. You have other options."

Sorrow crossed her arms. "This discussion is pointless. At the moment, I don't even have genitals."

"Not human genitals," said Vigor. "But reptiles aren't lacking in reproductive organs. I can train you on their function."

Sorrow grimaced, feeling an urgent need to change the subject.

"How would we find this walking castle?"

"It's on Podredumbre, but you can't find it," said Zetetic. "It finds you. Luckily, once you know that the castle feeds on souls, it's not difficult to trick it into appearing. I murdered an old woman from a village on the edge of the swamp to summon it."

"That's reprehensible!" said Sorrow.

"She wasn't long for this world," Zetetic said. "She was too weak even to scream when I stole her from her bed."

Sorrow stared at him, her jaw slack.

"Human sacrifice seems a bit extreme," said Brand. "Is there no other way?"

"There is a way that doesn't require you to harm another," said Walker. "If you're bold enough to risk it."

"I've my failings, but a lack of boldness isn't among them," said Brand.

Bigsby looked puzzled. "Why do you care if Sorrow finds Avaris? Shouldn't we be more focused on clearing our names?"

Brand shrugged. "When we sailed into the Silver City, I thought I was about to be trapped in a life I didn't truly desire. I've learned to enjoy my time as an adventurer. Hunting for an ancient witch seems like a more entertaining goal than waging a war with our-step mother over who is going to oversee the manufacturing of barrels."

"I admire that you understand your priorities." Walker chuckled as he stared into the young man's eyes. "I shall meet you all on Podredumbre. Who am I to stand in the way of your goals?"

CHAPTER TWELVE

MAMA KNUCKLE

PORT HALLELUJAH WAS much as Sorrow remembered it. She'd been fifteen when she came here, a young witch hungry for knowledge, impatient for power. The bay was surrounded by rolling hills where white brick houses with red tile roofs stood atop one another in a chaotic jumble. It was evening, and the tropical air was thick with the haze of a thousand lit stoves as the town prepared dinner. The wind smelled like charcoal, bringing with it the sweet scent of plantains roasting and the savory aroma of oysters cooked in their shells.

The Isle of Podredumbre had been conquered by the Brightmoons two centuries ago. Everywhere she looked, Sorrow saw the spires marking places of worship for the Church of the Book. In the Silver City, grand cathedrals could welcome tens of thousands of worshippers under a single roof. Here, two hundred years of colonization hadn't quashed the lingering tribalism of the populace; you couldn't gather a hundred people under a roof without at least some of the members attempting to kill each other over ancient grudges. Thus the hundreds of smaller chapels, each offering services to a few families.

"We've got company," Sage announced as a launch approached the *Circus*.

"Tax collectors," Gale explained. "They'll make a show of searching our ship, then slap a tax on our cargo.

"We don't really have cargo," said Brand.

"That won't matter. They'll inform us there's a tax on the wasted space in our hold, or fine us for having excess barnacles on the hull. No ship escapes free of charge."

"Should we be nervous that these are representatives of the king?" asked Brand. "There's been time for word to spread to be on the look out for us."

Gale shook her head. "The main law here is the law of the greased palm. After we make a show of protest over their fees, we'll slip the inspectors a few moons and a bottle of rum and they'll be on their way. There's an art to these things."

Sorrow interrupted their conversation and said, "While I'm certain that bribes can handle this situation, before they board I'm going to slip off the ship. I've got an old friend to visit."

"You have a friend?" Brand asked. He winced as soon as he said it. "Sorry. I didn't mean to sound so surprised."

Sorrow ignored the slight. "After you buy provisions, leave the city along the western road. When you arrive in the village of Two Mile Ditch, ask for Mama Knuckle. I'll be waiting for you there."

"Got it," said Brand.

By now, the inspectors had pulled alongside the *Circus*. Sorrow slipped over the other rail, which was on the shadowed side. She'd not gone swimming yet with her new body, but instinct kicked in once she hit the water. Even weighted down with her glass armor, her powerful tail had no difficulty propelling her across the calm bay. The setting sun painted the ripples spreading out from her in colors of flame. If anyone spotted her monstrous body swimming toward the river that fed the bay, they failed to call out an alarm. By the time it was dark, she was well up river and able to slither out of open water into a long, marshy field of reeds.

Even though the moon was only a sliver, she had little problem finding her way among the canals that cut the landscape into a neat patchwork. In most farmlands, the canals would be for irrigation, bringing water to parched crops, but in Podredumbre, the canals were used to drain water from old swamps, leaving behind spongy black soil. Most of the cotton traded in the Shining Lands came from these fertile fields, and other parts of the island were famous for rice. All dry land was officially the property of King Brightmoon, meaning the workers here were trapped in permanent poverty, eternal squatters living on shacks build atop stilts in marshes and other marginal lands unfit for producing profit. The king made a show of generosity, keeping any able-bodied person who wanted work busy on the farms or working to reclaim new lands. He paid just enough to avoid the abject misery that might stir his subjects to rebellion, but not enough for them to have excess money they might save to escape to a better life.

It was well past midnight when she slithered into Two Mile Ditch. The landscape seemed unchanged from a decade ago. A few shacks lined the western road, next to the ferry that crossed the eponymous ditch, nearly two hundred feet across. She followed the ditch toward the oaks in the distance. Such old, tall trees were actually a rarity in Podredumbre, outside the most treacherous depths of the swamps. Most trees that could easily be reached had been felled to provide firewood and building materials. But thickets stood here and there, protected by various quirks of geography, fate, and luck. This particular patch of trees was lucky enough to be home to Mama Knuckle. No one who knew that name would ever touch the timber.

Sorrow squinted as she looked into the shadows of the gnarled old oaks. There were corpses sitting against the tree trunks, their arms limp by their sides, their crow-picked eyes turned in her direction. Sorrow bowed and said, "Uncles, I'm grateful you watch over this weary traveler. Do not rise from your rest; I'm a friend."

The corpses said nothing.

Sorrow slipped past unmolested, which was a much less interesting arrival than her first visit here, when she'd barely escaped the clutches of Mama Knuckle's guardians.

Though it was late at night, there was a soft glow from the window of the shack sheltered by the trees. Mama Knuckle kept nocturnal hours, working throughout the night, sleeping through the day.

Sorrow slithered up to the house, preparing to knock, but the door swung open on her approach. She crouched to slip through the doorframe.

"Come in, girl. As much of you as will fit, anyway." Mama Knuckle stood in front of a wood stove, stirring a large black pot. A monkey skull bobbed in the bubbling broth, which Mama pushed under with a heavy wooden spoon.

She wiped her hands on her cotton apron and turned to Sorrow. Her dress looked out of place amid the spooky hut, with its furniture all formed of twisted wood and wired bones. The fabric was a pattern of bright red flowers against a field of blue, slightly threadbare, but clean and well mended. Mama had lost much of her hair in the last decade. Only a few threads of pure white lay across her leathery scalp. Her eyes, failing when Sorrow had trained here, were now twin white moons. Though the cataracts had certainly robbed her of all ordinary sight, she smiled and said, "I never thought I'd be so happy to have Sorrow cross my doorstep."

"Did you know I was coming?" Sorrow asked.

"Girl, you're crawling around on Rott's own tail. Ghosts are gonna talk." Mama's dead eyes scanned the length of Sorrow's body. "I wasn't sure I believed 'em. The dead get a little stupid after their brains fall out. But it's true. You've got two souls inside you now. You're half-dragon. It's what you always wanted, I guess."

Sorrow shook her head. "I never wanted this."

Mama smiled faintly. "The day you first came here, girl, you were all about power, power, power. You were gonna overthrow kings and topple churches. If you're only goal is to make things fall down, it's only natural that you partnered with Rott."

"I don't consider this a partnership," said Sorrow. "I consider it an unpleasant side-effect. I was hoping you might know how to reverse it."

"Have you considered taking that sliver of Rott's tooth out of your brain? I've got a good salve you can put on afterward. Armadillo fat. Seals up any wound."

"If I remove the nail, I lose the power," said Sorrow. "There's no guarantee my body will return to normal."

"No, but you won't lose any more of your human bits, that's for sure."

"Those I have lost will have been lost in vain. I'll be no closer to saving the rest of you from the systems that oppress you."

Mama Knuckle shook her head as she placed a lid on the pot. "Girl, I'd hoped you'd outgrow such talk by now." She took a cane from beside the stove and used it to steady herself as she crossed the small room to a rickety rocking chair. The chair creaked as she lowered her bony frame into it. "It's natural to be angry at the world when you're young. Anger's just part of the blood then. But it should have boiled out of you by now."

"How can you not be angry? You live in a country where a foreign king has stolen your land and reduced your kin to little more than slaves. A church that no one truly believes in imposes its tithes and forces women into lives of subservience."

Mama Knuckle shook her head. "Girl, ain't no church did that to women."

"I've seen how free women are among the Wanderers. They're treated as equals, not house servants."

"Wanderers are different," said Mama. "The men and women are stuck together on the same ship along with their kids. It's easy to divide up the duties. But in the rest of the world, the men labor outside the house all day, or are sent to the ends of the earth as soldiers. Women stay at home to raise the children not because they're oppressed, but because they're the only ones who can be trusted to do it right."

"There's no reason it has to be this way."

"Once you carry a baby around inside you for nine months, you see things different. That child is your flesh and your future. It's no burden to dedicate yourself to being a mother."

"But—"

"It's nature girl. Haven't you opened your eyes a single day in this world? It's not a human invention that mothers care for their children. The lion, the eagle, the alligator... the females take care of the babies. It's the great wheel of life, girl. I'm sad for you that you haven't decided to ride it."

"This conversation isn't going at all like I expected," Sorrow said, crossing her arms.

"I suppose not," said Mama. "Sorry to be scolding you. I just thought you'd learn your lesson after all these years."

"Why didn't you tell me these things when I was here the first time?"

"I did, girl. Every day! But you only hear the things you want to hear."

Sorrow shook her head. "I didn't know you thought so little of me. Am I truly such an awful person?"

Mama sighed. "Oh, child, you ain't so bad. You're just a little turned around. Your father got you all twisted up long before I got hold of you. You went out into the world thinking you knew something about the truth, and you did. You did. But there's more than one truth, girl. And if you don't understand that, then the one truth you do know will turn into a lie."

"My one truth is that my father and the system he represents are wicked," said Sorrow. "Is this a lie? Is it?"

"Not always."

"I thought you of all people would understand."

Mama nodded. "I do understand. The world could be a better place. Maybe you can make it so."

"I have to try."

"You didn't come here to see me. To the island, I mean."

"Avaris is here. Somewhere in the swamps. Why didn't you tell me? You knew ten years ago I wanted to find her."

"Avaris is dangerous, child. She's got bad things in her heart. Hate and bitterness and pride, poisons of the soul."

"She has reasons to be bitter," said Sorrow. "She was once a queen. She was beloved by thousands of women. The church killed almost everyone who was loyal to her, because they couldn't stand the thought that there was someone offering a better way of life."

"She was a queen, yes. But she ruled by fear. Maybe she started with good in her heart, but she made pacts with terrible powers that turned her spiteful and cruel."

"Those are the lies the church tells," said Sorrow. "You can't believe everything the victors of war say about their enemy."

Mama Knuckle lowered her head, looking weary. "When you came to me, girl, I knew I had to train you. I could see in your eyes that nothing would stop you from finding the answers you sought. I taught you many things, but you never learned mercy. You never learned love."

"I show mercy constantly," Sorrow said, thinking of how she'd spared Eddy, the river pygmy who'd betrayed her, from suffering a moment more than necessary. "As for love, I don't know that you can teach something that may not even exist."

"Oh, child," Mama sighed.

"Love is just a mumbo jumbo word used to hide our animal natures," said Sorrow. "Between men and women, it sanitizes lust. Between a mother and child, it's a pretty word for an instinct that, as you say, even wild animals possess. Between a child and her parent, it's simple dependency that forms the bond. We romanticize these feelings, blend them together, and label them love. We attempt to make something noble out of mere biology."

Mama Knuckle rose and hobbled back to her stove. She lifted the lid and a cloud of steam rolled out. The fat from the marrow of the monkey bones had turned the broth a dull yellow. Mama Knuckle pulled down a bundle of dried chilies that hung near the stove and tossed them into the pot without bothering to chop them. After stirring the concoction in silence for a few moments, she said, "I took you into my home, girl, when you were nothing but a hungry little runaway with a scalp full of oozing wounds. I nursed you to health and taught you my secrets. I cared for you even though the guardian spirits told me to kill you. They said you were sharp with anger, the way a porcupine is prickly with quills. Touch that girl, they told me, and you'll bleed."

"I don't deny I'm angry. What I've never understood is why everyone else isn't. Why is the world so blind?"

Mama Knuckle fixed her unseeing gaze on Sorrow's face. "If the rest of the world can't see the things you see, do you think they maybe don't exist?"

"Don't be absurd. The cruelty, the injustice, the hatred... they're the facts of the world, even if no one else has the courage to see it."

"But because you're blind to love, you think it doesn't exist."

Sorrow grimaced. "Fine. I'm honest enough to admit I may have a few blind spots. What does it matter?"

"It matters because the world is in balance, Sorrow. You see only the bad things. I remember how you would walk through the cotton fields and come home to tell me how you saw workers sagging under the weight of their burdens. You'd tell me how hungry the children looked. You never told me about walking through the village in the evening and seeing the men and women dancing. You never talked about the children running around like wild things in the alleys, laughing with their friends. There's good in this world. Ordinary people can bear their heartaches because they're lifted by their joys."

"You think I can't feel joy?" Sorrow asked.

"Can you?"

Could she? She'd felt excitement, obviously, like the anticipation she'd experienced finding the Witches' Graveyard. She could feel satisfaction, like the sense of accomplishment she felt when she constructed a particularly useful golem. And she could certainly feel amusement. She'd been able to laugh when Slate had been confused about Bigsby's gender. Weren't these things joy?

Thinking about Slate, she said, "We've talked about me long enough. I've questions of a more practical nature."

"Yes?"

"I've met... a man. Who has no aura."

"Is he lethargic? Sad? Sometimes the soul perishes before the body."

"He's anything but lethargic. While he's a bit moody, he certainly smiles more often than I do."

"Perhaps some magic masks his soul?"

"Maybe," said Sorrow. "Do you know how to create such a mask? Would you know how to remove it?"

"I've not had much reason to mask souls," said Mama Knuckle. "But I know it can be done."

"So do I," said Sorrow. "Apparently, there was an animating spirit locked into the woodwork of the *Freewind*. I spent weeks on the ship and never suspected. I was told the soul had been masked to hide it from Rott. That ship was destroyed, but the soul lingers on inside the figurehead. The family is wanting me to help move the spirit into a new ship. I've no clue how to do this."

"Blood, child. Spirits flow with blood."

"I know this. But there's no body, only wood."

Mama nodded. "Then someone from the family would have to supply the blood."

"I'm sure there would be volunteers," said Sorrow. "How much blood would we need?"

"Enough to soak each board of the new ship."

"That would take gallons! No one has that much blood."

"The blood could be diluted in wine. Still, to remain potent spread across an entire ship, you would probably need all the blood from an adult."

"I doubt that's going to happen. I imagine any of the Romers would be happy to bleed a little for the cause, but it makes no sense for one of them to sacrifice their life to free one ghost."

"Without understanding love, it's impossible for you to judge these things," said Mama Knuckle.

Sorrow stretched her arms out to the side and yawned. "You've given me a lot to think about. Maybe some of it will make sense to me in the morning."

"Will you stay the night here?"

"We both know I won't."

"Why not?"

"Because if you don't want me going to see Avaris, you have a hundred different tricks to stop me. You once showed me the recipe for that paste you put on sleeping men's tongues to destroy their will and render them obedient. Going to sleep in your presence wouldn't be very smart."

"Sorrow! You trust me so little? I would never harm you. Though you'll never understand it, I love you, girl."

"Even though I scare you? Even though you think I'm corrupted by ambition?"

"Everything in balance, child. You may be blind to the good in life, but I see the good in you. The ghosts tell me you helped save the sun. The world would be a cold, dark place without you."

"I played some small part in ensuring that we'd still have daylight, yes. I can't pretend that was a particularly difficult moral choice."

"If not for your ambition, you would never have had the power to do this important thing. If not for the coldness in your heart, you wouldn't be able to stay clear-headed and focused in the face of danger. You're as close to fearless as anyone I've ever met."

"Not so fearless. If you offered me a cup of tea, I wouldn't have the courage to bring it to my lips."

Mama Knuckle laughed. "That's wisdom, not fear."

"I've seen what you've put in your teapots," Sorrow said, also laughing.

*　　*　　*

SORROW SPENT THE remainder of the night and much of the morning sleeping in an old barn on the edge of Two Mile Ditch. Perhaps it came from seeing Mama Knuckle, but she felt a wave of nostalgia sweep across her as she curled up in the loft, away from prying eyes. In recent years, she'd had the money needed to live in relative ease. She lived as a vagabond, but a comfortable one, able to afford the best rooms in the best inns, or her choice of cabins aboard ships. But for most of the first few years following running away from home, she'd slept any place that kept rain off her head—under bridges, hiding in cellars, haunting old houses half-way fallen down. She'd fed herself by stealing from gardens and, when hungry enough, from the scrap heaps of taverns. A wriggling rat had been a horrifying meal, but it wasn't at the top of the list of the worst things she'd put in her mouth.

She rolled her eyes, thinking of those starvation meals, amazed at the things one could feel sentimental about.

She spent most of the day watching the main road through a gap in the boards. At last, she saw Brand, Slate, and Bigsby approaching town in an ox-wagon. Most surprising of all, Jetsam was with them, sitting next to Brand on the bench.

Sorrow slithered out of the barn. Though it was getting late in the day, the light was still strong enough that there were men working the fields. They fled as she undulated toward the road, most heading in the direction of Mama Knuckle's hut. Hopefully the necromancer would calm them down.

As she reached the road, Brand called out, "Sorry we're a little late. Arranging to have the *Circus* restocked took longer than I planned."

"What are you doing here, Jetsam?" Sorrow asked. "Wanderers can't come onto land!"

"Technically, I'm not on land. I'm on a wagon. Abyss doesn't seem to have a problem with us walking around on boats or docks. A wagon is kind of a land-boat."

"What if someone knocks you off?"

Jetsam shrugged. "Hopefully I'll have time to get airborne and make it to water. Besides, if I lost the protection against drowning offered by Abyss, I know it would break Ma's heart, but I really don't think I'd be worried. I can walk on water. I'm more likely to break my neck tripping over a wave than I am to drown."

"But why risk coming here at all?"

"Ma has a letter she wants me to give Avaris."

"I could deliver the letter."

"Ma says she can only trust a family member."

Sorrow frowned. She didn't like that Gale was doing things involving magic without consulting with her.

Slate stood up in the back of the wagon. He was dressed in the form-fitting, black glass scale-armor Sorrow had crafted for him, though he wasn't wearing his helmet. "Have you found Avaris yet?"

Sorrow shook her head.

"Any sign of Walker?" Brand asked.

"No."

"Perhaps we should have asked him to explain his plan in more detail," said Brand.

"What's the point?" said Bigsby, clanking as he stood. "The more he talks, the more confused I get." He was once again dressed in the chain mail he'd worn when he'd thought he was a princess, only without his breast plate. It also looked as if he had lined his eyes with black make-up. At least he wasn't wearing his wig.

"We're still a few miles from where the road ends in the swamp," Sorrow said. "My understanding is we'd find him there."

"Lead on," said Brand.

Sorrow led them to the ferry. The riverman fled as she approached, but he left his pole behind. Jetsam flitted ahead to grab it. Shortly after the wagon was secured, he had the ferry free from its moorings and pushed off from shore.

"I'm a little surprised to see you geared up for battle," Sorrow said as she glanced at Bigsby.

The dwarf looked at his mace as if he was also surprised to find it in his hands. "I've been thinking a lot about what Equity said. About having the courage to be who you want to be, no matter what the world thinks. There was something deep inside me that wanted to be a warrior. I mean, I had my armor made up long before I went crazy. The legend of the missing Princess Brightmoon has been going around for a while, and it was fun to daydream crazy scenarios where I might be her."

"I can assure you that you're not," said Sorrow. "Infidel was the true Princess Brightmoon." As soon as she said it, she wondered if that was the sort of thing she was supposed to keep secret.

"Hah!" Jetsam said.

"You don't believe me?" asked Sorrow.

"Of course I believe you!" Jetsam laughed. "It makes perfect sense."

Sorrow couldn't tell if she was being mocked.

Bigsby said, "I was used to being bullied in Commonground. For release, late a night, when I was alone in my shop, I used to dress up in armor and my wig and beat the living snot out of straw men with my mace. But the odd thing is, when I went crazy and got into some real fights, I did okay. Maybe I'm more of a natural fighter than I thought. Maybe Equity was right. All I've been lacking is courage."

"I think Equity was talking about the courage to wear whatever clothes you wanted," said Sorrow.

"I'll start with testing myself in combat. That seems much less daunting than going out in public wearing my wig."

"I notice you didn't throw that mop overboard like I suggested," said Brand.

"It's an expensive wig," said Bigsby.

They continued to follow the road on the other side of the creek. They soon left behind cultivated fields, and before long the road was flanked on both sides by marshes. Twisted trees rose from the water here and there. Blueherons perched in their branches: huge, ungainly birds that turned into graceful ballerinas once they took flight. Trunks fallen into the river were thick with black turtles, still catching the last rays of the vanishing sun.

As the light disappeared, so did the road. It came to an end with a row of pilings stretching off into black water, looking like the foundation of a bridge or a dock that had never been finished. Across the water, there was a thick forest of tangled trees. The air was cacophonous with frogs.

"I'm guessing this is where Walker will meet us," said Sorrow.

Jetsam jumped from the wagon and swam into the air. "What do we need him for? From what I know, Avaris lives in a walking castle taller than these trees. It seems like she should be easy enough to spot. At least, if the light was better."

"If her castle only walked this world, that would be true." They all turned toward the voice and found Walker sitting on the bench where Jetsam had just been.

"You seem to know a thing or two about walking between worlds," said Sorrow. "When I saw you on the Isle of Fire, I thought you were a ghost. Now you look solid enough. Are you a spirit, or a living man?"

Walker grinned. "Aren't we all ghosts?"

"I'm reasonably sure I'm not," said Jetsam, hovering above.

"Living men are merely bewildered ghosts, oblivious to their true nature," Walker said. "Were you not dead before you were born?"

Bigsby smiled. "I like having him around. It means I'm no longer the craziest person here."

Sorrow studied Walker. "I don't think you're crazy. I've been to the Sea of Wine and the Great Sea Above. I know that our reality is like the heart of an onion, surrounded by other layers. How is it that you move between them so easily?"

Walker's face suddenly turned serious. "I've paid a great price. Nothing of my existence is easy."

"What price?" asked Sorrow. "Who exactly are you? Why are you helping us? For that matter, the first thing you said to me was that you'd come from hell where you'd been chatting with demons. Why should we trust you at all?"

Walker shook his head. "I speak to demons for the same reason I speak to men. Infinity is a lonesome burden. Conversation offers a moment of relief. As for who I am, I was once called—" He suddenly let out a string of whistles that sounded like a bird call. "I was the shaman of the Spike Bark tribe. I was taught by my father to grind roots into a paste that I rubbed in my eyes. This allowed me to see the true nature of the world. For a long time, I served my tribe, helping guide the spirits of my dead brethren to the Realm of Roots."

"That's another afterlife?" asked Sorrow.

"I would not use the word 'after,'" said Walker. "Though even I made the mistake in assuming there was a distinction between the material world and the spirit world. I did not learn the truth until my wife died. In my grief, I tried to follow her spirit. But she was already tangled in the roots, being sucked back into what I thought of as the living realms. When I tried to follow her back, to discover how she would be reborn, I found myself... elsewhere."

"Elsewhere?"

Walker looked wistful. "It looked the same, my village in the trees, my children, my brothers, my sisters. But all was changed. I saw the truth for the first time. What I thought of as the 'real' world was only a waking dream, neither more nor less substantial than the Realm of Roots. The treasure I thought of as life was only a facet of the larger jewel of death. I was certain that I misunderstood what I saw, so I left my village to seek the wisdom of others. Eventually, as I was led through more and more abstract realms by my guides, all barriers between the worlds became visible to me. They're thin as tissue, and easily torn."

Sorrow had more questions, but Brand interrupted. "I'm sure that this would be a fascinating conversation under other circumstances, but I'm having a little trouble focusing while I'm being devoured by mosquitoes. Why don't we set up camp and get a fire going?"

"You didn't come here to camp," said Walker. "You came seeking Avaris."

"Any chance we'll find her while I still have some blood left?" Brand asked, slapping a bug that had alighted on the side of his neck.

"Her castle is near," said Walker. "I came here last night and sang for it. It enjoys music. It will return to listen once more for my serenade."

"Start singing. That sounds a hell of a lot easier than human sacrifice. I'm not sure why you thought that required a lot of boldness, however."

"Sacrifice will be required. The castle will listen to my song, but it will not leave the Black Bog unless it can feed."

"The Black Bog is the swamp?" asked Jetsam.

"The Black Bog is another realm of the dead," said Sorrow. "It's part of the local mythology."

"What kind of sacrifice?" Brand asked Walker.

"You must die, of course," the pygmy said. "But not for long. I'll guide your spirit back into your body once the castle crosses into this world to feed."

"So... what? I just slit my wrists and trust you to handle the rest?"

"The castle dislikes the taste of suicide," said Walker. "It prefers the flavor of murder."

"If we kill Brand, what guarantee do we have that the castle will notice?" asked Sorrow.

"It's here right now, watching us."

Everyone craned their necks toward the forest, searching the shadowy treetops.

"Come here," Walker said, motioning for Sorrow. "I'll help you see past the veil."

Sorrow leaned toward the pygmy. Without warning, he grabbed her by the back of her neck and pulled her forward. A shard of obsidian appeared in his hand, seemingly from nowhere. She cried in pain as he sliced the sharp stone across her eyebrows.

She punched him in the chest and jerked away. She grabbed her face with both hands. The wound across her brow didn't feel deep, but it hurt like hell. She wiped at the blood dripping into her eyes.

"Why did you do that?" she grumbled.

"Look to the trees," he said.

She did so. She grew still. Looming above the forest was a huge shadow, oval in shape, like a turtle shell large enough to encompass a village. Unlike a turtle, it was held aloft by four spindly insect legs, at least a hundred yards tall. At the front of the oval was a second, smaller oval, almost like a head. On that head were two narrow slits, glowing pale red, like eyes formed of embers.

She swallowed hard as she realized the eyes were looking directly at her.

CHAPTER THIRTEEN

DARK MIRROR

"WHAT IS IT you see?" Slate asked, hopping down from the wagon.

Sorrow said softly, "It's here. Her walking palace. I see it."

"Cut me," Slate said to Walker.

The pygmy stood on the seat of the wagon to comply.

Slate sucked in air through his teeth as he pressed his hands against the wound. He shook off his pain and looked up. His jaw went slack.

"Is it... a structure? Or a living thing?" he asked.

"Whatever it is, it's staring at me," Sorrow whispered. "I feel... I feel the way a mouse must feel when there's an owl on the branch above."

"I guess someone needs to kill me," said Brand. He looked at Walker. "Should they stab me?"

"Strangling would be best," said Walker. "Your body remains mostly undamaged, making it easier to return."

"Slate, you've got good strangling hands," said Brand.

"I'll not kill an innocent man, even if asked," said Slate.

"Me neither," said Jetsam.

Brand looked surprised. "You kill people all the time, Jetsam! I've heard you sing while you're doing it!"

"Yeah, but only to defend my family. Killing for any other reason means that when you make that final trip to the Sea of Wine, the Joyful Isles will forever retreat on the horizon."

"How about you, Bigsby?" asked Brand. "Do you have an appetite for fratricide?"

"No," said the dwarf. "How can you be so flippant about this? I know this is important to Sorrow, but why would you do something so stupid?"

Brand raised an eyebrow. "Stupid? I'm being offered a chance to experience death with the promise it won't be permanent. How can anyone with a healthy level of curiosity not be intrigued at the thought?" He turned to Sorrow and said, "Since you're the one wanting to see Avaris, I guess it's up to you to do the deed."

Sorrow heard a crashing, splashing noise as Brand spoke. She looked to the shadows and saw that the walking castle had turned tail and was running away.

"There's no point in anyone dying now," said Walker, shaking his head. "The castle has been spooked. It will not return, even if we offered it a dozen souls."

"No!" Sorrow screamed, slithering forward into the murky water of the swamp.

Slate splashed into the water beside her.

"There's no point in chasing it," said Walker. "It retreats further into the Black Bog."

"You can cross between worlds," said Sorrow. "You've taught Zetetic! Lead us!"

Walker laughed. "Zetetic practices seven disciplines of insanity each morning before breakfast. His mind is hardened against the blending of the real and the unreal. Untrained minds fall prey to nightmares and never escape."

Sorrow whipped back to the shore with the speed of a rattlesnake striking. She grabbed Walker by his shoulders and shook him. "Don't talk to me about falling prey to nightmares! I've seen things that would frighten your damned demon friends and come out stronger for it! Take me over!"

"If she goes, I go," said Slate.

Sorrow's hands suddenly lost their grip on Walker as his body turned to fog.

As he faded away, his laughter lingered in the air, along with his final words, "How can you go when you're already there?"

Sorrow drew back. To her horror, Brand, Jetsam, and Bigsby were dead, reduced to skeletons fallen across the ox-wagon. The ox, too, had become a pile of jumbled bones.

"We've crossed the veil," Slate said softly as he turned slowly to study the landscape. The swamp, once abundant with life, was reduced to dead trees and rotting marsh grass. Not a single frog chirp disturbed the still air.

Sorrow glanced back toward the walking palace. It was a mile away by now, only a gray silhouette against a starless night sky black as ink. Slate started to jump into the water once more, but Sorrow caught him.

"Careful," she said. "If the legends are correct, once you swim in these dark channels, you lose all memories of your mortal life."

"That would mean I would forget that I don't remember who I am," said Slate. "It sounds almost like a fate I'd welcome. If we don't enter the water, how are we to give chase?"

Sorrow sighed. "I wish I'd grown some damned dragon wings instead of this dumb tail."

As the words left her lips, she cried out in agony. It felt as if someone had just driven a sword into her back. She fell to the dusty ground, her body trembling.

"Sorrow!" Slate cried, kneeling beside her. "What's wrong?"

"Can't... breathe," she said through clenched teeth. It felt as if her armor was shrinking, crushing her torso. In desperation, she willed her glass armor to fall away, returning it to the sand from which it came.

Sorrow sucked in air as she sat up. She covered her bare breasts as she looked at Slate, who was staring at her with wide eyes. She nearly fell backwards. A terrible weight had settled on her shoulders. Throwing modesty to the wind, she reached both hands over her shoulders and discovered a giant bulge on her back, like a watermelon between her shoulder blades. The skin was so taut it felt as if it would tear open any second.

And then it did, with a sickening wet rip. She screamed, but the pain was followed instantly by relief. She looked over her shoulders and found black, bat-like wings spreading from her spine, large as sails. They were wet and slimy, like a newborn baby, and as they moved the cool air felt soothing.

She stood up, stretching her wings, wondering if they would be as simple to master as her tail had been. Then she realized she'd just stood up. She stared down at her bare legs, now restored to full humanity.

"You wished it," said Slate, "and it came true."

"So it would seem," said Sorrow, once again having the presence of mind to drape an arm across her breasts.

"I wish I could remember who I was," said Slate.

He stood silently for a moment, his face devoid of emotion.

"Did it... did it work?" she asked.

He shook his head.

"Maybe you have no memories to restore," she said. "I don't think my wings came out of nowhere. Instead, it's like I have a certain amount of dragon in me, and I was able to move it around, thanks to the dream-like nature of this place."

"Can you fly?" Slate asked.

"That's kind of the obvious question, isn't it?" Sorrow said, managing to muster a feeble grin.

She turned her head toward the skies, spread her wings, and, in a sensation that filled her with indescribable pleasure, she bent her knees and ankles to crouch. It felt good to have legs again. The muscles in her thighs and calves felt warm and powerful. She tested their strength as she jumped with all her might.

Her wings beat down, striking the earth, lifting her higher. She flapped again and shot up a dozen yards, leveling off, feeling the wind beneath her wings as she glided in a wide circle around Slate, who was gawking. It was an unwelcome sensation to have a man stare so openly at her nude body. On the other hand, if Slate had suddenly shed his clothes and grown dragon wings, would she have been able to turn her eyes away?

She scanned the skies. The palace could no longer be seen, but she knew which direction it had been heading. It would be simple to give chase.

"Will you be able to carry me?" Slate shouted.

Did she want to carry him? She'd always imagined she would be making the journey to see Avaris alone. She didn't even know why Slate was here. Yes, she understood his primary motive. Avaris might be able to explain who he was and why he had no memories. But then what? Would Slate swear allegiance to Avaris, grateful that her magic had given him life? Or would he attempt to kill her, reverting to the witch-breaking cruelty that she'd seen in the painting?

On the other hand, she'd been keeping journals for almost fifteen years and the one constant theme was her complaint that no one ever chose to stand by her side in her battles. She was in a nightmare landscape full of unknown dangers, and Slate wanted to be here with her.

In the end, it wasn't a difficult choice.

"Spread your arms," she yelled. "I'm going to swoop down and try to grab you from behind."

He did so. She wheeled through the air, then adjusted her flight with frequent small movements to keep herself on target. The horror she'd felt waking up with her legs replaced by a serpent's tail was replaced by a casual, matter-of-fact acceptance that she now had wings. Perhaps it was the dream-like nature of the abstract realms that explained how natural her new limbs felt. Here the impossible became the mundane.

But if flight had been second nature when is was her own body being carried through the sky, the second she slammed into Slate the absurdity of what she was doing was knocked back into her. She lost most of her speed on impact, with the wind knocked both from her wings and her lungs. Worse, while she'd managed to wrap her arms tightly around his chest, momentum was carrying them both toward the swamp. She had only seconds before she discovered if the mind-numbing properties of the water were true.

Of their own accord, her wings beat a mighty down stroke that altered her trajectory. Slate's boots left ripples as he danced across the water, dangling from her grasp. Her wings beat again and they rose, barely clearing the trees. He brought his hands to her wrists and grasped them with a death grip. She couldn't drop him now if she wanted to.

They continued to climb. The dead forest lay in shadows beneath them, a jumble of jagged trunks and limbs, twisted so that they looked like men frozen as they writhed in agony.

"I see it!" Slate shouted, pointing in the darkness.

His eyes proved superior to hers. She flew in the direction indicated for a full thirty seconds before she could distinguish the moving shadow.

The castle's back was to them. As they drew closer, she could see that her initial hunch that the structure resembled a turtle was accurate, assuming turtles grew to be a quarter mile across. Now that they were closer, she could see that the shell was bleached white. There were no obvious windows or doors.

"We'll have to go around to the front," she said. "Maybe we can enter through the mouth."

As she spoke, the castle shuddered. With startling speed, the beast whirled on its spindly legs until its glowing eyes faced her. It opened toothy jaws that would have been more at home on a shark than a turtle. Without warning, a jet of puss-colored fluid arced toward them. She banked hard, wincing as droplets of the yellow liquid spattered her wings, burning holes. Fortunately, her human skin was shielded by Slate. His glass armor proved well suited to defend against an attack of acid. Still, as she climbed higher, she said, "Okay, maybe not the mouth."

"Drop us on the center of the shell," said Slate. "The creature's head can't possibly turn to cover its own back."

Sorrow wasn't certain that was true in a place like this, but had no better strategy. She tilted her wings and they slowly dropped onto the apex of the beast's shell. She wasn't surprised to discover that this area was defended as well. As soon as Slate's boots hit the bone, the roof splintered for a dozen yards in every direction. Human skeletons rose from their bony matrix, their eye sockets turning to face the two interlopers, their jaws open wide in silent, outraged battle-cries.

"Let's try closer to the—"

Before she could compete her thought, Slate broke free from her grasp. Following the battle with the pirates, he'd expressed satisfaction with the results he'd gotten from Bigsby's mace, so she'd crafted one for him with a longer shaft and larger head that took advantage of his unusual size and strength. He tore into the nearest skeletons with a fury, reducing them to splinters with each blow.

Sorrow realized she would only get in Slate's way, so she leapt into the air before the remaining horde could reach her and patiently flew in circles for the handful of minutes it took Slate to pound his way through the last of the undead. She landed amid a cloud of chalky dust and said, "Sorry I wasn't more help. You looked like you were having fun."

Slate shook his head as he picked up a fallen skull. "These were men once. It's tyranny to enslave the living. How much greater is the crime of enslaving the dead?"

Sorrow didn't feel like debating the matter. Instead, she studied the roof they stood on. Her Rott-informed sense of the decay in all things kicked in as she studied the joints of the bone plates.

"It's weakest here," she said, running her fingers along a seam. "One good whack will split this wide open."

"Stand back," Slate said, bringing the mace overhead with both hands.

Sorrow shielded her eyes as he swung, sending a shower of needle-sharp bone splinters shooting toward her. There was a loud cracking sound, followed by a *WHUMP*. She lowered her arms to find Slate missing. Her toes were at the edge of an octagonal hole large enough for an elephant to fall through. She peered over into the room below.

Slate was on his butt in the middle of the collapsed roof. He'd fallen into what looked to be a library, with long rows of shelves lit by orbs of glass filled with what looked like fireflies. From her training in soul-catching, she suspected the lights were actually the souls of unborn children. They gave off a particularly gentle light when restrained.

She dropped into the library and looked around at the rows of leather-bound books.

"It would take a lifetime to read all of these," she said.

A single book near her feet said, "Read me before you read the others. My unread words burn within me, like a breath held burns the lungs. Release my words! Free them!"

Sorrow's eyebrows rose as she took a second look at the book, which plainly had a face. The leather binding, it seemed, had come from a man. His eyes were sewn shut, and his lips had once suffered a similar treatment, but the thread that closed the mouth had frayed, perhaps torn loose when the ceiling fell.

She turned away, pointing toward a door at the far end of the room. Slate nodded as he headed toward it.

"You can't leave me," the book cried, loudly enough that other books on the shelf awakened. Most of their lips were stitched together, reducing their pleading to incoherent whimpers. A fresh voice broke free of its binding, shouting, "There's no hell so dark as an unopened page! Read me! Restore my purpose!"

Slate paused, looking worried as he asked Sorrow, "Should we—"

"Ignore them. You could be trapped here for all eternity trying to satisfy them. The unread books of the world will always demand more of the living than can be given."

"But these aren't ordinary books."

"More ordinary than you think," said Sorrow, grabbing him by the wrist and pulling him toward the door.

She pushed it open. She wished she'd looked for another door.

Beyond was a chamber of horrors. There were double the shelves of the previous space, but rather than being filled with books, the space was filled with jars. And if the dancing fireflies in the lights were the souls of unborn children, the jars most certainly held their bodies. Pickled babies in various stages of development floated in pale gray alcohol. She'd seen such things before, curiously enough, in the collection of her father, who had a room of his mansion devoted to such oddities as calves with two heads and human babies with flippers instead of limbs. But this room contained thousands of the unborn. At least, she assumed they were unborn; some looked suspiciously large and well developed.

"Who would possess something like this?" Slate whispered.

"Try not to judge. It's disturbing to look upon, true. But physicians learn the skills they need to help the living by dissecting the bodies of the dead. I'm certain these bodies have some educational purpose."

Slate looked around. "Which way should we go?"

Sorrow shrugged. "It's not like I have a map. Just keep moving until we see a door. What's the worst that can happen?"

She regretted the question the instant it left her lips.

The next room was the kitchen. Sitting on the butcher's block was a child's head. It looked fresh. Slate looked as if he was going to be sick.

"You've seen decapitated heads before," Sorrow said, trying not to stare at the cutting board. Poppy's book had said that Avaris ate babies. This was definitely not a baby. It looked like a girl six or seven years of age. Why that mattered, Sorrow couldn't say. But could she even trust her eyes in a place like this? Or was she seeing a butchered child only because she'd been told she'd see them?

Slate covered the head with a towel, looking pale.

"We really can't know what happened here," said Sorrow.

"A young girl was killed, butchered, and eaten?"

"Maybe she died of natural causes. Or some accident that severed her head. Maybe she's been brought here to be cleaned up before burial."

"To a kitchen."

"Kitchens get used for lots of things."

"You cannot excuse this."

"I'm just saying we may not understand everything we're seeing. This isn't the world we know. We're in no position to judge the inhabitants."

"I believe I *am* in a position to judge," said Slate. "I'm a tolerant, patient man. But I've no mercy for those who would harm a child."

Sorrow ground her teeth together. She, too, thought of herself as a protector of children. Was she so hungry to learn from Avaris that she was ignoring plain evidence that Mama Knuckle had been right?

Slate marched from the kitchen, opening a door into a long hall.

"I may be turned around, but I think this leads toward the head," Sorrow said.

Slate moved down the hall with his mace at the ready. The door at the end of the hall was far more ornate than any they'd yet encountered.

"It would be nice if Sage were here to tell us what's behind the door," Sorrow whispered.

"After what we've seen, I'm ready for anything," Slate said. He leaned back and kicked the door open.

They'd found the throne room. A red carpet led to a throne of black bones. Perched upon it was a woman of breathtaking beauty. She wore a jeweled red gown that glistened like fresh blood on her ivory skin. Her hair was black as coal, held in place by a crown of teeth. She was fifty feet away, behind a crystalline orb nearly a yard wide. A black, bat-winged creature could be seen in the light moving within the crystal. It took Sorrow a few heartbeats to realize that the creature was herself.

The woman clapped her hands together in an exaggerated fashion as a large man in plate armor stepped from behind the throne.

"Bravo," she said. "A magnificent performance from both of you. Kicking in the door of my throne room was satisfyingly dramatic. I imagine it must have been quite cathartic for you as well. You came looking for Avaris, Queen of Weavers. You've found her. Now that the dramatic parts are past, may I summarize the rest of the plot? You'll growl a few threats. I'll respond with witty banter. We'll bargain. In the end, we'll all get something we want, and I'll spare the lives of your friends."

"Our friends?" Sorrow asked.

"The three you left behind," said Avaris. "The three who can't see my palace. I've turned us around so we can kill them. They'll die without ever knowing why."

"No one needs to die," said Sorrow. "I've come looking for answers, not to fight you."

"I'm not sure your companion agrees," said Avaris. "He's positively trembling with rage."

"We found a girl in the kitchen," Slate said.

"Part of one, at least," said Avaris.

"Did you kill her?" Sorrow asked.

"Heavens, no," Avaris answered. "Her body was given to me in exchange for favors."

"Favors?" asked Sorrow.

"Why would you traffic in the body of a child?" Slate asked.

"To eat it, of course," said Avaris. "I'm six hundred years old. Without a steady diet of youth, I imagine I'd be quite the fright."

Slate growled, brandishing his mace and charging. The large, armored man stepped forward, drawing his sword. The blade was pitch black, and as it left its scabbard the air was filled with the distant howls of souls in agony.

"Slate!" Sorrow cried. "It's the Witchbreaker!"

Slate showed no caution, however, charging the man and swinging his mace with both hands. Sparks flew as Avaris's defender caught the shaft of the mace against his blade. The iron in both weapons rang as they slid against one another, bringing the two men's faces inches apart. Slate wasn't wearing his helmet, while his opponent was wearing a helm that hid his face. Which was why everyone was surprised when Slate head-butted his opponent. The swordsman was knocked back by the blow. As the gap between them opened, Slate drew back his mace. But he didn't aim his blow at the warrior. Instead, he threw his weapon at Avaris. She was caught off guard by the attack, dodging at the last moment. The mace missed, smashing into the back of the throne where her head had just been. But the heavy iron handle slammed into the side of her head just above her ear, knocking off her crown.

Avaris tumbled to the floor, landing on one knee. She rose shakily, beating a hasty retreat toward the velvet curtains on the rear wall, and Sorrow gave chase. She was furious at Slate for losing his temper and attacking, and furious at herself for knowing that the crimes Avaris had just confessed to didn't change Sorrow's desire to talk to the woman. If Avaris had become a parody of evil, it was only because her enemies had made her thus.

Avaris slipped behind one of the curtains. Sorrow heard iron bars rattle down. She glanced back and saw Slate and the warrior still grappling. Slate was keeping close, where a two-handed sword like the Witchbreaker was nearly useless. Slate had managed to slip his hands beneath the warrior's helmet and was squeezing his foe's throat with all his might.

Sorrow pushed aside the curtain and reached out to touch the iron bars that blocked the doorway. With a thought, they crumbled to rust. She pushed through, her wings scraping against the edges of the doorframe.

She found herself in a luxurious bedchamber. A canopy bed sat in the center of the room, with gilded bedposts and satin bedding. All around the room were mirrors in frames of gold. Beside the bed was another crystal sphere, as large as the one outside. She could see the two warriors in the throne room struggling. Could hear them, too, the *clinks* and *clangs* of their armor echoing faintly from the crystalline surface. The room was almost silent other than this.

Almost.

There was an open door at the back of the room. The obvious path was to go through it. But in the relative silence of the room, she heard a noise. Her ears fixed upon a large wardrobe on the far wall. She moved before it, holding her breath to hear better. She furrowed her brow. Someone was definitely inside. And they were sobbing?

She yanked the door open. Avaris fell at her feet, her hands clasped around her bleeding temple, as she whimpered, "Please! Don't kill me! I'll give you anything you want!"

Sorrow raised her eyebrows. The woman seemed genuinely terrified.

"You were a queen once," Sorrow said. "Now you grovel at the feet of an unarmed woman?"

Avaris snorted. "You don't need to be armed. You've blended your spirit with Rott. You're destruction incarnate."

"I just expected... someone a little..."

"Braver? I fear death so much I've hid from it for six centuries. I live in shadows because I fear the scorn of those who remain in light."

Sorrow didn't know what to say to this. As she silently stared at the woman, she heard laughter from the crystal at her back.

A man's voice said, "I feel your hands grow weary. I see you've inherited none of my cleverness. How stupid must you be to try to strangle a dead man?"

Sorrow blocked this from her mind. If Slate bested his foe, he could burst through the door any moment and kill Avaris. If the swordsman bested Slate, he might prove a bit more courageous than the queen. In any case, she needed to speak quickly.

"I may be blended with Rott," said Sorrow. "But I'm having difficulty controlling my power. I'm hoping you can help. If anyone knows how to command the powers of a primal dragon, it's you."

Avaris shook her head. She ran her fingers through her black hair, pulling locks away to reveal an ugly bubble of scar tissue on the pale flesh beneath. "This is all that remains of my one attempt to master the powers of Rott. In the end, I gladly plucked the nail from my skull."

"You had the same powers?" Sorrow asked, unable to take her eyes off the scar. "And you threw them away?"

"I'd lost an even greater power," said Avaris. "Since I was young, men have done my bidding, seduced by my beauty. I lost that power when I blended my soul with Rott. No matter how I tried to blend the dragon's body with my own, I wound up repulsive, covered with scales. My once perfect mouth was ruined by fangs." She glanced up at Sorrow's nude body. "You've kept your figure better than I did. If you found a man who didn't mind the wings, you might still seduce him."

"I'd rather be part dragon than seduce men," said Sorrow.

"Truly? Because you may be ignoring your greatest natural gift. Women need no magic to enslave men. After I gave up on the false path of controlling the primal force of decay, I rediscovered the primal force of womanhood. I restored by body with bone-weaving and went on to seduce my greatest tormentor."

Sorrow almost asked who that was. She turned her gaze toward the crystal ball as a loud *clang* rang out. Slate had recovered his mace. He'd just knocked the warrior's helmet from his head.

The two men stared at each other in the aftermath. Save for the swordsman's deathly pallor and gray hair, they were as alike as twins.

"Lord Stark Tower," Sorrow whispered.

"The Witchbreaker," said Avaris. "My mortal foe, now my undead champion. Once I seduced him, perverting what little good remained in him, it was a simple matter to enslave his body and ferry his soul to hell. I keep his corpse healthy with a daily supply of virgin blood."

Sorrow started to ask if Avaris meant that Stark drank the blood, but decided she didn't want to know.

Avaris looked puzzled as she stared at Sorrow, "If you don't seduce men, how do you summon the procreative energies required for bone-weaving?"

"I don't," said Sorrow. "I've never learned the art. That's why I've been hunting for you all these years."

"Ah. Then we can make a bargain. I give you knowledge. You spare my life."

"We spare all lives," said Sorrow. "Call off your castle's attack on my companions. Tell Tower to spare Slate."

"You've asked just in time. The castle has found your friends, and stands above them now, unseen. It shall not strike unless I will it. As for Tower, he may be my slave, but his cruel streak exceeds my ability to control. He'll play with your friend until he grows weary. Slate will die in terrible pain. It would be tragic, I suppose, if he were truly a living thing."

"Slate isn't alive?"

"For all physical purposes, the man you call Slate is indistinguishable from a living man. But he's my creation, an exact duplicate of Stark Tower, woven from the original's blood. I magically endowed him with all of the original's prowess in battle, but warped other aspects of his mind so that he would be Tower's dark mirror. Tower swaggered around the world claiming to be the champion of good. I created Slate to be the champion of evil. Only, I had made the mistake of believing Tower's own myth. When my creation woke, he was not the scourge I had hoped for. Instead, in his mirror nature, he proved kind where Tower was cruel. He was selfless where

Tower was vain. While Tower hated mankind, Slate was quick to form friends, even with those who should have been his worst foes. In the end, I was forced to give the useless dolt a potion that destroyed his memories. I intended to find a wicked spirit in the realms of the dead more suited to my needs, and offer him Slate's impressive shell. Alas, these events unfolded in chaotic times. Though I soon made the true Witchbreaker my slave, his armies still overpowered my own, and I was forced to flee. Slate was left in stasis, neither alive nor dead, until such time that I could return for him. Of course, in my exile, I decided to change my tactics."

"How?"

"The kingdoms of the world rejected my rule. I came to understand they were never worthy of my time. Let the masses suffer under their false churches. What they believe was a victory against me was the beginning of their long doom. I'm now immortal. What does it matter to me if it takes my enemies centuries to fall?"

There was more laughter from the globe. Sorrow looked back to see Slate clutching his side, bleeding. Much of his armor was shattered. Save for his missing helmet, Lord Tower looked none the worse for wear.

"You're younger," Tower said. "Faster. Perhaps even a bit stronger. A benefit of still having a heartbeat, I suppose. What a shame that a living body so quickly grows weary. I do not miss pain. I do not miss the burning in my chest when breath grows short." He swung his sword overhead with both hands and chopped down. His blow didn't seem aimed to kill, but to maim, targeted on Slate's legs. At the last possible instant, Slate rolled aside, and the sword bit deep into the bone floor.

Sorrow looked back at Avaris. "How long will it take you to give me a nail of bone? I still wish to learn this art. It's said that bone-weavers can alter their forms. Can I not restore my humanity with it?"

Avaris shook her head. "The dragon spirit is stronger than mere flesh. You may rearrange your body, but only if you sever all ties with Rott can you be fully human. As for the bone nail, have the weaver arts decayed so far that you don't see the simple truth?"

"There aren't many witches left."

"But all should be bone-weavers."

"But I've never found a bone nail. I've never even discovered a bone-weaver's skull to study!"

"Fool! Peel away your scalp and what would you find?"

"My skull?"

"Made of?"

"Oh," said Sorrow.

"You were born with the tools. You merely lack the teaching."

"How long will I have to train?"

"A lifetime. I still discover new aspects to the magic. But there is a short cut."

"What?"

"You've already shown a willingness to blend your soul with a dragon. Would you be open to blending your mind with mine?"

"How?"

Avaris ran her fingers along Sorrow cheek. "I will take your left eye. I will give you one of mine in exchange."

Sorrow stared at the woman's face. Avaris looked serious. Her eyes were a perfect match for Sorrow's own emerald green.

Sensing Sorrow's hesitation, Avaris said, "It's only painful for a short time. After this, I will see all that you see. We can converse by thought though separated by miles and dimensions as easily as we speak now. I can guide you in the art of bone-weaving, and improve your mastery of other skills. I may even be able to guide you in dealing with the dragon spirit. I held the power for over a decade before rejecting it. I know a thing or two about control."

"And sparing your life is the only price?"

Avaris laughed. "No. No, I think not. Of course, you've already dedicated yourself to the thing I would find most pleasing."

"The destruction of the church?"

Avaris nodded. "My price cannot be something you would do on your own. So, I will make it simple. You will kill someone of my choosing."

"Who?"

Avaris shrugged. "I don't know yet. It may take me many years to decide."

Sorrow frowned. She thought about the decapitated girl in the kitchen. There were people in this world she couldn't and wouldn't hurt. She turned away. "I cannot accept your bargain. If you were to demand I kill a child, I could not obey you."

"Even if the child were Numinous Pilgrim?"

Sorrow pressed her lips together.

She was still thinking the offer over when Avaris said, "Fine. No children. Nor anyone you would consider innocent, though no such creatures exists. I promise when I name my target, you will agree that they have committed the most flagrant sins."

Sorrow nodded. "Agreed." She turned to shake the elder witch's hand. Instead, she found Avaris standing behind her. The woman's left eye was a barren socket. The woman grabbed Sorrow's face, bringing her mouth toward Sorrow's eye. The witch's teeth warped and grew into long blades. Sorrow screamed as the fangs gouged into her flesh.

CHAPTER FOURTEEN

JUST MAN

"SORROW!" A VOICE cried out. It was Slate, from the other room, still alive despite the odds. She couldn't look at the crystal ball, however. She couldn't look at anything. There was nothing but a veil of perfect blackness before her. Avaris' fingernail dug around within her left eye socket, removing dangling bits of flesh. The pain made her reflexively clamp her right eye shut, effectively blinding herself.

There was a terrible pressure in her skull as Avaris jammed something hot and wet into her bleeding eye socket. Suddenly the veil of black was full of dancing white sparks. Avaris removed her hand and Sorrow jammed her palms over her face. She probed as gently as she could and felt that she once more had two eyeballs.

With sheer force of will, she pulled her hands away and opened her eyes.

Everything in the room was doubled. She blinked, but it did little to improve her overlapping vision. She craned her neck. Avaris was nowhere to be seen. She rose on trembling legs, steadying herself on the bed frame. She glanced into the crystal ball. Through her doubled vision, she could see Slate still on the floor before the Witchbreaker. Judging from the deep scars across the floor, he'd rolled out of the path of dozens of blows.

"You're getting slower," Tower taunted as he raised his sword once more. "I can keep this up for all eternity."

Sorrow stumbled back toward the door she'd entered, placing her hand on the wall as she fought for balance. Her heartbeat pounded in her temples as she squeezed her eyes shut, fighting dizziness. The weight of the wings upon her back threatened to bring her to her knees. Just how much blood had she lost?

Taking a deep breath, she forced her eyes open once more. Her doubled vision snapped into focus as she stared at the bloodied handprint she'd left on the wall. Outside the room, she heard Lord Tower erupt into deep, booming laughter.

She stumbled into the doorway in time to see Slate once more roll aside as the Witchbreaker bit into the floor of the throne room. Slate's efforts at avoiding the enchanted blade had left an almost perfect circle chopped into the pale white bone that both combatants stood upon.

Slate was bleeding from a gash in his forehead and a slice across his right shoulder. He was drenched in sweat, his limbs rubbery as he managed to rise into a crouch.

"Don't you understand the futility of struggle?" Tower asked with a sneer. "Look upon my face. You're nothing but my reflection, a redundancy, a pathetic doppelganger stubbornly clinging to the illusion of life."

"Bold words," Slate wheezed, wiping sweat from his eyes, "from a man without a heartbeat."

Tower shook his head. "Hearts are a tremendous liability. Allow me to demonstrate!"

The knight swung the Witchbreaker high overhead. Sorrow leapt forward, spreading her wings, but in her weakened condition succeeded only in crashing to the floor.

Her flailing wings distracted Lord Tower enough to allow Slate to roll aside before the Witchbreaker once more sliced into bone. The knight looked at Sorrow as she tried to rise. He smiled as he said, "Gravity is not your friend."

"Nor yours!" Slate cried as he rose to his knees, wrapping both his arms around Tower's armored waist. With a gurgling grunt, he bent the undead knight backward, until Tower's leather boots lost their grip and the knight's heavy frame slammed into the center of the weakened circle of bone.

A loud *POP* echoed from the few inches of bone that remained intact around the circle. Cracks formed and broadened. Just as Sorrow made it back to her knees, the floor beneath the two warriors gave way and they dropped from view.

"Slate!" she cried, leaping forward, landing so that her body dangled out over the gaping hole.

The two men tumbled toward the earth a hundred yards distant. There was no time for her to even move.

From nowhere, a smaller airborne man dodged around the falling circle of bone, spreading his arms as he kicked toward Slate. Jetsam! From the smell of the humid swamp beneath, Sorrow supposed that they'd crossed once more into the material world.

Jetsam wrapped his arms around Slate's belly, kicking furiously to push toward the waters of the swamp. They disappeared into the ink-black waters.

The bone floor turned on edge and landed upright, punching into the ground immediately behind the wagon where Bigsby and Brand were sitting. The ox harnessed to the cart bolted like a startled rabbit, plunging them all into the swamp. Lord Tower's armored form landed in the rut of the cart's wheel and lay very still.

Sorrow climbed back into the throne room, feeling too weak to risk flying. She turned and found two overlapping images of Avaris directly behind her. The two raven-haired witches quickly resolved into one as Avaris drew back and delivered a powerful kick to Sorrow's gut. Sorrow was forced backward into the open hole.

As she dropped, she heard Avaris say, "Fledglings sometimes need a little nudge from the nest."

Sorrow twisted, spreading her wings, her fall slowing as she caught the air. She wound up in a dizzying spiral as the dark ground rushed toward her. Fortunately, her wings slowed her fall enough that when she landed in the marsh grass, she sank in the muck to her knees, but was otherwise unharmed.

She craned her neck toward the star-filled sky and watched as the walking castle lumbered back into the swamp, fading deeper into the shadows with each step. Within seconds, its feet no longer splashed in the waters of the material world.

She tried to will herself back across the veil to give chase; she had many more questions for Avaris. But her body remained stubbornly stuck in the realm of mud. With a loud *SLUCK* she pulled herself from the mire and stumbled back to drier ground.

"Walker!" she shouted. "Walker!"

"He's gone," Brand said. "Just faded away, until nothing was left but a grin. Then even that vanished."

With some effort, she focused her eyes on him. Brand was still dry, apparently having jumped from the cart just before it hit the water. He said, "Walker told us to be patient before he vanished. Jetsam was keeping watch while Bigsby and I caught a little shut-eye. Next thing I know I'm waking up with the damn castle directly overhead, people are falling from the sky, plus you've got wings, and, oh, yeah, legs. Care to explain what's going on?"

Sorrow didn't answer. What was she to say?

"Are you all right?" he asked, stepping closer. Brand's expression changed from consternation to concern. He placed his fingers on her chin and turned her head to get a better look at her eye. "By the sacred quill. I thought you just had mud on your face. I didn't realize you were injured."

"It's just a head wound," she said with a feeble smile. "I collect them to fill my idle hours."

"New body parts also seem to be a hobby," said Brand. "Wings?"

She shrugged. "My body was a bit more flexible in the Black Bog. I'm still halfway to dragonhood, but at least I can wear shoes again."

Brand took off his shirt and offered it to her. "You have more urgent things to cover than your feet," he said, glancing toward the swamp, where Slate and Bigsby were crawling up the bank. Jetsam was balanced on the surface of the water, kneeling before the ox thrashing in the mud, using his sword to cut away the beast's harness.

Sorrow looked at the shirt, baffled by how it would possibly work with her wings. In the end, she tied it around her hips to serve as an impromptu skirt, then crossed her arms over her breasts.

The dripping wet ox thundered past a moment later, galloping off across the field in a panic. From above, Jetsam said, "Sorry. Lost my grip on his lead as I was helping guide him back to land. I couldn't just let him drown."

"It's okay," said Brand.

"I'm not okay with it," said Bigsby, shaking mud from his limbs as he walked between the ruts left by the ox cart. "It's a long hike back to town." He came to a sudden halt as he encountered the armor sunk into the ground.

"Careful," said Sorrow. "He might not be dead!"

"From that height?" Jetsam said. "He's dead."

"Okay, yes, but he was dead before and it didn't slow him much."

Slate approached the fallen knight and dropped to his knees. He grabbed the knight's left shoulder and tried to turn Tower over onto his back. The man's arm came loose in his hands. Maggots writhed in the exposed tissue inside the iron sleeve.

Jetsam and Brand gagged as the stench of rotten meat billowed into the air. Sorrow wrinkled her nose reflexively, but was surprised that the stink didn't strike her as particularly foul. Perhaps sharing body parts with Rott had deadened her revulsion to such smells.

Bigsby also seemed oddly oblivious to the odor as he walked up to the body and stared at the face, which had been partially revealed by Slate's efforts.

"He looks… familiar," Bigsby said.

Brand pinched his nose shut and covered his mouth with his hand as he asked, "How can you stand so close to that stench, brother?"

Bigsby shrugged. "I ran a fish market for almost twenty years. I guess even nostrils can develop calluses." Looking back at the corpse, he asked, "Who was he?"

"He was me," said Slate, shaking his head mournfully.

"Explain," said Brand.

Slate told them what he'd learned, which meshed pretty well with what Avaris had told Sorrow. Apparently, Tower had been chatty during battle.

Everyone stared at Slate quietly after his tale. His expression was completely unreadable.

Finally, Brand said, glancing at Tower, "I suppose the decent thing to do would be to bury him."

"That sounds like work," said Jetsam. "Can't we just toss him into the swamp?"

"No," said Slate. "He may have been turned into a monster in death by Avaris, but in life he was a great champion of the church. He deserves better than to have his body tossed into some nameless swamp."

"I'll bet actual money the locals have a name for this place," said Jetsam.

"I'll build a coffin," Slate said. "I need to take his remains to a respectful resting place."

Sorrow couldn't hold her tongue. "Are you out of your mind? He tried to kill you! He was laughing as he tore new holes in your flesh!"

"You mistake the corpse for the man," Slate said. "Avaris perverted his remains. You witnessed her atrocities. You heard her casual boasts of wickedness." He glanced at her. "Or can it be, even with one eye nearly missing, you're still blind to her evil?"

Sorrow touched her face. With all the blood, Slate must have assumed that Avaris had attacked her. No one needed to know of the bargain made.

"You're right," she said. "I may have had, perhaps, an overly optimistic idea of the kind of person she was. But don't you see the same is true of Lord Tower? He was cruel in life as well as death. Disposing of him in the swamp is almost an insult to the swamp."

Slate pulled Tower's body completely free of the soft earth. The Witchbreaker was revealed in the dirt beneath. Faint howls of agony filled the night as Slate lifted the ebony blade. They fell silent as Slate slid the weapon back into its scabbard.

"A blade that that sends the souls of its victims to hell," said Sorrow. "Is that the weapon of a hero?"

"It is now," said Slate, slinging the scabbard over his shoulder.

"You're keeping the blade?" Bigsby asked. "I think having to hear those screams every time I used it would give me nightmares."

"A just man need not be disturbed by hell," said Slate. "After the events of this night, I understand the need for such a place, and the justice of it."

"Slate, listen to yourself!" Sorrow said, throwing her hands into the air. She quickly clamped them back over her breasts when she saw Jetsam's eyes bulge. She returned her focus to Slate, marching up and shouting, "You aren't a champion of the church! You're just a bit of magic that looks like a man. The church despises things like you and is dedicated to wiping them from existence!"

"However odd my origins, I'm a man," said Slate, remaining calm. "I may lack memories, but I have a conscience."

Sorrow sighed. She was confounded by Slate's reaction. But what would she want? That he would be outraged by his origins? Wouldn't that just make him hate witches? Did she desire that he be filled with despair? Of what use would he be if he were despondent, or suicidal?

"I'm sorry," she said. "You're right. You're a man, and a good one at that. I shouldn't have said that you weren't. I'm merely asking you to consider that, possibly, the real Lord Tower didn't quite live up to the ideals laid out in Poppy's book."

"That doesn't mean I can't," said Slate. "Whatever Lord Tower's sins may have been, I'm his second chance. I can live as the hero the world believed him to be."

"Is this settled?" Brand asked. "If we're going to build a coffin, that might take a while. I guess we can use wood from the cart, but we don't really have the right tools."

Sorrow shrugged. "If he must have a coffin, I can make one. With my wood weaving abilities, it won't take long."

She waded into the water to tear boards off the cart. The dark water was warm as a bathtub. She dipped beneath the surface to clean the blood from her face.

"And where exactly are we hauling him off to?" Bigsby asked.

"There's a vault for highly honored knights in the Cathedral of the Book," said Brand. "But going back to the Silver City is out of the question any time soon."

"Saints get air burials at the Temple of the Book," said Jetsam.

"Air burials?" asked Bigsby.

"The temple is high in the mountains of Raitingu," said Jetsam. "There's no real soil there, just rock, so bodies are left out for birds to devour. The left-over bones are put into an ossuary beneath the temple."

"It looks like the maggots aren't leaving anything for the birds," said Bigsby.

"The Temple of the Book," Slate said, as if he was trying to remember something. "That's where the One True Book was discovered? The birthplace of the church?"

"Yep," said Jetsam. "Kind of ironic, since now the place is surrounded by Stormies."

"Stormies?" asked Slate.

"The Isle of Storm is where Tempest dwells," said Brand. "For the last couple of centuries, the dragon has been worshipped as a god by the locals. Stormies isn't the most respectful way of addressing them."

Slate looked confused. "Why would men worship a dragon?"

"Why would men worship a book?" Jetsam asked.

"They don't worship a book. They worship its author," said Slate.

Jetsam held up four fingers, tapping them one by one as he said, "Church. Of. The..." He let the last word go unspoken as he stared at Slate.

Sorrow tossed the last of the boards she'd need onto the bank. She left the water, shaking her wings to dry them. Her strength had returned somewhat after her bath.

She began the work of fusing the coffin together. She took care to close the cracks in the old boards and smooth out any splinters. The cart had been in use for years, giving the wood a natural patina that sealed the pores. Once the body was inside, smell wouldn't be an issue.

Sorrow straightened up when her job was done, using her wings to shield herself from Jetsam's gaze from above as she stretched her back. "Once you gentlemen are done discussing religion, you can load the body. I trust you'll figure out how to get it back to the ship. I'm going to fly on ahead and rustle up some proper clothing."

She jumped, flapping her wings. She clenched her teeth, surprised by the effort required. It had definitely been easier to fly in the Black Bog. Back in the material world, climbing a hundred feet into the sky took almost as much energy as sprinting up a flight of stairs of equal height. She only made it to two hundred feet before she was forced to lock her wings as wide as she could and glide while she caught her breath. Her wings seemed to have the necessary power, but now that the rest of her body had returned to human proportions, her lungs felt inadequate to the task.

"People think flying's easy," Jetsam said, his voice just beneath her. She looked down and found he was doing a backstroke about fifty feet below. "But it's more like swimming. It wears you out fast if you aren't careful."

"I'll get better with practice," she said.

"You keeping the wings?" Jetsam asked. "I thought your whole reason for looking for Avaris was to return your body to normal."

"You saw how bloodied I was," said Sorrow. "Avaris wasn't exactly helpful."

"I hope you can explain that to Ma. She'll be upset I didn't deliver her letter."

"I'll talk to her," said Sorrow. "I'm sure she'll understand."

They passed over a freshly plowed field. Jetsam spun in the air until his back was facing her. He spread his arms and rose, just as air lifted her own wings.

"Follow me," Jetsam called out. "I know the types of land to watch for that produce updrafts. The air is full of currents. I can teach you how to ride them. You can cover twice the distance with half the effort."

"Lead on," she answered, as they swam among the stars.

IT WAS DAYBREAK when they returned to the *Circus*. Sage met them on deck. The second Jetsam's feet touched the planks, she said, "You still have the letter."

"You noticed."

"This surprises you?"

"Not in the least. Does Ma know yet?"

Sage shook her head. "She went to bed a little while ago. Go below and wake her."

As Jetsam ran below deck, Sage knelt and opened a satchel sitting beside her. "I noticed you've returned a bit altered. I hope you don't mind that I took the liberty of securing you some clothing."

"Mind? I'm unspeakably grateful!"

"Here are some pants. And I've cut the back from this blouse. You can slip it on from the front, then tie it around your neck and waist," said Sage.

"A seer and a tailor," said Sorrow, taking the clothes. "You're quite talented."

Sage shrugged. She said, in a neutral tone, "I count lip reading among my talents."

Sorrow froze for half a heartbeat as she pulled on the pants. She asked, "So, can you... can you see into the abstract realms?"

"Alas, no," said Sage. "You and Slate vanished from my sight the second you left the material world."

"Ah," Sorrow said, nodding. She smiled wistfully. "Too bad. You missed quite an adventure."

"I must have. It's not often that people leave this ship and return with entirely new body parts."

Sorrow looked up at her wings. "I don't think of these as new, so much as rearranged. I think my body still has the same amount of dragon mass. I was just able to move it into a more useful configuration."

"With the help of Avaris?"

"No, I pretty much did it just by wishing for it, but don't ask me how."

"So how did your meeting with Avaris go?"

Sorrow considered her answer as she tied her blouse shut behind her neck. "If you were watching, you saw that I returned from her palace with a rather nasty facial injury."

"True enough," said Sage. "But what's even more interesting is, you've returned with someone else's eye."

"What?" Sorrow asked, trying her best to scoff.

"Your left eye. It's different. Like it belongs to someone else entirely. You left with two auras and you've come back with three."

"Strange things happen in the abstract realms," said Sorrow.

"Strange things happen here as well," said Sage. "People my family trust have been known to betray us."

Sorrow didn't say anything.

"And I've been known to do very bad things to those who willingly place my family in danger."

"You've no reason to be worried about me. I can't explain what you think you're seeing, but, trust me, I'm perfectly fine. Everything's alright."

"No, it's not," a woman answered from behind. Sorrow turned to find Gale and Jetsam behind her. "Since we couldn't appeal to Avaris for aid, my mother is still trapped."

Sorrow nodded. "I'm sorry. But before I left for the Black

Bog, I investigated a solution to this problem. I explained things to Mama Knuckle, a highly skilled necromancer."

Gale's face brightened. "And she had an answer?"

"An answer, yes. A solution, probably not. Blood is ordinarily required to sustain souls. The *Freewind* had been prepared to house your mother's soul by having her blood dissolved in wine, which was used to soak the timbers. Unfortunately, while there may be some residue of your mother's blood in the figurehead, we'd never be able to soak a whole ship with it."

"Then there's no hope?" Gale asked.

Sorrow sighed. "I don't... I don't think so. Mama Knuckle said that it was possible for a family member to supply the blood. But it would require all the blood from an adult. Someone would have to die to restore your mother."

Gale shook her head. "A life is too high a price."

"Perhaps your mother's soul can still travel on to the Sea of Wine. You may see her again one day."

Gale still looked crestfallen. "I've failed."

"Grandmother had a good life, and was able to watch her grandchildren grow for many years after her natural death," said Sage. "You haven't failed her."

"I've failed everyone," said Gale.

"You've never struck me as someone prone to wallowing in self-pity," said Sorrow.

"This isn't self-pity. This is realism. The ship that was my family home has been lost. My family would have been broken up long ago if not for the *Freewind's* ability to sail the Sea of Wine. It kept us beyond the reaches of our enemies. Our supernatural speed meant that we could keep clients even as the oceans became increasingly dangerous to sail."

"We don't really need clients now," said Sage. "Brand's willing to foot the bills with his dragon-bone money."

"That's charity, not business," said Gale. She looked at Sorrow. "It's time to admit the larger truth. Even if the

Freewind hadn't been lost, my family would have been broken apart soon enough. Most Wanderer ships are crewed by forty or fifty people, with the core family supplemented by spouses and cousins and close friends who've outgrown the confines of other ships. I've extended a hundred offers to other ships to provide homes for excess crew, and been rebuffed each time."

"The pirate wars are still fresh in people's minds," Sorrow said. "In a few years, things will calm down."

Gale nodded. "But the calm won't lead others to join us. Instead, they'll accept us, one by one. Levi left our ship and married soon after. Sage, you've caught the eye of many a young man. How long before you're seduced away?"

"I wouldn't abandon you," said Sage.

"But don't you see? It wouldn't be abandonment. It wouldn't be betrayal. I've not created a ship where you can forge a future. I want you to be happy. I want you to know love, to form a family. If I'm honest with myself, I know that means you'll have to leave me. It breaks my heart, but it hurts more to think that you might not leave to pursue your own happiness."

"You certainly didn't take that attitude with Levi," Jetsam said, sounding skeptical.

Gale frowned. "I know I'm bitter. It's not as if the circumstances of Levi's departure were simple. He killed a man, then fled, then joined forces with some of our worst enemies."

"But only because he fell in love," said Sage. "And you know he thought he was defending you when he killed our dryman."

"You're not telling me anything I don't already know," said Gale. She sighed. "When he left, I still had hope that our friends and relatives would make peace with us. I felt like he left before I could really work things out. Now, I see I'll never make things right. All I can do is help each of you prepare for the day when you leave this ship to start your life anew."

"Is this why you keep making us call you Captain?" Jetsam asked.

Gale nodded. "I want you to have good habits for the day you serve on another ship."

"I don't think that's going to happen with me," said Jetsam.

"You say that now. But sooner or later, the lure of another ship will be irresistible."

"No," said Jetsam. "I mean, when I go, I don't think I'm going to live on another ship. The rest of you only see the world from its shorelines. I've been lucky enough to explore the landscapes of the islands we visit from above. I've got to tell you, the land looks a hell of a lot more interesting than the sea."

"Jetsam!" Sage said, sounding shocked.

"You would betray your culture?" Gale asked, her voice trembling.

"What's so special about our culture?" Jetsam asked. "I've been told since I was a toddler that Wanderers value individuality and freedom, but it seems to me like most of the other Wanderers look down on us because we're different. There's more than one way to live a life."

"If you feel that way, then go," Gale said. "Be like Levi. What's keeping you here?"

"Love," said Jetsam. "You mean the world to me. Everyone in this messed up family of ours is more important to me than all the stuff I've seen on land. Maybe one day our family will be scattered over a half dozen ships, pursuing different lives. But until that day comes, as long as the Romers man a ship, I plan to be part of that crew. That's just the way I feel, Captain."

He stepped forward and wrapped his arms around his mother. Gale hugged him back, tears in her eyes. "Ma," she said.

"Captain Ma," said Sage, as she wrapped her arms around the both of them.

Sorrow turned away, wiping her eyes. For some reason they were watering. At least, her right eye was. Her left eye was clenched into a contemptuous little slit, and despite all of her willpower she was unable to open it.

* * *

AFTER SLEEPING MUCH of the day, she went above deck in mid-afternoon. She knew that a winged woman walking around in plain sight might draw unwelcome attention to the *Circus*, but she and Jetsam had flown onto the ship together that morning, when the docks had been bustling with fishermen. By now, word that the *Circus* held monsters had to have spread to the far ends of the town.

What she didn't expect was to climb out of the hold and find the air cloying with the aroma of flowers and incense. Mako stood at the gangplank, arms crossed, looking annoyed as he stared at her.

"What?" she asked.

He nodded for her to look down the gangplank. The whole of the dock below was filled with vases of flowers, baskets of bright fruit, and hundreds of lit candles. Smoke wafted from incense burners scattered amid the colorful clutter.

"You've made an impression on the locals," said Mako. "They've been leaving offerings all day. A few have tried to get on the ship, but turn tail when I show my teeth."

"Offerings?" she asked, not sure she'd heard him correctly.

"Another name for Podredumbre is the Decaying Isles. Before he stopped manifesting bodily in the material world, Rott used to make his home here. Most of the locals publicly worship the Church of the Book, but in private they still live as if Rott is the lord of this place. Did you know that every year on the winter solstice, they dig up the bodies of their departed relatives and bring them back inside to sit at the table for a feast?"

"I've heard that," Sorrow said.

"Nice wings," said Mako.

Sorrow shrugged. "I haven't really had much of a chance to look at them." She walked down the gangplank. Some of the vases were made of blown glass, and a few of the incense burners were silver. She grabbed them and returned to the deck to make mirrors.

"You never struck me as the vain type," Mako said as he watched her turn to study herself in the looking glasses.

"This isn't vanity. It's curiosity." She ran her fingers along the inner folds of her wings. The scaleless flesh was smooth and soft as her inner thighs. "You'd understand if you ever grew a new body part over night."

Mako opened his massive jaws, his head tilting back so that his face effectively disappeared, leaving nothing but a gaping maw filled with rows of arrowhead teeth perched upon his shoulders. He closed his mouth and said, "I wasn't born like this, you know."

"You can't pretend you didn't spend a great deal of time studying your new mouth in the mirror," she said, as she stretched her wings to their fullest extent. Light seeped through the flesh at its thinnest points, revealing dark veins.

"I don't need to pretend," said Mako. "I don't look at myself in the mirror. Ever. The others may have gotten rewards from the Mer-King, but I've been given a curse."

"It can't all be bad," said Sorrow. "You seem to be a lot stronger than a normal man. I'm under the impression you can stay underwater a long time as well."

Mako shrugged. "Being strong and a good swimmer are normally things that girls find attractive. But girls stay far away from me. The few that do talk to me never stop staring at my teeth."

"I'm not a good person to talk to about romantic frustrations," said Sorrow, looking over her shoulder to study her back in the mirror. "I find the subject entirely uninteresting."

"You aren't interested in children?"

"In what way?" As she said this, the image of the head they'd found on the butcher block flashed into her mind.

"In having them."

"Oh. No. I think not."

"But you're estranged from your father," said Mako. "Don't you want a family of your own?"

She chuckled. "For now, I'll just keep borrowing yours."

CHAPTER FIFTEEN
STORMCALLER

By MIDNIGHT, THE dock next to the *Circus* glowed as bright as noon from all the candles. Along the waterfront, crowds had gathered, singing in a language Sorrow didn't understand.

At this point, all the Romers were awake and on deck. Mako seemed especially highly strung as he paced along the railing.

"Calm down," Sage said as she stared into her spyglass. "There's no point in getting worked up. I'll see if anyone tries to board, but I don't think anyone's going to bother us. Listen to the music. This isn't some battle anthem. It's a hymn. They aren't here to hurt us."

"It's still spooky," Cinnamon said from her perch in the rigging. "Look at all the coffins."

Sorrow had made note of them herself. The local mausoleums had apparently been emptied out. For all the living people in the crowd, there were just as many coffins, lids open, their skeletal contents lifted for a better view of the ship.

Poppy was balanced on the rail near the gangplank, steadying herself with a hand on the rigging. "If anyone tries to bring a coffin on board, I'm popping it to the moon."

"This might be a good time to talk about Slate," Jetsam said to Sorrow.

"Right," said Sorrow. Then, addressing the rest of the Romers, "Slate and the others are bringing back a coffin."

"I know," said Sage. "They're almost here. The crowds are slowing them down."

"I see them too!" Jetsam cried out.

Sorrow's eyes followed Jetsam's pointing finger. She couldn't make much sense of the jumble of humanity before her. Finally, she saw a coffin held higher than the others. She recognized the coffin she'd made, and watched as Slate and Brand pushed their way through the crowd to the dock. Each was holding up one end of the casket. Bigsby walked between them. He broke free as they neared the gangplank and rushed back aboard the ship.

"I thought I was going to be trampled to death," he said, gasping.

Slate and Brand marched up the gangplank and laid the closed coffin carefully onto the deck. Brand glanced at Sorrow. "So," he said. "You seem… popular."

"How can you be sure they're here to see me?"

"Because street venders are selling little winged dolls woven from marsh grass and cornhusks." He produced one of the dolls from his pocket. The cornhusk wings had been dyed black with squid ink. "They're saying the Death Angel has come to free them from their oppressors."

Sorrow eyed the spires of the nearest church.

"Don't," said Brand.

"Give me one reason why I shouldn't," said Sorrow.

"Because if you lead this mob on a church-burning rampage, you'll only be setting the stage for tragedy."

"I'll be helping to lift the colonial boot from their neck," said Sorrow.

"Let's say you spark a rebellion. Once news reaches the Silver City, the king will simply launch his navy to retake this town. Or maybe the Isle of Storm will hear about the rebellion and decide that now's a good time to stage an invasion. Maybe you'll get a thrill from watching these churches burn. Will you get an equal thrill when tens of thousands of people die from the war you trigger?"

Sorrow clenched her fists. "How am I at fault if there's war? The blame falls upon the king who claimed land not his own in the first place! For too long in this world, we've accepted that might makes right. Is it not better to die free than to live in fear?"

"That philosophy is the foundation of my life," said Gale. "But if these people long for freedom, they must seize it themselves. They have the power to set fire to a church or a jail. Instead, they light candles beseeching you to save them."

"If I have the power to save them, shouldn't I?"

"If you lead them to war tonight, are you willing to remain here for years to come to lead them into peace?" Gale asked. "Are you a builder? Or only a destroyer?"

Sorrow turned her back to the crowd. Her body felt like a spring that had been wound for fifteen years. Now was the time to release a lifetime of tension and achieve her first important victory against the church.

She took a deep breath, opening her hands, staring into them. She knew Brand had a point. The king would only send his navy. With all the wealth and worshippers commanded by the Church of the Book, any church she watched burn tonight would be rebuilt within a year. Leading these people might win a fleeting battle, but would do nothing toward winning her war.

"You're right," she said, tersely. "It's not worth the price. Let's depart for Raitingu before I change my mind."

"Raitingu?" Rigger asked. "Why, exactly, are we going to the Isle of Storm?"

Slate answered. "This coffin holds the mortal remains of Lord Stark Tower. I feel it's my duty to deliver them to the Temple of the Book."

"Stark Tower?" Rigger asked. "The Witchbreaker? Are you sure?"

Slate drew the ebony sword from the scabbard on his back. The howls of the damned gibbered around him. "I'm reasonably sure."

"That is so windswept!" Poppy said, jumping down and running up to stare at the blade.

"Windswept?" asked Slate.

"It means amazing, or wonderful," said Jetsam.

"Can I hold it?" Poppy asked.

"I don't think that's wise," said Slate as he slid the blade back into the scabbard. "Carrying the sword is a great responsibility. For now, its burden must be mine alone."

"Still, wow, we've got a magic sword and a quest to travel to a legendary temple," said Poppy. "This is just like the stories!"

Rigger cleared his throat. "Excuse me, but may I be the voice of reason and point out that Raitingu is an insanely dangerous place for us to visit?"

"When has that ever stopped us?" asked Jetsam.

"Our biggest advantage at sea is Ma's ability to control winds," said Rigger. "Maybe you're unaware the priestesses who serve Tempest are known as stormcallers? They not only control wind, they also command rain and lightning."

"And we control kicking butts," said Jetsam. "Let them try to mess with us."

"What about Levi?" Rigger asked.

That brought looks of concern to the faces of all the Romers.

"What about Levi?" asked Sorrow. "He was helpful when his hurricane came to our rescue north of Skell."

"If we meet him near Raitingu, he'll be defending the island," said Rigger. "Are we really going to go there and possibly fight our own brother?"

Gale walked toward the wheel. "If we face Levi in battle, it's because of choices he made, not us." She took the wheel in hand. "In the meantime, we're sailors. We go where the owner of the ship commands. So, Brand, what say you?"

"Sorry, Rigger," said Brand. "Going to Raitingu makes sense to me as well."

"Why? To bury some dead knight?"

"No. Because my father had business contacts there. I know several of them from a trip I took with my father when I was a teenager. Going there gives me a chance to make my case to them that my father's economic empire should belong to me and Bigsby, not that gold-digger living in his mansion."

"I thought you didn't want to run your father's business," said Sorrow. "I thought you were happy to start a new life where you could make your own fame and fortune."

"I am," said Brand. "But that doesn't mean I want some woman I don't even know to enjoy the fruits of my father's labor. She can't do what she's done to me and not expect to face the most horrible revenge I can dream of."

"You're going to kill her?" asked Sorrow.

"I'm going to sue her," said Brand. "There are hundreds of lawyers in the Silver City who would like a piece of the Cooper fortune. With a few letters and the testimony of my father's business partners, I'm going to wage a legal battle against my stepmother that will strip her of every last moon. She wants to use the law against me? Two people can play at this game."

"I didn't know you had a vengeful streak," said Sorrow. "I like it."

WEEKS LATER, EIGHTY miles out from Raitingu, the sea grew rough and choppy. Jetsam had been training Sorrow with daily practice flights since they left port, but the winds were so strong this morning that she kept being forced back into the rigging.

Jetsam stood in the ropes next her. She shouted, "It's getting too dangerous. We should just go back down."

"Oh?" He grinned. "You only want to fly in good weather?"

"Could you fly in this?"

"Sort of. It's more like body surfing, only the waves are invisible. Once the wind gets this bad, you ride where it takes you."

"When your mother wakes up, will she calm things down?"

"Maybe a little. But we're close to the city of Kaikou, at the mouth of the Ookawa river. That's where the cloud giants' hurricane ships anchor when they need to take on supplies.

They slow their winds when they're over the city, but even at their lowest speed it's like being caught in a tropical storm."

"Hurricane ships?" Sorrow said. "Do you think Levi will be there?"

"Maybe."

"I didn't really get to talk to him much, but he seemed nice enough. How did he wind up getting involved with the Storm Guard?"

"It's really more a matter of getting involved with a cloud giantess. Tempest forces all the cloud giants to serve in his military, even though they're by nature gentle creatures. But when you live on clouds, and the dragon who has absolute control over clouds asks you to do something, you do it."

Cold rain began to spatter against Sorrow's wings. Worse, Sorrow had gotten used to Gale keeping the ship reasonable steady. Up here in the rigging, the pitching and swaying of the ship left her stomach lurching.

"It might be time to go below deck," she said.

"Aw, it's just a little water," said Jetsam. "I need to stay on watch until Sage wakes up, but you go on down."

Sorrow climbed carefully to the deck. The rigging grew increasingly slick as the rain set in with a vengeance. She wasn't completely vulnerable to the elements. Bigsby had modified the cloak he'd made for her. It didn't fit over her wings, but it served as a hooded shawl that protected her shoulders and head. Still, even with her head covered, her body was quickly drenched. She saw Rigger at the wheel, standing beneath a canopy made of a loose sail stretched between taut ropes that shielded him from the rain.

He shrugged as he watched her shivering and said, "There's room for two."

She tried to shield herself with her wings as she traversed the rolling deck, but the wetter they got the colder she felt. Her teeth were chattering by the time she made it under the canopy.

"Who says you don't have sense enough to come in from the rain?" Rigger said.

She studied his face, unable to tell if she was being insulted. Though Rigger was only two years older than Jetsam, his thin face was marked by worry lines. He held out a steel flask. "Take a swig of this to warm yourself."

"I don't drink alcohol."

"It's only tea. I can't keep it in a cup or it would slosh out."

She took the flask, grateful for the warmth as she wrapped her fingers around it. She took a sip and nearly spit it out. It was unbearably bitter. "What is that?" she managed to ask despite the numbness spreading across her tongue.

"Just tea. A few cloves as well."

"It doesn't taste like tea."

"You've probably had the dainty version where you steep the leaves then drink the runoff. I crush the dried leaves into a fine powder before mixing it with the water. It gives it a little kick."

"Kick is right. My mouth feels numb."

"That's the cloves. They deaden my ability to taste anything."

"If you don't like the taste, then why—"

"Because it keeps me alert. When I'm hooked into the ropes, it's like my fingers are hundreds of yards long. I'm touching every part of the ship. I feel so much that it's easy to get distracted. The tea helps me focus."

Sorrow nodded. She had to admit, a single mouthful had certainly made her feel more awake. Sorrow gave the flask back to Rigger, who took a long swig before slipping it back into his pocket. His face showed signs of strain as he pulled the ropes wrapped around his arms.

"Is it tough sailing in weather like this?"

"Are you just making small talk?" he asked. "You can't possibly think that there's anything easy about sailing a ship this size by myself. It's difficult even in good weather."

"Maybe I am just making small talk. We've been at sea together for months since I first met you aboard the *Freewind*, but I don't think we've even talked for ten minutes."

"That's because I'm always working or sleeping. Did you know when I was born, the *Freewind* had a crew of forty-three people? My aunt Rosemary's family lived on board then. She has eleven children, and four of them were married by the time I came along."

"And the war drove them away?"

Rigger shook his head. "Ma tells people it was the war, but, really, it was me. Once she discovered I was all the crew she needed, she quit having to compromise and cooperate with other Wanderers in order to keep her ship in business. I kept taking on more and more responsibility, wrapping myself in more and more ropes, not completely understanding how tied up I was becoming. Everyone else on this ship gets to dream about one day leaving and starting a life their own. I'm bound to this ship until Ma quits, and that's not going to happen."

"You might be surprised."

"Nothing surprises me any more," said Rigger.

"Haven't I heard you proven wrong after saying that?"

"On the small scale. On the large scale, my life is depressingly predictable."

"If you feel that way, why don't you quit? I understand how another ship might not be eager to take on Mako, but any captain would have to instantly recognize your worth."

"I wouldn't go to any ship that wouldn't hire Mako," said Rigger. "And, while I gripe about mother's unwillingness to compromise, I couldn't work aboard a ship that transported slaves. Also, while another Captain might welcome me, would another crew? I suspect my presence aboard a ship might cause some resentment. My magical gift might be useful, but I don't pretend that I'm not a freak. Everyone aboard this ship is. So, my perfect job would be upon a ship that was anti-slave, welcoming to freaks, and where no one resented my talents." He managed a grim smile. "I know of only one ship that meets these criteria, and I already have a bunk there."

*   *   *

SORROW RETURNED TO the hold and sat in the dark and relative quiet, to be alone with her thoughts. Of course, her hope was for the exact opposite, which was to find company in her thoughts, via the link Avaris had told her would be established once they traded eyes. Since embarking for the Isle of Storm, she'd tried meditating several times daily, in hopes of quieting her own thoughts enough that Avaris could be heard. It hadn't worked yet.

It wasn't working now.

Hours passed before Gale and Mako could be heard in the hall, returning to the deck. Sorrow gave up on her futile attempt at finding Avaris within her own skull and decided to join them above.

"Can I go get some sleep now?" Rigger asked as his mother approached. "I should get a little rest before we hit the eye. We'll be needing to adjust the sails then."

"I'm afraid there's no time for that," Sage said, calling down from the crow's nest. "You don't need magic to see that we're coming toward the eye of the storm now."

Sorrow looked forward and could see the sky brightening in the distance. Gale guided the buffeting winds to the tail of the ship and pushed it toward the light. A few minutes later, the wind calmed and the rain gave way to sunlight. The eye of the hurricane was an almost perfect circle of calm several miles across. Ahead were two stone mountains, rising at steep angles toward the heavens. In between the two mountains was a valley cut through by a broad river. The banks of this river were thick with thousands of almost perfectly square buildings with roofs of woven bamboo. Roads rose up from the city, winding along the steep mountain cliffs, disappearing among the clouds. To Sorrow's surprise, rope bridges ran from the mountains out into seemingly thin air. Men moved along the bridges, guiding large goats harnessed to carts piled high with barrels and baskets. They vanished into a dense bank of roiling clouds that seemed to hang in a stationary position above the city.

"By the winds!" Rigger said, his eyes growing wide. "That's Levi's ship! The *Thunder!*"

"Wonderful," Gale muttered.

Sorrow stared at the heavens. "How can you tell? They look no different from any other clouds."

Sage traced her fingers in the air. "See those wispy white clouds? Kind of like little squiggles? They're the ship's markings."

Sorrow tried to follow Sage's gaze, but it was hopeless. All she could see were clouds.

By now, word had somehow spread below deck that Levi's ship had been sighted and all the Romer children came up top. Brand and Bigsby followed close behind.

Slate was the last to come on deck, shielding his eyes as he studied the city. They were close enough now that Sorrow could make out individual people. The city resembled an anthill in its frantic activity. Every street and alley was thick with men and women carrying loads back and forth.

"Why do they all look alike?" Slate asked.

"By law, all the citizens dress identically," said Rigger. "Male or female, they all wear gray pants, gray shirts, sandals and straw hats. Both sexes wear their hair in the same ugly bowl cut."

"It's worse than just clothing," said Gale. "Everyone here looks alike, at least within age groups. They practice infanticide against any child born with a visible flaw, even harmless birthmarks."

"Thank the divine author that I come from a more civilized society, where flawed babies are sold to carnivals instead of being killed," said Bigsby.

"Why would people live like this?" Slate asked.

"While the destruction of newborns is inexcusable, other aspects of the life here strike me as superior to life elsewhere," said Sorrow. "All the citizens are provided with matching clothes, identical houses, and equal shares of food. It's a society without wealth or poverty. It's far more fair than the feudal system of the Silver Isles, where a handful of families control the majority of the wealth."

"They may be equal, but they have no individuality or freedom," said Jetsam, hanging upside down in the rigging. "They're kind of anti-Wanderers."

"And Tempest is their king? They're ruled by a dragon?" Slate asked, sounding distressed.

"Tempest is their god," said Rigger. "From birth, they're ingrained with his philosophy. *The lone raindrop is powerless, but a storm can wash away mountains.* The people believe their lives only have meaning as tiny parts of a larger whole."

"But, to have no hope of advancement or growth…" Slate said, letting his thoughts trail off.

Rigger said, "They aren't completely without hope. Men can increase their status by joining the Storm Guard and rising in military rank. Women can serve in the shrines built to Tempest, and some go on to great honor as stormcallers."

"Speaking of which," said Sage, who was listening above, "we're about to have company."

Two ships were approaching, both packed with armed men. Unlike the gray, loose-fitting clothing worn by the townsmen, these men were dressed in tight black coats lined with brass buttons. Golden lightning bolts decorated their shoulders. They wore leather bucklers on their forearms and swords that hung from their waists to their ankles.

"Are we in for a fight?" Sorrow asked.

"I'm sure this is just a routine inspection like we faced in Port Hallelujah," said Brand. "Despite the uniformity imposed on the citizens, Kaikou is actually a fairly cosmopolitan port. Most of the world's iron is shipped out of here, so they're welcoming toward people visiting for business. Even among dragon worshipers, money trumps philosophy."

Gale nodded in agreement. "Also, the city makes a lot of money from the steady stream of pilgrims visiting the Temple of the Book. We'll tell them that's why we're here. They'll name a docking fee, we'll pay it, and that should be the end of their interest in us."

"I should get below deck," said Sorrow.

"That would have been an excellent idea about thirty seconds ago," said Sage. "Judging from the way the stormcaller on the lead ship is holding her spyglass, she's just spotted you. We'll have to tell them that you're a half-seed."

"Not that they're fond of half-seeds," said Mako.

"Things will work out," said Gale. "Everyone keep their mouths shut and let me do the talking and we'll be done with this in moments."

Slate crossed his arms and glared as Gale ordered Rigger to trim the sails, allowing the ships to pull alongside. Gale had Poppy and Cinnamon lower rope ladders to give the boarding parties easier access. She donned her captain's hat and buttoned her coat, standing beside Rigger with her arms clasped behind her.

Eight soldiers climbed aboard, four from each ship. They stood at attention beside the ladders as a woman climbed up from the ship on the starboard side and a man who was obviously an officer boarded from the port. The officer's uniform was identical to those of his men, save for three golden lightning bolts on each shoulder and a sword with a decorative scabbard, inlaid with blue stones forming a stylized dragon. The stormcaller wore black robes, and if Gale hadn't informed her that stormcallers were women, she wouldn't have known. The black robes hid the shape of her body, and her face was concealed behind an azure dragon's mask. She carried a three-foot rod carved from clear quartz crystal that glowed with an aura separate from that of the woman.

"Captain," the uniformed man said, bowing toward Gale. "Welcome to Raitingu. I'm Inspector Rim. My companion is Stormcaller Lotus. Please order all your crew and passengers to the deck."

"We're all accounted for," said Gale. "No one is below."

"Truly?" Rim asked, his eyebrows raised. "Such a small crew for a ship this size?"

"Our crew was once larger," Gale said. "We're doing what we can until I recruit more."

"What's the purpose of your visit?" Rim asked.

"This man is on a pilgrimage," said Gale, nodding toward Slate. "He carries the mortal remains of his father to the Temple of the Book."

Rim looked at Slate. "You would sail all this way to dispose of a corpse? He must have been a very important man."

"Important to me," said Slate.

Rim walked closer to Slate. Slate was once again dressed in his glass armor, which Sorrow had repaired after they returned to the ship.

"This is unusual armor," he said. "Are you a soldier?"

"A knight," said Slate.

Rim ran his fingers along the glass scales. "Is it dragon hide?" he asked.

"Just glass," said Slate.

Rim looked skeptical. He turned back toward Gale. "Unfortunately, it's illegal to transport a corpse to our land. We must confiscate the body."

"Illegal?" said Gale. "Since when?"

"Kaikou is a city of half a million people," said Rim. "Corpses can spread illness."

"Getting your drinking water from the same river you dump your sewage into might also cause a few sniffles," said Rigger.

Gale shot a glance at him.

Rigger shrugged. "Sorry, that just came out."

Gale sighed. "We're but humble Wanderers, Inspector, ignorant of your laws. If there are permits required to transport a coffin to the Temple, we understand. Would a fee of fifty moons acquire the necessary permissions?"

Rim chuckled. "Fifty moons? This man's dragon-hide armor is worth a hundred times that. A thousand."

"What if we give you the armor?" Gale asked, aware of its relatively humble origins.

Lotus interrupted, shaking her head. "Inspector, the knight speaks the truth. The armor is not dragon hide."

"You're certain?" he asked, sounding disappointed.

"The claw of Tempest caressed my cheek at our wedding," said Lotus. "I'm intimately familiar with dragon skin. This man does not possess it." Her masked face turned toward Sorrow. "This woman, however, does. Look at her wings."

Rim looked at Sorrow. "What manner of beast are you?"

"Just a half-seed," she said.

"There are no dragon half-seeds," Rim said. "The fetus would be fatal to any mother."

"What if my father was human and my mother was a dragon?" Sorrow asked, knowing Rim would probably find the answer insulting. She respected Gale's desire to talk and bribe their way past these guards, but her gut level hatred of men trying to exercise authority over her was nearly impossible to suppress.

He nodded toward his men. Two of them flanked him as they approached Sorrow. On an unseen signal, all three men drew their swords.

"I apologize for the woman," Gale said. "Her half-animal nature has left her dimwitted. Please ignore her babbling."

"Remove your hood," Rim said, as he fixed his eyes on Sorrow's face.

Sorrow smiled as she obeyed. The look on Rim's face as he spotted the nails on her scalp was quite satisfying.

"Witch!" Rim shouted. In unison, he and his men drove their swords into her belly. Luckily, her command over iron made her skin even better than dragon hide against their blades. The swords folded limply against her stomach.

"Down!" Lotus cried as the three men stood gawking at their ruined weapons. At her command, they threw themselves to the deck. Lotus pointed her crystal rod at Sorrow and shouted, "Khong!"

Sorrow spread her wings as brightness flared within the crystal, but suspected she wasn't going to get out of the way in time.

Slate threw himself in front of her as a loud *CRACK* filled the air. An arc of brilliant white light sliced into Slate's armored chest, vanishing as quickly as it struck. In the aftermath, Slate looked none the worse for wear. The stormcaller raised the glass rod toward the sky and began screaming out a prayer. Poppy dropped down from the riggings, balanced on the woman's shoulders for a heartbeat, then vaulted to the deck as the woman shot toward the clouds, her prayer changing to a shriek. Her azure mask and the crystal rod clattered as they fell to the deck.

Sorrow blinked and suddenly there were dozens of Storm Guard spilling over the rails. Rigger grimaced as a score of ropes snaked toward them. The soldiers proved remarkably coolheaded in the face of such a strange assault and deftly leapt over the dancing hemp, slicing ropes with their swords as they charged toward Slate and Sorrow.

The air around the *Circus* sounded like an orchestra of harps being plucked as soldiers climbed the rigging of their ships and began to shower arrows toward the *Circus*. A whirling wind knocked the missiles off their path as Gale cried, "Don't kill anyone!"

Mako froze with his jaws half an inch away from Rim's throat. "Are you serious?" he growled.

"If no one dies, we might still bribe our way out of this," Gale shouted. "If we kill anyone, we're going to have to flee this port. That's not what Brand hired us for."

Brand said, "I also didn't hire you to be pin-cushions. Do what you must to defend yourselves!"

"Storm Guard!" a voice thundered from above, so loud it sounded as if a giant had shouted it. "Stand down!"

Sorrow looked up. A giant *had* shouted it. A man one hundred feet tall was walking down a staircase of wispy clouds. He was dressed in a uniform similar to the one worn by Rim, but with so many lightning bolts they jagged together to form a chain all the way around his shoulders. In his open palm he carried the stormcaller. The front of her robes were flecked with vomit.

"Levi!" Jetsam shouted, as the storm guard lowered their weapons.

"That's Commander Leviathan to you," Levi said, as he stepped onto threads of fog that rose up from the sea. He lowered Lotus carefully back to the deck of her ship, then drew a crystalline battle axe that sparked with static from a holster on his back. The head of the axe was the size of a mainsail. He gripped the weapon with both hands as his eyes narrowed. "Did you really believe you could strike a beloved bride of Tempest and not face my righteous wrath? Surrender at once, or face destruction!"

CHAPTER SIXTEEN
PATH OF THE PILGRIM

LEVI RAISED HIS weapon overhead to strike. Sorrow bounded across the deck and grabbed the crystalline lightning rod. She raised it toward Levi, prepared to shout, "Khong!" but before she could finish inhaling, Mako tackled her, knocking the breath from her lungs. He pinned her to the deck, her wings folded painfully beneath her.

"We surrender!" Mako shouted, craning his neck toward the sky.

Sorrow was almost as shocked by these words as she was by the tackle. Mako wasn't known for avoiding fights.

"We most certainly do not surrender!" Gale shouted, raising her hands toward Levi, whose hair began to flutter in the wind.

"Brand!" Sage shouted. "It's your ship! Order Ma to give up!"

"Gale," said Brand, "Give up."

Gale clenched her jaw, her lips pressed tightly together.

Brand cupped his hands and called out, "I own this ship and I surrender!"

Gale turned her back to Brand, folding her arms across her chest. The wind that stirred Levi's locks vanished.

"A wise choice," Levi said as he sheathed his ax. He looked down at Inspector Rim's ship. "Carry on with your duties," he said. "I personally will take these foreign heathens into custody."

Rim frowned.

"Is something displeasing you, Inspector?" asked Levi. "Speak freely."

Rim looked like he was in pain as he said, "Should we trust these foreigners into the custody of someone who is himself a foreigner?"

Levi ran his fingers along the chain of lightning bolts encircling his shoulders. "That's Commander Foreigner to you, Inspector. Your trust is not required, only your obedience."

Rim bowed deeply. "As you say, commander."

Mako rose, freeing Sorrow, as Rim barked out orders for the two ships to leave.

"I'm sorry if I hurt you," Mako said.

Sorrow said nothing, ignoring the hand he held out to help her rise. There was a cold pit in the center of her belly. She worried that if she opened her mouth, dark energy would spew out and reduce Mako to bone.

A woman's voice screamed in her left ear, *Don't fear this power! Master it! You'll never learn to control Rott's power if you shun all opportunities to unleash it!*

Sorrow turned her head. No one stood beside her. Perhaps sitting quietly in the dark had been the wrong strategy for inducing Avaris to teach her. But this lesson would have to wait for another time. She breathed deeply, calming herself. The tension in her stomach seeped away. She took Mako's outstretched hand.

"Are you alright?" he asked.

You're a weakling and a coward!

Mako showed no reaction to the angry voice, though it was so loud Sorrow was surprised other people couldn't hear it.

"I'm fine," she answered softly.

As the two ships departed, Levi knelt next to the *Circus*. He smiled broadly and said, "Rescuing you guys is turning into a full-time job."

He placed his fingers on the deck of the boat and Poppy and Cinnamon ran up to hug them. Jetsam swam through the air to hover in front of his brother's face. "I knew you wouldn't hit us!"

"I needed to put on a show, though," said Levi. "Most of the Storm Guard are suspicious of me thanks to my foreign origins. They hate that I've become commander of a hurricane in such a short time."

"We knew you were a good sailor, but it's impressive that you've risen in the ranks so quickly," said Jetsam.

Levi shook his head. "It's all dumb luck. When I met Flutter and fell in love, I had no idea she was the daughter of Commander Rumble. He only accepted me as part of his crew because Flutter threatened to live out the remainder of her life on land with me if he didn't."

"That's romantic," said Poppy. "Like something from a story book."

"The story books skip over the hard parts, I'm afraid," said Levi.

"Like betraying your family by joining the armed forces of their enemy?" Gale asked, still not looking back at him.

"You're not seeing the story from my perspective," said Levi. "At the time, I'd lost my power to shrink back to human size. I'd been forced to leave behind my life as a Wanderer simply because there were no ships I could board without capsizing them. I thought I was fated to live out my life alone, on a desert island, until Flutter looked down and spotted me. My choice to join the Storm Guard had nothing to do with politics. It was my only chance to live a normal life."

"You live in a cloud," said Jetsam.

"Which feels curiously normal after a while."

Gale shook her head. "It's one thing to join their crew. Now you command their forces?"

Levi shrugged. "Again, dumb luck. What I didn't know about cloud giants when I went to live among them is that they might be huge as clouds, but they're also just as fleeting. They go from babies to adulthood in about six months. The average cloud giant lives only seven years. A few truly ancient specimens make it to ten. This means there's a lot of churn in the ranks aboard any cloud ship. In the human world, I'm still wet behind the ears. Among the giants, I'm practically an immortal, and treated like I'm in possession of some special age-imbued wisdom."

"Are you?" asked Jetsam.

"Only if heartbreak is wisdom," said Levi. "I live in a world where anyone who becomes important in my life passes away almost before I get to know them. I was seventeen when I met Flutter. She wasn't even a year old, but already considered something of an old maid among the giants. She passed away last year, just after her fifth birthday."

"Oh, Levi," Sage said. "I'm so sorry."

Levi smiled wistfully. "She had a good life. I've learned a lot about living for the moment. You have to drink every bit of life that flows into your cup today, because the cup might fall from your hand tomorrow."

"Why didn't you tell us this when you helped rescue us when the *Freewind* was sinking?" asked Sage.

"You guys had your own problems. I knew Ma's heart was breaking to lose that ship. I didn't want you to worry about me just because I'd lost someone I loved."

Gale's shoulders sagged. "I'm sorry for your loss," she said, turning to look at him. "But what about the loss of all those Wanderers who fought on our side during the pirate wars? Every day, we received reports of some new ship lost at sea to the Storm Guard's hurricane fleet. How did the lives of Wanderers become so cheap to you?"

Levi shook his head. "It's not that simple. I didn't start the war. Cloud giants don't even keep slaves. Pygmies just fall through the clouds. Even after you drink the zephyr elixir, you still need really big feet to get any traction on mist."

"We Wanderers didn't start the war either," Gale said.

"I'm almost entirely certain you did," said Levi. "And you had good reason to. Every time I return to this port, I watch Wanderer ships hired by slavers unload their human cargo at the pygmy market. It turns my stomach to see people in chains, sold to the highest bidder. If I'd already been commander when the war started, I would have done anything I could to tip the battles in your favor. Alas, I wasn't in command of the ships."

"You still could have changed things."

Levi nodded. "The question of what I should have done burns in my mind every single day. Unfortunately, what I should have done has to be weighed against what I could have done. Giants have learned the art of steering the winds and shepherding clouds together into semi-stable structures to live upon. But they don't actually make clouds. If they ever earned the wrath of Tempest, he could simply blink his eyes and the clouds we live upon would evaporate. The dragon holds the power of life and death over every last giant. As long as there are giants in my life that I cherish, that means Tempest controls me."

Sage asked, "Did you have children?"

Levi shook his head. "No. I don't know if humans and giants can't interbreed, or if there was just something about the two of us. But even though we had no kids of our own, her brothers and sisters were quite prolific. There's about three hundred cloud giants who call me 'uncle.' If I were to openly defy Tempest, it would be bad for all of them."

"Giants need not live on clouds," said Gale. "As a race, you could free yourself from Tempest's power just by moving back to land. It's where giants lived long ago, before discovering the zephyr potion."

"True enough," said Levi. "And Wanderers could avoid the whole slaving controversy just by giving up the sea."

Gale didn't respond to that.

Levi said, "Just because my new family is important to me doesn't mean I don't still love you guys. Why have you come here? What can I do to help?"

Brand stepped forward to explain his situation and tell Levi about Slate's quest.

Levi answered, "I'll tow the *Circus* to the slave market. There's a dock next to it reserved for ships under quarantine. We can anchor you there and no one will mess with you. I can arrange the proper travel permits so a few of you can leave the ship. I suppose we need three, for Brand and Bigsby and Slate?"

Four! Avaris shouted, so loud that Sorrow flinched.

Her sudden motion caught Levi's eye. "Yes?"

"I need a permit as well," Sorrow said. "I'm going to the Temple of the Book."

Slate looked at her with unmasked suspicion.

"What?" she asked. "If I wouldn't burn churches at Port Hallelujah, do you think I'm dumb enough to walk into the most sacred sanctuary of the church and try to pick a fight?"

"Then why would you come?" asked Slate.

Tell him you love him and cannot bear the thought of not being at his side.

"I most certainly will not," said Sorrow.

"I'm confused," Bigsby said. "Are you going or aren't you?"

Men are simple creatures. You'll gain great power over him if he thinks you desire him.

"Shut up," Sorrow said.

"I'm just asking," said Bigsby.

"I just... I guess I'm still a little scatterbrained from where Mako banged my head into the deck."

"I said I was sorry," said Mako.

"Apology accepted," said Sorrow. "So, let me be clear, I'm not going with Slate because I in anyway find him attractive."

Eyebrows shot up around the deck. Slate looked especially surprised.

"I'm going because I've spent my whole life hating people who worship a stupid book. And I've never even seen this book. I mean, what if there's something about this religion that I'm just not getting because I haven't taken the time to really try to understand?"

"This is... open-minded of you," said Brand.

Sorrow shrugged. "A lot of things changed in the swamps of Podredumbre. It's not just my body that got rearranged. I'm starting to see I might have the same vulnerability to blind faith that I accuse my enemies of. I give you my word I'm not going to this temple looking for trouble."

"That's twice you've mentioned Podredumbre," said Levi. "You wouldn't have anything to do with the uprising there, would you?"

"What uprising?" Sorrow asked.

"We've gotten reports that the residents killed King Brightmoon's governor two weeks ago. The whole island is in a state of anarchy."

"That's just after we left," said Jetsam.

"But we didn't start a revolution," said Sorrow. "Not directly, at least. And, I promise, I'm not going to start anything here."

Slate still looked skeptical, but said, "The path of the pilgrim is open to anyone who cares to walk it. I cannot tell you to remain on the ship."

They believe your words, said Avaris. *We both know you're going to the temple with malice in your heart.*

"I'm going because you told me to!" whispered Sorrow.

"What's that?" said Bigsby.

"Nothing," said Sorrow.

As Levi grabbed the jibboom in his massive hand to tow the *Circus*, Sorrow turned and ran below deck, whacking her wings against the edge of the hatch as she descended. Once she was out of earshot of the others, she said, "Now is a fine time for you do decide to speak to me. You've been inside my head for two weeks. Why haven't you said anything?"

I saw no purpose. By now you must have noticed that Rott's power tries to enter your body during moments of stress. You've spent the last two weeks in calm meditation. And out at sea, if you'd summoned Rott's powers, there was no one to harm but your shipmates. Now that you're in a city of enemies, you'll have more suitable targets to focus your power upon.

"Fine," said Sorrow. "But couldn't you have explained things before now? Have you been watching and hearing me this whole time? Why haven't I seen or heard things you've experienced?"

You haven't experienced my senses because I do not wish you to. As for whether I've been watching you continuously, I've actually given you little thought. As you've just learned, events in my corner of the material world have been turbulent. Many have sought my aid. No evening goes by when the child of some colonial master isn't presented to me as an offering. My castle has engorged itself with their fat souls.

"Are you trying to provoke me?" Sorrow asked. "Are you purposefully boasting of such evil deeds as some sort of test?"

It would be convenient for me if you believed that it was only a test, wouldn't it?

Sorrow clenched her jaw. Just what kind of creature had she made her bargain with? But knowledge was knowledge, and Avaris obviously knew more about magic than anyone else Sorrow had ever met. A man who trained in the use of a sword could use that skill either for murder or for the defense of his family. Just because Sorrow would learn from a person with corrupted morals didn't mean that she herself would follow the same path into darkness.

The first thing you must do is protect the rod you've stolen.

Sorrow had almost forgotten about the lightning rod. She looked at the yard-long crystal she carried. Here in the shadowy hold, its inner light was quite brilliant.

Stormcallers can sense the weapon and will soon send enforcers to recover it. You must mask it at once with bands of negation. Since you weave iron, I assume you know how to make these?

"Yes," said Sorrow. She found one of the swords she'd used when training with Slate, tore off fist-sized wads of metal and molded them into rings around the shaft. Most energetic magics were baffled by iron barriers.

Excellent. The lightning rod is more than just a powerful attack. It absorbs any lightning directed toward it. Even Tempest could not harm you with his electrical bite.

"Will the rod work even with the negating bands?"

No. But you can remove them with only a touch.

Which was true enough. Of course, she hadn't come here to fight stormcallers or Tempest.

"I assume you want me to make use of Rott's powers when I go to the Temple of the Book?"

Why be timid? You command the power to decimate armies. You've spent your whole life wishing to strike a blow against the church. Wouldn't destroying the sacred book itself bring you satisfaction?

Sorrow felt her heartbeat quicken. The thought of tearing through the temple on a rampage of destruction certainly appealed to her. But she felt unprepared for the aftermath. She didn't know how the world might change once the book was gone. Would she be opening a path to a golden age, or would she only be inviting anarchy?

Don't concern yourself with the effects of your destruction. You're now a force of nature. Greatshadow devours stands of trees with insatiable hunger, leaving only barren land in his wake. Yet new growth sprouts in earth made fertile by his rampage. If you burn through all of civilization, leaving only ashes, you will create fresh soil for a new world to grow.

"I know you're right. I still feel unprepared. If you'd only spoken to me earlier, we could have formulated a better plan for me to enter the temple." A board creaked overhead. From the weight, it had to be Slate. "I'd rather fly ahead and leave Slate behind. If things turn violent, I'd as soon not have to fight him as well."

So you do have feelings for him.

"Yes. I feel like he practically knocked my damn head off the first time I fought him. Also, he didn't do a bad job of taking down your unstoppable bodyguard. It's wise to keep him at a respectful distance. The only problem is, if I fly toward the temple, I'm bound to be seen. I'll have a whole army of knights and truthspeakers waiting for me by the time I arrive."

You need not fear armies.

"I'm glad you're so confident in my abilities. I'd feel more encouraged by your words if the army you want me to fight didn't scare you so badly you live in another reality now."

Fine. If you fear being spotted in the air, walk.

"That doesn't help," said Sorrow. "It's not like my wings disappear when I'm walking. They're too damn big to hide with just a cloak."

Then change your body to something that can be concealed.

"How? I was able to alter my form in the Black Bog, but I can't just wish away my wings in the material world."

True. The body of Rott that bleeds through from the abstract realms can't be gotten rid of. But with bone-weaving, you could still alter your form.

"What? And go back to the tail?"

You could spread the dragon mass evenly across your body. I did so briefly. It was monstrous. Even your face will be covered with scales. Your hands will be hideous talons. You'll be much larger than your current stature, but not inhuman in size. You could conceal your body beneath a cloak and a veil, and hide your talons with gauntlets.

"Trade my wings for full body disfigurement? You really know how to sell a plan."

You're the one who came to me to learn the art of bone-weaving. Now you reject the very tool that would help you reach your goals? Slate's lack of memories and confusion over his origins leave him vulnerable to emotional manipulation. You could bed him this evening. Given his enviable physical attributes, you'll no doubt find the experience to your liking. As your body fills with procreative energies, I can guide you in the transformation of your form.

"I was just thinking that, if I did decide to experiment with physical contact with a man, there's nothing I'd want more than to have a disembodied bystander watching the whole thing and shouting out advice."

If you reject all my suggestions, I've nothing to teach you.

Sorrow hid the lightning rod amid her blankets. "I know," she said. "Just… give me a little while to think about this."

As you wish.

BY NIGHTFALL, THE *Circus* was in quarantine and Levi had gone to secure the necessary papers. He wouldn't be back until the morning. The Romer children were in good spirits after seeing their brother, but Gale was still pensive as she stood vigil near the wheel, staring at the docks nearby.

Sorrow joined her. She followed Gale's gaze and saw that she was staring at the slave market, barely fifty yards away. The place was a long dock with a warehouse upon it, with iron bars over every window. A lone ship was unloading, with a string of thirty pygmies walking down the gangplank, their legs in shackles.

Gale shook her head. "I thought I'd raised him better."

"Levi isn't to blame for this," said Sorrow. "Slavery is as old as mankind. We live in a world designed to corrupt. He's as much a victim of the system as those poor pygmies."

"I risked everything to oppose that system."

"As have I. Don't despair, Gale. The world that exists today is built upon a foundation of lies and oppression. Place the right weight upon it and that foundation will crumble, as it has in Podredumbre. Change is coming. Faster than you think."

Gale glanced at Sorrow. "I've heard your speeches before. You're fighting for a cause larger than yourself."

"I'd like to think so."

"And your battle places you in great danger. Just by allowing you on my ship, I'm placing my family at risk."

"I won't deny it. But you're tough enough to bear the burden of associating with me. You've spent the money I've paid in the past to charter your ship happily enough."

"Happily isn't exactly the sentiment," said Gale. "But it's not that far off either. I'd rather be ferrying a revolutionary dreamer around these isles than another load of cotton or booze. I like you, Sorrow. I hope I can help you reach your destination."

Sorrow tilted her head, not sure if she'd heard Gale correctly.

"Don't look so surprised. We're both people who act as if our beliefs matter, even as the world around us tries to make us abandon our most deeply held values. No matter how hard the headwinds become, no matter how rough the sea, you push forward. I've no patience for the poor souls of this world who get driven off course the moment they encounter a patch of bad weather. You're never going to turn away from your goals because the going gets rough."

As Gale's words sunk in, Sorrow smiled.

"This isn't something you should smile about," said Gale. "Having the courage to stand up for what's right when the rest of the world is determined to drag you down is a terrible burden."

Sorrow smiled even more broadly. "I know. But I didn't know you felt this way. I just... I never meet anyone who approves of my goals. I'm used to people telling me I should let go of my anger. I'm used to people looking at me as if I'm crazy!"

Gale shrugged. "Perhaps we're both crazy. I sometime think that what the world accepts as sanity is merely the capacity to grow numb to outrage. I find sanity to be a depressingly common commodity. Your anger exists for a reason, Sorrow. I admire that you still have the capacity to feel it. I admire that you're willing to risk everything in order to try to put the world right."

Sorrow couldn't control herself. She threw her arms around Gale and hugged her with all her might. Gale hugged her back, and whispered, "You're more my daughter than Levi is my son."

"Oh, Ma," Sorrow answered, as she choked back tears.

* * *

IT WAS LATE at night when Sorrow knocked on Brand's door. Sage had gone to sleep. Mako was on watch in the crows nest.

"Risk everything," she whispered. "Don't be afraid of a patch of rough water." She took a deep breath as she heard Brand's footsteps approach.

Brand's hair was wet when he opened the door, his face pink and freshly shaven. Before he could speak she pushed him back into his cabin and closed the door behind them.

"I suppose it was a bit optimistic to imagine it might finally be Gale paying a visit," Brand said with a sigh. "What can I help you with, Sorrow?"

Sorrow swallowed hard. She didn't look him directly in the face as she said, "The... the same thing you were hoping Gale would want from you."

Brand laughed softly. "I don't think you know what you've just asked of me."

"I believe I do."

Brand stopped smiling. "This is... an unusual request."

"Is it? I was under the impression you'd had multiple sexual partners."

"I was under the impression you hadn't," said Brand.

"Your impression is correct," she said. "But circumstances have changed. You were present at dinner with Zetetic. He told me that sexual release was an important source of magical energy. I've decided I can no longer afford myself the luxury of ignoring it."

"I can tell you that I've felt something very much like magic during, uh, the requested activity. So maybe there's an energy in the act that you'll know how to use. But I really can't help you."

"Why not? I'm willing to pay you."

"I'm not a prostitute, Sorrow."

"I ask as a favor from a friend."

"There's a lot you need to learn about friendship." Brand crossed his arms.

"If you overlook the wings, am I not attractive?"

"For what it's worth, the wings make you even more interesting. There's also an appealing honesty about your look. You don't go out of your way to fool men with make-up or fancy clothes. There's an innocence about you that's almost irresistible."

"Then, why—"

"I'm in love with Gale," he said, shaking his head. "You know this."

"But she's not in love with you."

"She feels what she feels. It doesn't alter what I feel. I gave her reason to mistrust me by sneaking a stowaway aboard the *Freewind*. I'd love to win her heart with some big gesture, but I also accept that it may take me years to earn back her trust. I'm willing to wait."

"Gale never needs to know anything happened between us," said Sorrow.

"I would know. If you ever loved anyone, you'd understand."

Sorrow shook her head. "What I'm asking has nothing to do with love. It need not involve any emotion at all. I'm asking only for physical assistance. It need be no more a betrayal of Gale than if you were to scratch my back."

"Emotionless sex isn't anything I'm interested in. One day you'll understand it's not what you're interested in either."

Sorrow's shoulders sagged. She'd been certain that Brand would help her.

"Ordinarily, I'd give you a hug and tell you things will be okay," Brand said as he sat on the edge of his bed. "But I'm worried you might misinterpret any physical contact. You've denied your sexuality for so long you probably have a very steep learning curve ahead of you."

"I was hoping you would be a good teacher."

"Sex is one of the few things where your first lessons are probably best learned from other beginners. Have you approached Slate?"

"No!"

"That's surprisingly emphatic."

She waved her hand as if she were swatting away his words. "He's not my type."

"Tall, dark, and handsome isn't your type?"

"He's so empty it frightens me. He's so desperate to fill himself with something. He's trying to serve a religion he doesn't even understand. I'm certain he would find sex outside of marriage to be a sin."

"The original Tower didn't."

"And he's Tower's opposite."

"And you don't want to corrupt him."

"Corrupting him is very high on my agenda," she said. "I'd hoped to turn him into an ally against the church, but he seems to be going in the opposite direction. He'll probably be a saint one day."

"Why... oh, wait. I get it. Since Slate has no memories, you've been able to project all your hopes and dreams onto him. Despite your protests, you imagine him to be perfect. He's the man of virtue your father failed to be. Having sex with him would shatter that illusion, and make him merely human."

"Is this more of your carnival act? Just take anything I say and tell me I meant the opposite?"

"How's it worked so far?"

Sorrow turned to the door. "I'm sorry to have wasted your time." She paused as she took the latch in her hand. "Brand, can I ask—"

"I won't say a word about this. Good luck with your lessons."

Sorrow left Brand's cabin. Her arms were wrapped tightly across her breasts. The night air was cold enough that her breath came out as fog. Pale moonlight filtered through the clouds, painting the deck a ghostly gray. A shadow moved before her. Her body tensed as it drew closer. She looked up and found Mako in the rigging.

"I... underestimated Brand," he said, softly. "I thought he was only toying with my mother's affections. I didn't realize how deeply he felt about her."

"You heard us?" she asked, mortified.

"Sight isn't a terribly important sense for a shark. But they can hear a wounded fish flopping on the surface from many miles away. Usually there's so much sound in the world I have difficulty making sense of everything. But late at night, on a sleeping ship, a single hushed conversation is difficult to ignore."

"Did you also—"

"—hear when Sage and Mother spoke to you about Grandmother's ghost? I did. Why they don't simply include me in their confidence is no mystery. How did mother phrase it? That I have freakish hearing? That no girl would ever want me because of my teeth? She's seen the thing I become when I smell blood in the water. It's hard enough to know that no girl will ever trust me. It's harder still to know that my own mother fears me."

"She still loves you. As do all your siblings."

"And I love them. Still, the love of my family only serves to remind me that I will likely never have a family of my own. It's a lonely thing, to be a monster."

Sorrow folded her wings about her, and ran her fingers along the fine scales that covered the leading edge. "I know how you feel."

Mako dropped to the deck before Sorrow. He said, "Ma would lash me if she knew I'd left my post."

"We can't have that," Sorrow said, turning her back to him.

He placed his sharp-nailed hand between her shoulder blades. His fingers were rough and callused as he lightly scratched her back. "This need not involve any emotion at all," he murmured, inches from her ear.

She shuddered as his inhuman mouth pressed against the nape of her neck. She could feel his saw-toothed jaws beneath his cold lips as he kissed her. His hands moved to rest lightly upon her hips.

She placed her hands upon his, feeling the soft webbing between his fingers. She turned to face him. His eyes were dark as the ocean's depths.

"Some things are best learned from other beginners," he said, as he brought his lips toward hers.

CHAPTER SEVENTEEN

SAFE PASSAGE

THE FOLLOWING MORNING, Sorrow waited on the dock in front of the *Circus*. Slate appeared on deck dressed in his black armor, standing patiently as Rigger helped outfit the coffin with a rope harness. Slate wrestled the coffin onto his back and headed down the gangplank. Through the holes in his helm, she could see his eyes fixed upon her. She knew he didn't recognize her. She was outfitted in a suit of full iron plate complete with a jousting helm. Mirrored glass shaded her eyes. She now stood nearly as tall as Slate, and carried an iron mace almost as large as the one she'd crafted for him. He watched her closely as he approached, seeming more wary of her than he was of the trio of Storm Guard next to her.

Of course, the Storm Guard weren't terribly impressive. None stood even as tall as Sorrow's shoulders. She also noticed this morning how uniformly thin the residents of Raitingu appeared. Apparently, Tempest believed in keeping his worshipers a bit hungry.

One of the guards bowed toward Slate. He held out a scroll, similar to the one he'd already given Sorrow. He said, "Good morning. I'm Agent Nori. I've orders to guide you to the city gates. Beyond, this permit will provide you safe passage as a pilgrim."

Slate took the scroll, but his eyes were still fixed on Sorrow.

She cleared her throat and said, "You seem fascinated by my new armor."

"Sorrow?"

She nodded. She could tell from his eyes he had a thousand questions, but he wisely held his tongue as he turned to Agent Nori and said, "We're honored to have you serve as our guide. Lead on."

The three guards formed a triangle around the two as they passed through the bustling city streets. The roads were paved with gray gravel and were remarkably clean. Every block was attended by old men with rakes, who worked to smooth out the gravel in the wake of passing carts. The same attention to maintenance was shown in the buildings. Unlike the worn, shabby atmosphere of Port Hallelujah, each building in Kaikou looked freshly painted, albeit in unappealing shades of cloudy gray. Small gardens graced the fronts of each house, but were devoid of flowers. Instead, each was a merely a box of raked sand, sporting a few round stones of random size and placement. A few boxes also featured a single gnarled juniper tree, severely cropped to stand no more than a few inches tall. The gardens reminded her of sand-boxes where children played in the Silver City, but she saw no one playing. What children she spotted were all engaged in labor, mending thatched roofs, sweeping doorsteps, and running chamber pots down the steep streets to the river.

At length they reached the city gates. The frame of the main gate was carved in the fashion of a giant dragon's head, requiring them to enter the jaws in order to reach the barred doors at the back of the throat.

"This is where we must part," Agent Nori said as he bowed. "I hope you find safe passage beyond these walls."

"Why would we not?" asked Slate. "We've been granted permission, yes?"

"Bandits don't bother with permits," Nori said.

"Bandits would be fools to bother with us," said Sorrow.

"As you say," Nori replied, with a bow. He turned to depart, with a final blessing: "May the clouds always protect you from the oppression of the sun."

Slate and Sorrow passed through the iron gates as they slid open. As they walked through the tunnel of the dragon's mouth on the other side, Slate whispered, "What happened to your wings?"

"It hurts like hell, but I was able to fold them beneath my arms and around the front of my chest. It's why my armor is so barrel-chested."

"Your voice sounds different," he said. "Deeper. Gruffer."

"It's probably just my helm that makes it sound different. There's an echo in here."

"I can't help but notice that you're taller as well. And apparently much stronger, given how swiftly you walk in that armor and how lightly you carry that mace."

She chuckled as she tossed the mace back and forth between her iron gauntlets. "The mace is hollow; it's mainly for looks. As for my height, it's a simple thing to add a few additional inches in my boots and to the top of my helm. The weight of the armor doesn't matter because I'm wearing almost nothing beneath. My magical control over any iron I touch means I'm moving the armor with my magic, not my muscles. Going on this pilgrimage as a winged witch was only going to cause us both a lot of grief. Going as another knight, I'll barely draw attention."

They stepped from the dragon gate as she spoke these words. Immediately a mob of filthy men and women in ragged clothes rushed toward them and threw themselves groveling at their feet.

"Knights!" a woman cried as she stared up at them with tears in her eyes. "Please! We're humble pilgrims seeking to reach the temple! Have mercy!"

Sorrow sighed, reaching for the purse on her belt. The woman's left arm was nothing but a bandaged stump. She felt pity enough to spare a few moons.

The woman shook her head as Sorrow produced the coins. "It's not moons we want. It's protection. We've all attempted the journey and been turned back by violence. We've lost everything but our lives."

Slate nodded. "We were warned of bandits."

"Bandits?" the woman said, shaking her head. "There are no bandits on this road. The Storm Guard shows no mercy to their ilk."

"Who has reduced you to this state?" asked Slate.

"The Storm Guard themselves! They place barriers in the most narrow gap of the mountain pass and demand a toll to pass. Even if you pay the price they demand, they still take from you anything of value."

"They took my daughter and stripped her bare before me," said a man with an empty eye-socket. "She was only eleven. I tried to protect her honor, but they beat me and tossed me into a ravine, leaving me for dead. I almost wish I had died when I hear her terrified cries in my dreams."

"You may journey with us," Slate said, his voice trembling. "We will protect you from such atrocities!"

"Hold on," said Sorrow. "We aren't the only warriors to travel this road. From what I understand, the temple is defended by hundreds of knights. Why don't they protect the pilgrims?"

The one-eyed man shook his head mournfully. "Tempest forbids them to intervene. If the knights were to take action against the Storm Guard, Tempest would direct his wrath against the temple itself. The first priority of the knights is to protect the One True Book from harm."

"The code of the knight requires him to be a defender of all men of virtue," said Slate. "Protecting a book is no excuse for turning a blind eye to the suffering of fellow men."

This is why I buried the poor fool.

Sorrow jerked her head to the left, but of course, Avaris was nowhere to be seen. Sorrow grimaced. She'd thought that her iron helmet might hide her senses from the elder witch.

Of what use is a warrior who takes pity on the suffering of others? He lacks the hardness required to do all that is needed to achieve victory.

Sorrow didn't answer, partially because she'd learned her lesson about talking to herself, and partially because the opinions of Avaris didn't matter. What Avaris took for Slate's weakness, Sorrow saw as his strength. She'd worried he would stand in the way of her goals. Now, she realized, he'd be key to achieving them.

She looked up the mountain. "We've many miles to go," she said, placing the coins back into her pouch. "Together we shall reach the temple, and no thug with a barricade is going to stand in our way."

"Forward," Slate cried, his voice a strange mix of optimism and outrage. Sorrow smiled. If Gale was right, and sanity was merely the capacity to grow numb to outrage, Slate might prove crazy enough for her needs after all.

THE FIRST THIEVES they encountered were shopkeepers along the way. Bamboo shacks selling noodles and barbequed rock lizards were scattered along the route. In most of the world, such a simple meal would require the exchange of a few coppers. Here, a single bowl of noodles cost an entire moon. Sorrow was tempted to test Slate's temper, to find out if she could provoke him into stealing to feed the score of hungry pilgrims who traveled with them. Instead, while she contemplated what she might say that wouldn't seem like outright manipulation, he surprised her by producing a bag of coins and buying food for everyone.

"You shouldn't pay these thieves such prices," she said, as the pilgrims hungrily slurped noodles.

Slate shrugged. "Brand gave me a purse before I departed and insisted I keep it, just in case I found myself in a situation where I'd need a few coins. I won't miss money that wasn't truly mine to begin with."

"So you're just going to pay the toll when we encounter the Storm Guard?"

Slate nodded toward the old woman stirring the pot of noodles. "These people didn't threaten us to gain our money. They had something we wanted and offered it to us for a price. Perhaps an unfair price, but we had the option to move on."

"But the Storm Guard have something we want as well," said Sorrow. "If this is your attitude, why shouldn't they be allowed to set a price?"

The one-eyed man wiped his mouth on his sleeve and said, "There's the treaty. King Brightmoon granted Tempest control of a few islands south of here in exchange for a promise that the path of the pilgrims would remain open. The Storm Guard ignores the law because no one dares to punish them."

Slate had his helmet off, looking lost in thought as he nibbled absent-mindedly on a lizard thigh. He glanced at Sorrow, who still had her helmet on, and asked, "Aren't you going to eat?"

"I'll do it later. You know why I don't want to reveal my head in front of others," she whispered.

"Right," he said. "Sorry."

THE MOUNTAIN PATH they followed was barren of vegetation. When night arrived, they had nothing to use to build a fire. The pilgrims huddled together beneath an outcropping of stone, shivering as the wind howled up the steep path.

Slate lowered the coffin he carried to the ground and sat beside it, pulling off his helmet with a weary shake of his head. Sorrow stood before him.

"Aren't you weary?" he asked.

"Not as much as you might think," she said. "My armor has done most of the walking. I'm just kind of along for the ride. Except for my wings feeling bruised, I'm still pretty fresh."

He nodded. After a moment of silence, he asked, "Why are you here, Sorrow?"

"I told you on the ship. I've been rethinking a lot of assumptions in my life."

Slate stared at her. "It would be easier to judge your words if I could see your face."

"Who appointed you as the judge of my words?"

"I fear... I fear that you may not be undertaking this pilgrimage with the best of intentions."

"Allow me to try Brand's little trick. When you say you mistrust my intentions, you mean you mistrust your own."

Slate cocked his head to the side as he puzzled over her response.

"I saw your expression when that pilgrim told you that the knights didn't defend travelers. You're wondering if I'm right, and if the code of the knight in Poppy's book isn't just a romantic fiction. The body you're carrying in that box belongs to a knight who certainly failed to live up to Poppy's standards."

"What do the actions of others have to do with my intentions?"

"Because, at heart, you share the same basic emotional quality that defines Gale and myself. You still have the capacity for righteous anger. You might be mad that the Storm Guard abuses pilgrims, but you expect evil from them. However, the idea that supposedly good men stand by and do nothing... that outrages you."

"What if it does?" he asked.

"You find yourself in the same position I've been in ever since my grandmother stood on those gallows. You'll come to see that the true problem with the world isn't the wickedness of a few, it's the unthinking acceptance of the many. You either surrender in the face of their apathy, or you let the anger build inside you until you have no choice but to fight."

"Fight who? Brother knights whose only sin is inaction?"

"What makes them your brothers? The fact they pay lip service to a faith you imagine you believe in? Or will you wake up and realize that you're more kin to the Romers? Your true family is found among those who would give everything in defense of what they believe."

Slate lowered his head. He sighed. "We can't know that it's apathy that holds back the knights of the temple. It would be unfair to judge them based on the testimony of others."

"Fine," she said. "I just ask that you maintain the courage to accept what you see, instead of what you wish to see."

"Who are you to demand this of me?"

She removed her helmet. In the moonlight, her still human face reflected in the polished steel.

"I'm your friend, Slate," she said. She glanced toward the pilgrims. From the sound of their collective snores, they'd fallen asleep quickly. She slid her finger along her breastplate and peeled it open, shrugging it free, then lifted her arms to spread her wings. She willed the legs of her armor to open and stepped out barefoot on the cold ground. Goose bumps quickly covered her body. Her arms were bare. She wore only a simple cotton slip that hung to the upper part of her thighs.

"You've no idea how good it feels to be out of that suit," she said, stretching her aching wings, savoring the soothing cold.

"The transformation is remarkable. You looked quite mannish in that armor. I much prefer this look."

She sat beside him and pulled her breastplate near. She ran her fingers along it, stoking the metal into a red-hot glow. He scooted closer to her, until their legs were touching, as he stretched his hands out over the glowing metal.

"So, you prefer me this way?" she asked. "Wings and all?"

Perhaps it was the red glow of the iron, but it looked as if Slate were blushing as she looked into his face.

He smiled softly and said, "Aye."

"The wings don't bother Mako either," she said. "He kissed me last night."

Slate's eyebrows shot up.

"Don't be jealous. Nothing happened. There was just a... momentary misunderstanding."

"What cause have I to be jealous?" he asked, tersely.

"Oh. I just thought... there have been moments...."

"Aye. There have been moments."

"Under different circumstances, I think... if I were to ever feel for a man, it would be a man like you." She sighed. "But these aren't different circumstances. My life has been the only life I've lived, and my heart is the only heart I have. It shattered a long time ago. I don't think I'll ever be able to feel anything like ordinary love."

Slate shrugged. "Is there anything ordinary about love?" He stared at his hands as he rubbed them together. They were covered with thin white scars from where he'd fought the bone dragon. "I think about you stitching me up after battle, the tenderness in your touch, the concern in your eyes, and I sometimes believe you're an angel sent by the Divine Author to grant me happiness. Then I listen to you make excuses for monsters like Avaris, and I wonder if you aren't a devil. Perhaps the warmth I feel in your presence presages the fires of hell."

"Hellfire?" Sorrow chuckled. "That's harsh."

"Aye," he said, managing half a smile. "Perhaps I exaggerate. I get a bit addled in your presence. You're a very confusing woman, Sorrow."

"Aye," she said. "And a confused one as well."

He placed his hand upon hers where it lay on her bare thigh. She shivered.

"Art thou still cold?" he asked.

She grinned and said, "A little too warm, actually."

She pushed his hand aside and stood, stretching her wings once more. She stepped back into her iron legs and willed them shut.

Coward. Bad enough you rebuffed the boy. Now you miss the chance to enslave the heart of a man who may yet prove to be your greatest enemy?

"I'm an honorary Romer," said Sorrow. "I don't believe in slavery."

"What does slavery have to do with anything?" Slate asked, completely befuddled.

"I was merely thinking that I couldn't shackle anyone, without feeling shackled myself."

You try to frame your avoidance of sex as a matter of independence, but we both know you merely lack the courage.

"I think I'm displaying courage by following my own path," Sorrow said softly as she placed her hands on her iron-clad hips.

Your words would be more convincing if you weren't wearing what must certainly be the world's largest chastity belt.

THEY SPENT MOST of the next day struggling up the steep mountain path. Progress was slow, as the pilgrims had to stop and rest often. The cold was getting worse, and Sorrow worried that frostbite awaited many of the pilgrims. She felt guilty in the comfort of her armor, whose temperature she controlled with only a thought. Looking behind her, the city they'd left the day before was still visible, though the white sails of the ships in the harbor were no larger than snowflakes.

Looking up at the thick clouds directly overhead, she wondered if she wouldn't soon have actual snowflakes on hand for comparison. The trail ahead led directly into the cloudbanks.

They pressed on, the visibility growing worse with each step. Soon the fog was so thick she couldn't see her hand when she held it before her face. The pilgrims all locked arms to move forward, with Slate in the lead, sure-footedly finding his way along the all-but-invisible rocks. Sorrow brought up the rear of the group. Partially this was to defend against anything that might try to attack unseen, and partially because the mass of her armor provided an impassible barrier if any of the pilgrims slipped and fell.

Suddenly, there was a blinding flash, followed by a loud rumble, and the wails of the pilgrims before her. Gravity lost its hold on Sorrow as she fell. The sensation was very much like falling to sleep. An electric blue swirled in front of her, blotting out the snow.

When her vision cleared, she sensed that she was no longer on the mountain, but was once more falling toward the waters of the convergence. She spread her wings and soared above the waves. Looking back along the length of her body, she found she retained her now familiar dragon-winged but otherwise human form. Unlike before, the convergence was dark and sunless. The sky above was filled with clouds, the lightning within providing the only light.

"You're the interloper the others whisper about," a deep voice rumbled. "The human who usurped the power of Rott."

"And you, I presume, are Tempest," she said.

"Rott's elemental essence is omnipresent," said Tempest. "I cannot exclude him from my earthly domain. But Rott's intelligence has been absent for centuries. I'm not happy to see the human mind that now directs his powers finds my earthly empire worthy of her attention. Why have you invaded my home, usurper?"

"I mean no disrespect. I'm not here to confront you. I accompany a companion on his quest to the Temple of the Book. Once we're done, I'll leave this land as fast as humanly possible."

"That is not much of a promise from one who can walk through the realms immaterial. You could leave in the space of a heartbeat. And before coming, you could have summoned me to the convergence to ask permission to walk through my domain. Instead, you forced me to bring you here."

"There's a lot of this dragon stuff I'm figuring out," said Sorrow. "If you have any suggestions on how I can learn more, I'm willing to listen."

"Bah. I wouldn't waste such knowledge upon you. I see now that, while your mind has touched Rott, you are not yet the sole vessel of his essence. You're still merely a mortal. It would be a simple thing to kill you."

Sorrow's heart skipped a beat. Could one dragon attack another in the convergence? She suddenly felt very alone, and wished that Stagger was here to refresh her memory of the rules.

As she thought this, the dark waters below began to brighten. She looked up and saw a pink glow breaking through the clouds above her. The storm parted and a shaft of golden sunshine burst down through the clouds.

"Sorry to interrupt," a voice said.

"Stagger!" Sorrow shouted.

"The second usurper," the thunder grumbled.

Stagger's voice came from high above the clouds "I felt a tug to come here, so I did. I've been practicing looking into other realms, and even tried my hand at crafting avatars. Perhaps now that I'm here, Tempest, you could offer a few pointers?"

"I think not," growled Tempest. A draconic head formed from the roiling clouds and fixed its gaze upon Sorrow. "I believe that you visit my kingdom intending no malice toward me. I will overlook the trespass... this time. Complete your journey with haste, then depart. We shall not speak again."

There was a flash of light that washed away Sorrow's sight and a clap of thunder that deafened her. She blinked and shook her head and the white persisted. Her body felt strangely heavy. She turned her head and the white shifted. She suddenly realized the lenses of her helmet were covered with snow. Somehow Tempest had pushed her back to the real world.

"Sorrow!" Slate was shouting from above. "Sorrow!"

She wiped the snow away from her visor and managed to sit up. Her legs were wedged between two massive rocks at the bottom of a steep slope. She pulled herself free with a grunt.

"Sorrow!" Slate shouted again, his voice slightly further away.

"I'm down here," she yelled back.

"Are you alright?"

"I think so," she said, examining the slope. She could see dark splotches among the fresh snow where she'd tumbled down. "I must have slipped and knocked myself out."

Slate came sliding down the slope through the swirling snow. He was carrying a stout rope, one he'd had wrapped around the coffin.

"I've been looking for you for ten minutes! I worried you were dead, like the others."

"Dead? What others?"

"The three pilgrims ahead of you. They were killed when the lightning struck!"

"Lightning?" she said. She shook her head. Her visit to the convergence seemed so unreal. Had Tempest really just paid her a visit that had proved fatal to bystanders? Or had she gotten jolted into unconsciousness by standing too close to a lightning strike and merely dreamed the whole conversation?

"Grab the rope!" Slate said as he reached her. "We can't waste more time. I've sent the surviving pilgrims on ahead. If they stop moving in this storm, they'll freeze..." His voice trailed off.

"What?" she asked.

"Your chest."

To see what he was staring at, she removed her gauntlet and placed her hand on his helmet, willing the glass to form a mirror finish. The light was dim, but good enough to make sense of what she saw.

Her breastplate was scorched in three jagged parallel slashes. It looked for all the world as if a dragon had raked its claws across her chest.

THEY RECOVERED TOWER'S coffin after they climbed out of the ravine, each lifting an end rather than wasting time wrapping it with ropes once more. They pressed forward at the quickest pace they could muster, their feet slipping in the mounting snow. Yet despite the misery of their condition, the light was definitely getting brighter. Had they climbed so far in the last few hours that they were now rising above the clouds?

This proved to be the case, as the snow faded into fog that changed instantly to ice as it splattered against them. The coffin grew increasingly heavy as the ice built.

The clouds came to an abrupt end as the path they traveled led into a long gap between two steep cliffs. The span between the cliffs was no more than fifty feet across. The sun was red as it sank into the ocean of clouds at their back, painting the cliff walls a deep crimson. Ahead, they saw the pilgrims on their knees, huddled before a wall of men in heavy fur coats who stood as a living barrier to their passage.

"Storm Guard?" Sorrow asked.

"Who else could it be?" answered Slate. They moved forward. Sorrow counted thirteen guards. She couldn't tell if they wore armor beneath their coats, but could see that they were armed with heavy hammers and battleaxes. In contrast to the clean-shaven, slender soldiers of the city, these were large, burly men with thick black beards and bushy eyebrows. Their coats were silver and brown, pieced together from the hides of wolves.

Slate lowered his end of the coffin. Sorrow set her end down. They marched through the kneeling pilgrims, who had their hands clasped before them in prayer.

The largest of the armed men stepped forward and shouted in short, guttural syllables.

"Do you not speak the Silver Tongue?" asked Slate.

The pilgrim who was missing an eye said, "They demand twenty moons for safe passage, and that you surrender your weapons."

"Tell him my weapon is a sacred relic that will not be relinquished."

The man frowned. "If I tell them that, they definitely won't let us pass unmolested. They'll steal the relic and hold it for ransom."

"So be it," said Slate. "Tell them."

The man swallowed hard. With a look of pain, he choked out a string of syllables.

The leader smiled as he barked back a response.

"It's as I feared," the one-eyed man said. "He now demands we turn over the relic in exchange for safe passage."

"Tell him…"

Before Slate could finish, the leader barked out a new jumble of sounds.

"He says that if you cause trouble, his men will kill all of us. He asks that you weigh your answer carefully."

Slate looked at Sorrow. "Are you ready to give our answer?"

"I'm ready if you're ready," said Sorrow.

Slate removed the Witchbreaker from its scabbard. The walls of the narrow canyon echoed with the howls of the damned.

Sorrow dropped her mace and allowed her gauntlets to crumble to rust.

"Anything you want to teach me, now's the moment," she said.

Slate replied, "Just follow my lead," not guessing that she hadn't been talking to him. He said to the translator, "Tell them to clear our path, or face destruction."

"There are thirteen of them," the man answered weakly. "There are only two of you. You're gambling with our lives!"

"You're the ones who begged to join us," Sorrow snapped. "Just tell him what Slate said."

The man turned pale as the looked back at the warriors and gave his answer.

The thirteen warriors roared in unison, raising their axes and hammers. Before they could finish inhaling, Slate leapt forward and drove the Witchbreaker deep into the belly of the leader. A soulful wail of terror filled the air, though nothing but bloody gurgles escaped the dead man's lips.

A half dozen of the warriors leapt toward Slate as he kicked the leader free of his blade. The rest of the men charged the kneeling pilgrims, with only Sorrow standing in their path.

Breathe flies, Avaris commanded. *You will feel a door open within your belly. Do not let go of this door!*

Sorrow was familiar with the sensation, having used this power to dispatch a band of warriors she'd faced in Hush's lair. She pulled her helmet free as the pressure built within her stomach. In her mind's eye, she saw the small black portal in her center, wobbling and warping as flies boiled into her belly.

She was vaguely aware that a warrior was three strides away from smashing a warhammer down on her bare scalp. She opened her lips and the man's face disappeared in a tornado of flies that erupted from inside her. The hammer dropped as his fingers went limp, and he fell to his knees before her, his body collapsing against her legs. She looked down and found his face was nothing but a skull writhing with maggots.

Don't allow yourself to be distracted! Do not lose the door!

Sorrow found the disembodied voice screaming at her far more distracting than the dead man rapidly falling to bits around her feet. The boundaries of the black gate grew fuzzy. Suddenly, she lost all sense of where its edges lay.

Fool! You've just allowed more of Rott's essence to bleed into your physical body. When you open a door, you must have the discipline to close it properly!

"Good advice," Sorrow said as she watched the other warriors near her fall to the ground, tearing at the maggots writhing under their skin. "Maybe if you hadn't waited to tell me until one second before I needed to know, I might have found it useful."

She was snapped back from her argument with Avaris to her present danger by a head bouncing past her.

Slate had finished off four of the Storm Guard and was currently driving his blade into the fifth. Unfortunately, the sixth had bolted, and had run quite some distance up the path. She couldn't allow him to bring reinforcements.

She glanced back at the pilgrims, whose mouths gaped in horror at the maggot-ridden body before her. She felt something tickling her lip and brushed a fly away. If they'd witnessed this, there was no reason to hold back. With a thought, her armor fell away and she leapt into the air, still carrying her mace. The guard made it another hundred feet before she dropped onto his back, driving the mace into his neck with all her strength. Unfortunately, she hadn't been lying when she'd said the mace was hollow. Her victim still struggled beneath her, and if he made it to his back and freed his arms, he might yet cause her grief.

She placed her hand upon the nape of his neck. She imagined the black portal once more, this time opening in her shoulder. She focused as dark energy flowed down her arm and the man's flesh liquefied in her grasp. She never took her mind's eye off the portal. Clenching her jaw, she willed the pulsing black circle to grow smaller, then smaller still. With a final gasp, she closed it completely.

She raised her hand, wrinkling her nose at the pink gore that coated it.

Well done. If you maintain such discipline in the future, you may grow powerful indeed.

"And if I don't?"

You'll lose the last of your humanity as Rott consumes you.

Sorrow nodded. The risks were clearly laid out. Before, she'd been frightened by the uncertainty of what dangers she faced. Now she knew what the risks were, and could push through the fuzzy veil of fear into the firm embrace of pure terror.

CHAPTER EIGHTEEN
A BIT OF CLEVER MAGIC

THE WIND HOWLED through the narrow stone gap as Sorrow stared at her gore-covered hand. She knelt and wiped her fingers on the man's wolf coat, then headed back down the pass to retrieve her armor before she froze to death.

Slate stood over the maggot-ridden bodies of the men she'd killed. The pilgrims were all huddled together, still on their knees, their eyes wide as they stared at Sorrow. At least, most of them were staring at her. Quite a few eyes were focused instead on Slate, who still held the ebony sword in his grasp, filling the air with faint cries of agony.

"What magic is this?" Slate asked as she drew close. "These men have been reduced to skeletons!"

"You knew I had tapped into Rott's power," she said.

"When we fought the pirates together, your methods were less... disturbing."

Sorrow arranged the components of her discarded armor and molded her now ice-cold iron shell back into position. She commanded the metal to warm, but her teeth were still chattering as she said, "I don't think you're in any position to declare my methods disturbing. You just sent your enemies' souls directly to hell."

As if to prove her point, the screams of torment that echoed from the sword grew louder.

"Is this not an appropriate fate for the wicked?"

"I'm not certain it is," she said. "First, the Storm Guard have a very different conception of the afterlife from the Church of the Book. I'm not up on my theology, but I'm pretty sure they didn't feel like their actions were going to earn them an eternity in a fiery pit tormented by demons."

"The failings of their belief system are unfortunate," said Slate. "Without the fear of hell, how are men of weak morals to be brought to the path of righteousness?"

"So you admit that this church you're so enamored of uses fear and the threat of torture to ensure obedience?"

Slate frowned. "It's not as simple as that. Men who behave in compliance with the Divine Author's will are rewarded with paradise. The possibility of hell is merely..."

When he seemed at a loss for words, she said, "It's merely a threat to catch the few poor souls who aren't swayed by bribery?" She nodded toward the blade. "I'll never worship a god who built a place that sounds like that."

He said nothing as he slid the Witchbreaker back into its scabbard, silencing the cries.

She tucked her wings under her arms and closed her armor. "Besides, I thought everything that will ever happen is already recorded in the One True Book. Why have this whole system of punishment and bribes to control men when every last choice they're given has been decided by the Divine Author? By the very tenets of your faith, these men were only in our way because it was His will that we kill them." She pointed to the huddled pilgrims. "These poor fools have lost possessions, loved ones, and limbs because your god thought it would make a good story."

Slate crossed his arms. "I'm a knight, not a theologian. I'm sure there are others at the temple who can explain our beliefs more eloquently than I can."

Sorrow donned her helmet once more and moved to stand beside Slate as he stood before the shivering pilgrims.

"It's almost nightfall," he said to the pilgrims. "But these guards must have a camp nearby. If any guards remain there, we'll take it by force. Tonight, you'll sleep in the beds of those who caused you grief."

The one-eyed man cleared his throat. "We've decided to turn back. We'll complete our journey another time."

Slate glanced over his shoulder at the corpses behind him. "Have we... frightened you?"

"We... we didn't understand... what manner of creatures... we journeyed with. We'd heard stories of demons who disguise themselves as men—"

"We're not demons," said Slate. "I'm a knight. My companion is... unusual in appearance, but human."

"He's right," said Sorrow. "We're both human. Which means we're even more dangerous than demons. If you want to turn back, turn back. You wanted a roadblock removed and we removed it. What direction you go from this moment is entirely up to you."

"You all have reasons for being here," said Slate. "Your faith has brought you this far. You can't turn back now."

And yet, one by one, the pilgrims stood and began to walk back down the path, toward the churning clouds at the mouth of the gap, linking hands as they vanished into the storm.

"They were slowing us down," said Sorrow. "Don't look so dejected."

"It was as if they feared me as much as you," Slate said, shaking his head. "We fought to save them and they hate us for it?"

"Welcome to every damn day of my life."

NIGHT HAD FALLEN when they discovered the camp of the Storm Guard, a tight cluster of stone huts with hide roofs. Someone shouted out an alarm as they approached, and a moment later they were attacked by five warriors.

The fight was brief.

They spent the remainder of the night in the largest of the huts, warming themselves in front of a stone furnace fueled by coal. Sorrow stared into the flickering flames, wondering if she might dream of Greatshadow once more. Slate looked glum, and even though the hut was well stocked with dried meats and fruits, he ate nothing. He silently removed his armor and stretched out on the ground beside the stove, covering his massive form with a heavy blanket pulled from one of the bunks. His eyes were locked on the Witchbreaker, which rested atop his armor.

Sorrow welcomed his silence. She had worries of her own. The familiar itchiness had returned to her skin, this time concentrated in her arms and hands. She'd shoveled a load of coal into the furnace when they'd arrived, leaving her hands black with dust. Now, as she watched, the blackness hardened on her fingers, growing shiny. Her nails grew longer and thinner, turning into hard claws.

Seduce him and I'll teach you bone weaving. You cannot rid yourself of the dragon's essence, but you can push it to less visible parts of your body.

"I know," she whispered. "But it's not going to happen."

Why not? I see the way you glance at him. You're not immune to his charms.

Sorrow rose and walked to the far side of the hut. "I want to end our agreement. I'm sorry if I've inconvenienced you, but I don't feel that you're the best teacher for me."

You've more than inconvenienced me. You invaded my home, assaulted me, and destroyed my companion. You cannot turn away from my teachings now.

"Are you teaching me? Or punishing me?"

There may be some overlap. It doesn't change anything. You promised me you would take a life at my request. Until this promise is kept, our bargain remains in place.

"What if I tell you I don't intend to kill anyone just because you ask me to? Can we end our bargain then?"

If you betray me, you forfeit all the power I've taught you to use.

Sorrow started to argue that wasn't very much, but thought better of it as she contemplated the possible ways Avaris might remove the knowledge. The old witch probably knew exactly what parts of Sorrow's brain to probe with a long fingernail in order to scrape away her memories. For now, she was still trapped in her bargain.

Why the doubts now? You were the picture of confidence when you battled your way into my castle.

"I don't have doubts. I have... finality. There's no real time left to learn anything before tomorrow."

Tomorrow you will reach the Temple of the Book.

Sorrow nodded. "Tomorrow, I'm going to cripple my enemies with a blow they can never recover from. I... I intend to win tomorrow's battles, but I'm not kidding myself. There's a strong possibility that tonight is my last night alive."

All the more reason to seduce him.

Sorrow shook her head. "No. If I'm to die, I intend to die true to myself. I've lived with the certainty I had no need of men. It's the wrong moment for second guesses. But if there is anything you have to tell me about Rott's power that I don't yet know, now is the time to reveal it. You have to want the church to feel pain as much as I do. Now's your chance to turn me into your weapon for revenge."

Your father has already done that work for me.

Avaris began to laugh inside Sorrow's skull. It wasn't a pleasant sound.

DURING THE NIGHT, Sorrow had held out some slender hope that the changes to her hands weren't as bad as they seemed. The coal dust and the darkness of the hut perhaps made her skin appear darker and rougher than it truly was.

In the pale light of morning, she had no reason for hope. She melted snow in the iron bowl of her helmet and washed her hands, if they could still be called hands. Her pinkies had fused with her ring fingers and all of her digits had become longer and banded by scales. Her nails were now claws, tapering to razor-sharp hooks.

When she heard Slate stirring, she hastily pulled on her iron gauntlets, willing the metal to stretch to hide her deformity. She folded the now empty pinkies of the gauntlets closed and fused them, hoping no one would notice their lack of motion.

Slate looked even more exhausted than he had when he went to sleep.

"Rough night?" she asked.

He shook his head. "Climbing this mountain with a coffin balanced on my back has drained me. From what the pilgrims told me, the temple is only a few hours walk. I look forward to divesting myself of my burden."

"It's a burden you placed upon yourself," said Sorrow. "We could have buried Tower in the swamp."

"Tower had already suffered the abuse of having his corpse reanimated as a slave of Avaris. The hero of Poppy's storybook deserves a better ending."

"He's dead no matter where his body winds up," she said. "His ending is already written."

Slate didn't look directly at her as he rose to dress. He buckled his armor without saying a word.

"I guess this conversation is over?" she asked.

"This conversation is impossible."

"What does that mean?"

He sighed. "Only that I will never be able to explain myself." He walked to the coffin and knelt beside it, placing his hands upon the wooden surface. His voice was soft as he said, "I was created from Tower's blood. I'm like a branch snapped from a tree that's taken root in new soil. Is the new tree a double of the old, or an extension of it? I'm not Tower's duplicate. I'm his continuation. Who else in all of history has borne the burden of having to bury himself?"

*   *   *

Sorrow had expected the Temple of the Book to be a more imposing structure. In fact, it wasn't a structure at all, just a number of dark holes chiseled into a cliff of solid white quartz. The landscape surrounding it was windswept and barren, nothing but rough gravel over frozen gray soil.

The dark holes led into the mountain, and she could see shadows flickering across the well-lit interiors. They were still several hundred yards away, but from the flurry of activity, she gathered they'd been spotted.

A horse galloped out of one of the uppermost holes, bearing a rider upon his back. The horse was a pure black mare, well-muscled to support the heavily armored knight upon her back. Glorystone horseshoes shot beams of bright light down from the mare's hooves, and the horse raced across the sky upon these columns of radiance. The knight was armed with a crystalline lance, which had a pale blue glow similar to the lightning rod Sorrow had stolen. He wore a flowing purple cape trimmed with golden silk. There were words embroidered within the trim, but Sorrow couldn't make them out at this distance.

The horse charged toward them in eerie silence, coming to a stop roughly a hundred feet up in the sky.

"Halt!" the knight shouted.

Slate halted. Sorrow felt an almost uncontrollable urge to step forward, so she did.

"I said, halt!"

"What right do you have to prevent anyone from walking the path of the pilgrim?" she asked.

The knight flipped up the visor of his helmet. He was a square-headed man with bright blue eyes and a thick gray mustache that hung several inches below his jaw. "Don't pretend you don't know who I am," the knight answered. "I'm Sir Forthright Castlebridge, the Fist of the Book, the rightful protector of Utmost Humble, the Voice of the Book. For thirty years I've defended this sacred place with the power of my mighty steed, Sunracer, my legendary lightning lance, and my unflagging faith."

"Horses don't live thirty years," said Sorrow.

"This is Sunracer VI, though that doesn't matter," said Castlebridge. "What matters is that the Voice of the Book is the sole authority to decide who may enter the temple, and I am the enforcer of his will. I command you both to lay down your arms and surrender."

"We command you to take your lance and shove it up—"

"Sorrow!" Slate snapped. "Is there a reason you're being so disrespectful of a duly appointed defender of the temple?"

Sorrow clenched her fists, then relaxed them. "I don't like men bossing me around. You talk now."

Slate lowered his coffin to the ground. He knelt and said, "Good sir, we come on a mission of peace. This coffin holds the mortal remains of Lord Stark Tower, the famed Witchbreaker. He was a great hero of the church. I've delivered him so that his bones may rest in a place of honor surrounded by his fellow saints."

"Whatever your intentions," said Castlebridge, "you killed an entire camp of Storm Guard yesterday. We received word of your crimes this morning. The Voice of the Book has decreed that you will be turned over to representatives of the Storm Guard to face punishment."

Slate rose. "We killed only thugs who were molesting pilgrims unjustly. Is it not the duty of any knight to defend the followers of the Book?"

"The first duty is to defend the Book," said Castlebridge. "This is a dangerous land. We are but an island amid a vast ocean of enemies. Our peace with Tempest is a fragile one. In seeking to punish a handful of greedy men, you place the most sacred ground of your faith in danger of invasion."

"This is madness!" Slate cried. "Are there no men among you willing to stand up to evil?"

"Standing up to evil is a vice if it harms the greater good," said Castlebridge. His eyes lifted from Slate to look down the road. Sorrow turned and saw a large group of men on shaggy horses loping up the trail.

"Grant me permission to speak to the Voice of the Book," Slate said.

"Permission denied," said Castlebridge, pointing his lance at Slate. "The only matter left for debate is whether the Storm Guard will take living men into their custody, or corpses. If you wish to make a show of defying me in order to provoke my attack, I understand. Storm Guard justice is known for its brutality. The death I unleash shall be swift and merciful."

"How do you want to handle this?" Sorrow asked. "Should I devour him with flies, or do you just want me knock him off his horse so you can chop off his head and condemn his soul to hell?"

"I'll not use the Witchbreaker upon a fellow knight," said Slate.

"So, flies?"

"I haven't come here to harm the defenders of the temple!"

"Have you come to surrender to the Storm Guard?" she said, looking at the approaching horses. "Because you've got maybe two minutes left to make a decision."

"I'm going to speak to the Voice of the Book!" Slate shouted at Castlebridge. "Do not stand in my way!"

He stepped forward. Castlebridge lowered his lance. Sorrow willed the iron sheathe of her mace to crumble away, revealing the lighting rod within. There was a loud *CRACK* and a flash that left her blinking her eyes. The crystal rod she held was hot and brightly glowing. In the sky, Castlebridge was frowning.

"I don't need my lance to deal with you," he bellowed, flipping his visor down as he dropped his lance and drew his sword. The sword was blood red and had an aura separate from that of Castlebridge. As the knight charged down from the sky brandishing the blade, she had the flicker of an idea that perhaps she should delay her attack in order to learn what enchantments the blade might possess. But the idea vanished as she felt the familiar pressure in her belly of Rott's power bubbling up from the abstract realms. She quickly found the edges of the portal and focused as she widened the gap. Her body convulsed as she threw her helmet aside and snapped her jaws open. A black whirlwind swirled into the air, engulfing Castlebridge and the horse he rode in on.

To her great consternation, Castlebridge and Sunracer VI emerged from the whirlwind unscathed. Castlebridge leaned in his saddle and swung his blade toward her. She jumped aside, but the tip of his sword sliced through her armor as if it were mere fabric, leaving a three-inch gash along her right bicep. She clamped her hand upon the wound as she sucked air through her teeth. The pain was nearly blinding as the blood gushed between her fingers. Worse, the shock of the blow had once more distracted her from properly closing the energy gate. The dose of dark magic dissipating through her set her nerves jangling from scalp to toes.

Sunracer VI turned swiftly, targeting Slate. Slate stood with his legs spread to steady his stance. The horse seemed aimed to collide with Slate's chest, veering at the last possible instant to allow Castlebridge to aim his slashing sword at Slate's neck. Slate's hand shot out and grabbed Castlebridge by the wrist, halting the blow and knocking the older knight off balance. Slate yanked Castlebridge from his saddle and threw him to the ground. Castlebridge's helmet tore free from its clasps as the knight rolled across the rocky earth. He wound up on his back, looking dazed, his arms spread to his side. The red sword was still in his grasp. Slate jumped toward the fallen knight, driving his boot into the wrist that held the blade.

"Yield, and face no further harm," Slate said.

"Fool!" Castlebridge's face twisted with fury. "You don't know what you're doing! It's you who must yield! Your companion's already dead!"

"Wrong," said Sorrow, walking toward them. "Still alive."

"A fleeting condition, witch!" Castlebridge said as he stared at her scalp. "The wounds inflicted by the blood blade never heal. You'll bleed to death soon enough."

Sorrow looked toward the approaching horsemen. She wasn't feeling confident about trying to use Rott's power again, and twenty men on horseback seemed like a lot even for Slate to handle.

"Let's get inside the temple," she said.

"I'll fight to my dying breath to stop you!" growled Castlebridge as he rolled to his side, struggling to free his arm. Fortunately, he was in full plate armor. On the ground, his movements were somewhat reminiscent of a turtle.

Sorrow knelt. She still had one hand clamped onto her arm to slow her blood loss, but she placed the hand of her wounded arm upon Castlebridge's armor. She could feel enchantment within the casing, perhaps a protective spell that had spared him from her power earlier. Enchantment or no, the armor was made from iron, so it was a simple matter to force Castlebridge once more onto his back. She ran her hand from joint to joint, crimping the metal, swiftly turning his armor into a prison.

She tore his cape free. Now that it wasn't flapping, she could see the embroidered letters spelled out 'Castlebridge.' For some reason, this increased her pleasure in tearing the cape into shreds.

She willed her own armor to fall into rust. She wouldn't be needing it anymore. She handed Slate the strips of cloth and said, "Bandage me. Make it tight."

"Your hands…" he said, staring at her talons.

"I know. You can stare at them later. Just bandage me."

He tied the strips around her arm, pulling the cloth so tight it was painful. But the pressure had the desired effect, as the blood loss slowed to a seep.

By now, the horsemen were in full gallop toward them, no more than half a mile away and closing quickly. She looked back and saw an army of knights pouring out of the Temple of the Book. She noticed Sunracer VI returning to the hole she'd originally seen him launch from. Apparently, the steed didn't like Castlebridge anymore than she did.

She turned Slate away from her and wrapped her arms around his chest. "Hold tight!" she shouted as she spread her wings. Her most powerful flap failed to lift them. For her to carry him, she'd need to already have some momentum.

"Run down hill!" she cried as she pushed him. "Keep your arms out to your side!"

"I can't leave the coffin!" he protested.

"We'll be the ones needing coffins if you don't trust me!"

Slate looked unhappy, but he nodded to indicate her argument made sense. He spread his arms and ran downhill, even though this meant he was now charging directly at the mounted Storm Guard. She waited until he was thirty yards away before running after him, then kicking off with all the strength she could muster. She could feel the weariness of her sleepless night draping over her like a heavy blanket, weighing her down as she flapped as furiously as she could manage. It was enough for her to catch air beneath her wings. By now, Slate was a hundred yards down the slope from her. She glided toward him, building speed, the ground flashing by mere inches beneath the tips of her wings. Slate and the horsemen were only yards apart when she caught him and jerked him into the sky. His left foot caught the lead horseman in the face, knocking him from his saddle and stripping Sorrow of a bit of momentum. Gritting her teeth, she flapped so hard she feared her wings would tear from her shoulders. The effort paid off, and soon she was soaring well above the heads of the thundering Storm Guard.

She banked and cut a long arc through the air. Drawing on Jetsam's lessons, she found the edge of a steep slope exposed to the rising sun and caught the wind that pushed up from it. She spiraled higher on the updraft, her sweat turning to beads of ice upon her skin. At last she climbed higher than the temple. She tilted toward it, intending to glide the remaining distance. Unfortunately, as she approached, she saw archers in every window. She wasn't certain she could dodge missiles while carrying Slate.

A curious thing happened as she came within range. All the archers lowered their bows in unison, and vacated the windows of the temple, leaving her a choice of landing sites. She aimed for the largest opening, filled with the brightest lights. It was the only one wide enough to accommodate her wingspan.

"This might get rough!" she called out to Slate. They were flying too fast. Landing at this speed was going to be painful, but if she tried to slow her flight they would drop below the window and crash into the face of the cliff. She would have to turn her wings into parachutes the second they were safely inside. She'd practiced rapid landings with Jetsam, but never carrying an armored knight.

But it wasn't her lack of practice that endangered her as she flashed through the window. Instead, the second she entered the room beyond, her left eye went blind. She crashed into a chandelier comprised of hundreds of tiny glorystones linked together by fine silver chains. The unexpected net entangled her wings and she crashed to the stone floor. Slate tore from her grasp as she bounced upon the white quartz. The glorystones beneath her tore into her like glass shards.

The world swirled slowly as spots danced before her. No matter how hard she blinked, she had no sight at all in her left eye. She tried to rise on her hands and knees but failed, collapsing to the floor, weak as a baby. It was more than just exhaustion or blood loss. It was as if half the life had been sucked from her body.

Slate had fared better. He was already on his feet, studying their surroundings. As near as Sorrow could gather, they were in a long hall lined with doors. At the end of the hall, she saw a large iron door swing open. A man in black robes stepped through, pausing to lock the door behind him. He walked toward them, his hands clasped behind his back. He was old and thin, with thick curls of snow-white hair that hung about his shoulders like a lion's mane. His expression was a curious mix of sternness and serenity as he approached them.

"I apologize for telling the archers to stand down," the man said. "I saw no need for them to get hurt."

"Apologize?" asked Slate.

"The two of you have a thirst for attacking lawful authorities," the man said. "A man of your description killed several guards in the Silver City only weeks ago. You're obviously the same ruffians who abused the port inspectors earlier this week, and I heard you confess to Forthright that you killed the Storm Guards who camped at the pass."

"You heard... how?"

The man shrugged. "I've lived in this place a very long time. I'm spiritually attuned with the very rocks you stand upon. There is nothing that takes place upon this mountain of which I'm not aware."

"Then, you must be—"

"Utmost Humble, the Voice of the Book," he said.

Slate knelt before the man. "Sir, I'm a knight of the book, seeking permission to inter the remains of—"

"A knight?" Utmost said, with a scoff. "Stand up."

Slate stood.

"You're not a knight. You're not even human. You're a bit of clever magic that has broken free of the control of its caster."

"The blood of Lord Stark Tower beats within my veins," said Slate. "His soul is my soul."

"You should be grateful that statement is untrue. Avaris killed Tower with his own sword. The poor man's soul has burned in the deepest pits of hell for nearly five centuries," said Utmost, shaking his head as if recounting it was distasteful. "Take comfort that, when you die, you'll face no such torments. Nothing but oblivion awaits you. It's almost a peaceful fate, if you contemplate it."

"It's not a fate I accept," said Slate.

Utmost sighed. "I understand. You're not to blame for the travesty of your own existence. I'm sure you would prefer to live a life that had some semblance of meaning. And perhaps you will."

Sorrow's head had cleared somewhat by now. She rose to her hands and knees, contemplating the blood on the stone beneath her. Utmost turned his face toward her and said, "You will lie back down."

She did so, though she fought with all her will to rise.

"What meaning?" Slate asked. "What meaning can my life have if I am soulless?"

Utmost gave a feeble smile. "When I turn you over to the Storm Guard, your torture and torment will occupy them for a while. It will give tensions time to ebb. Nearly daily, I'm faced with the emissaries of Tempest, threatening to invade this sanctuary and destroy the One True Book. Ordinarily, I would lend no credence to his threats. But after our mission to kill Greatshadow ended in failure, and our plan to kill Glorious left a human intelligence in command of an elemental power, Tempest has become quite anxious."

"Because he believes he's your next target?"

Utmost laughed. "No. He's not our target. He's our ally. He approached us with a plan to eliminate the other primal dragons. His Storm Guard were the raiders who stole the Jagged Heart. He gave us advice as to which abstract realms would provide the most advantageous battlegrounds. Now that our first two assassinations have gone awry, he's blaming us for the failures."

"What? Why would Tempest ally himself with you? Why would you ally yourself with him?"

Utmost shrugged. "This island has been the birthplace of many religions. Tempest knows that even primal dragons may be slain. He wishes to escape death by transcending his draconic nature and becoming a god."

"And why would you assist him in this?"

"If we trust the truth of our faith, then we trust the truth he will fail. For now our goals are aligned, as he helps us target other primal dragons. Also, there's the not inconsequential matter that he does hold this temple hostage at the moment.

The Storm Guard society doesn't function well. It's corrupt, built upon an unsustainable economy of slaves, and fails even to feed its own people. The Silver Isles would have conquered this land long ago, if not for Tempest's threat to destroy this sacred place." He nodded toward the door he'd entered. "The One True Book lies beyond that door. This holy ground is protected by wards that bar elemental spirits, but, even so, the dragon would only have to extend his power a few hundred feet to destroy it forever."

"Then move the book!" Slate said, sounding completely exasperated.

"The book is too holy for human hands to ever touch," said Utmost. "Until the Omega Reader opens its pages, men's souls are too sullied by sin to survive a brush with the divine power the book contains. They would burn like a leaf placed upon a red-hot forge."

"But—"

Before Slate could argue further, Sorrow finally regained some control of her limbs. She rolled to her side, then sat up.

"You will lie down," said Utmost.

She did, cursing beneath her breath.

"Any advice?" Sorrow shouted.

"What advice do you seek?" asked Slate.

"Avaris can't hear you here," said Utmost. "She's dwelled in the Black Bog so long, her dark soul withers when exposed to the radiance of the glorystones."

"You know about Avaris?"

"And of her plot to reclaim Rott's power."

"You may have some mistaken information," she whispered as she strained to lift herself from the floor.

"You're the one who's been deceived. Avaris once before attempted to steal Rott's power. Of course, Rott's intelligence was far more active then. He resisted her control, and began to control her. She cut herself free from his power before her personality was completely devoured. Now she's watching you to see if Rott's will has decayed sufficiently that her mind could dominate."

"The flaw in that theory is that I'll be one controlling Rott's power."

"Avaris could crush your spirit with no more effort than it would take me to crush a snail. You're no obstacle to her plans, girl, only a stepping stone. At least, you were going to be, before you embarked on your pathetic plan to barge onto this sacred ground and attempt to destroy the One True Book. It's a pity your intelligence doesn't match your audacity."

Sorrow had tucked the lighting rod into a cotton sash around her waist. She felt it beneath her hip. If she could move only a few inches, she could aim it toward Utmost and release its power.

"I can almost hear the gears whirring in your head, witch," said Utmost. "Instead of thinking of desperate schemes of escape, might I suggest this would be a good time to contemplate repentance?"

"It's not escape, I'm scheming," she said through clenched teeth as her talons strained to touch the rod.

"You will go limp," said Utmost, shaking his head.

Every muscle in Sorrow's body fell slack.

Utmost sighed. "You can't say I didn't give you the opportunity to confess your sins and plead for the Divine Author's mercy." Utmost turned toward Slate. "Draw your sword."

The now familiar howls swirled through the air as the blade left its scabbard.

"You imagine yourself to be a continuation of the famed Witchbreaker?" Utmost asked. He didn't wait for Slate to answer. "For one brief moment, allow me to indulge your fantasy." He pointed toward Sorrow.

"There's a witch. *Break her.*"

CHAPTER NINETEEN

RUMBLE

Sorrow held her breath as Slate turned toward her. She managed to lift her head half an inch from the floor before Utmost cried, "You will remain still, witch!"

Sorrow's head banged onto the stone floor. She couldn't even move her jaw to speak. If she opened the dark portal within her to channel flies, would she be able to release them safely, or would they simply tear through her face? She had to try. But despite the full force of her will calling it, the black portal failed to open. The wards that protected this place were too strong for Rott to overcome.

Slate's boots drew closer. From her vantage point, her cheek pressed to the floor, she could only see the two men's feet. Then, unexpectedly, Slate's boots turned from her.

"Don't turn back," Utmost said. "Kill her!"

Slate walked toward the Voice of the Book. The Witchbreaker fell silent as Slate slid it into its scabbard.

Utmost stammered, "Wh-what are you—"

He was silenced by a sudden WHACK. Sorrow couldn't see the source of the noise, but a moment later Utmost crumpled to the floor with blood streaming from his mouth. Sorrow jerked her face off the floor as her body returned to her control.

"You've no authority over me," Slate said, standing over the old man with his fists clenched. "You've no authority over anything!"

"How can you defy me? I'm the highest of the truthspeakers!" Utmost shouted, blood spraying from his torn lips.

"I defy you because you're the lowest of liars," Slate said.

"You've confessed as much with your own lips. The true Voice of the Book would defend his faith with all his body and soul. You've thrown away your authority through compromise and bargains with false gods."

"For the greater good, you fool!" Utmost cried. "Our bargain with Tempest is ultimately a trap for him! When his usefulness to us exhausted, he, too, shall die!"

"So you deceive him?" said Slate. "You befriend him with the intention of stabbing him in the back? These are not the actions of an honest man."

"Who are you to judge me?" Utmost spat out bright red spittle. He wiped his lips and said, "You're nothing but a motherless abomination."

"Whatever my origins," Slate said, "I strive to be an honest man. As Poppy's book teaches, a single honest man outnumbers a legion of liars."

"We'll find out!" Utmost said, before screaming, "Help! Help!"

Slate grabbed Utmost by the back of his robes and pulled him to his feet. "Silence! I'll let you live if you open the door to the One True Book."

"I'll do no such thing!"

"I saw you place the key within your robes. We may both preserve a bit of dignity if I'm not forced to strip you bare to find it."

"What are you doing, Slate?" Sorrow asked as she limped toward him, still pulling shards of glorystone from her skin.

"I'm setting things right," he said. He glanced at her. "Perhaps there was truth to your words. The church has become corrupt, willing to accept evil in the name of maintaining the status quo. But you're wrong to think that the church deserves to be destroyed. It needs instead to be cleansed. We must drive the false prophets from the temple and return the One True Book to the hands of righteous men."

By now, Utmost had his key ring in his hand. "You simple-minded fool. The One True Book must remain in this temple."

Slate pushed him forward.

Utmost continued, "No man may touch the book without destroying his soul. We know the truths within only through prayer and meditation. No man has prayed longer and more intently than I have!"

"Just open the door," Slate said, pushing the aged cleric up to the heavy iron portal.

Utmost toyed with the lone key on the ring. It was a small key for such an imposing door, no longer than a man's thumb. The head of the key was remarkably simple, merely three stubs sticking out from the shaft.

"Stop playing with your key and open the door," said Slate.

Without warning, the key ring fell from Utmost's grasp and clattered on the floor. Sorrow glanced at the iron ring and realized it was empty. Before she could act, Utmost tilted his head backwards as he shoved the key into his mouth.

He fell, choking, both hands upon his throat.

Slate shook his head as he reached for the hilt of the Witchbreaker. "I'd hoped this could be done without any further decapitations."

"That won't be necessary," Sorrow said, placing her hand on the iron door. She willed it to crumble to rust, and was thrown back as a jolt of energy crackled through her, landing hard on the floor, cutting her lip open.

Utmost laughed wetly as he finished swallowing the key. His eyes were filled with something like delight as he watched her writhe in pain. He said, with a raspy voice, "These doors are forged from the same hell steel as the Witchbreaker. That iron nail in your head is useless against its abstract nature."

Sorrow crawled back toward the door. Tears ran down her cheeks. Each inch she moved was agonizing, but Utmost's sadistic laughter spurred her on. When he died, it wouldn't be with a smile on his face.

Her hands fell upon the iron key ring. She rose on rubbery legs as she crushed the ring between her palms and rolled it into a shaft. Despite the claw-like nature of her hands, she still retained her gift for sculpting. It took only seconds to pinch and pull and snip the metal into a duplicate of the key she'd seen.

She slid the key into the lock and turned it. There was a soft, but satisfying, *click*.

Utmost fell silent as his face turned ashen gray.

"You don't look like you're feeling well," she said, as she pushed the door open. "Was it something you ate?"

Utmost didn't answer. Sorrow grew quiet herself as she turned her eyes to the chamber beyond, a simple oval of rough cut white quartz with a low ceiling. The floor was smooth and polished from centuries of use. A a circular groove, ten feet around the central pedestal, had been worn into the stone by innumerable truthspeakers, who had over the years knelt there and pressed their heads against the floor in prayer.

Upon the pedestal of quartz was the One True Book.

The tome failed to impress her. She'd heard the book was as tall as a man, but this was only the size of an atlas: large for a book, but small for a legend. Rather than being bound in the pure white skin of an angel, the book was bound in aged leather that perhaps had once been white, but had long since turned a dull yellow. The pages, rumored to be trimmed with gold, were merely parchment, brown with age. The cover and spine were wordless.

"This is it?" she said, placing her hand upon the wall to steady herself. "This is what caused all the suffering for so many centuries?"

"This hasn't caused suffering," said Utmost. "Suffering is the natural state of mankind. This book is the source of hope. It's the promise that all our earthly travails have meaning, that everything that happens unfolds for a reason."

Sorrow took a stumbling step toward it.

"Go no further," said Slate.

She glanced at him.

"You came here to destroy the book. I will not allow it."

"I don't need your permission," she said. "You should want this as much as I do! Can't you see the mere existence of this book is partially to blame for Utmost making deals with dragons? He loves this pile of parchment so much he cherishes its survival more than he values the lives of pilgrims. Ridding mankind of this vile tome is the only hope of creating a just world."

"You cannot speak to me about making deals with evil," said Slate. "Just what happened when you chased Avaris into the farther room? How many of your nonsensical mutterings have been private conversations with the Queen of Witches?"

"What do you think happened? I made a deal with her. She would teach me to use Rott's powers safely and instruct me in bone-weaving."

"What did you give her in exchange?"

"Nothing. Yet. Just a promise."

"Was destroying the One True Book the promise made?"

"No."

"She couldn't destroy it if she tried," said Utmost. "The second she touches it, her soul with perish!"

Slate tossed Utmost to the floor and walked toward the pedestal.

"What are *your* plans, Slate?" she asked. "You seem to have gotten a bit side-tracked from your plan to lay Stark Tower to rest."

"Small injustices must be ignored in the face of larger ones. I'm going to do what should have been done centuries ago. I'm going to carry this sacred book from this land of dangers and deliver it to the Cathedral of the Book in the Silver City. There it may be defended by men of greater character than those who dwell here."

Slate held his hands over the book.

"D-don't," whispered Utmost. "The divine power within will surely destroy you."

"I'm an abomination not born of woman," said Slate. "I've no soul to risk."

He placed his hands upon the book. Sorrow's heart skipped a beat as he lifted it. Despite her hatred of the book, she half expected Slate to fall over dead. Instead, it was Utmost who clenched his chest with both hands, his face twisting in pain as Slate lifted the tome from its pedestal. The old man's eyes rolled back in his head as his body went limp.

Slate turned toward the door and said, "I'll send anyone who attempts to stop me straight to hell."

Sorrow sighed, her shoulders sagging. "I won't try to stop you. You asked what price I promised Avaris. I promised her I would kill one person she asked me to kill. But I won't harm you. You may be a motherless abomination, but you're also the first honest man I've ever met. I won't have your blood on my hands."

Slate nodded toward the door. "I was talking to them."

Sorrow turned and found the chamber beyond filled with knights. Slate walked toward them, despite being outnumbered at least fifty-to-one. Sorrow tried to summon flies to help clear his path, but still felt no connection to the dark energy.

As Slate approached the knights, one by one they lowered themselves to their knees and took off their helmets, staring at Slate with an expression best described as awe.

The nearest Knight said, "It's said we live in the final pages of the Book. Some believed a child named Numinous was the one who would open the sacred tome, but it's rumored that he failed the tests. Are you the final prophet? Are you the Omega Reader?"

"No," said Slate.

"But you disobeyed the truths spoken by the Voice of the Book. You could not do so unless your truths were greater than his."

"It's foretold that the Omega Reader will be a flawless man, devoid of sin. I'm not that man. These sacred words must wait for their final reader. I'm taking the book to the Silver City. With the book safe, Tempest will no longer be able to corrupt the church."

"You'll not travel alone," said the knight. "My name is Steadfast Plowman, a knight of the book. I didn't take up arms for my faith with the intention of living like a coward. For years, my brother knights and I have seethed in silent anger as our superiors commanded us to ignore the wickedness of the Storm Guard. We're men of true hearts willing to give our lives for your cause."

"Then rise and take arms. The road before us is long and steep. I do not expect our journey to the sea to go unopposed."

"We need not take the road," said Steadfast. "Follow us."

"Give me one more minute to catch my breath," said Sorrow. Slate shook his head.

"I fought beside you believing you were my friend, when all along you plotted with Avaris behind my back. I... do not hate you. I believe that, like Utmost, you possessed good intentions. In the name of a greater good, you've allowed yourself to embrace evil. I won't kill you. You still have hope of redemption. Perhaps one day you can turn from the dark path you've chosen. For now, we must part ways."

Sorrow slid down the wall to rest upon the floor as Slate left the chamber. She didn't have the strength to chase him, and definitely lacked the will to argue with him. She'd spared his life because of his honesty. And because of that honesty, his words had been hammers driving nails of truth into her aching skull. As she sat with her wings pinned beneath her, staring at her clawed hands, she understood that it wasn't her body that had become a monster. She was just as corrupt and compromised as Utmost. She thought her eyes had been forever tuned to see the evil that others were blind to.

In the end, she was the one who'd been most blind. Like her father, she held her principles so dearly, so tightly, that she'd smothered them.

She still had the key she'd used to open the door. She pressed it between her fingers until it became a razor sharp scalpel. She brought the knife toward the left side of her face, until she could no longer see it. In this temple of truth, her left eye was already blind.

In this temple of truth, there was more than one way to undo a bad bargain.

SHE USED THE silver threads from the fallen chandelier to stitch her wounds shut. The wound inflicted by the blood blade continued to ooze despite her efforts, painting her arms in red tendrils. She used the lightning rod as a cane as she hobbled toward the large window they'd flown through.

She steadied herself with a hand on the wall as she looked down. The cliff face below her was sheer. She jerked her head up as battle cries broke out above her. Horses erupted from an unseen window, leaping out into open space and landing on columns of light that shot from their glowing horseshoes. The horses continued to jump until there were more than she could count, each bearing a knight upon its back. She called out "Slate!" as she spotted him in the middle of the pack astride a magnificent black stallion. Whether he heard her or not, he didn't look back.

She looked at the ground once more. With only one eye, her depth perception was too poor for her judge the distance, but in the end, what would it matter? She would either leap and find the strength to fly, or fail and plummet to her death. Whether the distance was fifty feet or five hundred didn't truly matter.

She tucked the lightning rod back into the cotton sash she'd tied around her waist, then held her arms clasped together before her, preparing to dive. She spread her wings and fell forward. The second her toes left the white quartz floor, she felt a surge of strength flow through her. Her connection with Rott had returned! Draconic power pulsed through her veins, feeding her wings. They caught the rushing wind and threw her across the sky, in hot pursuit of the galloping horses.

What foolish thing have you done, girl?

"Avaris?" she cried in shock and dismay.

Did you think that eyes alone sealed our contract? You may pluck out an eye, but you cannot pluck out a soul. I'm part of you until you've fulfilled your vow!

"Fine," said Sorrow. "For the time being, all I want you to do is shut up. I've got my hands full at the moment." Which was true enough, as she reached behind her and grabbed the lightning rod. She paused for a heartbeat as she found a patch of rough scales along her hip. The return of Rott's power had brought further changes to her body, it seemed. She had no time to inspect herself, however. The knights were galloping directly toward the bank of clouds beneath them. Flickers of lightning lit the churning gray mass. She dissolved the iron rings around the rod to protect her from any stray bolts.

Her prescience paid off, as a gray-skinned cloud giant rose from the storm below with a quiver full of glowing javelins strapped to his back. He hurled one at the closest knight, who was thrown from his saddle as a bolt of lightning cut his horse from beneath him. The giant drew a second bolt, but before he could strike, Steadfast Plowman, whom she recognized from his coat of arms, broke free from the pack of knights and charged with blinding speed toward the giant, his lance set to strike. Sorrow winced as Steadfast drove his weapon into the giant's eye. The giant toppled, ripping the lance from Steadfast's grasp, disarming him just as three other giants climbed atop the clouds, javelins at the ready.

Half the knights peeled off to engage in combat while the core of knights surrounding Slate closed even tighter as together they plunged into the clouds. Thunder rumbled as lighting crackled across the sky. Sorrow aimed toward the area of greatest intensity, the lightning rod held before her. Its glow flared as it sucked power from the charged air. Sorrow's wings were quickly soaked by the torrential rain within the cloud, and the winds spun her about like a chicken caught in a tornado. Suddenly her momentum came to a bone-jarring halt as a giant hand wrapped around her, squeezing her torso until she felt ribs snap. A pair of enormous fingers approached her head, looking ready to pinch it from her shoulders.

Her body was already ruined. She opened the dark door inside her, letting the entropic force flow. Flesh sloughed from the giant's hand, leaving only fingers of bone, which loosened their grasp.

Sorrow fell, sucking in wet air, shivering as mixed rain and snow froze on her exposed skin. She managed to spread her wings just as she tumbled out of the clouds. She was mere yards from a snow-covered slope, and it was more luck than skill that allowed her to swerve out of the path of the largest boulder before she slammed into it.

She flapped her wings with all her might, shaking free the ice that coated her, and flew on beneath the rumbling storm. She craned her neck from side to side but couldn't see Slate or the knights anywhere. Had they met their ends inside the cloud? Somehow, she doubted it.

She hurtled down the mountainside at speeds she'd never dared before. The wind froze her arms as she held them before her, turning her skin gray. Or were her limbs turning dark for other reasons?

At last she broke free from the worst of the rain. Before her, she could see the port, and her eyes scanned the rim of the bay looking for the *Circus*. Her heart sank when she found towers of flame rising from that very area. But as she drew closer, she saw that the *Circus* was half a mile out in the bay, all sails set, smashing through the waves.

The flames were coming from the slave market. The whole of the complex was ablaze. A bucket brigade had been formed, but its efforts were too late. The pitch-soaked pilings that supported the dock were the source of the most energetic flames. The firefighters threw down their buckets and ran as the docks groaned, tilting and twisting beneath the weight of the structures upon them. Within seconds, the last half of the dock collapsed, sending great whirlwinds of embers roaring into the sky.

Sorrow flew around the columns of sparks, gritting her teeth as the winds tossed her side to side. Closing on the *Circus* was slow going until she caught the gusts that Gale had summoned to drive to boat to full speed. She rode the wind toward the deck, tilting her legs down to land on the aft-castle.

Gale, Sage, and Rigger were at the wheel, along with Brand. Most of the other Romers and Bigsby were occupied with what looked to be a hundred pygmies, helping them steady themselves as they descended the stairs to below deck. Mako was the only one not visible.

"Get ready for full speed!" Gale called out as she held he hands above her head, fingers spread wide.

"This isn't full speed?" Sorrow struggled to stay on her feet on the pitching deck.

"Sage saw you coming. I slowed down so you could catch us."

Brand turned pale as he looked at her. "What happened?" he asked, studying her face.

She touched the crusted stitches over her empty eye. "I feel like I should have a witty reply, but I don't."

"This has something to do with our conversation?" Sage asked.

"Something, yes."

"Oh. I didn't even notice the eye," said Brand. "I was talking about the scales."

Sorrow let her talons fall to her cheeks. She found her skin was now covered with smooth, hard beads.

"These things happen," she said. She glanced toward the pygmies. "And apparently, a lot of other stuff has happened as well. How did your business meetings go?"

Brand steadied himself against the rail as the wind lashing the ship grew even stronger. He shouted, "One of dad's associates was a slave-trader named Price. I spoke to him for about five minutes before I realized that the only favor I wanted from the sleazy bastard was to watch him suffer and die. But he was thrilled enough to meet me that he gave me a tour of the slave warehouses. From one of the windows, I could see the *Circus*. After that, one thing led to another."

"Where's Mako?" Sorrow asked.

"I'm right here," Mako said as he pulled himself up over the railing, dripping wet. He tossed an auger to the deck, and whipped his head to fling his long, slick hair out of his face. "While Jetsam and Ma got the fire going, I was making certain any ships that might pursue us had holes in their hull."

"What about cloudships?" Sorrow asked.

Gale said, "I'll take Levi at his word that if he'd been commander during the thick of the pirate wars, he would have taken actions to tilt the battles in our favor."

Sorrow looked up. The sky directly above them had patches of blue.

Amid this blue, a trio of horseman could be seen in silhouette, galloping toward the *Circus*.

"They're attacking from above!" Jetsam shouted.

"It's Slate!" Sage called out. "Ma, calm the deck so the horses can land!"

Gale lowered her arms.

"Another delay," grumbled Rigger. "Am I the only one in a hurry to get onto the high sea before Tempest intervenes?"

"Tempest isn't going to pay attention to a few missing slaves," Mako said. He had his eyes fixed on Sorrow. She turned away, feeling awkward. His feelings had been so hurt when she'd spurned his advances. But after her conversation with Gale the other night, she wasn't going to betray the woman's trust by engaging in loveless sex with her son.

"What will it matter if we're on the high seas?" asked Brand. "There are storms at sea as well."

"True," said Gale. "But that's also the domain of Abyss. We could ask for his protection."

Slate and the trio of knights reached the deck. The horse's hooves clomped loudly on the wood as they tried to steady themselves.

"Windswept!" Poppy shouted as she ran toward the steeds. "I've never gotten to touch a real horse!"

"Stay back," said the knight on Slate's right, who wore a green tunic over his armor. "Our steeds are exhausted and nervous after what we've been through." He dismounted, stroking his horse's neck. "I wouldn't want you risking injury."

"I've always dreamed of riding a horse!" said Poppy.

"The experience isn't as pleasant as you might think," Slate said as he dismounted, standing on rubbery legs. He had the One True Book clasped beneath his left arm. It looked a bit waterlogged.

"I can teach you to ride sometime," said Bigsby. "I'm an excellent equestrian."

Everyone looked at him.

"Um," said Brand, "that was the princess who was jousting as a toddler, not you."

"I know," Bigsby said. "But I learned to ride while I was with the circus. I was so good I could stand on horseback and juggle knives as I rode around the tent."

"Wasn't the owner of your carnival killed with a thrown knife?" Brand asked.

"And I made my escape on horseback," said Bigsby. "There's probably a lesson to be learned there." He glanced back at the now distant city, toward the smoke rising to mix with the churning storm front. "Having been an unwilling employee, it does my heart good to see a place like that burn. I only hope Price didn't make it out alive."

"He didn't," said Jetsam, as he guided the last of the pygmies to the stairs.

The pale green pygmy looked forlorn and frightened until

319

Bigsby clicked, clucked, and whistled something to him. The pygmy smiled gently as he went below deck.

"What did you say?" asked Jetsam.

"The smallest men walk away from the longest falls," said Bigsby. "It's an aphorism forest pygmies use to cheer themselves when faced with hard times."

By now the knight to Slate's right, who wore a tunic of gold embroidered with a large red lion, had dismounted. He said, "I thought the cloud giants had the best of us. I can't understand why they suddenly retreated when we were so outnumbered."

"Indeed," said a thundering voice that rolled across the bay. "It's quite the mystery. I look forward to learning who issued such a command once I'm finished retrieving my property."

The thunderhead above the burning docks writhed as a whirlwind spun out to form a long, serpentine neck. Sheets of clouds spread across the sky, shaping themselves into wings. Shadows fell across the *Circus* as Gale raised her hands to summon winds. The sails caught air with a loud *SNAP* and smashed into the rising waves as Tempest emerged from the clouds, a massive gray dragon far larger than their ship. The great beast easily outpaced the *Circus*, looping around before it with the grace of a creature that had dwelled for centuries in the sky.

Tempest's mouth was full of lightning as he said, "You've stolen something from me. I would like it back."

"We'll never give you the slaves!" Brand said, leaping onto the bowsprit and shaking his fist at the sky-monster. Before waiting for the dragon's reply, Brand glanced back at Gale and grinned. "Any of this turning you on?"

Gale smiled. "I'd answer, but I don't want my children to blush."

"Oh, Ma," said Sage.

"The slaves are of no concern," rumbled Tempest. "You've stolen the One True Book. Its presence in my kingdom brings me a great deal of power."

"You've no right to this sacred tome!" the green knight

shouted, drawing his sword. Sorrow was puzzled as a woman's voice suddenly filled the air, singing a rousing battle-hymn. "My singing sword and I shall defend this holy book to our dying—"

There was a flash. A mound of molten slag burned into the black circle on the deck where the knight had stood as flecks of green fabric drifted through the air. The singing sword landed on the deck, still calling out its battle-hymn, until it was drowned out by the wave of thunder that washed across the lurching ship. Sorrow was thrown to the deck. The impact knocked the lightning rod from her hands. It rolled across the planks, bouncing as it went, until she was certain it would fall into the sea. As luck would have it, Bigsby fell in front of the rod and caught it, though Sorrow couldn't tell if he'd leapt to make this catch, or merely lost his footing on the pitching deck.

Tempest whirled around the boat once more, giving everyone time to study the burnt spot that had once been a man. His voice again thundered through the rigging. "Place the book upon the spot I've marked, turn away, and I shall spare you."

Gale shouted, "Hold steady for the mouth of the bay!"

"Have we thought about giving him the damn book?" Rigger asked. "What's it to us?"

"If he wants the book badly enough to chase us, he can't capsize the ship without losing it! If we turn the book over, we've nothing to shield us!"

"You've nothing to shield you now," Tempest said, as he turned his gaze toward Gale and opened his jaws wide. Sorrow could see straight down his gullet as the lightning arced toward them.

CHAPTER TWENTY

FLESH AND BONE

BIGSBY MADE IT to his feet a few yards in front of Gale just as lighting erupted from Tempest's jaws. The lighting rod flared as thunder cracked so loud it rattled Sorrow's teeth. In the aftermath, no one was harmed.

Tempest's eyes narrowed as he glared at the dwarf. He flapped his wings forward and the waves rose in towering whitecaps, crashing across the deck. Sorrow was swept from her feet by the wall of water. As she was washed over the rail, ropes snaked through the surf to wrap around her arms and legs. She jerked to a halt, yelping in pain as her stitches tore, and wound up choking on a mouthful of brine.

As Rigger dragged her back aboard, she saw Slate was gone. Had he been washed overboard, or had he gone below to place the One True Book in a safer location? Two of the horses skittered in the air a yard above the pitching deck. The third horse charged toward Tempest with the red-lion knight in the saddle. A tight shaft of brilliant ruby light beamed from the tip of his lance and left a path of burnt scales across Tempest's face. The dragon roared, punctuating his pain by spitting lightning. Knight and horse fell toward the water, trailing smoke.

"I gave you a fair chance to surrender the tome!" Tempest cried. "You shall pay the ultimate price for your defiance!" Lightning arced from his jaws once more, targeting the front of the boat, well clear of Bigsby's rod. The top half of the foremast toppled into the crashing waves, the sails in flame.

Tempest circled the ship, whipping his tail, leaving waterspouts in his wake. Hail pelted Sorrow like shot from a sling. She was too rattled by the assault to think clearly. She could feel the dark energy building in the center of her being, but didn't dare attempt to release it while she was so muddled.

A chunk of hail the size of a fist slammed into her forehead, knocking her flat. She blinked stars from her eyes as she stared up at the churning clouds. Without warning, the clouds tore in twain and a giant man dropped from them. It was Levi, grown to half a mile in length, splashing into the bay with a wave that threatened to turn the *Circus* on its side. Levi wrapped his arms around Tempest's neck, dragging the massive reptile down into the sea.

Instantly, the waterspouts collapsed upon themselves. Sorrow grabbed the railing and struggled back to her feet as the wind lessened and the hail stopped pounding her. Tempest was apparently as susceptible to distraction as any other living thing.

"Go!" Levi shouted as the backwash swirled the *Circus* past his thighs. "I can't hold him for long!"

"You can't hold me at all!" cried Tempest as an enormous claw closed around Levi's throat. With a rapid slash, he slit Levi's jugular.

"Levi!" Gale cried as her son fell toward the *Circus*, clutching his windpipe.

Levi's eyes were unfocused, but with his last flicker of thought he lurched to the side to avoid crushing the ship. Blood sprayed across the *Circus* as he fell, speckling the sails with crimson as his enormous body splashed into the water. The *Circus* rose atop a wave that lifted the ship to the clouds.

At last the wave broke, dropping the ship into the brine red with blood. Sorrow held her breath as the ship plunged beneath the surface. She couldn't see a thing for half a minute, until the *Circus* popped above the bloodied water like a cork.

"That son of a bitch!" Rigger cried, turning the wheel hard. Every rope on deck rose, until the ship resembled an inverted jellyfish, its tendrils probing for a meal of dragon.

"What are you doing?" Brand shouted.

"I'm going to drown that bastard!" Rigger answered. "The waves are the domain of Abyss! Tempest will be weakened if he doesn't make it back to the sky!"

Rigger's hope of revenge came to a rapid end as Tempest swam away from the *Circus*, his body whipping through the water. When he finally spread his wings, they caught the wind and lifted him from the whitecaps. Tempest flew nearly a mile away from the ship before turning. His mouth glowed as he opened his jaws once more. There was a loud *crack*, but again his lightning failed to rake the deck. Instead, Sorrow saw the arc stop a few hundred feet before the dragon's gaping mouth. She narrowed her eyes, squinting through the squall, cursing her half-blindness.

She spotted the thin columns of light cast by a knight's horseshoes. Only it wasn't a knight in the saddle. It was Bigsby, lashing the steed forward, holding the glowing lightning rod above the long, flowing locks of his bright blonde wig.

"Is he committing suicide?" Sorrow shouted.

"When the hell did he get the wig?" Brand asked.

Rigger fought the wheel as the ship slid down a mountain of water. "He said he was going to shove the rod down the dragon's throat! If he can rob the beast of his lightning, we stand a chance!"

The dragon assisted Bigsby in his mission by thrusting his neck forward and snapping his jaws shut, swallowing the horse in a single gulp.

"Now!" Cinnamon shouted.

Sorrow turned in time to see Poppy balanced on her sister's shoulders. The girl jumped off and Cinnamon shot into the air, tracing a perfect arc toward the dragon's nose.

"No!" Gale cried as she watched her daughter fly.

"Yes," Sage shouted from beside Poppy. "I helped them aim! She's going to hit her target!"

"It was Cinnamon's idea," Poppy said, defensively. "She's going to make the dragon so sick he can't fight!"

"Have you both lost your minds?" Gale cried.

Sage knelt and ran her fingers along the deck. It looked as if the planks were awash with wine. "I've never seen things more clearly." She turned and ran for the hold just as Slate emerged from below deck, Witchbreaker in hand.

Sorrow had no time to follow what was happening on the ship. Instead, she watched Cinnamon land dead center of Tempest's snout. The dragon's eyes grew wide. His jaws snapped open as his tongue shot from his mouth as if it was trying to escape. Bigsby tumbled out of the dragon's mouth, plummeting toward the sea, leaving his wig fluttering in mid-air. He looked to still be alive to judge from his flailing limbs, but he was falling from a quarter mile up. His odds of surviving the impact weren't favorable.

Just before Bigsby hit, Mako shot from the waves like a missile, wrapping his arms around the dwarf, absorbing some of his momentum as they splashed into the froth.

Tempest whipped his head back and forth, his body convulsing as he gagged. Cinnamon lost her grasp on his scales and was tossed aside. Sorrow hoped Mako saw her as the girl plummeted. Instead, it was Jetsam who came to her rescue, jumping from wave to wave, sprinting and vaulting until he neared her. He used the momentum of a cresting wave to kick into the air, spreading his arms to catch his sister before they both disappeared.

Tempest cut a long, slow arc through the air as he probed his jaws with his claws, plucking free the lightning rod.

"Poppy!" Slate shouted. "Pop me!"

The girl leapt into the riggings and jumped onto his shoulders. Slate zoomed into the sky, brandishing the Witchbreaker. Tempest turned his back toward the knight and lashed out with his tail, batting Slate back toward the ship. Rigger snared him in ropes as he fell, but Slate still hit the deck hard enough that Sorrow felt the impact.

Sage came back from the hold, dragging the masthead of the *Freewind*.

"Levi hasn't died in vain," she announced. "His life energy is soaking every board! It's the same aura that used to envelop the *Freewind* when we'd cross into the abstract realms! We have to get Grandmother in place on the bow! If we free her, we can escape to the Sea of Wine!"

"Give her to me!" Rigger shouted, wrapping his ropes around the wooden figure. "I can lash her to the hull in seconds!"

Sorrow headed toward the front of the ship. "Contact with the blood may be enough to free her, but I'll use my powers to blend the old figurehead to the ship!"

The figurehead was directly above Sorrow, carried forward by ropes. Without warning, a reptilian claw stretched from the clouds and tore the wooden bust from Rigger's grasp.

"Was this precious to you?" Tempest snarled as he whirled above them. The sea began to swirl as he swept around them, sending the *Circus* in a dizzying spin. "As precious as the book was to me?"

"Where's Jetsam?" Mako asked as he leapt over the rail, dragging Bigsby by the collar. The dwarf gasped loudly as he hugged the deck.

"He brought Cinnamon on board then went back into the air," said Sage, "but he can't fight the dragon alone!"

"He's not alone," said Sorrow, clenching her talons. She spread her wings, allowing the hurricane winds to snatch her from the deck. She didn't want to be touching the *Circus* for what was coming next.

Tempest turned his jaws toward her. Lightning glowed in his mouth.

She opened her jaws and a jet of flies shot forth. They quickly burnt to ash as Tempest unleashed his lightning. Sorrow's human skin felt as if it was boiling away.

But not from the lightning.

Because the second her feet had left the deck, she'd focused on the nexus of the dark energy, seeing it clearly in her mind's eye like a wobbling black disk. She grabbed the portal with the fingers of her mind and stretched it as wide as possible. Her blood turned to ice as she stared into the void beyond.

The void stared back, with eyes devoid of all emotion other than hunger.

"Come out," she whispered.

And it came.

Every time she'd killed by releasing flies, she'd wondered in morbid curiosity what it must feel like for those caught on the edges of her assault. These poor souls survived the initial wave of acid spewing insects only to have the few that burrowed into their skin multiply and devour them from within. Now she understood, as a billion unseen teeth chewed her muscles and gnawed her bones, erupting from her skin in black boils, until the whole of her body was covered in a shell of flies, gleaming black and chitinous. Her body swelled, doubling in size, then doubling again. She flapped her wings out of pure instinct, keeping airborne as she recovered her wits enough to scream.

Only, as the air rushed through a windpipe now several yards long, it erupted from her toothy jaws as a roar. All pain vanished as unearthly strength flowed through her new muscles. During her transformation, she'd lost sight of Tempest. She banked, curving her serpentine neck enough that she could see her new draconian form.

Pain returned suddenly as the plate-like scales along her ribs began to burn. Thunder nearly deafened her as it crashed into her eardrums, now larger than dinner plates. Tempest spit another gob of lightning, blowing a hole in her thigh. The damage would have disintegrated her human body, but she was now more massive than a whale, and the burnt crater in her side felt like nothing more than a solid punch.

There was no blood. She felt a flicker of panic as she realized that she had no heartbeat, but the panic quickly changed to understanding. Rott's body was already dead, and had been for centuries. The strength she felt in her limbs was not the power of life, but the unstoppable elemental force of decay.

She blinked as she turned back toward Tempest and realized she was now seeing him through two eyes. Had she finally broken her connection with Avaris? She had no time to contemplate this, or anything, as she sailed through the sky toward the dragon.

Tempest's jaws again glowed. She belched out a cone of swirling flies that met the lightning, the survivors flitting onward to speckle the storm-dragon's blue gray hide. Sorrow glanced down to make sure the *Circus* wasn't directly beneath them. She saw Poppy balanced on Slate's shoulders, but the ship was in the clear if she or Tempest fell.

The distance between her and Tempest closed in seconds. Before she could understand what was happening, Tempest's jaws snapped around her throat. If she'd still needed to breathe, the blow might have been fatal. Her fear that they would crash into the sea proved unfounded as a powerful whirlwind swept around them both, pushing them higher in the sky. She wrapped her tail around the storm-dragon and raked at his belly with her hind claws. Rott's power flowed through her limbs and the storm-dragon's scaly flesh sloughed away in massive strips of putrid meat. Her mind went clear, all thoughts silent as lightning boiled her blood from snout to tail. But as her human mind faltered, Rott's draconian hunger came to the fore and she sank her jaws into the meaty flesh of Tempest's powerful shoulders. Tempest's jaws loosened on her neck from the shock of the blow and she vomited flies into his gaping wounds. Maggots bubbled up along the length of Tempest's spine as he writhed in agony.

Sorrow was vaguely aware of something slamming onto her back, near her hips. She ignored the blow, focusing on the entropic energy surging through her jaws into her struggling victim. They lurched through the sky as one of Tempest's wings suddenly tore from his shoulders, spiraling off, leaving a trail of engorged worms. The storm-dragon's howls suddenly went silent as a loud, wet, gurgle came from his back. The

JAMES MAXEY

maggots had eaten through his skin to open his lungs to the air. Tempest went still as Sorrow released his now skeletal form, and watched it fall lifelessly to the sea.

The bust of Jasmine Romer also plunged into the waves. She caught a glimpse of Mako leaping into the chaotic water. She spread her wings wide in the buffeting wind to keep from joining him. She climbed toward the roiling clouds. The weight that had slammed into her hips now shifted to the center of her back and clung there.

Then, to her dismay, the clouds bulged downward, as a dragon's face took shape from the billowing vapors.

"Fool!" Tempest thundered as the clouds turned into jaws large enough to swallow Sorrow whole. His eyes glowed like twin suns as he turned his gaze upon her. "I am the will of the whirlwind! The heart of the hurricane! The soul of the storm! I am the lord of wind itself, a god of this world! Do you think you can stop me by destroying mere flesh?"

His new jaws shot toward Sorrow. She opened her mouth to release more flies, but to what end? If she destroyed Tempest's body yet again, he would merely grow another one. Her touch could destroy all material things, but how could she attack his soul?

As she hesitated, the weight upon her back lifted and what felt like tiny footsteps ran the length of her neck. As Tempest closed his jaws around her, ready to bite her in half, Slate suddenly ran between her eyes and along her snout, the Witchbreaker held above his head with both hands.

He leapt, shouting, "It's not your flesh my blade thirsts for, monster!"

He landed upon the creature's gray tongue and plunged his blade into the roof of the dragon's mouth as it closed. She heard the blade bite through bone, plunging into the gray matter beyond.

Tempest's teeth turned to mist as they sank through the scales on Sorrow's back. She could see nothing around her but gray

329

haze as the interior of the storm-dragon's mouth changed once more to clouds.

Her body dove almost before she understood why it was doing so. She emerged from the clouds and spotted Slate falling toward the ocean. She flapped her wings to overtake him, snatching the knight from the air with her hind claws, leveling off as she charged toward the *Circus*. Ropes still snaked into the air around the ship. Did they understand that the black dragon approaching them was her?

She dropped Slate as she passed over the ship, counting on Rigger's reflexes to catch the knight. She spun around and tried to call out, "I'm Sorrow! I won't hurt you!" but no sound escaped her lungs. She'd forgotten to breathe since exhausting her lungs earlier.

Needing a moment of stillness to ponder her new condition, she landed in the sea. When she'd first encountered Rott, he'd been swimming through the Sea of Wine, so she didn't fear sinking. The sea was calming as the clouds began to dissipate. It felt like mere minutes had passed since she'd leapt from the Temple of the Book, but the sun had only been low on the horizon then. Now, the moon slowly emerged from the thinning haze. The enormity of what she'd just done slowly sank into her.

The *Circus* pulled alongside her. The clown figurehead was gone, and Mako and Jetsam were at work with hammers, fastening the bust of Jasmine Romer beneath the bowsprit, guided by Sage, who balanced on a rope beside them. Gale and Brand stood at the wheel. Brand's arms were wrapped around Gale, who sagged into his embrace, tears in her eyes. Bigsby was up in the riggings, stretching his stunted arms as far as he could manage, his fingers spread wide, as he snatched his fluttering wig from the air.

Cinnamon, Poppy, and Slate stood at the rail, staring down at Sorrow.

"You saved us!" Cinnamon shouted.

"I thought the horses were windswept!" Poppy called out. "I didn't know you could turn into a dragon! By the seven stars, you have to give me a ride!"

"You'd ride her even smelling like that?" Cinnamon asked.

Sorrow wondered what was wrong with the way Poppy smelled, until she realized that Cinnamon was talking about her. Her sense of smell and taste were mercifully absent. She remembered Rott's putrid aroma from the Sea of Wine and was grateful for her missing senses.

Sorrow lifted her head from the waves and made the conscious choice to breathe. "Perhaps another time," she answered with a deep, guttural voice she didn't recognize as her own.

Slate removed his helmet. He looked heartbroken as he asked, "Can you... can you change back?"

"I don't know how. I think... I think I may be spending the rest of my life this way." Assuming *life* was the correct word. Her voice caught in her throat as she thought of it. She'd lived so long consumed by anger and grief that she'd never noticed the wonder of her mere human life. But as she looked at Slate and the others, she understood that her humanity was the most precious thing she'd ever possessed. She now had all the power she'd ever wanted, and more. She'd become the Destroyer that Walker had come to witness. She now had the strength to topple churches and crush kingdoms. She possessed the pure force to put an end to everything she hated.

She would have traded it all to be once more standing on the ship on human legs, with the music of a heartbeat pulsing through her.

"What will you do now?" Slate asked.

"I don't know," Sorrow whispered, or at least as close to a whisper as she could manage from her gargantuan throat.

I know.

"No!" Sorrow cried in anguish.

"What's wrong?" Slate asked.

"It's Avaris! She's still in my head!"

We made a bargain, girl. Until you kill the person of my choosing, I'm part of you. But don't despair. It's time for me to name my chosen target. Obey, and you shall be free.

"It cannot be anyone upon this ship! Our bargain was that it would be a person I agreed to be guilty! Someone worthy of death! All aboard this ship are innocent!"

But what of those who swim beside it?

Sorrow swallowed hard, a very long and dramatic gesture given that her neck was nearly as long as the *Circus*.

Kill yourself, Sorrow.

Sorrow didn't answer.

You've nothing left to live for. You've lost the last of your humanity. You've become the monster of flesh that you long ago became of the soul. Death will be a sweet release from the torment of the sins that burn inside you.

"How can I die?" she screamed. "This body is already dead!"

Slate could end your misery. He wouldn't deny your request.

Sorrow stared at the clearing sky, toward the stars above, which took on halos from the dampness of her eyes. Avaris had chosen her victim well. Sorrow couldn't dispute that she was deserving of punishment for all the things she'd done. But as she looked back at the *Circus*, and saw Slate studying her with tears in his eyes, she thought of his reaction on learning of his inhumanity. He'd left the Black Bog not in despair, but with an attitude of atonement. He'd chosen to fight for redemption.

She couldn't surrender all hope. Whatever had happened to her body, her soul was still her own. Perhaps she'd trapped herself in this strange half-life, but she still could think. As long as she had free will, there was hope. Slate wouldn't have given up, nor would any of the Romers.

Kill yourself now, or forfeit all!

"No!" Sorrow shouted. "I defy you!"

Once again, laughter filled her skull from the inside. She lost all sensation from her tail, then her limbs, then her torso. Her eyes lost all sight as she found herself gagging breathlessly in the foulest atmosphere imaginable. Despite herself, she filled her lungs in amazement as she realized that she once more had human arms and legs... even if they were encased in quivering acrid slime.

Suddenly, she found herself flying at great speed. Her sight returned as she passed between massive black teeth and emerged into the night sky. She tumbled head over heels, slime flying from her limbs as she skipped across the ocean, until at last she sank beneath the water.

She gasped as she kicked back to the surface. She ran her hands along her scalp and found that Rott's nail was gone. There wasn't even a scar. The whole of her head was smooth as she probed it frantically. All her nails were gone! Her reborn body at least had two eyes, and all her many wounds were healed, even the one left by the blood blade. But she was utterly powerless as Avaris rose from the waves in Rott's body, her hind claws finding the bottom many leagues below. The ancient witch stood like a tower, her mighty lungs sounding like giant bellows as she inhaled, before setting the sea shuddering with her laughter.

"It's mine once more!" she cried. "Rott's will is completely absent! At long last I have the power to avenge the indignities I've suffered!"

Slate rocketed into the air toward the dragon-witch, propelled by Poppy. Avaris reacted with the speed of thought, snatching him from the air with one claw, plucking the Witchbreaker from his grasp with the other.

"Your glass armor insulates you well from my touch," she said. "A pity it won't spare you from your own blade!"

But as she fumbled with the weapon, tiny in her massive claws, it slipped from her grasp. Before she could snatch it back, a rope whipped out from the *Circus* and wrapped around the hilt. A dozen other lines knotted themselves around her claws, straining to pull Slate free.

Sorrow spat out seawater as she bobbed in the waves caused by the thrashing dragon. A muscular arm wrapped around her waist as Mako shouted in her ear, "Don't struggle!"

In a dozen powerful kicks, he dragged her back to the *Circus*. He grabbed a rope and they rose toward the deck.

He didn't look at her directly as he softly said, "I'm sorry... the other night when I kissed you –"

"It's okay," she said. "You've nothing to apologize for. It was a confusing night for both of us."

Then they were both back on the deck, which lurched sharply as Avaris tugged at the ropes that tangled her.

"I can't free Slate!" Rigger shouted. "The dragon's too strong!"

"We'll have to depart without him!" Sage answered.

"We can't leave him!" Poppy screamed as she ran toward Sorrow and draped a blanket over her naked shoulders.

"Leave for where?" Sorrow asked as she pulled the blanket around her. "What's going on?"

"Levi's blood has soaked every inch of the hull," Sage said. "He died to save us, and in his sacrifice he's given new life to grandmother as well. We can travel once more to the Sea of Wine!"

"It seems remarkably cool-headed to think of freeing your grandmother after the shock of watching your brother die," said Sorrow.

Sage nodded. "We'll all grieve later. The important thing at the moment is to make sure no other Romers die today."

The main mast creaked and groaned as it bent like a fishing pole. Avaris had stopped thrashing randomly against the ropes and was now coolly pulling the ship toward her.

"We can't wait any longer!" Gale cried as she knelt on the deck. "Whatever Sage did, I can sense mother's spirit spreading through the hull once more. We have to cross into the Sea of Wine before the *Circus* is torn apart! I'm sorry!"

"No!" Sorrow shouted. "We can't flee to the abstract realms! Rott already swims the Sea of Wine. Avaris might be even more powerful!"

"We have to try!" Gale shouted, placing her hand upon the wine-colored wood. The whole of the ship gleamed in the moonlight. The glow encompassed Avaris as well.

Avaris suddenly turned her head to the sky and shouted, "No! I cannot leave now! I defy your summons!"

"Release the ropes!" Sage screamed. "She's crossing over with us!"

But it wasn't the *Circus* that tugged the witch-dragon toward the abstract realms. Instead, the sea boiled as Abyss, the dragon of the sea, rose from the depths behind the black dragon.

"No dragon may refuse the call," he growled as he clamped his turtle-beak onto her wing.

The material world grew ghostlike around Sorrow. She raised her hand and found she could see through her flesh to her bones.

CHAPTER TWENTY-ONE
CONVERGENCE

"SOMETHING'S GONE WRONG!" Sage shouted. "We aren't passing cleanly to the Sea of Wine! It's like we're caught in some vortex!"

The sea churned as Abyss's island-sized body changed suddenly to churning whitecaps. Rott's body trembled, then collapsed, changing into a dragon sized mass of writhing maggots that fell toward the frothing waves.

The night vanished, replaced by bright, dazzling sunlight. Sorrow clamped her eyes shut. She blinked and saw Slate tumbling through the sky toward the deck. Rigger was apparently blinded as well; no ropes moved to catch the knight. He slapped into the mainsail, his armor tearing the fabric as he slid down it, before dropping ten feet to the deck with a *THUMP.*

Sorrow ran to see if he'd survived the fall, but was distracted as her vision cleared and she recognized her surroundings. "This is the convergence!" Sorrow shouted as she looked around at the tropical seas. "It's where the primal dragons meet to talk to one another!"

Sorrow craned her neck to see which dragons were present. Greatshadow's smoke poured up from the sea, as did Kragg's stony spine. A massive iceberg rose from the northern waves, as a tropical jungle screaming with the cries of a million animals rose to the south.

The ship groaned as it shuddered to a sudden halt, run aground on an island of wriggling maggots that clotted beneath them. Beside the ship, a larger mass of maggots climbed skyward, hatching into black flies that took on the form of Rott.

The central sea bulged upward as Abyss rose from the depths, lifting his head to stare in the direction of the *Circus*. "This is not your first time here, witch. You cannot claim ignorance of the rules. When you are summoned to the convergence, you answer."

Sorrow thought Abyss was speaking to her, but before she could think of a response, Avaris roared, "Don't speak to me of rules, sea-dragon! I'm destruction and ruin! The death of all who displease me is now the only law!"

Hush rose from the iceberg to the north and turned her face toward Avaris. "Destruction and ruin are the order of the day, witch! Tempest has been slain!" The ice-dragon's eyes narrowed as she looked around at her kindred. "I warned you all of the dangers! I warned you that mankind was a threat to each of us! With Tempest slain, can you still be blind to the consequences of inaction?"

"I witnessed his death," said Abyss. "Tempest could have avoided his destruction simply by ignoring the humans. He brought his end upon himself by meddling too deeply in the affairs of men."

"Believe as you wish," said Hush. "But your voice is only one among many. I bring you all here to ask again, shall we destroy mankind? I say yes!"

"No!" Greatshadow roared as he rose in a whirlwind of smoke and sparks from his volcanic home. "Tempest brought his fate upon himself. We cannot punish mankind for his hubris!"

"Agreed," said Abyss.

"I vote for death!" rumbled Kragg. His mountainous form shifted, sending rocks sliding from his limbs into the sea. "First Verdant, then Glorious, now Tempest? I would be done with this danger that I might slumber in peace."

"Abundant!" Hush demanded. "What say you?"

"Men are still beasts," she said, folding her arms across her chest. "I cannot condone their extinction. Can we not be satisfied with destroying all they have built? Let us tear down their cities and burn their fields. Let us strip the clothes from their backs and force them naked into the forests, where they may root and forage to survive. These arrogant beasts have forgotten their animal nature. It would be satisfying to remind them."

"No!" shouted Hush. "Humiliation is not enough! Destruction is the only solution!"

"Agreed," said Kragg.

"Then we are deadlocked," said Greatshadow. "No opinion has the majority!"

"I vote for destruction!" Avaris said, rising up on an island of maggots. "The men who dwell within the world are corrupt and pitiful creatures, worthy only of disdain! Let us wipe them from creation! In my home within the Black Bog, I've labored for centuries to perfect a new breed of men. These are superior to their predecessors in every way, and completely obedient to my will. Under my guidance, these new men shall never endanger another dragon!"

"You get no vote!" Abundant growled. "Rott's mind is still silent. You're nothing but a human puppet master, making his jaws move. And you've brought other men! You sully these sacred seas with their presence!"

Avaris turned her gaze upon toward the *Circus*. "These pests? They will bother us no longer."

Avaris inhaled deeply, her torso swelling. With a buzzing roar, a wave of flies churned from her jaws and shot toward the ship.

Sorrow's eyes turned toward the golden disk above. "Stagger!" she yelled. "Now would be a good time to help!"

"I was just thinking that myself," a voice said from the heavens. Fingers of golden light beamed down, shaping into a hand that closed around the flies. When the hand opened, the cloud of pestilence had vanished.

Sorrow shielded her eyes as Stagger knelt upon the island of light above the convergence, smiling as he leaned over the edge to look down. Avaris turned away from his outstretched arm, shrieking. Stagger caught the dragon by the tail. In scale, he was like a man catching a cat.

"No!" Avaris sobbed as she clawed the maggots beneath her. "No! Let go! Let me go!"

"You're the one holding onto something that isn't yours," Stagger said.

Rott fell silent, his body collapsing limp upon the worm island as black smoke bubbled from his nostrils. The smoke shrieked as it coalesced into the shape of a woman before flying off over the waves.

"She gone!" Sorrow cried. "Utmost told me Avaris couldn't stand the light of glorystones. Stagger's whole body is a glorystone!"

"Her vote still counts!" Hush cried.

"No," Kragg grumbled. "It would be base hypocrisy to pretend that the witch spoke for Rott. We continue to be deadlocked."

Stagger sat on the edge of the sun island, dangling his feet as he looked down. "Permit me to undeadlock you. Allow me to introduce myself. My name is Stagger, and I'm the new sun. It's a pleasure to meet you."

"You're just another interloper," Kragg said.

"And you violate the sanctity of this place by attacking a dragon!" Hush screamed.

"Rott's none the worse for wear," said Stagger. "I just helped rid him of a parasite."

"Using power that you've stolen," said Abundant. "The stink of humans is on everything these days."

Stagger stepped down from the sun to stand amid the dragons, a glowing giant with skin too bright for Sorrow to look at directly.

Stagger crossed his arms and said, "I know that none of you are happy I'm here, but I suggest you get used to it. I've been practicing this avatar trick. I know how to get into your little clubhouse any time I want."

"You shouldn't speak to us so boldly, human," said Kragg. "It's not so long ago you were a living man. There are still things in this world that are precious to you. Things that dwell in our domains."

Stagger nodded. "Agreed. I don't deny you have the power to hurt me. I even acknowledge that, collectively or alone, you have the power to wipe mankind from the planet. I know I couldn't stop you. But I also know, if you decide to do so, I could make things very uncomfortable for all of you."

"Was that a veiled threat?" asked Hush.

"Allow me to unveil it. This convergence seems like a pretty nice place, the green waters warm and sparkling in the sunshine. And guess who owns that sunshine? I have the power to turn my back on you all. I can simply leave the sky and make the world a very dark, unpleasant place in the aftermath. The seas will freeze. The trees and animals will wither and die. You'll win a world free of men. You'll simply lose daylight, forever."

"Eternal winter is what Hush desires!" Abyss bellowed.

"So she's happy. What about the rest of you?"

"I'm not happy being threatened, human," said Kragg.

"Nor am I," said Abundant. "I recognize you have the power to carry out your threat, but you cannot protect humanity forever. You've seen by now that no dragon is immortal. Why do you believe you will outlive us?"

"I'll worry about how this ends another time," said Stagger. "For now, the only thing I ask in exchange for sunrises and sunsets is that men be left to live however they wish."

"Very well. I vote with Greatshadow and Abyss," said Abundant. "Mankind shall be spared. For now."

"We're concluded here," said Abyss. He swam toward the island of maggots that the *Circus* was beached upon, sending a bulging wall of water onto the shore to lift the ship. The waves crashed upon the hull, forming an inhuman voice that gurgled, "Leave and do not return!"

"Hold tight!" Gale shouted as the *Circus* rocked upon the tide, the hull bumping along Rott's submerged and lifeless body. "Let's get to the Sea of Wine before we lose our bottom!"

"We've only made the journey by moonlight," Rigger said. "What's going to happen if we try to make the jump in sunlight? Do we even know that we can get there from here?"

"Do we have a choice?" asked Mako. "Do it!"

Gale knelt and placed her hands on the boards.

Instantly, daylight changed to darkness. Sorrow couldn't even see her hand before her face. Everything was quiet until Brand flicked open his glorystone pendant.

"Where are we?" he asked.

"Nowhere," said Sage, staring into her spyglass. "We... we've crossed into a place beyond all dreams or myths." Her face turned pale. "This is limbo."

Sorrow looked over the rail. The ship wasn't floating in water. It hung in mid-air, supported by nothing. Nor was it falling; there was no hint of any breeze or motion.

"I've got an idea," said Bigsby. "Let's go somewhere."

Gale still knelt on the deck, her shoulders trembling as she pressed her hands against the boards. "I'm trying to push the ship across the abstract barriers, but this place... it has no edges! It has no barriers to cross."

"We got in," said Mako. "There must be a way out."

"Those poor pygmies in the hold," said Cinnamon. "They've kept so quiet through all of this. They must be terrified."

"You're not?" asked Bigsby.

The girl shrugged. "We're all still together. Romers can figure out anything."

"But can we figure out nothing?" asked Jetsam, scratching his head as he studied the surrounding void.

Sorrow suddenly remembered Slate. She ran back to the main mast and found him sprawled there, face down, completely limp. She knelt and turned him onto his back.

"Is he alright?" asked Rigger. "I didn't even know he'd made it back onboard."

"Avaris dropped him as we passed between realms," said Sorrow. "I can't tell if he's breathing!"

She pulled off Slate's helmet. He had a knot on his forehead the size of an egg. Blood was caked around his nose. She held her fingers over his lips and felt no air.

She pressed her cheek to his chest, but couldn't hear a heartbeat through the thick glass. She tried to will the glass to dust, but it didn't respond. She was truly powerless.

Except...

She'd always had the power of bone-weaving. She didn't know exactly how to access these powers. But perhaps there was a reason why, in storybooks, curses were always lifted with a kiss.

And so she kissed him, placing her lips tentatively against his at first, then more firmly. Long seconds passed as she felt heat grow where their faces touched.

And yet... with their lips pressed together, there was no mistaking the fact that he wasn't breathing. She placed both hands upon his cheeks and opened his mouth, breathing into him as her tears flowed.

The air she filled him with left his lungs as a soft groan. She pulled her face away, uncertain if she'd heard the sound at all. At last he inhaled on his own. His eyes fluttered open as he lifted his fingers to touch where Sorrow's tears trickled down his cheek.

His eyes focused on her face, still only inches from his. To her great shock, he placed his hand on the back of her neck and pulled her lips to his once more. Her eyes grew wide.

He opened his eyes as well and she pulled away. "Forgive me," he said. "I'm just overjoyed to see that you're human once more!"

"No apology necessary. I'm happy to see you too. But... we perhaps should celebrate our mutual joy someplace a bit more private?"

She looked around to find all the Romers gathered round them, illuminated by the light from Brand's locket. Brand and Gale were holding hands; was it just to comfort each other, or had Brand finally won Gale over?

"Don't stop on account of us," said Jetsam.

Gale slapped him on the back of the head.

Mako turned and walked off into the shadows.

Slate rose to his elbows and looked around. "It's quiet. I take it we defeated Avaris?"

Sorrow nodded. "We sent her running home with her tail between her legs."

"I'm not sure *we* did much of anything," said Rigger. "Stagger did all the work. I guess it pays to have friends in high places."

"But Stagger's in a high place because I put him there," said Sorrow. "We wouldn't have won if not for steps I've taken in the past."

"You can't pretend that Stagger's intervention was part of some master plan you had," said Rigger.

Sorrow shrugged. "I planted the seed that brought us victory. I don't see why I can't take credit for the harvest."

"Good to see your ego hasn't taken a hit just because you're powerless," said Brand, staring at Sorrow's scalp.

"I'm hardly powerless," said Sorrow. She ran her fingers along Slate's stubbled cheeks and said, with a gentle smile, "I've everything I need to take up bone-weaving."

Brand's eyebrows shot up.

"And what's more," she said, standing and helping Slate to his feet. "I'm human again. I've a sound body and a keen mind, and that makes me one of the most powerful forces of nature imaginable. I'm ready to take whatever life throws at me." She held a clenched fist before her face to illustrate her words. She lowered her hand as her eyes drank in the unending blackness that engulfed them. "Not that this does me any good in limbo."

"Limbo?" asked Slate, looking around at the surrounding dark.

"We didn't make the leap between realms cleanly," said Sage. "We've wound up literally nowhere."

Slate shook his head, looking forlorn. His shoulders sagged. "In seeking to protect the One True Book, I've placed it in even greater danger."

"We'll think of something," said Poppy. "We're Romers! We get out of tight spots for a living."

"But we're not in a tight spot," said Sage. "We're in no spot at all. I didn't see things ending like this." She sighed. "I'm so sorry."

"I'm the one who made the jump," said Gale. "Long ago, mother warned me she could only find her way across to the spirit realms at night. Sunlight blinds her to the path. I pushed her anyway."

Sorrow snapped her fingers. "Sunlight!"

She marched toward Brand and grabbed the locket at his throat. She thrust her lips inches from the glorystone and shouted, "Stagger! We're in limbo! Help!"

Brand looked at her as if she'd gone insane.

"The glorystone is part of the sun," she explained. "Just as Greatshadow can see through every candle, Stagger, in theory, can see through every glorystone. But, there are thousands of little fragments like this. I just want to be sure we catch his attention."

"There's only one sure way to catch Stagger's attention," said Bigsby. He tugged on Brand's shirt. "Bend over."

Brand did so, and the dwarf cupped the locket in both hands and shouted at the top of his lungs, "Battle Ox has just tapped a fresh keg and I'm buying 'til it's dry!"

Bigsby looked around. Everyone was quiet. The dwarf sighed. "I thought for sure that would work. Anytime similar words were spoken at the Black Swan, he'd fly through the doors so fast he'd knock tables over."

Everyone jumped as wood banged against wood all around the deck. The ropes overhead began to rattle in the pulleys.

"Rigger?" Gale asked.

"It's not me!" he called out, spinning around to see who had hold of the ropes.

Sorrow's jaw dropped as she saw horned demons flying in from the edges of limbo to light upon the deck of the *Circus*, where they grabbed at the rigging. They were monstrous creatures, with skeletal human bodies and animal heads. They were dressed, curiously enough, in sailor uniforms identical to the ones worn by the Romers.

"You might need this," Rigger said as he thrust the Witchbreaker into Slate's hands.

"Someone's at the wheel!" Gale shouted, racing into the shadows. Sorrow gave chase, though Mako beat them both to the wheel, cursing as he tried to grasp the pale, wraithlike form he found there. Sorrow squinted in the darkness, seeing a short, light-colored head just behind the wheel. Bigsby? As Brand approached, the light fell upon an albino pygmy who smiled at Sorrow with a familiar grin.

"Walker!"

"Sorrow. I'm happy to have found you at last. Stagger's guidance was most helpful. It's a shame you waited so long to call to him."

"Not that we're ungrateful, but why were you looking for us?" Brand asked.

"Because you've created an atrocious mess," said Walker. "It would be unfair to task others with cleaning up your mistakes, not that many haven't tried."

"What mistakes? What are you talking about?"

"Twenty years ago, you robbed most of the world of their faith in the One True Book. The Silver Isles have sunk into outright despotism in their attempt to maintain order. War, famine, and pestilence are daily life for most men now. But as bad as the material world has become, your greater error was to provide Tempest a doorway to a place he did not belong. The dragon has used the intervening decades to craft a new empire, one with a far larger population than his old one. I'm weary of hearing my demon friends grumble about the new management, and have persuaded a few of the more rebellious ones to join me in rescuing you."

"Wait, wait, wait, wait," Brand said, "Twenty years? We've barely been gone twenty minutes!"

"I informed you earlier that time isn't constant between the various realms," said Walker. He spun the wheel hard to the left.

"Where are we going?" shouted Gale.

They splashed into a broad river between smoking black banks of gravel. For an instant, given the horrid heat that wrapped around her, Sorrow thought they were riding on a lava flow back on the Isle of Fire, and expected the boat to burst into flames. The sky above was a writhing mass of angry clouds, crackling with lightning.

"The river!" Jetsam called out as he leaned overboard. "It's pure blood!"

"Nonsense," Walker said with a giggle. "Nothing here is pure."

"This isn't blood," Sage said as she looked around the landscape. "It's memories!"

"You've good eyes," said Walker. "What else would fill the rivers here? Nothing burns its way down a parched throat like memories."

Sorrow went to Slate's side and took his hand. He squeezed her fingers gently as he stared down into the red currents lapping the hull.

"I've never felt such thirst," he whispered. "Even knowing all that I now know of my origins, I still ache for memories."

She placed her fingers on his chin and turned his face toward her. She stood on tiptoes to kiss him gently. "We both have a fresh chance to make new memories." She looked across the wasteland. "Though, I admit, making good ones in a place like this might prove to be a challenge."

Bigsby climbed up the rigging for a better look. "I give up," he said. "Where the hell are we?"

Walker's fingers slipped from the wheel as he fell to the deck, laughing as tears ran down his cheeks.

ACKNOWLEDGEMENTS

Witchbreaker wouldn't be the book it is without the hard work of my wise-readers, a select band of rugged individuals who are willing to slog through my early drafts and gaze unflinchingly upon my naked prose. It's seldom pretty. Without their critiques and encouragement, writing would be a very lonely business indeed. Thank you, James Marsh, Cathy Bollinger, Ada Milenkovic Brown, Laurel Amberdine, Joey Puente, Jenney O'Callaghan, and, of course, my wonderful wife, Cheryl Maxey. Special thanks to artist Adam Tredowski, for gracing the book with a truly amazing cover. Thanks also to my editor, Jonathan Oliver, and everyone else at Solaris who has worked so hard on this series, including Ben Smith, Michael Molcher, and Simon Parr. In previous acknowledgements, I've given credit to the various writing workshops and critique groups that have helped me hone my skills over the years. But two people I haven't acknowledged get most of the credit (or blame) for launching me on this whole writing kick a long, long time before I was even consciously aware of it. So, let me rectify my oversight: It's probable I wouldn't be a writer today if not for my grandfathers. Both of my grandfathers were poor, but both were readers. On my mother's side, my grandfather Allen Henkle had excellent taste in trashy periodicals. Not pornography, but weirdness, magazines like *Fate* that talked about UFOs and telepathy and bigfoot. He also had a stash of men's adventure magazines, with lurid stories about cannibals and secret jungle temples and "real life" survival tales of men who crash on the side of mountains and survive by sawing off their gangrenous leg and hopping back to civilization with nothing to slake their thirst but their own urine. And my mother's family were natural storytellers, always ready to recount a ghost story, which made quite an impression on me since when you looked out the back window of their house you saw a graveyard. (I also remember a huge collection of *Reader's Digests*, but all I ever read in them were the jokes.) My father's father, Sidney Maxey, Sr., had books stacked in every room of his house, and when he ran out of room in the house, the books spilled out onto his porch in giant mounds of mildewed paperbacks. I don't know if my grandfather read every one of these books or if he just bought them in bulk from Goodwill stores and flea markets, but they were on every subject imaginable. It was sitting on his porch digging through paperbacks that I first read writers like Ursula K. LeGuinn and Isaac Asimov. I also remember reading about the Bermuda Triangle and ancient astronauts, but these sensationalist paperbacks were balanced out by every issue of *National Geographic* in print since 1929. I devoured these magazines, gaining a perspective on the vastness of the world beyond my rather narrow view from the southern Virginia mountains. I don't want to oversimplify things, but in some ways my maternal grandfather's reading material shaped my imagination, hooking me on the desire for there to be things hidden from ordinary understanding. Because of him, I retain an insatiable curiosity about the fringes of human knowledge. But it was on my Grandfather Maxey's porch library that I learned to be fascinated as much by the natural world as I am by myths and legends. Pictures of fish photographed from bathyspheres were even weirder and more wonderful than the aliens hand-drawn in the pages of *Fate*. To be a writer, you must first be a reader. Thanks to these two men, I am.

ABOUT THE AUTHOR

James Maxey lives in Hillsborough, NC with his lovely bride Cheryl and a clowder of unruly cats. He is the author of the *Bitterwood* fantasy trilogy, *Bitterwood*, *Dragonforge*, and *Dragonseed*, as well as the superhero novels *Nobody Gets the Girl* and *Burn Baby Burn*. His short fiction has appeared in dozens of anthologies and magazines such as *Asimov's* and *Orson Scott Card's Intergalactic Medicine Show*. The best of these stories appears in the collection *There is No Wheel*. For more information about James, visit dragonprophet.blogspot.com.

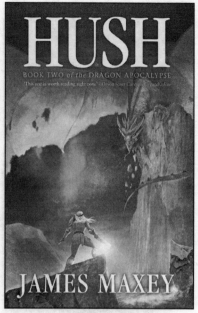

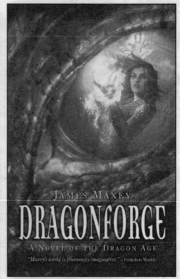
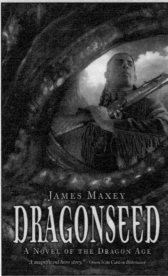